Dedication

In Memory of George Eichler

*"All Things Truly Wicked
Start From Innocence."*
Ernest Hemingway

THE INNOCENT ASSETS CONSPIRACY©

Roger Quinn

Pp
PROSEPRESS

ACKNOWLEDGMENTS:

This book would not have been possible without the support of my wife, Barbara.

I owe a deep sense of gratitude to my story editor, Richard Gale. Rich patiently guided me with character development and story transition.

I am especially grateful to the following:
Kathy Hughes and Linda Pombo, for editing Chapters Two and Three.

Jim Rudge, who reviewed 400 pages of line edits.
Prose Press publisher and designer, Bob O'Brien, for his acuity.

Also:

Peter Manchee, contributed hours of his time, diving log and expertise.

Philip McGrath, for his recollections of exploring the U-853.

Captain Bill Palmer, *Last Battle Of The Atlantic,* for his insights into the controversial last hours of the U-853.

Glenn Allen, for directing me to the U-853 divers.

David Straka, who provided memories of life on board a US submarine.
Lenny DiGregorio, who helped me write about logistics management.

John Jett, who contributed photographs of the Patchogue Hotel, the Post Office and the Village Memorial.

My loyal readers of *THE TRINITY CONSPIRACY*, who encouraged this sequel.

Please attribute errors or omissions to me. A few typos remain to pique your curiosity.

Preface:
Berchtesgaden, Germany
Spring, 1945.

It was a simple home in Berchtesgaden at the foot of Hitler's infamous retreat. Manfred Bartel and his wife, Gertrude, were ordered to report there from Berlin. Bartel, a German naval officer with the rank of Korvettenkapitan (Lieutenant Commander) remained on station in Berlin when Admiral Dönitz became Commander in Chief of the German navy in 1943. Dönitz's operational headquarters was located in Flensburg, Germany.

Bartel initially perceived his orders as a welcome relief. The constant air raids, rumors and intrigue covered Berlin with a pall of impending doom.

Gertrude Bartel was slowly succumbing to the tension and constant turmoil. Nevertheless, the directive was very specific. The officer's wife was perplexed and made anxious by the urgency. They were ordered to travel by automobile following a specific route from Berlin to Berchtesgaden. This trip required special precautions. They traveled at night in a chauffeured Mercedes accompanied by an SS officer. The Bartels were very special. They were the keepers of the secret.

The Bartels visited Berchtesgaden once before. Those were happier times. Now as the Russians moved closer to Berlin, transportation was at a premium, petrol rationed and restricted to high-level officers and party leaders.

Manfred was shocked by the devastation from the British fire bombings and American daylight raids. The Allies' strategic bombings were slowly working into the rural areas. Surprisingly, Berchtesgaden had been spared. It wouldn't be long before Allied bombers would target the palatial homes of the Nazi elite along the winding road up the mountain. Without warning the Mercedes came to a stop.

"We will have to wait for this convoy to pass," the chauffeur said.

The SS officer snickered. "The exodus is on. We've been ordered to safeguard destroyed and abandoned estates, while the party elite disappear into the shadows before they are captured. To speak of desertion or surrender is treason and punishable by death. The cowards are on the run. Posts unguarded." The SS officer pointed to a deserted checkpoint.

The SS escort's remarks startled Bartel. "You could be shot on the spot without a trial or court martial for saying that," Bartel exclaimed.

"You will soon discover it is common knowledge SS soldiers are deserting their posts. They are ransacking local homes and discarding their uniforms. With so many men captured or killed there is no shortage of civilian clothes."

The Mercedes finally arrived at its destination. The Bartels, along with their escort and the chauffeur, climbed the steep winding stairs to the front porch.

Upon entering the home they were greeted by two uniformed SS officers. Bartel recognized their distinctive uniforms from his brief visits to the Reich Chancellery. The skeleton key symbol on their uniform designated the elite SS Panzer Corps. These two still wore the operational Adolf Hitler cuff titles. They were part of Hitler's personal bodyguard still stationed in Berchtesgaden.

The shorter of the two SS officers stepped forward, examined the naval officer's papers, and abruptly dismissed the chauffeur and escort.

"Do you know why you were ordered to report here?"

"No." Manfred looked at Gertrude. Her face was pale and she began to tremble with fear. Something was wrong.

"The Lebensborn certificate number."

Bartel's posture stiffened. "What about it?"

"The certificate and number," demanded the officer.

"We gave the certificate to the family along with the child years ago," Manfred insisted.

"We have no other documents," said Gertrude. "And the child?"

"The child is safe but the hillside home was destroyed. The family has left."

"The Lebensborn may have a duplicate registration card." Gertrude's trembling increased.

"You were instructed to memorize the number." The SS office grew agitated. He unbuttoned his field blouse and withdrew a scrap of paper. "Now, tell me the authentication number."

Bartel slowly recited the birth registration. "SS – 1 – 3128."

The SS officer smiled, turned to the second officer and nodded his satisfaction. At that, Manfred and Gertrude Bartel were directed to separate bedrooms. Manfred reluctantly followed the short SS Officer into the bedroom. The door closed, the SS officer swiftly unholstered his pistol, and fired a single round into the naval officer's head. A second gunshot resounded from the adjacent bedroom.

So began the *Innocent Assets Conspiracy.*

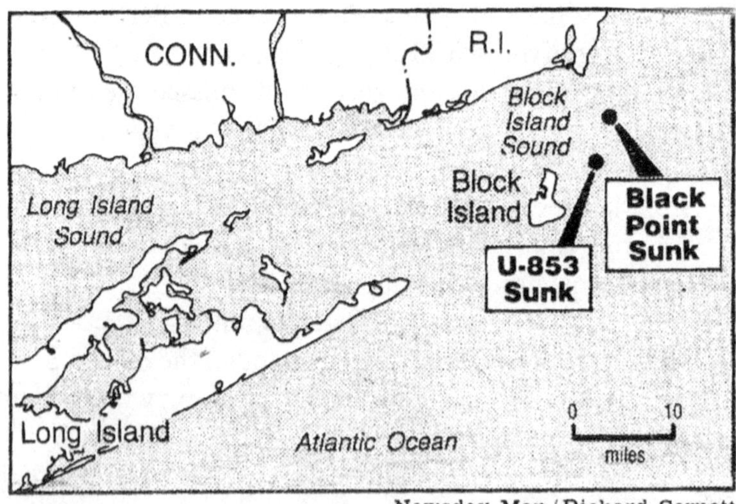

Newsday Map / Richard Cornett

Book One

Chapter One:
A Chance Encounter
Farmingville/Lake Ronkonkoma, New York

The county dispatcher activated Farmingville's tones at 0905. It was an ambulance call, a 24 on a 16-23-MVA to Ronkonkoma. In plain English the nearby community of Lake Ronkonkoma requested an additional ambulance and crew for a motor vehicle accident. Timothy "Doc" Clawson rolled over in bed groping the nightstand top to reset his screeching pager. This was no way to start the New Year's Day, but "Doc" was on call. Drifting snow and high winds slowed his response time. The other two members of his crew, Rich Sanders and Al Perry were waiting in the ambulance.

"Hey, we almost blew the call," said Perry. He slowly pulled out of the truck bay and with lights flashing and, siren blaring, ambulance 5-18-16 headed west.

"What kept you, Doc?" asked Sanders. No one around the firehouse called Clawson by his first name, Tim. His nickname "Doc" was stenciled across his gear and embroidered on his company shirts. Clawson earned the name back in 1968 as a Marine corporal in Vietnam.

It was February 6, 1968; Doc's platoon was fighting its way toward Thua Thein Prison. It was part of the concerted effort to rout North Vietnam Army regulars and Viet Cong from Hue City. During those bloody days, Navy corpsmen were prime targets for enemy snipers. Though not a corpsman, Tim Clawson used his limited medical skills to help wounded comrades. Soon Clawson was christened "Doc," and the name stuck.

"Are you OK, Doc?" asked Rich Sanders, as the ambulance approached the scene.

"Sure. I need to get my mind into it. Rough night."

Ronkonkoma was into the call when 5-18-16 arrived. Ronko's Chief directed them around a large van. On the far side, a dump truck and Cadillac sedan were fused together. A crew worked the Jaws of Life cutting away mangled steel. The truck driver was uninjured, but inside the Caddy were three trapped occupants. The three Farmingville responders went into action. Doc directed the extrication of the passengers.

Rich Sanders climbed through a cleared side window and started triage. Across the back seat slumped the limp body of a woman. Rich checked for an airway. Ronko's extrication team freed the rear door and placed the woman on a gurney. Rich began life support even as the woman's lifeless eyes stared back at him.

The driver regained consciousness and called for his companions. Rich, still in the rear, turned to stabilize the driver. The man had a severe head wound. A portion of his scalp was torn away. He wasn't wearing a seat bet. The impact vaulted the driver into the sunroof panel. His head took most of the impact.

While Rich tended to the driver, Al Perry gained access to the front passenger. The man was breathing, but Al sensed the man had serious chest injuries. Suddenly, the driver cried out and began to flail.

"I need some help here," Al shouted. The extrication team cut the door and removed it.

"Who are you?" demanded the confused driver. He was a strong man and appeared to be in his late eighties.

"I'm an EMT. You've been in a car accident. Please allow me to help you."

The man nodded. Doc worked to stabilize the patient's head wound. *He's got to have serious internal injuries.*

Ronko's chief called to Doc. "Take the driver to Stony Brook. I've already notified them we have three ambulances headed to their facility."

Once Doc's patient was secured in 5-18-16 Doc called out "Let's roll."

"How are my friends?" asked the Cadillac's driver.

"They're on their way to the hospital," said Doc.

"What's your name?"

"Doc. Doc Clawson. And yours?"

"Price. Jack Price." the driver responded as he attempted to lift himself on the gurney. "My head is killing me."

"You've been in a serious accident."

"I've seen worse," Price responded.

Doc sensed the man meant it.

"Is this yours?" asked Al. He held out a gold pocket watch. An eagle and the letter "M" were inscribed on the cover. "One of the cops found it."

"Ah yes. It belongs to my friend. The other man in the car."

"Hold on to it for him," said Al as he made a note on the bottom of Price's "run sheet." Al placed the watch in Price's jacket pocket.

Rich Sanders raced 5-18-16 toward University Hospital. Within minutes they were in the emergency receiving area. Doc felt the adrenaline rush wearing off. The nurse administrator initialed the paper work when an attending nurse called out.

"The attending physician asked you guys to remain with the patient until he goes into surgery."

The three EMT's looked at one another and shrugged.

"OK," Doc said.

"It's the patient's request. He claims you saved his life. He's had significant blood loss. They want to stabilize the guy."

An hour later 5-18-16 departed Stony Brook hospital.

❧

Several months passed when Doc received a note from Jack Price. Price was recovering at home and asked Doc to visit. On the following Saturday, Doc drove along the winding Harbor Road, passed Head of The Harbor, an exclusive community nestled between St. James and Smithtown. He turned into a secluded driveway and approached an electronic security checkpoint. A voice greeted him.

Doc responded: "Tim Clawson to see Mr. Price."

The gate opened and Doc continued along the winding road. It led to a beautiful building with expansive landscaping. *This reminds me of a German castle.*

A man walked toward his car. His dark blue suit and demeanor reminded Doc of an FBI agent he knew.

"I apologize for the security check," the guard said. "One quick sweep with the wand. It's a precaution. You understand, sir. Can't be too careful these days."

Doc wasn't sure what the guard meant.

"Presley, sir. I'm assigned to Mr. Price's security detail."

Security detail? What is this place? Why would Price need a "security detail"?

Presley led Doc through the building's main entrance into a huge elegantly- decorated foyer. Two portraits hung on the far wall.

Doc's inquisitive look caught Presley's attention. "This facility once served as headquarters for a corporation. They've outgrown it and moved on. They maintain it, now that Mr. Price is a guest."

" What company is it?"

"I'm sure you've heard of it, Mr. Clawson. Trinity Pharmo Dynamics. They're a huge international company. They manufacture pharmaceuticals and medical supplies."

Doc knew the name, all right. *Their logo is on half the medical equipment on our ambulance.* "And the portraits?" Doc pointed.

"The first is Walther Liechtenauer, the company's first director. The other is Ashton Pickering, the current director. Rumor is Pickering may soon step down."

Presley led Doc along a corridor to an elevator. "The second and third floors are administrative and private facilities. Mr. Price's apartment is on the third floor. I might caution you, Mr. Price isn't well, but you'll discover that soon enough. Please try not to look too surprised. Mr. Price requested we remove the mirrors from his living quarters." Presley frowned. The elevator door opened. Presley pressed the third floor button.

Price's apartment was plush with mahogany paneling and plush tapestries.

"Through here, Mr. Clawson." Presley pointed to a doorway. It led to a bedroom equipped with a hospital bed and medical supplies. "Please wait here."

Doc didn't know what to anticipate, but his curiosity was short lived.

"Greetings, Mr. Clawson."

Doc turned to see Presley pushing Price in a wheel chair. "I've just completed my daily treatment. Presley, please help me into bed. I'm tired. I apologize, Mr. Clawson. The initial treatments seemed to be a breeze, but now I'm not so sure. Thank you Presley." Presley left the room.

Doc sat on a chair beside the bed. On the nightstand was a photograph of Price and two others. Along side was a gold pocket watch. *Al Perry handed Price the watch after the accident back in January, Doc recalled.*

"The photograph is from years ago," said Price. "Do you recognize them? The two in the photo were in the car the day of the accident. The Pokels were my closest friends. Price turned his head in a feeble attempt to conceal tears. The photograph captured a younger Price. His athletic build and youthful appearance suggested an adventurer or soldier of fortune. "And you recall the watch?" Price asked. Price coughed and from time to time placed a suction wand into his mouth to remove the saliva. The facial lacerations were healing. His head was covered with a surgical skullcap. An IV line was taped to a shunt in his right arm. A vital signs monitor measured life signs. The Trinity PharmoDynamics inverted-sword logo emblazoned on the device.

"And the watch?" Doc asked.

"Ah, the watch. Now that's a long story. It is a relic from an awful time." Price paused and reached for a small device. He pressed it several times. "Morphine. They pour on the shit. Look at this machine. The whole idea is that it limits the amount of morphine I demand. The doctor doesn't want me to become an addict." Price laughed and choked.

"First, let me tell you about my friend, Kurt Pokel. It was the mid 1930's. Kurt's old man, Gus, was a bastard and a bully. He joined the German-American Bund. On weekends Gus and Kurt rode the Long Island Railroad to Patchogue. A bus went from there to Camp Siegfried in Yapank. The old man let me come along a couple of times," said Price.

"I remember the camp entrance. Two flags flying side by side. A huge Nazi swastika flag overshadowed the American flag. Kurt cautioned me not be frightened. 'I don't want to be here, but my father will punish me if I refuse to come.'"

Price told Doc about brown-shirted Storm Troopers on parade with wooden rifles. The weekend events drew thousands of people.

"I still remember the uniforms, the bands, and the singing. The people loved it. Not Kurt. He didn't buy into any of it."

Price paused his tale for several seconds, perhaps to gather his thoughts.

"And then what happened?" Doc asked.

"The old man moved to Germany and took Kurt. Just disappeared. Gus didn't tell his wife until he got there."

"How does the pocket watch fit into all of this?"

"Go ahead. Pick it up." Price motioned his approval. Doc took the watch off the table.

"It isn't a pocket watch. It's a stopwatch used for timing torpedo runs. A diver recovered it from a sunken U-boat off Block Island. When Pokel heard about it he paid the diver a small fortune for it. The mechanism is damaged."

"I remember reading about a sunken U-boat some place off Montauk."

"Block Island. It rests in about 120 feet of water," said Price.

"Wasn't it the last German U-boat sunk at the end of World War II?"

"The U-853. The sub rested there for years until sport divers rediscovered it. Divers began taking gruesome souvenirs. During one exploration a crewmember's skeleton was removed."

"Really? Are you serious?"

"Check for yourself. My point is…well let me put it another way. Presley informed me you are a Vietnam veteran."

"You ran a background check on me?"

The old man waved his hand as though brushing the question away like an annoying fly. "Forgive me, Mr. Clawson, but it's routine," Price responded.

"Please let me continue my thought. How would you feel if you read of an American aircraft downed during the war being ravaged and desecrated?"

"I'd be pissed off. Still, I know it happens."

Price continued. "Next came the professionals. They call it 'airlifting.' Air is pumped from a surface vessel through a rig made from PVC and flex hose. Water pressure forces silt into the pipe along with anything else it picks up and it's deposited in a catch basket. The turbulence scatters the crew's remains." Price's story abruptly ended.

"That's it?" Doc asked. *There had to be more to the story. Price was obviously moved by a compelling personal issue. With all the talk of MIA's, why would the US government allow airlifting on a sunken U-boat?*

A monitor hung over Price's bed. The display flashed. An alarm sounded. The bedroom door opened and Presley returned.

"That's it for today, Mr. Price. I thought we had an agreement. No excitement."

Wearied Jack Price didn't argue. "Thank you for coming, Mr. Clawson. I hope to see you again."

Doc nodded in agreement. *Something about this place makes me uneasy.*

Presley re-set Price's monitor and the pair were about to leave. Doc glanced back at the photograph and the gold stopwatch. He was captivated by Price's tale. *How much was fact?*

❦

An hour later Doc climbed the stairs to his apartment. *I've gotten myself into something I have no business being in. Searching for clues to a mystery will complicate my life.*

Doc was a recovering alcoholic. He lived life one day at a time. Doc knew he had to keep things simple. His previous life had been filled with turmoil and broken promises. Doc never could fully acclimate to civilian life after Vietnam. In 1975 Doc was on the back end of a nasty divorce. He accepted the blame. Doc's drinking changed his personality. He was filled with anger and resentment. His fists were always clenched. In late spring Doc's school district placed him on administrative leave for excessive absences. Lonely, nearly broke and depressed, Doc bottomed out.

Then one morning a friend revealed she was a recovering alcoholic. The friend persuaded Doc to enter rehab. Following discharge he began attending AA meetings. With the encouragement of his sponsor Doc began to reclaim his sense of humor and purpose. By the following semester he was able to return to work. Eventually, Doc joined the volunteer fire department and trained to be an EMT.

◈

Jack Price and the U-boat were low on Doc's list of priorities. Then for some unexplained reason, Doc took a renewed interest in the sunken U-boat. He would spend his Saturday mornings at the Sachem Library reading newspaper accounts of German U-boats in the North Atlantic.

The U-853 was sunk on May 6, 1945, not far from Block Island, Rhode Island. The newspapers speculated the U-boat captain was a diehard Nazi fanatic. He risked his crew and vessel to sink a coal freighter in shallow waters hours before Germany's unconditional surrender. The compelling issue confounded even the Navy. Admiral Dönitz, Hitler's successor and commander of the U-boat fleet, issued a surrender order. U-boats were directed to surface under a black flag, The U-boats were not to be scuttled.

Why didn't the U-853 surrender? The question perturbed Doc.

One afternoon a call came.

"Mr. Clawson, this is Presley, Mr. Price's personal assistant. I regret to tell you, but Mr. Price is declining. He asked if you would visit again."

Doc agreed and the next weekend returned to the so-called retreat. The electronic gate was all that remained of the once-tight security. The interior still maintained its elegance, but Doc felt a somber atmosphere as he entered the building.

Presley greeted Doc. "Please try to avoid talking about U-boats."

Doc was puzzled by the request, but agreed.

Presley and Doc rode the elevator to Price's quarters. The bedroom suite resembled a fully equipped emergency room. An attending nurse sat in the far corner reading a magazine.

Doc was surprised by Price's appearance. His once-penetrating blue eyes were sunken. Price's hand trembled and fell as he reached out to greet Doc.

"Surprised, Mr. Clawson? This dying business is hard. Please excuse us for a bit, Presley," whispered Price. Presley motioned to the nurse to leave the room, also.

"So what did you discover?" Price asked.

"Discover?" Doc asked. He knew Price meant the sunken U-boat. "If you mean the U-853, not much." Doc had read a few old newspaper clippings. "The captain was on a suicide mission," Doc answered.

"Nonsense!" Price tried to raise himself a bit in his excitement, but lacked the strength.

"That's the gist of what I read. I did come across a couple of articles about divers exploring the sub. You're right. There is quite a controversy surrounding divers taking souvenirs."

"I'm telling you there's more to the story than what the papers printed in 1945. The whole thing is a government cover-up."

Doc glanced at the vital signs monitor. Price's blood pressure and heart rate were fluctuating. "Presley asked me not to discuss the U-853. I can see why."

"Don't mind Presley. This is important. What's your gut feeling?"

Doc hesitated for a moment. "The U-853 is surrounded in mystery. The initial reports stated the captain was a fanatic. I have no idea. One thing I did find odd, however."

"What?" Price asked impatiently.

"The war was a few hours away from the official surrender. A signal was sent from the German Admiralty for U-boats to surface under a black flag and surrender. The U-853 was in 120 feet of water with no place to go. Why not surrender?"

"Exactly," responded Price. He tried to roll on his side to retrieve the stopwatch from the rolling medication table. He winced with pain. "Please hand me the watch."

Doc handed Price the prized possession.

"You're missing the key point," said Price.

"That's all I know," Doc shot back.

"I'm sure you know much more than you realize. The key point…the captain never surrendered. It's my guess he never was given a chance. The pursuit tenders dropped eleven magnetic mines and over one hundred and eighty depth charges. After a while they lost count. Don't you see?"

"See what?"

"They never wanted the U-853 to surrender."

"They? Who didn't want the U-boat to surface?"

Price never had the chance to answer. His vital signs were fluctuating to the point the alarm was sounded and both the nurse and Presley rushed back into the room.

"Mr. Clawson, please. Mr. Price, you promised no talk of submarines," admonished Presley.

"We weren't talking submarines or flying saucers," replied Price struggling to regain the authority he had lost to Presley weeks ago. "I deserve a degree of privacy."

"Very well, Sir. I'm cautioning you; I'll be watching the monitor in the other room."

Once the pair left Doc said, "I think it's time for me to leave, too."

"Mr. Clawson, please take the stopwatch."

"I can't." Doc insisted. "What would I do with it?"

"Take it. I don't have a family. No close friends. I rely on you, Mr. Clawson."

"To do what?"

"One day you must return it to its rightful owner."

Doc was confused, but caught by Price's mesmerizing smile. "Are you asking me to place it back on board the U-853?"

"Yes. I trust you, Mr. Clawson. One day you will have the opportunity."

"I'm no diver. The Bonn Government issued a protest. They have declared the U-853 a war memorial. It's off limits from further exploration. Our government seems to be cooperating."

"Of course our government will cooperate. They don't want any further exploration of the U-853 for their own reasons."

"I haven't read any reports along those lines. I don't believe in conspiracy theories," Doc replied.

"Neither do I, Mr. Clawson. But I have participated in several intrigues." Jack waved his hand to imply they were secrets best kept in a vault.

"The stopwatch, Mr. Clawson. Guard it with you life. Forget the newspaper stories and government fabrications about the U-853. Our government invents the news and the media substantiates it. We share a reality; a truth greater than fact."

Doc looked perplexed. "I feel as though I am entering a role-playing game of sorts." Price motioned for Doc to come closer.

Doc leaned over the bed.

Price grasped Doc's hand and whispered, "Go to the book case." Price pointed to a floor to ceiling bookcase on the far side of the room. "The middle shelf. That's it. Count over five books."

Doc's fingers walked across the books. He stopped at book five.

"Go on. Take the book."

As Doc removed the book a small compartment opened. A surprised Doc looked at Price.

"Go ahead. Reach inside. You'll find two journals." Doc removed a small leather- bound journal from a watertight plastic bag labeled "U-853."

"Is this a ship's log?" asked Doc.

Price nodded.

The log's cover was wrinkled and water-stained. The bindings had been restored. Doc leafed through the pages, but paid little attention to the contents. Many of the pages were washed away and others smeared. Remarkably, many pages appeared legible.

"German," said Doc. "I struggled with German in high school."

"Now open the other book."

"What's this?" asked Doc.

"Look for yourself." Doc opened the second leather-bound journal. The entries were written in English.

"Is this an English translation?"

"In part. However, I've added annotations. You'll find it interesting reading. I'm entrusting you with both journals." Price motioned for Doc to bring the books to his bedside. "This is no game, Mr. Clawson. You hold the keys to an historic secret. Guard them. Men have died to preserve less. I trust you, Mr. Clawson."

"Secrets? Are you sure you have the right man? You hardly know me."

Price's grip loosened. Doc felt a cold sensation as he watched Price's eyes close. The morphine had taken hold. Doc took the stopwatch and the two journals. He walked to the door then paused to look at Price one last time. Doc placed the stopwatch in his jacket pocket.

Presley was waiting in the anteroom. "Thank you for coming, Mr. Clawson. Mr. Price was eager to see you." Presley glanced at the journals in Doc's left hand, but didn't comment.

Odd. I wonder if Presley knew Price would give me the journals?

Doc and Presley shook hands. Doc smiled and nodded.

Doc's mind wandered as he drove home. At some point he pulled into a 7-11 parking lot, turned off the engine and sat there. The leather-bound journals rested on the passenger seat.

Did I just hear Price's confession? Price admitted no wrong. Was Price's conversation a concoction of morphine fantasy? Did Price just hand me a burden he could no longer carry. Did I accept it?

Doc's mind flashed back to Thua Thein Province and his dying comrades. Doc fought the memories. He desperately needed a drink. Drops of sweat burned his eyes. Or were they tears?

Eventually, Doc Clawson regained his composure. He reached into his pocket and retrieved the stopwatch. He hefted the heavy timepiece and placed it in the glove box along with the journals. *What the hell have I gotten myself into?*

Chapter Two

Eva Braun and Magda Goebbels
Hitler's Estate, "The Berghof"
Berchtesgaden, Germany
1943

Sometime in late winter or early spring Eva Braun, Adolf Hitler's mistress, slipped into a depression. There were rumors Braun had attempted suicide early in her relationship with Hitler. Eva was lonely. She struggled with Hitler's preoccupation with the war.

"Your increased absences haven't helped. You use me as a showpiece. We rarely have time alone. We haven't been intimate in months. I am so lonely."

"What is this nonsense?"

"I watch you with other women. You invite their children to the retreat."

"Get to the point," Hitler demanded.

"I want a child."

"Impossible. My duty to the Fatherland comes before our personal lives."

Hitler's stamina and sex drive had all but vanished. Braun blamed Hitler's personal physician, Morell, for the Fuhrer's impotence. Hitler suffered from stomach ailments, gas, frequent battles with constipation and diarrhea. Gilbert Morell came to Hitler's attention for his unconventional treatments. Morell began treating Hitler and soon became part of the Fuhrer's entourage.

"It's Morell. Isn't it? He increases your injections each day. What concoction is he giving you? You explode at nothing. Lost all interest in me. I have my needs too. I am a kept woman." She began to cry hysterically.

Hitler's mind flashed back to an earlier romance and his former lover's suicide attempt. She later succeeded in 1931. Eva had attempted suicide as well. He wanted no more distractions.

"Our arrangement is more your doing than mine. You seem to relish the attention and the rewards of being at my side. A child isn't a puppy to be given away. You grow bored. You're weary. This is another of your episodes." He walked to the window and looked down the hill. "Is it your wish to humiliate me?" He repeated the question. Again, no answer. He turned to find Eva had left the room.

Eva Braun could manipulate Hitler, but only to a point. She recognized his fine line of rage. She played on his vulnerabilities – a need to be loved and the fear of abandonment.

Two nights later Hitler gave in to Eva's request for a child.

There was little possibility of Eva becoming pregnant. Dr. Morell's injections seem to aid Hitler's stomach problems, but he could no longer sustain an erection. Impotency was a subject even Eva feared to discuss. Hitler was convinced Eva didn't want to be pregnant or be confined by the responsibilities of motherhood.

The next morning Hitler met with Dr. Morell.

"Eva insists on a child. She enjoys the good life. She loves the spotlight. She flits through the Tea Room with her camera. Eva wants to be a Hollywood star. She has no time for a child," Hitler insisted.

"I will speak with her," said Morell.

"She'll never listen to you, Morell. She blames you for my impotence."

As Hitler and Eva spoke over breakfast the next morning Eva protested. "I will not meet with Morell. I find him disgusting."

"He is safeguarding my health," answered Hitler. "Your demands for a child are unrealistic. You are so moody. Morell may be able to prescribe medication."

"My dear, Morell's farts smell worse than yours."

The Fuhrer threw his arms into the air. "You go too far. I'm sick of your constant tantrums. You will meet with Morell. I order it."

Eva stepped back. She stiffened to attention. She had reached the fine line between her lover's anger and the Fuhrer's rage. She backed off. "All right. I will meet Morell next week when I return from visiting my sister in Munich."

Hitler slammed his fist on the table. "Why must you always have your way?" Suddenly, a pained expression covered his face. He pushed back from the table and rushed to the bathroom. He was struck with stomach pains, the precursor of a bout with diarrhea.

Several hours later Hitler told Eva he was returning to Berlin to meet with his General Staff. "I will be gone for quite some time."

"Fine. I will join my family in Munich." Eva frequently visited her family in Munich during Hitler's ever-increasing absences. On one of the visits Eva telephoned Magda Goebbels, the wife of Joseph Goebbels, Hitler's propaganda minister.

"Magda, I trust you. I need to talk with you."

Magda was a provocative woman. Years before she married Goebbels, Magda had married a man twice her age. Not quite twenty years old, she was dazzled by his success and wealth. Less than a year into the marriage her husband began to spend less time at home and more time away on business.

Magda confided in her sister. "I've had an affair."

"Who is he?"

"Never mind. My god, he's in fantastic shape. He's a wonder in bed. Always something new to explore. You can't believe the passion."

"And your husband?"

"The man spends more time on business than he does in our bedroom."

"Does he suspect?"

"I have no idea. My lover makes me feel appreciated. "

"Magda darling. Look around. You are surrounded by wealth any woman would envy. Be careful, sister."

Magda was convinced her husband tacitly condoned the affair as opposed to a scandal and divorce. Nevertheless, two years later they divorced. Then she met Goebbels.

Magda's marriage to Joseph Goebbels was tumultuous. Goebbels was a notorious womanizer and his constant public affairs humiliated Magda.

"My dear, Joseph must be giving you some pleasure. For heaven's sake, you have six children by him. You two are rabbits."

"He's brutal in bed. I give in just to get it over. Believe me it doesn't take him long. Besides, Himmler demands German women to have more babies for the Fatherland. I'm under constant pressure to maintain an image of the perfect wife in an ideal marriage."

One morning Magda found Hitler sitting alone in the atrium.

"How are you Magda?"

"Not well, I'm afraid."

Hitler looked puzzled.

"I want a divorce from Joseph. I will be discreet."

"There will be no divorce."

"Then I will take the children and leave the country."

"I forbid it."

Two days later, Magda was apprehended at the Swiss border.

"I want Magda kept under constant surveillance even within her home."

Albert Speer told his wife. Magda spends days at Hitler's residence while Goebbels travels on party business." "I suspect Hitler and Magda have a special relationship,"

Speer's wife chuckled. "The women gossip. The think Goebbels exploits the relationship to maintain close contact with the Fuhrer."

Eva Braun was aware of Hitler's affection for Magda and the Goebbels children. Consequently, she turned to Magda following a series of disagreements with Hitler.

"It is too dangerous to discuss delicate matters over the telephone Eva," Magda cautioned. She closed the sitting room door.

"I have an urgent problem. I need your help," said Eva.

"Best you come to our home," replied Magda.

"Berlin?"

"Yes. The children and I have moved into Paul's hideaway on the outskirts of Berlin." Magda rarely called Goebbels by his first name, Paul. He disliked his first name. Magda antagonized Goebbels by calling him Paul.

"Hideaway? Oh Magda how do you endure it?"

"Enough for now. Call when you are able to visit."

Magda replaced the phone and slumped into a wing back chair. She began to weep.

How could the Fuhrer do this to me? I've been so loyal. Why would he make me continue to live like this? Why won't he grant me a divorce from the pig?"

"Is everything all right Frau Goebbels?" asked the maid.

"Yes, fine thank you." Magda dismissed the maid. *She must have been eavesdropping at the door. I know she's an informer. No doubt the girl is servicing Joseph on occasion. How could the Fuhrer deny me a divorce? He must know Joseph is s pig.*

Clearly, Magda had begun to distrust Hitler. *He listens to his small group of advisors. They are all yes men and tell him what he wants to hear. I refuse to behave that way, too.*

Chapter Three
Magda and Joseph Goebbels
Berchtesgaden, Germany
1943-44

Goebbels' prestige and power stemmed from his relationship with Hitler. As the war progressed the Fuhrer reduced Goebbels's substantive pre-war authority. Goebbels continued to play upon the Fuhrer's apparent attraction to Magda. In turn, Goebbels maintained his entrée to Hitler's inner circle. The Goebbels family visited Hitler's Bavarian mountain retreat, the Berghorf, outside Berchtesgaden with increased regularity.

On one occasion Eva caught Goebbels standing in the entry to Hitler's library.

"Good day Joseph," said Eva. She caught Goebbels off guard. He was so attuned to a conversation between Himmler and Speer. Seeing Goebbels and Eva, Speer and Himmler stopped the chat.

"Ah, Dr. Goebbels. Come join us," said Speer. Eva left the room.

Speer and Himmler continued. The two were discussing the treatments Morell was giving Hitler. The Fuhrer's health seemed to be declining. His temperament was erratic.

"Morell is pumping Hitler with an aphrodisiac of sorts," Himmler chuckled. "Rumor has it Eva is lonely and longs for his attention."

Goebbels couldn't believe what Himmler had just said. Goebbels had recorded Magda's telephone conversations. He recalled the desperate call from Eva. *So the Fuhrer is* impotent. *Magda, that bitch, knows more than she's telling me.*

Goebbels listened as Himmler arrogantly revealed his information.

"Morell was treating Hitler with an amphetamine concoction. The potion was mixed with strychnine."

"What proof do you have?" Speer asked.

"Speer, you always underestimate me. I have a lab report. I had a syringe conveniently removed from Morell's' bag. Strychnine, beyond a doubt."

"Himmler, that's a serious accusation. You must inform the Fuhrer," Speer urged.

"Morell is a dangerous man. He has Hitler under a spell. Such an allegation might cost me dearly."

Speer simply shrugged and ended the conversation.

⌘

Later that afternoon, Goebbels was dressing. He designed a uniform for special occasions. Today, he was invited to attend a meeting with the Fuhrer's "inner circle", Bormann, Himmler, and Speer.

Magda showered while he brushed his uniform jacket, one last time.

"Please hand me my robe. It's on the bed," she called stepping from the shower.

Goebbels picked up the negligee, but waited for her to come into the room.

"My dear you look exquisite," he said running his eyes up and down her tantalizing body. "Nevertheless, I'm quite angry with you."

"What now?" Magda asked as she slipped into her silk negligee.

The depraved lust in his eyes disgusts me. She turned her back on him.

"Why didn't you tell me the Fuhrer and Braun were experiencing romantic difficulties?" Goebbels demanded.

"How would I know? Ah. Don't tell me. You've been monitoring my telephone calls. You are despicable."

"You fool, Magda. I listened to your conversation with Eva.

I won't tolerate treachery."

"Earlier today, I heard Himmler and Speer talking in the library. The Fuhrer is taking an aphrodisiac containing Strychnine. Now that's an odd concoction,"

"Strychnine. My god, Joseph that's a poison," Magda gasped.

"Only when taken in large doses. In smaller doses it may act as a stimulant. The formula is critical," Goebbels said.

"We must inform the Fuhrer immediately," Magda insisted.

"You will not."

"Are you crazy? Dr. Morell is going to kill the Fuhrer."

Goebbels grabbed Magda's arm.

"You're hurting me, Joseph. Let go. You will frighten the children."

"They are busy entertaining Eva and the Fuhrer." He squeezed her arm tighter and shoved Magda on to the bed.

"As for the Strychnine, you will not tell the Fuhrer. I want no controversy. I've been cut out of too many high level meetings. I won't infuriate Hitler or Himmler."

"They don't consider you their equal," Magda laughed. "Look at you. Dressed in that ludicrous outfit. You're no officer. You'd be nothing without Hitler."

Suddenly Goebbels' anger succumbed to lust. He tore open her negligee and threw himself on top of her.

"Get off me you club-footed animal." Magda struggled. She pummeled him. He laughed. Magda's fury aroused Goebbels. Goebbels bent her arm as he fumbled with his pants.

Magda thrust her knee between his legs and into his groin. Goebbels yelped more from pain than excitement. Suddenly Goebbels' body quaked in a violent swift ejaculation. He rolled off Magda and on to his back. Magda pushed herself to the edge of the bed.

"I'm warning you. If you ever hurt me again, I will go straight to the Fuhrer. He may deny me a divorce, but he won't allow me to be physically abused. He loves our children. I may have to live with you, but I don't have to sleep with you. Save that for the house keeper and your whores."

Goebbels got off the bed. His uniform pants were soiled. He

stumbled over the dressing table chair. "We'll see," he said as collided with the closet door.

⸏

Magda's anger with Goebbels began to fade as a plan came to mind. A wicked smile crossed Magda's mouth. *So Hitler is impotent. No doubt Morell's daily injections are complicating matters. Dr. Morell, l I have a task for you and your reputation if not your life depends on its success.*

The next morning after breakfast Magda and Eva went for a walk.

"Joseph wasn't at breakfast. Is he ill?" asked Eva.

"Oh, the fool. He fell over the dressing room chair. To make matters worse he walked into the bathroom door. I just don't fathom what his whores see in him."

"Power. They relish Joseph's access to forbidden places."

"I imagine."

"Didn't you at one time? You have six children, my dear. Need I say more?"

"No. Tell me. Why is it you want a child so desperately?"

"Hitler refuses to marry me. I am nothing more than his mistress. I'm certain others laugh and scorn me. Never to my face, however."

"Many do. Others are afraid," Magda replied.

"A child will seal our bond. He loves your children and Speer's children, too. He finds pleasure in visiting the school in Berchtesgaden."

"Sometimes I wonder. Joseph insists the Fuhrer pose for pictures with children for propaganda. I don't trust my husband's motives."

"I know he loves your children, Magda and Speer's children, also. He's told me so," Eva assured Magda.

Magda smiled. *Eva rarely refers to Hitler as Adolf. I find it so difficult to picture Eva's intimate moments with him.*

"I have noticed that lately Joseph plays less of a role in Hitler's decision making. Bormann, Speer and Himmler are the Fuhrer's unofficial cabinet. Martin Bormann is a pest. He is constantly under foot. We have no privacy. Bormann panders Hitler and plays to his ego. He constantly refers to the Fuhrer as the "wolf," a name Hitler savors," Eva complained.

"Be cautious," Magda urged. "Someday we my need Bormann."

"I told you. I despise the man. He controls every aspect of our lives. His estate looks down on our home. He pictures himself the chess master."

"Bormann is the Fuhrer's personal secretary. We need him."

"For what?" Eva stopped and turned toward Magda.

Magda smiled. "I have a plan to resolve your dilemma, my dear. Listen carefully." During their walk Magda told Eva the news about Morell's injections. She convinced Eva to meet with Morell.

"I know about the strychnine. I warn you. I will tell the Fuhrer. Himmler is convinced you are poisoning Hitler. Now my good doctor will you enthusiastically promote my request for a child?" Eva could see fear in Morell's eyes.

Six days later Hitler called Admiral Dönitz. "Speak with Himmler. Have it appear one of your officers is adopting a child. Himmler will make the arrangements. It must be a girl, Eva's concession to me. Once the paper work is complete deliver the child to a family in Berchtesgaden. You will receive their name. No one must know the child's ultimate destination. Any questions, Admiral?"

"No my Fuhrer."

In turn, Admiral Dönitz delegated the responsibility to one of his adjutants, Lieutenant Commander Manfred Bartel.

Chapter Four
Himmler's Lebensborn Program
Steinheoring, outside of Munich, Germany

Lieutenant Commander Bartel and his wife Gertrude were stationed in Berlin. Within days orders arrived for Bartels to travel to Steinheoring, a small town near Munich. Germany's birthrate was declining. Himmler devised the Lebensborn program to encourage unmarried Aryan woman to mate with SS and Wehrmacht officers. Steinheoring was Himmler's first Lebensborn. The Lebensborn program would produce blond, blue-eyed children to lead the master race. Steinheoring (SS-1) served as the model for the subsequent Lebensborn facilities throughout occupied Europe. Himmler turned to Steinheoring to find a child for Eva Braun.

Himmler personally selected the child, a baby girl, identified only as SS 1-3128. It was forbidden to officially name Lebensborn babies. Two documents were created for each child, an SS Lebensborn card and a certificate of Aryan purity. The father's name did not appear on the certificate. In most cases the biological father was an SS officer or German soldier. In the final days of the World War Two Himmler ordered Lebensborn records destroyed. Nevertheless, the identity card for SS 1-3128 existed.

The identity card for baby girl, SS 1-3128, listed Anna Bruns as the biological mother. Bruns was an unwed woman in her early twenties. She was accepted by the Steinheoring Lebensborn and continued to work there after her child was born. Mothers visited with their children several times each day. During each visit Anna secretly whispered her child's name, Nadine, into her baby's ear.

It was mid-morning on a chilly spring day when the Bartels

arrived in a chauffeured Mercedes limousine. The Lebensborn administrator greeted them. The Bartels waited in a simply-appointed private room off the reception area. The director instructed Anna to prepare the discharge document for the Bartels.

"Which baby is leaving?" Anna asked.

"SS 1-3128," replied the administrator.

No. Not Nadine. Without notice they are taking my daughter. No opportunity to hold her one last time. No farewell kiss.

For a brief moment Anna nearly betrayed herself. Her face paled.

The administrator looked at Anna. "Is something wrong, Anna?"

"I am fine," Anna responded. Any hesitation or reluctance would have warranted an immediate reprimand or dismissal. *Of course something is wrong. You know SS 1-3128 is my daughter. How can you be so callous requesting me to deal with the paperwork? I must maintain my composure.* Anna smiled in compliance. A few minutes latter she returned with the Lebensborn discharge folder. Standing beside the Bartels was a SS nurse. She handed the baby to Gertrude Bartel. The Bartels' were impatient to leave. Gertrude bundled baby Nadine for the next part of their journey. Anna didn't dare cry or show expression. The administrator accompanied the Bartels to the front foyer and the coupled departed. The memory of the Bartels limousine driving away haunted Anna.

Anna returned to the administrative office. There on the desk was the duplicate identity card. It was Anna's responsibility to index the card in the security vault. She slipped the card into her skirt pocket and hurried to her room. *Life ended today.* She cupped her eyes and sobbed.

The Bartels were the keepers of the Fuhrer's secret as they embarked on the second part of their mission.

Chapter Five
The Bartels and
SS-1-3128

The Bartels' chauffeur was given a specific route to follow for their trip to Berchtesgaden, in the German Bavarian Alps, a short distance from Salzburg, Austria. Hitler vacationed for several months in the region in 1925. According to Martin Bormann, Hitler wrote a portion of *MEIN KAMPF (MY STRUGGLE)* while living in the region. Bormann moved to gain Hitler's favor and significant control of the complex Nazi Party. Bormann consolidated his power when he was appointed Party Secretary.

Bormann's next move was to create a lavish compound for the Fuhrer and selected Nazi leaders including Albert Speer and Hermann Goring.

Bormann became impatient with the intransigence of some property owners and their reluctance to sell. "I don't give a damn. I want them off the property. If they won't sell force them out. Make an example of one or two. Level the homes."

Eventually, Bormann purchased all the surrounding land for the complex known as Obersalzberg. High on the winding road, Bormann built a magnificent estate. From his vantage point Bormann looked down on the Fuhrer's home and the other residences. The height of Bormann's accomplishment was The Eagle's Nest, a retreat constructed at the highest point on the winding road up the mountain. On a mountaintop nearly 3000 feet above the village of Berchtesgaden the hideaway, with its magnificent view frequently shrouded in clouds, was considered an architectural prize. It was built with Party funds and presented to the Fuhrer as a gift of the people.

It was a crisp, clear evening when the Bartels arrived on the outskirts of the small mountain village. As ordered, the chauffer parked in a designated area near the Nazi complex. The Bartels waited for their contact to arrive. The Mercedes' occupants could not have imagined the horror and despair destined to befall this pristine mountain community in the not too distant future. As Nazi Germany began to fall, the great estates were abandoned.

The Allies did not bomb the entire Berghof complex until April of 1945. At that point they were afraid Hitler would use the mountainside complex for his final stand. By then Hitler and Eva Braun were ensconced in the Fuhrer's bunker beneath the Reich Chancellery.

"How much longer must we wait? The child is hungry," complained Gertrude Bartel.

"We will sit here until our contact arrives. Stop complaining," Manfred snapped.

"Sir, we still have a container of warm milk for the baby," said the chauffer as he peered into the basket on the front passenger's seat. He passed it Gertrude.

"This will have to do my dear. Our contact must be delayed," Manfred said.

It was not long before a man and woman approached the car from a small alleyway. They were dressed in civilian clothes. The man was dressed in a blue suit. The woman wore a dark grey overcoat. The man tipped his hat. The chauffer acknowledged him by rolling down the driver's side window.

"Good evening," said the man. "My name is Richard Klein and this is my wife Sonja."

Manfred immediately exited the car. "Your papers, please." he demanded.

"Ah, yes. And now?" asked Manfred.

"Your mission is complete, Commander Bartel. We will take the child the rest of the way. You have the documents?" Klein asked.

Manfred opened the rear door of the limousine and retrieved the Lebensborn discharge folder. "This folder has two documents, nothing more." Bartels was impatient to deliver the child.

"And what is her name?" Richard asked.

"SS 1-3128," replied Bartel." He handed Klein an envelope.

An unspoken recognition flashed across Klein's face. *A Lebensborn baby!*

"She has no given Christian name. My wife calls her Edith."

Lebensborn baby SS 1-3128, secretly named Nadine by her mother, and was now baby Edith. Her name would change one more time. The Lebensborn identification number SS 1-3128 never changed.

"Thank you, Commander. I was instructed to tell you to return to your hotel in Munich this evening. Enjoy your leave. However, you are to return to Berlin by train. I must emphasize you and Mrs. Bartel must be discreet. Your mission is a closely guarded state secret. It would be best if you changed into civilian clothes for your trip home."

Manfred smiled. Richard Klein was unaccustomed to this sort of encounter. Manfred sensed Klein was not used to being dispatched on secret missions or giving orders. "We will exercise complete discretion," he responded.

"And now, the child," said Klein. He motioned for his wife to step forward.

Manfred opened the car door again and reached inside. Gertrude slid across the leather bench seat and carefully passed the bundle to her husband.

"Here is the baby," Manfred said. Sonja Klein reached out and took the bundled baby. Manfred heard a car engine start. An official SS limousine with a uniformed driver slowly approached.

Sonja Klein turned toward the approaching vehicle to display the baby. The driver immediately got out and opened the rear door of the car for the couple. The Kleins and baby SS 1-3128 were quickly whisked away. Manfred returned to his limousine.

"Return to Munich," ordered Manfred.

"As for you, my dear Gertrude, do not concern yourself with our recent mission. I sense it is best forgotten."

Chapter Six
Martin Bormann's Berghof Estate
Berchtesgaden
Prior to the Arrival of SS-1-3128

In accordance with the Fuhrer's Order, Bormann was charged with finding a home for baby SS-1-3128. He decided it would be with Richard and Sonja Klein. Richard Klein was employed by Martin Bormann to manage his Berghof estate. The Kleins were childless. They had talked about adopting. The Fuhrer encouraged large families for the promotion of the Fatherland. On the other hand, managing the huge estate was demanding. Martin Bormann, a micro manager, was increasingly caught up in the matters of state. Richard Klein often had to postpone routine decisions until Bormann approved. One evening Sonja complained that Richard's personality was changing.

"You are irritable and short tempered," Sonja protested.

"And you? All you do is complain. You don't appreciate the fact that the estate is short-handed." Richard slammed his fist on the kitchen table. "I work long hours. I work from sunrise to sunset. I enjoy sitting in front of the fireplace drinking my beer. I deserve my rest."

Sonja stormed out of the kitchen.

◈

Bormann's magnificent property was designed to be a self-sufficient farm. It was one of several models Bormann designed and established. The Obersalzberg farm sat on about 150 acres. Unfortunately, the mountainside location wasn't suitable for farming.

Klein worried the stables and barns no longer served as

Bormann's prototype for the model farm in the new Reich. One aspect of the farm was evident, the shortage of workers. Except for the contingent of SS forces, the workforce was recruited from Berchtesgaden at the foot of the mountain enclave. The residents of the remote community lived and worked within the confines of the town. Many of the men worked in the neighboring salt mines. As the pressures of the war increased, men were conscripted into the German army. Consequently, the available labor pool diminished. Life became increasingly difficult for the families left behind. One morning Martin Bormann sent an invitation to Richard and Sonja to luncheon with him at the main house. The Kleins were bewildered.

Bormann was in an especially serious, yet hospitable, mood when he met with the Kleins.

"I appreciate your devotion to the estate. It's no easy task managing an endeavor of this size. Nevertheless, I am about to add to your responsibilities."

Richard and Sonja anxiously awaited Bormann's next remarks.

"There is a child I want you to care for. There will be all sorts of questions from your friends and others."

"Are you requesting us to adopt a child?" Richard asked.

"Oh no. You will be the child's guardians. I have prepared official documents. In every way the child, an infant, will be your child. She will join you at community functions and live with you."

"Sir, I am fifty years old. Sonja is forty-nine. I feel we are too old and busy with the farm."

"Nonsense Klein. You are the ideal couple. I assure you every effort will be made to assist Sonja. All expenses will be paid through the estate fund. There are several considerations, however. From time to time Fraulein Braun will visit the farm. These occasions will be discrete. She may also invite the child to visit the Fuhrer's home to socialize with other children."

Again, Richard asked Bormann to reconsider.

"I can not. I recommended you and Mrs. Klein to the Fuhrer. I emphasized your loyalty. The Fuhrer seemed pleased knowing one of my trusted employees would be caring for the child. The arrangements have been made."

Richard knew his employer. Further discussion was useless.

"When will the child arrive?" he asked.

"Very soon. Tomorrow, you must go into town. Purchase what you must for the child. Whatever else you need order directly from Salzburg."

"Sir, there are all sorts of shortages in town."

"Not to worry. Everything will be provided."

Klein pressed Bormann. "My wife has many responsibilities. A child will need a lot of attention."

"I agree, Klein."

"And what will we tell our friends and the townsfolk?"

"Tell them what you know. The father was killed in France and the mother can no longer care for her. I've asked you to care for the child. They need no more. No less."

Sonja Klein's silent consternation disturbed Bormann. "Our conversation is confidential and remains here." Bormann stood and walked behind Sonja Klein. He placed his hand on the back of the chair. "I am counting on your complete cooperation Frau Klein."

Sonja scowled at Richard. "I understand."

Bormann walked to a table next to the huge picture window. He raised a pair of binoculars and began to scan the hillside below. "I can see everything from here. I must remain vigilant in protecting our Fuhrer." Then he dismissed the Kleins with a simple "Thank you for our meeting."

One week later Bormann telephoned the Kleins. "The child will arrive tomorrow. I will send a car for you. The following day Baby SS1-1328, once Nadine, but now Edith, arrived on the Bormann estate.

⌘

Eva Braun visited the Klein household on one occasion. Sonja Klein was ill- tempered. Richard was troubled by Sonja's complaining. He was afraid Bormann would consider his wife's behavior a betrayal. Richard spoke with Sonja, but she continued complaining about the burden of caring for a one-year-old. On her initial visit Eva Braun spent less than an hour with Edith.

Before she left the Kleins, Eva said, "Frau Klein, I will speak with Bormann. This child is very special."

After Braun left, Richard Klein turned to his wife. "Now you've done it. She will speak with Bormann. Why must you always be so disagreeable?"

"I don't want to care for a baby."

"Sonja, the war isn't going well. Please. You know Bormann is apt to rage or worse if he learns of your insubordination," Klein pleaded. *Why can't she be content? We have work, a fine home and food on the table. There's nothing unreasonable about Herr Bormann's request. He is our employer. Others have been asked to make great sacrifices.*

Chapter Seven
Ursula Grasse and Edith

Several days later a young woman from the village arrived at the Klein home. Ursula Grasse was nineteen years old and looked like the ideal Aryan woman. Ursula Grasse lived with her parents in Berchtesgaden. Both her husband and father were serving in France. Ursula's mother took in laundry and cleaned a neighbor's home. Food was scarce. Ursula tended a small garden and bartered for basic commodities.

Once before, Ursula had applied for work in the Bormann household as a maid. The interview went sour when Ursula rebuffed Bormann's advances. He had a reputation as a womanizer. It was public knowledge that he had a mistress. Bormann kept his wife, Gerta, and the children isolated on the farm.

Late one afternoon while Ursula was helping her mother with the laundry an SS officer arrived from the Bormann estate. A note offered work as a nursemaid for Edith. Ursula was perplexed.

"Don't be foolish," her mother said.

"Bormann frightens me, mother."

"You won't be working in the Bormann home. I've met the Kleins. Mrs. Klein is harsh and difficult. Mr. Klein seems meek and not the type to make advances. With your husband and father gone, we have no support."

Ursula had no choice. That evening after dinner, her mother set out Ursula's best dress. "You must look your very best."

At six thirty the next morning a limousine from the estate arrived. Ursula was driven to the Klein's home.

"Good morning. My name is Ursula Grasse."

"What do you want?" asked Sonja.

"I have been retained to be a nursemaid in your household."

"By whom?"

Before Ursula could explain Richard walked into the foyer. "Ah. Good morning. Didn't you apply for a position in the Bormann home?"

"Yes sir. My name is Ursula Grasse. I live in Berchtesgaden with my mother. My husband and father are in the army."

"Please come in," he said.

Klein turned to Sonja and winked. "My dear, this may be the help you have been requesting."

"Fine. I would have appreciated some advanced notice," Sonja shot back.

The three walked into the small living room. Ursula presented the letter from Martin Bormann. "Please sit down," Klein said.

Sonja paced the room. "Well, what does it say?"

"Herr Bormann has retained Frau Grasse to help you with Edith."

"I will arrive each morning by seven o'clock and return home each evening."

"Do as you wish," said the ungrateful Sonja.

"Why do you sound so unappreciative, my dear?" asked Richard.

"Are you hard of hearing? For the last time, I don't want to be the child's guardian."

Ursula began to nervously fidget. *I feel very uncomfortable.*

It was considered impolite for German couples to disagree or bicker in public. Ursula sensed it would be difficult to work for the quarrelsome Sonja Klein. *I feel very sorry for Mr. Klein.*

"Please understand. My wife is not the nurturing type. Come with me. You can meet Edith." Klein led Ursula up the staircase to a second floor with three bedrooms. There was one large room with two gabled windows. The other two were small with sloping ceilings. Klein pointed to the smaller of the two. "This is Edith's room. It's not much of a nursery. Herr Bormann provided all the furnishing."

Ursula opened the nursery door and peeked in at Edith.

"She is a quiet child."

"Too quiet," said Klein.

They returned downstairs. "The car is waiting to take you home."

Ursula thanked Klein. "With your permission, I will start work tomorrow morning," she said.

Klein smiled. He called for Sonja, but she refused to answer. Ursula still couldn't believe a chauffeured limousine was waiting to take her home. Each day from the spring of 1943 until early fall 1944 an SS limousine arrived at 6:30 in the morning to drive Ursula Grasse up the mountainside to the Bormann farm.

Ursula sensed the Kleins were especially guarded about Edith. The child demonstrated some disturbing behavior. *She's been through a lot.*

Many women returned to Berchtesgarden along with their children as the Allies advanced. They escaped urban centers and towns where significant fighting was taking place. The children clung to their mothers. Loud noises frightened them. Like their mothers, the children couldn't sleep. They were moody or sullen. Ursula spoke with Mrs. Klein about Edith's behavior.

"The child is always tense, Frau Klein. He tiny fingers are always clenched. She bangs her head against the crib."

"There's nothing we can do. You'll find out soon enough."

Nevertheless, over the next few months Edith began to smile. Edith grew attached to Ursula. The child became more animated. Edith and Ursula would sit on the carpeted floor near the fireplace and roll a small yellow ball back and forth. Ursula was a blessing for Edith. Sonja Kline grew even more resentful of the child's presence. Ursula was becoming Edith's surrogate mother.

Ursula's presence was, to an extent, a relief for Richard Klein. He looked forward to Ursula's smile and thought of her as a daughter. As summer approached Eva Braun's visits to the Bormann farm increased. On each occasion Ursula would always be present. On occasion, several wives and children of Nazi party officials visited the farm. During those visits Ursula was excused and found herself either in the kitchen or walking back to the Klein's home until the call arrived summoning her back to the Bormanns' mansion to retrieve Edith. At first Ursula thought nothing about the arrangement until one morning Frau Klein received a telephone call from Eva Braun.

"Change into something presentable, Ursula. You've been directed to bring Edith to Berghof. A car will be here at noon," ordered Sonja Klein.

⁊

Eva Braun was an avid photographer. Following the war, the US Army captured hundreds of Eva Braun's personal photographs. They also discovered dozens of reels of Eva's home movies. Dozens of photographs and reels of film show Hitler playing with small children and several infants.

Historians differ over the intent of the footage. Some suggest they were propaganda photos orchestrated by Joseph Goebbels. The Propaganda Minister encouraged the Fuhrer to visit the children of Berchtesgaden. "It was important to be seen among the townsfolk especially when they are hurting." Goebbels assured the Fuhrer. Others contend Hitler actually enjoyed being with the children. In either case, there are a number of photos of children including a series with the Albert Speer's children at play. One particular photo shows the Fuhrer with two small children. The youngest child in the photo may be Baby Edith. Eva's home movies taken at the Eagle's Nest and the little known Teahouse show Hitler with an unidentified child and a young woman in the background, most likely Baby Edith under the watchful eye of Ursula Grasse. Baby Edith was a welcome visitor at the Berghof as the fall of 1943 approached.

Baby Edith turned two years old in 1944. Thanks to Ursula, Edith was showing great strides. The child walked. She smiled. She was a chatterbox. Sadly, the children of the town below the Berghof were not as fortunate.

Berchtesgaden was showing the signs of suffering and shortages felt throughout the Fatherland. The school curriculum was closely scrutinized and followed the Nazi dogma. Jews and regime critics including clerics were dismissed from all levels of German education. Nearly all the teachers belonged to the Nazi Teachers' Association (The National Socialist Teachers' League). Few men and woman did not belong to the Nazi Party.

The political and social life of the community changed drastically. A pall covered the local school and churches. They were previously the focal points of celebration and community social life. Public meetings were strictly regulated. An air of suspicion and trust gripped the town. Church attendance diminished. Inflation gripped the nation as food supplies dwindled. Paying jobs were scarce. The number of widows increased. The residents of Berchtesgaden were terrified to express their worst fear – Germany faced disaster.

Chapter Eight
The Spy
Patchogue, Long Island, New York
1942

It was 6:55 on a Friday evening in 1942 when Sean Cummings stepped from the Long Island Rail Road train onto the platform of the Patchogue station. Indistinguishable from the other passengers, Cummings crossed the tracks and headed toward the Patchogue Hotel on East Main Street. He was dressed in a plain grey suit. A worn fedora covered his closely-cropped red hair.

The rain stopped. Cummings tossed his raincoat over his left shoulder. He carried an overnight bag in his right hand. He walked at a casual pace. His first stop was a stationery store on South Ocean Avenue. He purchased a copy of *The Advance* and a pack of Lucky Strike cigarettes. He approached the intersection of Ocean Ave and Main Street. At the "four corners" he turned right and walked east. He stopped in front of the Post Office. It was too late to check his lobby box. He placed his suitcase on the Post Office steps and dropped his coat on top of it. Cummings casually opened the pack of Lucky Strikes. He placed the cellophane in his suit pocket and withdrew a pack of matches. Cummings' training instilled a constant vigilance. He crossed East Main Street and climbed the hotel steps. Sean Cummings, a hotel regular, followed the same routine on the first and third Fridays of the month. The hotel porch bustled with guests waiting for taxis. The staff readied the huge ballroom for a Chamber of Commerce party.

"Good evening, Mr. Cummings," said the receptionist.

"Good evening." Cummings recognized the woman but didn't know her name. *She was quite attractive.*

"Did Mr. Silver take the night off?" Cummings asked.

"No sir. He enlisted in the Army."

"Please tell Mr. Silver good luck for me, when next you hear from him.

"Yes. My name is Paula Evans."

"Pleased to meet you. Is it Miss Evans?"

"Yes Sir."

Paula Evans caught Sean's smile. She blushed and quickly averted eye contact.

"Your room is ready." She turned and stretched to retrieve the key from the pigeonhole box. Her conservative dress failed to disguise her sculptured body. *A real prize, but now I have more important business.*

Sean nodded and said "Thank you."

Sean Cummings was a spy of the most unusual sort. He was born and raised in Limerick, Ireland. Cummings' father, Tom, an alcoholic, died when Sean was five years old. Tess Cummings nurtured her two sons through years of poverty. Sean inherited the indelible hatred for all things British from Tess. Sean followed his older brother's example and joined the Irish Republican Army. Timothy Cummings disappeared one March night in 1939. His body was discovered several days later. One look at the corpse left few doubts. Timothy had been tortured. By May, 1940, Sean Cummings had been recruited as a potential spy or saboteur for Nazi Germany. He'd do anything to avenge his brother's assassination. Sean Cummings soon joined an elite cadre sponsored by the Abwehr.

A demonstrated talent with small arms and explosives earned Cummings a respected position within the IRA. He also garnered high points from his Nazi patrons. German intelligence reports noted Cummings' talents. He was soon recruited for a special assignment in the United States.

Cummings' case officer in Berlin was Lieutenant Walter Kappe. Before returning to Germany in 1939, Kappe was active in the German American Bund. Unfortunately, he became entangled in the political structure. Kappe lobbied against Fritz Kuhn, the Bund's leader, and lost. Months later he moved his family to Germany and joined the Abwehr, Germany's intelligence agency. Kappe recruited Irish dissidents, including Sean.

Kappe arranged for Sean to enter the United States. He used a forged passport and several letters of sponsorship from Nazi sympathizers living in the New York area. A Nazi sympathizer arranged a job for Sean on the payroll of a New York City printing firm.

Cummings projected the persona of a naïve country boy though he had never set foot on an Irish farm.

"Mr. Cummings looks like my cousin who died at Pearl Harbor," Paula Evans whispered to a friend. I love his Irish accent."

Older women enjoyed Sean, also. They were lonely and found pleasure in seducing a younger man. He reveled in their fantasy, pretending to be led astray. His brooding eyes aroused their appetite. He sensed their hunger. He preferred a slow touch to a ferocious appetite.

Sean told his case officer, "I enjoy women. Sex is a release. I've learned to be guarded against attachments and entrapments. Alcohol, sex and relationships could cost a spy his life. My one vice is cigarettes."

Sean had a unique awareness of his surroundings. He observed a strict regimen. Monday through Thursday evenings he dined in different restaurants. He was careful to watch his apartment building before entering. A staircase led to his one-bedroom Brooklyn flat.

While the FBI monitored suspected Nazi spies living in Manhattan, an elusive Sean Cummings remained at large. He led a simple life in the shadows of the city's skyscrapers. Sean's orders and monthly contingency funds arrived at P.O. box 360 in Patchogue, sixty miles away.

The spy's first assignment involved an espionage plot called Operation Pastorious. A team of saboteurs was in route from Germany. On Friday morning June, 12, 1942 Cummings left work early. He took a train from Penn Station to the Long Island Rail Road Station in Jamaica. He waited for the eastbound train to Patchogue. He entered the third car from the end and waited for his contact. Just as the train was about to leave, a man stepped on board and walked toward the end of the car. He appeared to struggle with a small leather case. He searched for the agreed-to signal, a June copy of *LIFE* magazine featuring film star, Hedy Lamarr, on the cover.

Sean held the magazine conspicuously as though hiding behind it.

"Excuse me. Are you a friend of Walter Kane?" the man asked.

"No. I am a friend of Pastorious," said Cummings. The contact was made.

The man was Heinrich Franz. A German-American, Franz was a trained psychologist. He was enroute through France and on to Berlin via submarine.

Franz was dressed in a blue suit. His only possession was a leather briefcase.

The pair got off the train in Patchogue. Cummings had called ahead. The accommodating Paula Evans was all too happy to have Cummings' room ready for an early arrival. Cummings and Franz went to room 201. Cummings tossed his bag on the bed. He walked to the window and pushed the curtain slightly aside. The window faced East Main Street and the Post Office. Franz used the bathroom.

"Let's go," Cummings called. As they left the room Cummings placed a sliver of paper between the door and the frame.

"Just checking for visitors," he told Franz.

Sean stopped at the front desk. "Good evening, Miss Evans." Paula smiled.

Sean returned the smile. "Please post a note for room service to skip my turndown service this evening."

Paula looked surprised and was about to comment when Sean abruptly turned to his companion and said, "Let's go."

The two men walked across the street. Franz waited while Cummings checked his P.O. box. He peered through the tiny window of the brass door. *No mail.*

Next they walked to a luncheonette at the intersection

of Main Street and Ocean Avenue, opposite Swezey and Newins Department Store.

"What time does our train depart?"

"We have over an hour to wait for the eastbound train to Amagansett."

The platform was packed with weekend commuters heading for Montauk."

A man who called himself "Joe" met them at the Amagansett station.

There was an unexpressed tension between the two men as they sat silently for the ride to Amagansett station.

"Are you a friend of Walter Kane?" Joe asked.

"No. I'm a friend of Pastorious," replied Cummings.

The three men stepped from the platform and walked to Joe's car.

"I live in Montauk, a short distance away."

Cummings had an uncanny sense that Joe was another IRA recruit. The three men waited in Joe's car until dark. Gas was rationed in 1942, but Joe had obvious connections. His gas tank was full. His old Plymouth had been recently repainted. The once-worn seats had been reupholstered. A new set of "retreads" was the "giveaway."

Joe turned off the highway and drove to the beach. The Plymouth passed a cemetery. A heavy fog rolled off the ocean. Joe had driven the assigned route several times. He turned off the headlights.

"The Coast Guard patrols the beach," Joe explained to Cummings.

Joe parked the car parallel to the beach.

"You two wait here," said Cummings. Drive away at the first sign of trouble. I'll work my way back to the cemetery." He darted for the dunes and knelt in the sand searching for a signal. The fog shrouded the entire beach. He could hear the surf breaking. For an instant Cummings thought he heard a thud or thunder clap in the distance. Cummings fell forward to hide in the sand. *What the hell was that? The Coast Guard will be along any minute to investigate.*

Several hundred yards off shore a German U-boat silently waited. Then the signal appeared. A light flashed three times from the water's edge. It barely penetrated the dense fog. Cummings signaled three short bursts with his flashlight. Then he signaled his waiting conspirators. Franz climbed out of the Plymouth and rushed to the beach.

"Good luck," said Cummings.

"We will meet again," Franz said. Franz crept along the dunes. Cummings heard voices from the beach. Franz disappeared into the night. Cummings didn't wait. He ran back to the car.

Joe cautiously followed the route back to the highway. The Plymouth turned left and headed west. "Late-night travel raises suspicion," Joe warned. Joe finally pulled off the Montauk Highway and parked behind a building.

It was nearly six in the morning when they arrived at the Patchogue Hotel. The village was beginning to stir. Sean exited the car a block from the hotel. As he reached the front steps the janitor was sweeping the steps. Cummings nodded. The hotel lobby and the reception desk were empty. Sean peeked into the kitchen and found the clerk brewing coffee.

Cummings was exhausted. He climbed the staircase and carefully approached his room. The telltale sliver of paper was gone. He cautiously unlocked the door. The room was dark with the exception of the glow of the streetlight below. He hesitated then reached for the light switch. Paula Evans was stretched out on the bed.

"What the hell are you doing in my bed?" he demanded.

"I've made a fool of myself," said Paula. She pulled the sheet up to her shoulders.

"For god's sake, Miss Evans. This is ridiculous."

"It's my first time."

"Your first time? I'm a stranger." Cummings hesitated then dropped his jacket on the floor and began to unbutton his shirt. "Are you sure about this? You look frightened."

Paula folded back the sheet revealing her slender naked body.

It was a little after noon when Cummings awoke. Paula was

gone. *She is crazy. Insane. How the hell did she get out of here without being caught? The discreet, shy Miss Evans was hot. What made her do it?*

He ordered rye toast and black coffee from room service. He remained in his room until four that afternoon. He packed his bag and walked down the main staircase to the reception desk. Paula Evans had just arrived.

"I'll be checking out, Miss Evans." He placed the room key in her hand.

"The weather?" she asked.

"Yes. I might as well head back to the city. I'll be back in two weeks," he said.

"Very nice. We look forward to your visits." She smiled.

"Perhaps we might share coffee or lunch one time, Miss Evans." He leaned ever so slowly on the counter. The day manager was watching.

"Oh, that would be nice, but I'm afraid hotel policy prohibits employees from socializing with guests." She rolled her eyes to acknowledge the eavesdropper.

"Yes of course." Cummings laughed. He knew her rejection was really a "yes."

✍

Cummings stared out the dirty passenger train window. Paula Evans muddled his thoughts. He had one more part to his mission.

Cummings was instructed to meet an anonymous man in the lobby of Manhattan's Governor Clinton Hotel on the following Thursday evening. Cummings worried that the FBI might have the building under surveillance. Thirty First Street bustled. Cummings looked at his wristwatch. The contact failed to show. *I'll risk going inside.* He approached the registration desk.

"I'm sorry, sir. It appears Mr. Day has checked out," said the clerk.

"Strange. I was to meet him in the lobby tonight. We had a

dinner engagement," Cummings said.

The meeting never took place. George Dasch, alias Mr. Day, was one of the U-boat saboteurs. He betrayed his comrades. Dasch contacted the FBI. Next, he persuaded his partner, Burger, to accompany him to Washington, D.C. Both men surrendered to the F.B.I. Dash gave the authorities the locations of the remaining members of the Pastorious operation. Luckily, Dash never knew the name of his New York City contact. Cummings was safe.

Friday, June 12 and Saturday June 13, 1942 marked significant dates for the United States and Germany.

The President signed the executive order establishing the Office of Strategic Services (OSS), the forerunner of the CIA.

In Germany, the Nazi research team led by Werner Von Braun launched its first V-2 rocket at Peenemunde.

The Abwehr landed the first of two spy teams on Long Island. Heinrich Franz departed Amagansett on board the same German U-boat, thanks to Sean Cummings' work.

Returning to his apartment, Sean Cummings wondered what new missions lay ahead. The Allies and Axis were engaged in a total war. At Walter Kappe's direction, Cummings continued to follow his routine visits to Patchogue. He awaited his next assignment. It didn't come until the spring of 1945.

Chapter Nine
The Berghof
Winter 1944

The winter of 1944 was especially cold. In Germany many families were forced to share housing, food and other basic commodities. Nevertheless, there were no shortages among the Nazi leaders on the mountainside. Along with ample food, there was an abundance of intrigue. Whispered exchanges questioned the Fuhrer's bizarre behavior.

Hitler's personal physician was falling under suspicion. Morell, the persistent charlatan, had come up with a new scheme. Morell did everything possible to belittle Eva Braun. One evening Morell had too much to drink. He took a great risk and revealed Eva Braun's desire for a child to a colleague, Heinrich Franz. "I helped Braun persuade Hitler to bring a child to Bormann's home."

Heinrich Franz was the American psychologist who escaped Amagansett on board the U-202 with the help of Sean Cummings.   Since arriving in Germany, Franz had gained Hermann Göring's attention. Franz called his research "brain change." The technique incorporated the use of electroshock and drugs. One of Franz's favorite psychotropic drugs was mescaline. There was total disregard for his brain change experiment subjects. Follow-up studies would have revealed the children experienced ensuing physical and emotional disorders including epilepsy and depression.

Nevertheless, Franz convinced Hermann Göring to fund a spin-off project at the Hermann Göring Institute. Göring assembled volunteer Luftwaffe pilots for the study. These experiments involved behavior modification techniques. Franz assured Göring, "I'm convinced my techniques will give your pilots unmatched skill and commitment."

Franz's enthusiasm persuaded Morell, too. "I'm on the verge of unlocking the secret to totally altering an individual's personality. Can you imagine the unlimited potential?"

Morell smiled and listened with envy.

"Envision a human being programmed to obey an imbedded command without weighing the personal or moral consequences," Franz told Morell.

"Would this procedure work with children?" asked Morell.

"The younger the better. I've already begun experiments with a group of Hitler Youth. The younger the subject the easier it is to alter perception, cognition and behavior."

Morell smiled. "Ah, Heinrich. I believe I have just the subject for you."

"And who would that be?"

"The child Eva Braun keeps as her play thing. I will arrange a visit." Morell laughed.

◈

One morning in 1944, two strangers arrived at the Klein home on the Bormann estate.

"My name is Doctor Theodor Gilbert Morell. I am the Fuhrer's personal physician. This is my colleague Doctor Heinrich Franz. We would like to meet the child in your care."

Richard Klein was alarmed. "Is something wrong with the child?"

"Not at all," said Morell. "I've observed the child at play. She is a wonderful girl. However, the other afternoon the Fuhrer expressed concern that Edith appeared sullen and withdrawn on the last few occasions."

"But, is all this attention necessary? After all, Edith is only a child," said Klein.

Morell and Franz continued to visit the Klein home numerous times between February and late May. Richard Klein insisted Sonja and Ursula be present during the visits. Sonja frequently acquiesced to Franz's request to meet with Ursula and Edith alone.

"What goes on when you meet with Franz?"

"Dr. Franz shows the child drawings. He asks questions and takes notes. I don't understand what this is all about," said Ursula. Dr. Franz seems to pay close attention to Edith's behavior. The child seems afraid. When I pretend to leave the room Edith runs to me. She clings. Franz smiles and beckons to the child. I feel very uncomfortable.

"It doesn't matter what you like. Dr. Franz is here on official business," Sonja replied."

Ursula's suspicions grew as Franz' visits increased. There were times when Franz asked to be alone with the child. Ursula spoke with Sonja Klein. Sonja demanded Ursula not tell Richard. Frau Klein seemed mesmerized by Franz.

Soon Franz's visits increased to twice a week. One day Franz would spend with Ursula and Edith and the other with Sonja. The visits always took place while Richard Klein was attending to farm business. A suspicious Ursula confided in her mother. "I think Franz and Frau Klein are having an affair."

"Don't tell anyone," her mother cautioned. "You might be dismissed. Mr. Klein will find out soon enough."

Ursula began to notice subtle changes in Edith's behavior. Edith displayed mood swings. Playtimes at the Berghof appeared less fun. Eva Braun was spending less time with the child. Little did Ursula know of the growing tension between Hitler and Eva Braun.

One evening Eva asked Magda Goebbels, "Do you feel a growing tension among Hitler's advisors?"

"My dear it's the move," Magda replied.

"What move?'

"The Fuhrer plans to return to Berlin in July."

"He plans to leave me here.

"Are you sure?'

And what about the child?"

"I overheard Morell tell Joseph yesterday."

Eva turned and looked for Hitler. "How could he plan to leave without telling me? Morell knew. I didn't."

"You are too fragile, Eva," Hitler replied.

"And what of the Edith and Doctor Franz? Will they remain?"

"Franz. I've never heard of him."

"Franz is Morell's colleague. Surely you've met him. He has been visiting the Kleins' home several times a week for months supposedly at your request.   He spends hours with the child and her nursemaid, Ursula Grasse."

"Believe me, I have no time for such nonsense, my dear. I'm certain with Morell's supervision, your Doctor Franz is performing wonders for the child. Your obsession with Morell has to end. Morell is going with me to Berlin. I need him."

"Something is wrong. I'm sure of it," Eva sobbed.

"I'll ask Bormann to check into Franz. Now that's the end of it."

Eva suspected Martin Bormann might be withholding information about Hitler's health. *Why would Hitler find Morell so indispensable? Surely Bormann is aware of Franz's visits to the Klein home. Bormann watches everyone.*

∾

Eva waited several days before approaching Bormann. Bormann had an office at the Berghof. Hitler had told Bormann to anticipate Eva's visit. Franz's dossier sat on the corner of Bormann's desk.

"Heinrich Franz is unique," said Bormann. "He divides his time between Berchtesgaden and the Göring Institute.

"May I read the file?" asked Eva.

"I'm afraid that's not possible. Several portions are top secret? Bormann read selected sentences to Eva. "Franz holds an Abwehr clearance. Göring is sponsoring the man's work at the Institute. I would need the Fuhrer's permission to show you the entire file."

Bormann dropped the file to his desk. *Information is power.*

Bormann suspected Franz's Thursday visits were timed to Richard Klein's trips into Berchtesgaden. Bormann was certain

Sonja Klein and Heinrich Franz were enjoying an affair. Their dalliance intrigued him. *Franz is so much younger than Frau Klein. She must be a wonder.*

"I understand your concern for the child," Bormann assured Eva Braun. "Morell has tremendous influence with the Fuhrer. Believe me, I have no idea what Franz is doing.

"I have my suspicions about Frau Klein."

"I will look into the matter. I must be discreet," Bormann assured Eva.

After Eva left, Bormann sat at his desk to review Franz's personnel file again.

Bormann gloated over a minute notation he had overlooked. It referenced a directive from Admiral Wilhelm Canaris, chief of Hitler's military intelligence. Canaris promised Franz a position within the Abwehr's counterintelligence and research component in return for information about Dr. Morell's relationship with the Fuhrer.

Bormann chuckled. *So Canaris is a potential Franz patron. His work must be important.*

Bormann instinctively disliked Canaris. Bormann suspected he was involved in a conspiracy to grab control of Germany from Hitler.

"Canaris must be watched," Bormann warned Hitler.

On July 20,1944 a group of conspirators attempted to assassinate Hitler. A bomb was placed under the conference table. Hitler was severely injured. Several high-ranking staff members were killed. The coup failed. The Gestapo subsequently rounded up 7000 suspects. The main conspirators were immediately shot. Others were hanged. Nearly 5000 were executed. Prominent among those put to death was the Abwehr's chief, Admiral Canaris.

The Wolf's Lair incident was the sixth attempt to assassinate Hitler. Eva Braun became obsessed with Hitler's safety and her own vulnerability.

"I must be with Hitler in Berlin, " Eva protested.

"It is too dangerous," Bormann warned.

Eva telephoned Hitler. "I must have a will," she told Hitler. "Why?"

"I doubt you will marry me. I would die for you. You do not return my affection."

"My dear, you think too much. There's something else troubling you. What is it?"

"I've created a predicament. You warned me. It's the child, Edith. What will become of her? Please, you must save the child."

"The Reich is on the brink of disaster and you want me to save one child?"

"You must. You owe it to me."

"I'm too tired to argue. I yield. I plan to return to the Berghof for the holidays. I will tell Bormann to make the arrangements for the child."

Late the same evening Hitler met with Bormann. "I promised Eva I would help shield the child. You must come up with a plan. It's clear the Russians are closing in. I have no intention of leaving Germany. We will spend Christmas in Berchtesgarden. After the holidays we will return to Berlin and the Fuhrer Bunker to personally direct the defense of Berlin. Eva will accompany me."

"My Fuhrer we must have options for your safety. Months ago I took it upon myself to plan an escape route for you. You have allies in Brazil and Argentina. A U-boat has been selected for this very purpose."

"Nonsense, Bormann. I just told you. I have no intention of leaving. Make provisions for the child."

❧

Hitler and his entourage arrived at the Berghof in December. "We must prepare for a massive counteroffensive immediately," he instructed his General Staff. "We must be ready to act no later than mid-December."

Bormann arrived a day after Hitler. He went immediately to the Berghof rather than his own estate.

"The Fuhrer has been stricken with a bout of stomach

cramps," said one of the servants. "He is in a cranky mood."

Bormann was used to Hitler's chronic pains and attacks of diarrhea and so he braced for the unexpected. Bormann coughed several times to alert Hitler to his presence. Hitler turned and said, "Ah, Bormann. I am glad to see you. Do you have a plan for the child?"

"I do. It is risky and may sound far-fetched but it will succeed, if the order comes from you." Bormann handed Hitler a document outlining a plan to secure Edith's safety.

"Bormann, surely you are joking. You want me to order a U-boat transport to the United States. This is insane."

"The U-boat has already been selected. It was part of my plan to take you to South America."

"But why such extravagance to save one child?"

"My Fuhrer. Please, listen. The U-boat could be delayed."

"Never."

"Then allow me to proceed with the operation."

"Very well."

Bormann handed Hitler a pen.

Hitler signed the order and Bormann stamped the document with the Fuhrer's personal seal.

"Mein Fuhrer, you order will be followed. The plan will succeed."

Within days Hitler left for Berlin. Some of the bloodiest fighting of World War Two was about to begin.

Joseph and Magda Goebbels followed Hitler to Berlin and eventually resided in the Fuhrer bunker. In the end they would murder their children and fulfill a suicide pact. Magda contended, "I would never submit her children to the humiliation of capture by the Russians."

Berchtesgaden remained relatively safe from airstrikes until April 25, 1945 when American and British planes bombed the Nazi compound on the Obersalzberg. The following day units of the 101st Airborne and a tank battalion reached the Berghof. By then most if not all high ranking Nazi's had left the mountain.

By then Martin Bormann was ensconced with Hitler in Berlin. Bormann remained until the Fuhrer committed suicide.

He disappeared into the rubble of Berlin.

Hitler's physician, Morell, accompanied Hitler to Berlin, also. He left the bunker as the Russians closed in. He later committed suicide.

The mysterious Heinrich Franz managed to escape.

When Allied bombings destroyed the Bormann estate, Richard and Sonja Klein escaped the authorities by hiding in a friend's home. Eventually they surrendered to a US military police unit, but, were later released.

The Kleins never told the authorities about baby Edith. Edith was alive and in the care of a Naval Officer's family outside Flensburg, Germany.

Chapter Ten
The Flensburg Event
German Naval Training College,
 Four miles from the Danish-German border.
 Flensburg Germany

Admiral Karl Dönitz was unable to sleep. Dönitz was the commander of all German Naval Forces including the feared U-boat wolf packs. By this point in the war the U-boat service had suffered tremendous losses, including the deaths of the Admiral's two sons. Dönitz initially handpicked his U-boat captains. Many were vanquished. Young crews were dying in their iron coffins. Nonetheless, the loss of seventy percent of U-boat crews did not deter Dönitz from dispatching a final round of submarines on what he knew would be a disastrous mission.

Affidavits from the Nuremberg trials clearly show Dönitz remained a committed follower of Adolf Hitler. Hitler's will and final executive order named Dönitz as his successor. Since a failed assassination attempt months earlier, the Fuhrer's emotional and physical health had deteriorated. The incessant Allied air raids had demoralized the German population. Hitler's "thousand year Reich" was turning to rubble.

Admiral Dönitz telephoned Albert Speer, Hitler's key infrastructure advisor. "A failing transportation network denies my U-boats the needed fuel to carry out long missions to the US Atlantic coast," he told Speer. Dönitz knew better than to voice his fears. *Germany was faltering to the point of surrender. The Fuhrer's advisors are looking out for themselves.*

"The Fuhrer is doing his best, Admiral. We all are." Speer ended the call by shouting "Heil Hitler."

∽

Admiral Dönitz's U-boat fleet suffered mounting losses in the days following his call to Speer. Dönitz was shocked when a courier delivered the first of Adolf Hitler's Fuhrer Orders.

The order directed Dönitz to secretly contact General Eisenhower. The Fuhrer was prepared to negotiate safe-passage for an individual within his circle. Hitler promised Eva he would try to save Edith from the Russians.

Hitler wrestled with his decision. *What would Eisenhower demand in return?*

It was a bold move, but not without precedent. Few members of the Nazi leadership or the General Staff were aware of six Axis-Allied prisoner exchanges. The logistics were handled by so-called neutral nations in Europe and Latin America. The first exchange occurred 1942. A secret US-Japanese swap in 1943 repatriated 2500 US civilian and government officials. Perhaps more than 5000 civilians and government officials were exchanged prior to President Franklin D. Roosevelt's death.

Martin Bormann suggested the bold effort. "It has to be a daring plan. Perhaps a flight to England or Portugal."

"Out of the question," Hitler responded. "No, I have a better idea. I trust Admiral Dönitz. We'll need one of his U-boats and a stalwart crew."

"Such arrangements may take months."

"Nonsense, Bormann. Work out the details. I'll sign the Fuhrer Order."

Dönitz was dismayed when he read the order and questioned the directive's authenticity. There were too many variables including the lack of sufficient fuel to a U-boat to travel to the Long Island coast and return safely.

Perhaps this was a trap to test my loyalty. The Gestapo lurked in the shadows. He wanted no part of a conspiracy or coup. *These are perilous times. Even the slightest suspicion of intrigue will be disastrous for my staff and me.*

Dönitz contacted Martin Bormann. "Bormann, I'm calling regarding the authenticity of the Fuhrer Order to transport four passengers to the United States."

"Yes, I assure you it is authentic," said Bormann.

"The details will take six months or more. Fuel is in short supply. To implement the order requires extensive modifications to an existing U-boat."

"Phase one will begin immediately. An overture has been sent to Eisenhower. You must be ready by February. The Russians are moving north. Our forces are reinforcing Norway. The Fuhrer will remain in Berlin."

The next morning at breakfast Bormann informed Hitler of the Admiral's call.

"The Fuhrer order must be obeyed. What part of my order did Dönitz questioned?"

Bormann was about to answer when Hitler began to rant. "Be vigilant, Bormann. I know my most devious of enemies have unquestioned arrangements. Even my closest supporters are deserting me. They are scheming my demise."

Bormann was apprehensive. *The Fuhrer can't stay focused. I fear this U-boat business is doomed to failure.*

Bormann knew the end was near. Was it coincidental that Allied bombings focused on transportation and marshaling yards rather than industrial centers? The IG Farben Building stood untouched. Bormann ordered the arrest of one prominent industrialist who stated, "The world's financial powers have large pre-war investments in Germany. These assets must remain intact." The man's remarks reinforced Bormann's suspicions. *The Allies are designating certain locations as "off limits" for aerial bombardment. The Allies are protecting their pre-war financial investments in Germany as the war draws to an end.*

Bormann was beginning to protect the Fuhrer by withholding information. *The stress has become too much. The Fuhrer Order to transport four passengers to the United States seems doomed to failure. Is Hitler going mad?*

❧

At the Naval College in Flensburg, four days passed while

Dönitz delayed taking a U-boat out of service for modifications. It was a calculated risk, but he waited for Albert Speer to authorize the needed fuel for a long-range mission. Without adequate fuel, U-boats dispatched to the US coastline would never return.

The admiral was also troubled with the precarious position the Fuhrer had placed him in. He cupped his head in his hands brooding. He was ordered to prepare a U-boat for a one-way mission. The U-boat carried a crew of 52. It would have to be refitted to accommodate four passengers including a child. *How can such a directive be accomplished without raising suspicions? The Reich was rampant with fear and plotting.*

It was too late. Late one evening Bormann telephoned Dönitz.

"No more delays. We have received word through the Swiss Embassy that the Americans are willing to negotiate a deal."

"I must be involved in the negotiations, also?" asked Dönitz.

"Yes. Find a way to start clandestine negotiations via intermediaries."

"I detest dealing with Danish partisans."

"You have your orders, Admiral. The Fuhrer directed me to request the Swiss contact General Eisenhower. If Eisenhower responds positively, you will act immediately. In any case proceed with the U-boat modifications."

"I surmise the OSS (Office of Strategic Services) will play some role in the discussions."

"Perhaps. You must have one of your staff fully briefed and ready to meet with Eisenhower's agent. Admiral, may I remind you these talks must be kept secret. Do not reveal the Fuhrer Order to the Gestapo or the Abwehr."

"I understand."

Bormann abruptly terminated the call without his usual "Heil Hitler."

The next morning, Dönitz met with his aide-de-camp, Commander Hoff. The Admiral was somber as he briefed Hoff. Dönitz anticipated Hoff's immediate reaction.

"I have authenticated the order at the highest level. It must be obeyed. There is no room for failure."

"Sir, the order requires six or seven months of preparation. You have been given three."

"The Danish partisans have signaled the Allied response. Intelligence reports an OSS (Office of Strategic Services) agent parachuted into Denmark in December. He is now working with the Copenhagen partisans," said Dönitz.

"How will we coordinate meetings with Danish partisans?" asked Hoff. Hoff's tone always respectful echoed skepticism. *The Gestapo and sympathizers are everywhere.*

"Very carefully," Dönitz bluntly replied.

"Have you selected your representative? This will be a perilous assignment, said Hoff.

The Admiral turned and gazed at a huge map of the North Atlantic. "I have. You are my choice, Hoff."

"Sir. With all due respect, why me?"

"You speak excellent English and Danish. This is bound to be an OSS operation. The agent will be an American. You are an excellent match. Rest assured, the burden will not fall entirely on you. I trust you."

Dönitz sensed Hoff was reluctant to voice his objection. "Realistically, there is no turning back. We have our orders."

"Sir, you know the Gestapo and the SS scrutinize the General Staff. They trust no one. The Fuhrer must realize it will be impossible to maintain a curtain of secrecy."

"Everyone is under suspicion, Hoff. We must proceed with deliberate speed." The Admiral returned to the huge wall map. "The Russians are closing on Berlin. The Americans have advanced into Belgium."

"Sir, the Fuhrer's fury alone will not hold back the advancing armies."

Dönitz looked askance. "Are you prepared to deliver that message to the Fuhrer?"

"No, sir."

Dönitz turned and walked to his desk. He removed a document.

"Bormann dispatched an addendum to the original order. I suspect more will arrive. We will modify a U-boat for the evacuation of a child, the guardian and two adults. The order designates a specific vessel, the U-853."

Hoff was perplexed. "The U-853? What is its present location?" asked Hoff.

"Stavanger, Norway, undergoing repairs. Its commander was severely injured and his executive officer is the temporary commander."

"It is rumored our leader is quite superstitious. The U-853 has a reputation for getting itself out of close scrapes," the Admiral answered.

"Sir, when will I learn the complete details?"

Dönitz paused. "I will tell you. The secret may cost your life."

Hoff stepped back.

"Sir an IXC/40 U-boat calls for a crew of fifty-five. How will she accommodate three adults and an infant to the United States?" *This is an impossible plan.* "Is this another Abwehr scheme? Our crews suffer the consequences. You were opposed to Operation Pastorious."

"Yes, it was disastrous. We nearly lost the U-202. All eight agents were captured and presumed executed," said Hoff.

"I'm not so sure they are all dead, Hoff. The FBI's Director, J. Edgar Hoover, is a devious adversary. No, Hoff, this is not an Abwehr scheme. This is a Fuhrer Order. No more questions for tonight. You have your orders. I am depending on you to carry them out at all costs. That will be all for this evening. We will meet tomorrow at 0900 hours." The officer came to an abrupt attention and saluted the admiral.

Dönitz was left alone to ponder the New England coastline.

Chapter Eleven
Denmark December 25, 1944

It was Christmas day 1944 when OSS operative, code name "Robert," parachuted into Denmark. William Robert Mallory was a 24-year-old Yale graduate student when a college professor recruited his favorite student for the OSS. Mallory had all the makings of a spy. William Robert Mallory was a track star, first chair French horn musician, and Phi Beta Kappa scholar with an Aryan profile and a keen eye for a beautiful co-ed. Mallory spoke fluent German, but little Danish.

Mallory spent nearly a year in training for his first mission, a parachute insertion into Denmark. The training was intense. Mallory soon became incommunicado to his family and friends. The transformation from William to "Robert" was stressful and exhausting. One day at a time, William Mallory's personality faded as "Robert's" identity emerged. There were times when Mallory was uncertain who he was. At one point following a mock interrogation he thought of quitting. He didn't. In turn, Mallory was assigned to the Special Operation Unit, a tough behind enemy lines component of the OSS.

Mallory's intense training began with a six-mile run through Prince William Park adjacent to the Marine Corps Training base at Quantico, Virginia. One US official called the rigorous training appalling. The simulations crossed over the line to severe beatings and sleepless nights. "Once captured you will be tortured. Partisan lives depend on you." Mallory completed nearly all his training without injury. One accident jeopardized his efforts. He caught a trip wire and detonated an explosive tied to a nearby tree. The explosion knocked him unconscious. Undeterred, Mallory morphed into "Robert" a ruthless saboteur. There was one caveat. An instructor scribbled a note on Mallory's file:

"Mallory is scrupulous to a fault. However, he has the instinct for survival. I concluded he would not hesitate to kill if the mission were in jeopardy. His is remarkable at practical combat shooting and field craft. My one concern: Mallory is a Roman Catholic. His religious beliefs might prevent Mallory from committing suicide. His determination to fight to the death might lead to his being wounded and imprisoned by the enemy."

One Friday morning while planning for a well-deserved leave, Mallory was summoned to Colonel Barnes's office.

"Mallory, we have an important assignment for you. You will be part of a three-man team. Your objective is to connect with elements of the Danish Freedom Council. You're being promoted."

"Promoted, sir?" Mallory held the provisional rank of Lieutenant in the Naval Reserve, although he had never attended the Great Lakes training. Once, while visiting the newly completed Pentagon Mallory saw a tailored officer's uniform. He smiled. *Perhaps one day I'll have one made. For now I don't need the expense.*

"Your assignment demands the rank of Commander," Colonel Barnes replied.

Each day a new part of the mission was revealed. Mallory met the other two OSS operatives. These two would be inserted into Denmark prior to Mallory. Danish partisans would unite the team at a safe house outside of Copenhagen. Only Mallory knew the mission's ultimate goal. One of the team was killed during the parachute jump. The second man, a communication specialist, was also injured and being held in Gestapo Headquarters in Copenhagen. By the time OSS headquarters in London was informed Mallory was on the ground in suburban Copenhagen.

Hours prior to departure from England Mallory received his final briefing. He was to conduct a successful negotiation with Admiral Dönitz's envoy. Mallory's superiors concluded this mission was simply a prelude to the Admiral's interest in conditional peace negotiations. German forces were pushing into the northern region of the mainland. They occupied Denmark and Norway.

⌇

Mallory and a member of the Danish Freedom Council, code-named Mikkelsen, waited on a hill above a remote location on the Danish border. They peered down at a secluded fisherman's cottage. The remote cottage was the agreed-to location for their first encounter. Neither party trusted the other. It might be a trap. A number of partisans had been betrayed.

"The rendezvous time has past," warned Mikkelsen. Mallory and the agent grew uneasy. Then from the dock below came the signal. The two men descended the bluff. They could see the outline of a man standing alone on the dock. Mallory returned the man's signal. The man on the dock cautiously approached the cottage and opened the door.

"You go in," said Mikkelsen. "I'll cover you."

Mallory nodded in agreement and cautiously entered the room.

The abandoned cottage turned out to be a fishermen's refuge from bad weather. The windows on each wall were covered with ragged burlap. Wind whistled through the broken panes of class. Before the war fishermen used the structure as a shelter from the harsh winds and cold weather.

Mallory stepped back. *The smell of rotting fish entrails is making me gag.* A huge rat startled by Mallory's flashlight scurried across the floor. The flashlight's red lens cast a strange glow, but made it easier to see under the dark conditions. Mallory stepped further into the open. Mikkelsen followed.

"That's far enough," came a voice from the shadows. "What is the password?"

"Blue Dawn," replied Mallory. "And your response?"

"Phoenix rising," the German naval officer shot back.

Mallory's eyes were glued on the emerging figure. *This guy is nervous. His hands are shaking.*

"My torch doesn't have a red lens. It will next time, said the man as he moved toward the center of the room. A long workbench separated the three men.

"We are unarmed as agreed," said Mallory.

Mallory stepped forward, but Mikkelsen hesitated. Mallory turned to Mikkelsen, "Step closer."

The German stood at attention, clicked his heals and gave a military salute. Mallory expected a Hitler salute.

"Commander Wilhelm Hoff. I am Admiral Dönitz's adjutant and representative."

Mallory returned the salute. "Commander William Mallory, United States Navy, attached to the Office of Special Services."

"We know who you are, Commander. Your two companions were not as fortunate as you. Your communications specialist was injured during his parachute landing. He was taken to a hospital. He is now the guest of the Gestapo at Shell House. Hoff turned to Mikkelsen and asked, "You do know Shell House?"

Mikkelsen remained expressionless. *Off course I know Shell House you bastard. It's Gestapo Headquarters and torture chamber.* Hoff saw Mikkelsen's fists tighten. The Commander smiled. His remark had triggered a reaction.

"You boys need more low altitude parachute experience," replied Hoff. Mallory didn't like the gaff. Hoff was sparring. Several chairs and a stool were against the wall. The men remained standing.

"The four mile crossing was quite precarious. Rough water tonight," said Hoff. Mallory guarded against casual conversation. Hoff looked directly at Mallory as though memorizing the crevasses in his face. Then Hoff observed Mikkelsen. Both men nodded and exchanged tight-lipped smiles reminiscent of gladiators facing off in the Coliseum. Mikkelsen watched the exchange. *My days were numbered once this mission was completed. One way or another, the Gestapo will discover my role in this plot.*

"Commander, the Admiral signaled London that he wanted to discuss a substantive issue, an exchange of sorts. My superiors in Washington concluded the Admiral's intention was peace negotiations. Rudolf Hess is a prisoner in England. MI6 and the Allied Command found Hess's peace proposals totally unacceptable. There will be no conditional surrender. Please assure the Admiral."

"Admiral Dönitz owes an allegiance to the fatherland and then to Hitler. We are not all rabid Nazis. I assure you Admiral Dönitz understands the military and political realities."

"Berlin will fall," said Mallory.

"Not without a major battle, Commander. Nevertheless, I am not here to discuss peace negotiations. The Admiral informed me you are interested in a specific 'package.'"

"Your Admiral started the ball rolling, Commander. He wants something in exchange," retorted Mallory. "What is it?"

Hoff was authorized to tell Mallory the essential parts of the Fuhrer order.

"I will share all the details once we have an understanding, Commander. What does your government demand in return?" Hoff asked.

"My government wants a research scientist. We know him by the name Otto Bruns. He is a virologist. He was a faculty member at Berlin University. Our intelligence agencies believe Bruns is attached to Himmler's bio-research institute."

"I know nothing about Himmler, the SS, or his research. Why this particular scientist? What makes this Bruns so important?" asked Hoff.

"A ventured guess?"

Hoff nodded a "Yes."

"From my briefings, I suspect Bruns is the lab chief of your government's leading bio-weapons program on Riems Island."

"I recognize the name, but I know nothing about bio-weapons."

"It doesn't matter whether you know about bio-weapons or not. My assignment is to deliver Bruns to the United States. Admiral Dönitz has conveyed his willingness to negotiate."

Mallory was withholding information from Hoff. Army Intelligence had briefed Mallory prior to his mission. Mallory's target, Otto Bruns, was a key figure at the Nazis' Entomological Institute. He supervised a unit researching remedies against insect diseases. Hitler warned Himmler to avoid biological warfare. Himmler and others circumvented the directive by conducting defensive research. There is a fine line between defensive and offensive disease research. Himmler had dispatched Bruns to Manchuria.

"Again, I know nothing of Bruns or his activities," insisted Hoff.

"My superiors claim Bruns observed Japanese experiments on human subjects conducted Unit 731. The Japanese used ticks, fleas, and mosquitoes to spread disease. Bruns utilized this information for technical upgrades and expansion at Himmler's Riems Island facility. Bruns narrowed his research to mosquitos known to transmit malaria to humans.

"I assure you, Admiral Dönitz knows the urgency of these negotiations," said Mallory. His last coded message read: "Imperative we snatch Bruns before the Russians enter Berlin."

"Again, I assure you, Commander, I know nothing about biological research. I am naval officer. Naturally, I will convey the urgency of your message to the Admiral."

Mallory heard a boat engine start in the distance. "You understand the importance of obtaining Bruns?" Mallory insisted.

Hoff nodded his agreement. "It is time to leave."

"One question, Commander. How will I know you are ready to negotiate?"

"Look for a trawler flying a black ensign. It will sail near the shore. Be alert. We will meet here at sundown the same day."

Mikkelsen and Mallory returned to the distant safe house. A partisan sentinel was posted to watch for the trawler. Several days passed. January was nearly over. The winter of 1944 was especially harsh. Travel was difficult.

One evening, Mikkelsen received word of the American captive at Shell House. His interrogators were growing impatient. The prisoner was kept in solitary confinement and denied medical treatment.

"You are a spy and will be treated as such," shouted a Gestapo interrogator. "You will break. I assure you." The wires attached to the prisoner's testicles sparked. The second interrogator flipped the switch. The OSS officer screamed.

"He is unconscious, sir."

"Throw water on him," said the commandant.

On Thursday, January15, 1944, two officers from Gestapo headquarters in Copenhagen arrived at Admiral Dönitz's headquarters. They showed the Admiral a transcript taken during the captured OSS agent's interrogation.

"The prisoner is an US Navy communications specialist. He will break soon. Is there any possibility you have a traitor on staff, Admiral?" asked one of the officers.

"My staff is totally trustworthy, " Dönitz said indignantly. *They are fishing.* "Is my loyalty in question?" Then Dönitz added "It's regrettable your vigilance didn't extend to the attack on our Fuhrer."

Both officers' posture stiffened, but their faces remained expressionless.

Dönitz, a man of controlled composure, was angry. He struggled to regain his poise.

"Very well, Admiral. It was not our intention to cast aspersions on your staff. These are treacherous times. Be cautious."

There was no way Admiral Dönitz would reveal knowledge of Mallory. To inform Shell House would betray the Fuhrer's orders. The Gestapo officers departed.

When Hoff met with Dönitz, the admiral ordered: "Get on with the negotiations. Hold nothing back. Time is precious. Dispatch the trawler at first light. Fly the signal ensign. The Gestapo has picked up our scent."

The Admiral was alarmed, especially concerned by a decoded message on his desk:

"January 20, 1944: RAF dropped 2300 ton bombs on Berlin." *The pressure is building.*

At his next meeting with Mallory, Commander Hoff insisted German Naval Intelligence was unable to locate a biologist named Otto Bruns. "Yes, a scientist named Bruns had been at the Berlin Institute, a satellite of the University. I reviewed his file," said Hoff. "We have no record he was an observer at Japanese medical experiments in China. Yes, he works with rockets and biological weapons deployment. Our dossier shows he is an expert in offensive aerosol dispersal of anthrax. Is this your man?"

"All I know is Otto Bruns is my target. My orders are to extract him. Your job is to deliver my target. Admiral Dönitz initiated these talks. He assured my government he would provide for the exfiltration operation. Do you understand, Hoff?" Mallory shouted.

"I have told you everything I know, Commander," Hoff responded.

"Time is running out. My mission and my life are in peril. One man is dead. Another is a Gestapo prisoner. Admiral Dönitz has one more week, Commander. No more."

"You are in no position to make demands, Commander. And how do you propose to leave Denmark without the Admiral's help? You are a dead man." Hoff looked at Mikkelsen. "And you my friend are…" Hoff stopped.

"One week. Every thing must be in place. We must depart in February. March is too late. The war will be over," replied Mallory.

❧

Several more days passed when again the black ensign flew from a passing trawler.

"I spoke with a partisan from Copenhagen," Mikkelsen told Mallory. The Gestapo suspected an informant on the

Flensburg staff.

Mallory was determined this would be the last opportunity for negotiations. At this meeting Hoff carried an envelope.

"Memorize the documents," Hoff said. "Then destroy them." Then Hoff turned to Mikkelsen. "He must wait outside."

"He's right, Mikkelsen. The mission depends on secrecy. "I trust you, but the Nazis are merciless interrogators."

Mikkelsen frowned. He put on his coat and his satchel. "I'll find shelter outside."

"The Admiral insists that in exchange for Otto Bruns the United States will guarantee safe passage for two unidentified passengers. The journey will begin in Stavanger, Norway," said Hoff.

Mallory already knew the U-boat base was of great value to the Admiral. It was impossible for the mission to begin in Flensburg. Mallory also knew Allied bombers controlled the air and posed a danger to U-boats in the area.

"Otto Bruns will be delivered to Stavanger shortly before departure along with the other passengers. The U-853 will leave Stavanger and follow an indirect route across the Atlantic," Hoff continued.

"Then what?" Mallory demanded.

"Once the U-boat is at a point off Groton, Connecticut, the U-boat's captain will receive further orders."

Will we receive an escort?"

"Perhaps, two additional U-boats will depart Stavanger on a direct course to the rendezvous off the New England coastline. Our fleet is severely damaged. We may not have two available vessels."

Hoff questioned Mallory until almost sunrise.

"Commander, it is time to destroy the documents," Hoff insisted. "Too many lives depend on our secret."

"The U-boat captain will receive his instructions prior to departure. That's all you need to know."

⚓

In early January 1945, Hitler's General Staff advised the

Fuhrer to move his forces from Norway to increase Germany's defenses. Dönitz opposed the move. The submarine pens were vital to the Naval High command. "Norway is vital to our efforts against the Allies." As disaster became inevitable Dönitz issued the order: "All remaining U-boats in Norway will deploy in the event Germany surrenders"

Dönitz feared a troop withdrawal would hold serious ramifications. A retreat would jeopardize the Fuhrer Order. It was imperative the U-853's modifications be completed before it departed Norway.

An intercepted message between Martin Bormann and Dönitz revealed Hitler refused to abandon Stavanger. Secretly, Dönitz had devised a contingency plan for his remaining U-boat fleet. He told Hoff, "I've reserved several U-boats in Stavanger's pens as part of a diversionary plan. These U-boats would be dispatched to the East Coast to raise chaos on American shipping. It will be a costly and desperate mission." (5)

Commander Hoff assured Mallory, "Even as we speak, efforts are underway to ready the designated boat – the U-853. It is undergoing critical modifications. The captain and his executive officer are supervising the work."

The U-853 had a distinguished war record. The submarine was commissioned in June 1943. U-boats were compact killing machines. Designed with an inner and outer hull, the U-853 was 251 feet long with a beam of approximately 22 feet. Her draft – 15 feet -would play a critical part in the U-853's destiny. Her speed was 19 knots surface and a bit over 7 knots submerged. The U-853's range was nearly 16,000 miles traveling at 12 miles per hour.

Prior to leaving Denmark Mikkelsen delivered a coded message to Mallory. The message confounded Mallory. Wooden crates were in transport to Stavanger U-boat base. Upon delivery at Stavanger the U-boat's Captain would be given a sealed envelope with a detailed manifest. The envelope was to remain sealed and secured in the Captain's quarters. Neither Mallory nor the Captain knew the crates' contents. Mallory read the cipher one last time then crumpled it into a ball, placed it in his mouth, slowly chewed the paper and swallowed hard. *The Captain faces a challenging task.*

It was the Captain's responsibility to refit the U-853 to accommodate the additional cargo. Along with a naval architect the Captain examined every inch of the U-853's design. The deck and interior storage compartments had to be refitted for the voyage. Every ounce of weight had to be calculated to allow for the four additional passengers. Vital decisions were made concerning the storage of food and ammunition. Then another challenge emerged.

A story circulated among the mechanics and welders working below decks. Shipyard workers speculated the U-853 was being modified as an escape vessel for Hitler to flee Germany. This would explain the need to modify the galley storage, the Captain's quarters, petty officers' room and the crew bunks. The Captain's modest quarters provided for a bunk and desk with locking drawer in place of a safe.

Ammunition boxes were bolted to interior walls. The deck gun's compliment of 180 rounds was cut to 80. Emphasis was placed on the deck-mounted anti-aircraft guns. The most precious commodity besides fuel was drinking water. The water tanks' capacity, however, were reduced by twenty-five per cent. In turn, the U-853 relied on being resupplied in mid-Atlantic by huge U-boats called "milk cows". Two were still hidden in the Stavanger submarines pens reserved for a critical mission.

⤟

On Thursday, February 10, Mallory directed Mikkelsen to send a coded message to London. "Robert in place. Move imminent."

On February 11, the OSS signaled Mallory to hold his position. An elite Norwegian infantry unit assisted by the British Marines would arrange to extricate Mallory in the event negotiations failed.

Mikkelsen warned Mallory, "The Gestapo has increased their activities. Someone is bound to break." Mallory was troubled. Mallory agreed. *Mikkelsen would be discarded, eventually detected and arrested.* The OSS considered Mallory the valuable asset.

Dönitz refused to provide safe passage documents for either man. He feared the passes might be traced back to him. This sealed a death warrant for himself, his family and any suspected collaborators.

All wasn't going well for the Admiral. A second Fuhrer Order arrived. He read the order again. Additional cargo weighing 29,397 pounds would be brought on board.

Admiral Dönitz ruminated. *The Fuhrer has gone mad. Transporting four passengers to a hostile destination is a suicide mission. Insane! The entire mission is headed for disaster.* Despite his misgivings, it was senseless to question the Fuhrer's personal directive. Dönitz recalled his prior meeting with the Fuhrer in the elaborate Chancellery bunker.

Hitler was moody. His sentences were slurred. Dönitz noticed Hitler would hold his left arm close to his side or place it at an angle behind his back. The Fuhrer displayed a constant twitch. About twenty minutes into the meeting Hitler's personal secretary entered the room. Hitler left. When the Fuhrer rejoined the meeting he seemed calm and focused. Hitler dismissed the other officers.

"Admiral Dönitz, please wait a minute." Hitler spoke quickly and with authority. "The U-boat Fuhrer Order must be carried out impeccably. Trust no one. Hess betrayed me. Göring thinks of no one but himself. You have your orders, Admiral."

"They will be obeyed," Dönitz assured the Fuhrer.

With that, Hitler left once again.

As Dönitz was departing the bunker he caught a glimpse of the Fuhrer entering the dispensary followed by his newly-appointed physician, Dr. Ernst-Robert Grawitz, a Parkinson's disease specialist Dönitz had met at a social gathering. *Strange. Why is Grawitz here?*

✍

71

On the evening of February 13, 1945, Dönitz sent a priority message to Berlin. He assured Hitler the U-853 would depart no later than Tuesday, February 22.

The ever-superstitious Hitler was particularly anxious concerning another February event. On February 14, 1945, one of Hitler's favorite cities, Prague, was accidentally bombed. According to official Army reports a formation of B-17 Flying Fortresses miscalculated their primary target, which was to be Dresden. Prague was bombed, instead. There were thousands of civilian casualties. Not one vital installation was destroyed. Two days later Dresden was obliterated. The end was at hand.

Pressure mounted. Hitler sent another dispatch. The U-853 had to get underway. It was now impossible for U-boats to safely depart Flensburg. Soon the submarine pens in Norway would also be out of commission. On the evening of February 19, 1945 a Junker 34 carrying a pilot and four passengers landed at the military airstrip in Stavanger. The passengers included three adult men and a child. They were quickly spirited away to the safety of a concrete bunker near the submarine pens. William Robert Mallory was last to arrive.

Mallory's journey from Copenhagen to Stavanger was strenuous and daring. Transported by boat, Mallory was constantly seasick and dehydrated. The danger intensified when the special unit arrived in Norway. Dönitz denied Mallory a letter of safe passage fearing it could be tracked back to him. On February 21, the special unit reached the outskirts of Stavanger where Commander Hoff waited. Hoff drove Mallory to Stavanger. The pair entered a Spartan concrete bunker adjacent to the rooms housing the other passengers.

Chapter Twelve
The Meeting

At 0530 hours on February 22, 1945, Mallory was awakened. It was Hoff.

"Your coveralls. Put them on," he ordered.

When Mallory first arrived at Stavanger, Hoff ordered, "Get rid of your clothes…all your outer wear including the silk scarf map. You can't escape from Norway. Then Hoff pointed to a brown sail bag. "Open it."

Mallory pulled out a baggy jump suit. Wear it at all times."

"What's this for?" Mallory asked. He laughed at the washed-out U.S. Army T-shirt with an American flag stitched to left shoulder.

"Wear the shirt at all times. It may save you from being shot as a spy. But I doubt it. Now open the envelope." Inside was a safe passage letter signed by Admiral Dönitz. Keep the letter. You will need it when you arrive in the states. The Americans may not believe your cover story and shoot you on the spot." Hoff laughed.

Mallory finished buttoning the jump suit. In the back pocket was a dark blue Greek fisherman's cap.

"If one of the guards challenges us, let me talk. Say nothing and don't smile." Hoff appeared unusually nervous.

"Is something wrong?"

"Yes. The outfitting has fallen behind schedule. The Admiral will be displeased. No more questions. Quickly, follow me," ordered Hoff. He led Mallory along a concrete walk to the entrance of a long winding concrete tunnel. The base consisted of three large concrete structures designed to accommodate thirty submarines. With the loss of France to Allied forces Stavanger was a strategic location. The two men walked several hundred feet along the passageway. The noise from the far end grew louder to the point where it was deafening.

"Where are we headed?" asked Mallory.

"The U-853," said Hoff. "There are a few hands on board. The others have been on leave. I wanted you to tour the vessel before the entire crew came on board. You'll appreciate your spacious quarters," Hoff said. He turned and looked at Mallory then laughed. "The Captain is on board. He is an ambitious young man."

The British bombardments of U-boat bases were intense. Allied raids on Lorient, France killed thousands of Germans and French civilians. In January 1945 the raids on the "pens" in Norway intensified. The Allies now possessed the "Tall Boy" bomb capable of penetrating the reinforced concrete U-boat shelters. Then, too, there was the feared two-man de Havilland Mosquito bombers which would attack at low altitudes in an attempt to skip their bombs along the waterway into entrances to the fortified docks.

Once again Admiral Dönitz instructed Hoff, "It is imperative the U-853 depart as soon as possible."

Once underway U-853 would travel at an operational speed of six to eight knots. Fuel conservation was imperative. The original plan called for a refueling in mid-Atlantic utilizing a XIV supply submarine called a 'Milch Cow'. There were no "operational" units available. Instead, a second U-boat, the U-300 was designated for the task. Then another setback was encountered. The U-300 was sunk off Spain on February 21, 1945. The U-853 with its precious cargo would have to be resupplied by a surface vessel or complete its mission without a refueling. This was a critical problem for the U-853's captain.

The noise within the huge concrete U-boat shelter intensified. "How in the world do these men work in here without growing deaf?" asked Mallory.

"Some suffer hearing loss. Some wear ear protection. Others stuff cotton in their ears. This is wartime. Here, try these." Hoff handed Mallory two sponge earplugs. "This is nothing. Wait until you are underway and the boat's twin diesel engines are running."

"It's a wonder the mechanics don't go mad," said Mallory.

" The Admiral handpicked your captain and his officers. The crew is young, but battle hardened. Your Leading Engineer is top-rated," Hoff added.

"Leading Engineer?" asked Mallory

"He knows every aspect of the U-853 maintenance and mechanical systems. He has an awesome responsibility." Hoff didn't tell Mallory the Leading Engineer also set the demolition charges should the U-boat have to be scuttled.

The Executive Officer, Lieutenant Commander, and Henry Beck unceremoniously escorted Hoff and Mallory on board the U-853.

"The captain is forward with the lead engineer checking on the newly-installed compartments," said the executive officer. His sentences were brief and guarded. The officer's demeanor revealed he had not been informed of the U-853's ultimate mission. Beck seemed uncertain how much of the U-853's interior he should show this stranger.

Mallory turned to take in his uncanny setting. *Here I am, a Navy Commander in the heart of a U-boat pen with two German officers. I'll never be allowed to tell this story. Even so, who would believe me?* Mallory's winter clothing irritated his skin. He perspired heavily.

Beck told Hoff and Mallory the Captain was concerned that the additional cargo could have a negative effect on the vessel. Every piece of equipment; food, water, ammunition, fuel, crew, and four passengers had to be painstakingly weighed.

Mallory quickly ran the numbers through his mind. *One million dollars in gold bars.* The cargo, 1,069 gold bars, weighed approximately fourteen tons. *I understand the executive officer's concern. Where will the captain stow so much gold?* (4)

"Our tactical and defensive maneuverability will be compromised if we are forced to fill our torpedo compensating tanks with additional fuel. How much weight does the Admiralty expect us to transport without endangering the lives of the crew?" asked the executive officer.

Hoff was taken aback. "The success of this mission is imperative," Hoff reminded Beck. "Surely you understand its importance."

"Other U-boats are barely operational, yet so much attention is being given to the U-853," replied Beck. "The Captain must make a number of imperative decisions."

"This mission takes priority," said Hoff.

"I understand, Commander, but each decision means a substantial sacrifice," said Beck. "Our fuel capacity is being reduced from 180 tons to 165 tons, barely enough to return if our mission is prolonged. Our batteries account for twelve to eighteen percent of our tonnage capacity. We have two batteries driving our electric motors. Each battery requires 140 interconnected cells. To gain increased space the Leading Engineer reduced the number of cells."

"How does that affect the crossing?" asked Mallory.

"We will depend less on electric motors to travel submerged and more on the diesels and the snorkel. We'll be traveling at four knots with the electric motors rather than eight to conserve battery life. A greater danger for exposure to fumes from the diesels," said Beck. "Surfacing unnecessarily exposes the U-853 to air attack and could betray the mission."

"A risk you encounter all the time, Beck," countered Hoff. "Battery fumes, the hydrogen and other gases are harmful, but not less the carbon monoxide poisoning from a blocked air exchange in the boat's snorkel."

"Exactly. Ventilation is the key," said Beck. "Our lives depend on the Leading Engineer and electricians' vigilance."

Hoff grew impatient with Beck's focus on safety issues. "Now for our guest's tour." Hoff pointed to the conning tower. "Let's start here," Hoff ordered.

Beck pointed to the control room. "Up there. That's where you entered the boat. All of the gauges and instruments comprise our mission control. You saw the two periscopes are further up that ladder." Beck pointed aft. We have aft torpedo and forward torpedo tubes. The officers' mess is just forward. You will have a very small compartment to be shared with another passenger. The crew's bunk space has been further reduced to accommodate what I am told is a young boy and his guardian." Beck frowned. Then added, "Once word gets out the crew bunks are further reduced, they won't be happy."

Mallory forced a poker-faced expression. *If the crew knew the child was a girl and not a boy there might be an uproar. Superstitious sailors don't want a woman on board.*

"Exactly the reason for extending their leaves," said Hoff.

While boarding the U-853 Mallory looked back across the dock. He spotted wooden boxes stacked along the far wall of the dock. *This must be cargo I was ordered to inventory.* Two crates at a distance from the others caught Mallory's attention. These boxes were larger and longer. *How will they manage to store the additional cargo?*

As the tour continued Beck noticed Mallory was a bit wobbly. Indeed Mallory felt claustrophobic and the mission had not yet begun.

"Are you all right, Sir?" he asked.

"I can smell diesel fuel," Mallory answered.

"Yes. And once we are underway the noise and the fumes intensify. Most of the voyage will be submerged. I mentioned the retrofitted snorkel. It rises several feet above the water. The air exchange allows the diesel engines to run while we are submerged. Again, this conserves our batteries. We have to constantly monitor the air inside the boat. We have no on board air conditioning. The temperatures go to extremes. The stench is stomach wrenching. We have one toilet. An additional macerator tank was added. The Captain is very concerned for the child's health. Fresh water is precious."

Beck pointed to the welders still at work. The Captain's quarters were confined and narrow. The bunk was about thirty inches wide. A curtain provide privacy and a poor baffle from the radio room's constant static and activity. Two additional radios have been added to monitor US commercial radio stations and military communications. Beck blocked Mallory's entry into the cramped radio room. Under no circumstances was Mallory to view the coveted Enigma device for sending and decoding messages. "This room will be strictly off limits to you, Sir, and the other passengers."

Beck continued. "Forward of the crews' bunks are the torpedoes. Just before we leave port two torpedoes will be loaded into the rear torpedo tubes. The remainder of the space will be for cargo. It will be impossible to reload the torpedo tubes. We've already removed the deck gun and the shells. It will improve our submerged performance. We've added anti-aircraft guns. Still our offensive measures are highly restricted," Beck added.

"Adding weight adds a horde of technical problems," said Mallory.

"Yes, Sir. Everything must be scrutinized if we are to survive," said Beck.

"This is not a wolf pack mission, Lieutenant Commander," said Beck. "I remind you again, your Captain has been instructed to avoid enemy contact." Hoff's reprimand in front of the stranger stung Beck. Becks' resentment was evident. Beck turned toward the conning tower ladder in an attempt to mask his anger.

Hoff looked at his watch. "Thank you, Lieutenant Commander, but I have an appointment in one hour and must escort our guest to his quarters."

Beck remained silent. He refused to acknowledge Hoff's remark. The three began to climb into the conning tower.

Suddenly, the piercing sound of the U-boat's alarm system sounded. Mallory heard the piercing scream of the main air

raid siren reverberating through the fortress' concrete walls. "Quickly. Inside. Before all three men could re-enter the U-853, bombs began exploding in the channel. A flight of Mosquito bombers swooped in low flying directly at the opening to the pens.

Several U-boats were docked at the exposed pier adjacent near U-853 waiting their turn to enter the shelter. They came under direct fire. Their crews scrambled to man the twin 20mm anti-aircraft guns mounted on the front gun platform. On the second bomb run a Mosquito flew head on at the two U-boats. The plane flew so low the U-boat gunners could see the crew. The U-boat gunners scored a direct hit. The intense anti-aircraft fire tore the wooden wing from the plane's fuselage. The Mosquito spun furiously out of control. It crashed into the eight-foot thick concrete roof directly over the U-853. The force of the subsequent concussion resounded through the pen. Several dockworkers were thrown against the walls. One was crushed when several wooden crates toppled and spilled open. Mallory, now on deck seized the opportunity and started to run toward the gangplank to examine the boxes.

"Those damn planes. Get in here," shouted Hoff. Then came the third strafing run. A Mosquito dove at the exposed U-boat. The crew retaliated its twin machine guns blazing. The plane flew away leaving the dead gun grew sprawled across the platform.

The heavy British bombers were overhead. Their targets included the railroad line, the docks and the shipyard. The intense bombardment continued for thirty minutes. Then as suddenly as it began the sirens announced the "all clear."

Chapter Thirteen
Preparations Continue

Mallory and Hoff looked at one another. "We must return to the barracks area," shouted Hoff. His head ached. He would soon discover fluid dripping from his left ear. His eardrum was damaged.

Mallory, undeterred, crossed the gangplank and sprinted towards the dead dockworker. One of the wood crates had broken open spilling its contents. The dead man's wide open eyes revealed surprise. A gold bar rested on the worker's chest. Horrified, Mallory did a double take. Hoff and Mallory struggled to move the broken crate to one side. They placed an intact box on top. "This will have to do," said Mallory. Several men rushed to aid the fallen dockworker.

Mallory looked at Hoff. "It's time for us to get out of here. We'll return later. We don't want to draw attention to ourselves."

Hoff nodded agreement. "Quickly, before they get a closer look at you." Then Hoff stood and shouted orders at the dockworkers. "You men. Two remain here until help comes. The rest gather up some other men and search the pier for the wounded."

Mallory and Hoff hurried back into the main tunnel. Hoff began to jog. "We have to reach the barracks area."

"In the distance smoke billowed. Several small trucks were burning. Ambulance personnel triaged patients at the end of the barracks. Mallory and Hoff ran toward room 146 where the guests were housed. It was a temporary bivouac. The military police assigned to safeguard the three passengers had run to a nearby shelter leaving the occupants helpless. When Hoff and Mallory arrived the two front windows were shattered. The door was still closed and locked. Hoff pounded on the door and shouted for the occupants to let them in.

A man came to the door. "The child and Lieutenant Pokel are sheltered in the bathroom. I can't get Pokel to come out. We heard the siren, but didn't know where to go. I opened the door. People were running and then dust and debris filled the air. We heard the planes. The child is frightened," the man muttered.

Room 146 was a two-bedroom apartment used by junior officers. Hoff walked through the small living quarters. "I'll find other quarters for you, Herr Bruns," said Hoff.

So this was Otto Bruns? Mallory had no photograph to confirm Bruns' identity. He doesn't resemble the profile sketch. The Otto Bruns standing before him was a rather timid man. Bruns did have a beard but it was more gray than black. Mallory stared at Bruns. Bruns unkempt beard covered a pockmarked complexion. The tell tale feature was the prized dueling scar. It stretched from Brun's ear to his lower jaw. *I can't imagine this man having the courage to hold a razor edge dueling sword. The scar had to be self-inflicted.* The thick lenses of Brun's wire glasses gave him the appearance of a bullfrog. *Enough for now. I will interrogate him later. Admiral Dönitz wouldn't dare double-cross General Eisenhower with a phony Bruns.*

"Mallory, I need you. In here," called Hoff.

Mallory walked across the room. Shards of glass protruded from the furniture. He found Hoff leaning over Lieutenant Pokel huddled in the windowless bathroom cradling a crying child. Pokel looked up at the two men.

"She is so frightened," he said. "The first blast took us by surprise. Thank God she was covered with this blanket." Tiny pieces of broken glass cover the blanket.

Mallory knelt in front of the lieutenant. Using his code name, Mallory said, "My name is Robert. I have been sent here to escort you to the United States."

Pokel looked at Hoff. "The piercing sirens, the noise and then the bombs. I can't calm her," sobbed Pokel. His eyes filled with tears.

"You have taken wonderful care of the child," said Mallory.

Hoff turned to Mallory. "Let me speak with him alone."

Mallory stood and left the room.

"Lieutenant. Stand up," Hoff said in a calm voice. Pokel didn't budge. He hugged the child closer. "Stand up," Hoff ordered. You were selected to protect the child and you have done well. You are not a coward. Stand up." Hoff stretched out his arms and reached for the child. Pokel was hesitant, but gently placed the child in Hoff's arms.

"Please forgive my behavior. I've never experienced such intense bombing," said Pokel.

Mallory waited in the hallway, but could hear the entire conversation.

"Lieutenant Pokel. Get yourself together. Gather your kit and the child's belongings. We will move you to new quarters." Hoff turned and left the bathroom. Pokel followed.

"Herr Bruns. We are moving to safer accommodations. There is no way you will be departing tonight," barked Hoff. The complexity of the mission and the unexpected bombing raid were beginning to show on the commander.

Mallory took a deep breath and slowly let it out. The adrenalin rush was wearing off. Mallory felt exhausted. The U-853 wouldn't be departing on February 22. The damage caused by the air raid would delay their departure for at least two days. Neither the supplies nor the gold were on board. The bombing had damaged one of the escort U-boats.

Hoff went directly to the communications room and called Admiral Dönitz on a secure line. "Admiral, the damage caused by the British bombers has set us back. And now we have a difficult task of storing the gold. Every space has been utilized for our four passengers."

"I suggested you use your imagination, Hoff," ordered Dönitz.

"Sir, ammunition boxes have been welded to the vessel's inner wall. Several ready boxes for 20 mm ammunition were moved to the conning tower for quick dispersal. Gold bars will replace ammo in the floor compartments."

"I am not pleased, but I recognize the urgency," said Admiral Dönitz "Be vigilant. You must obey the Fuhrer's order."

Dönitz telephoned the Fuhrer immediately.

The Fuhrer raged. "The twenty-fifth, Admiral. Two days Admiral. I want the U-853 underway on February 25. Do not fail me. Now, speak with Bormann."

"Admiral, every item loaded onboard must be inventoried. One other item, Admiral," Bormann paused. "I've received word, Mallory's Danish asset was captured by the Gestapo. He is being held at Shell House. I suggest you get on with the mission as quickly as possible."

"My God. The mission will be exposed, if he confesses," protested Dönitz. Our lives…our families will be arrested. You have placed innocent people in jeopardy, Bormann."

It took several hours for the Admiral to relay Hitler's demands to Hoff. Communications were continually disrupted. The Admiral understood Hoff's fear. Dönitz's family had suffered sufficiently.

"How was Mikkelsen detected?" asked Hoff.

"A partisan prisoner at Gestapo headquarters revealed Mikkelsen's identity," Dönitz responded. "The American prisoner is dead. The Gestapo knows nothing of the U-853's mission, yet."

de Havilland Mosquito Bomber

Chapter Fourteen
Stavanger, Norway
February 22, 1945

The crew and shipyard force desperately worked to repair the U-boats damaged during the previous day's raid. Few buildings remained untouched by the bombing raids. Hoff arrange new quarters for the U-853's passengers.

Otto Bruns was now housed in a barracks on the far side of the base. Two guards stood watch. Mallory insisted Bruns have limited contact with Pokel and the child. Mallory felt uneasy about Otto Bruns. Once Bruns was secured, Hoff led Mallory to another wing of the huge concrete bunker.

"You, Lieutenant Pokel, and the child will stay here," said Hoff. Mallory looked around the cramped quarters. The U-853 will depart the day after tomorrow."

"Will the escort submarines be ready?" Mallory asked.

Hoff smiled. "The Fuhrer's orders, Captain. They will be ready. Again, this is not a wolf pack mission. " Hoff paused then added, "At least not until the mission is completed."

"Ready or not, the U-853 departs in two days. There is no turning back," said the Mallory. He sensed finality in Hoff's remarks. Hoff held out his hand. The gesture caught Mallory by surprise. Mallory hesitantly shook hands with his adversary. Mallory never saw Commander Hoff again.

❦

From the far end of the hallway, Mallory heard the child crying. He knocked on the bedroom door. Pokel answered.

"Just checking," said Mallory, and walked back to the tiny kitchen. The cabinets were empty. *Not even a coffee pot.* For the second time he asked, "How the hell did I wind up on a German submarine base thousands of miles from home?" This time he asked the question aloud. Stress and uncertainty were taking their toll.

"Excuse me, Sir. I didn't hear your question," said Pokel.

"Never mind, Lieutenant. The bombing raid has me a bit crazy. I'm talking to myself," Mallory replied. "Have you recovered?"

"Yes, but I fear for the child. I must cut her hair and dress her in boy's clothes. Seamen are superstitious when it comes to having a female, even an infant girl, on board," said Pokel.

An orderly knocked on the apartment door. He brought a small tray of food.

"No coffee?" asked Mallory.

The orderly set the tray on the table and left without a reply. Rations were scarce and coffee was a luxury. A few minutes later the orderly returned with a second tray. " For the child," the orderly abruptly announced. "This will be a strenuous trip for a seasoned crew. I can't imagine how the child will survive."

Mallory found it difficult to sleep that night. All sorts of scrambled thoughts troubled him. Otto Bruns was a major concern. *Do I have the right man? Was this the prized virologist the U.S. government wanted? Lieutenant Pokel presents another dilemma. Is he an American traitor who returned to Germany to support the Nazis? U.S. soldiers had no tolerance for traitors.* The child puzzled Mallory most of all. Mallory wrestled with the possibility his OSS superiors had withheld the true nature of his mission. *Was the Bruns exchange simply a cover? Was the mission about the child?* Mallory grappled to push these questions to the back of his mind. *Does it make a difference? I am committed.*

Chapter Fifteen
"The Transatlantic Journey"
Monday, February 22, 1943.

At 0600 hours Mallory was awakened by a knock on the door. It was the same orderly from the previous night. "Here is some bread." The orderly slid a tray on to the table.

"What's in the tin cups?" asked Mallory.

The orderly winked. "A ration of coffee from the officers mess."

"And the child?" asked Mallory.

"I will scavenge the galley. I know provisions have been set-aside for her, but the boxes are sealed. I will speak with the Captain. We didn't expect the delay."

"Thank you," said Mallory.

The orderly handed Mallory a note. "This is from Captain Fromsdorf. I'll be back in a few minutes. Then I will take you to his quarters at 0800 hours."

The note was a directive for Mallory to accompany the orderly to the Captain's quarters at 0800. It was signed "Fromsdorf." Mallory placed the note on the kitchen table and smiled.

True to his word the orderly returned with a bowl of gruel much thinner than porridge. "It's the best I could do. I have a child of my own. I haven't heard from my family in months. I pray they are alive. "

Mallory thanked the orderly. He wanted to ask the orderly's name, but stopped. *Hitler and the German war machine had brought immense suffering.* The orderly was his enemy. Mallory turned and slowly walked away.

"Is there anything else I can help you with?" asked the orderly.

"No," Mallory answered without looking back at the orderly.

"That will be all."

The previous day's events and the lack of sleep accentuated a foreboding I haven't felt since my father died.

Mallory rubbed his chin with the back of his hand. *Time for a shave.* He had neglected his appearance the last few days.

He walked to the bedroom and gently knocked on the door. Pokel was awake. The child was asleep. Pokel tiptoed out of the room.

"What is it?" Pokel asked.

Mallory held out a bowl. "The orderly scraped up some gruel for the child. Not much but it's something," said Mallory.

"It can wait," said Pokel. "Let her sleep."

The barracks housing reflected the deteriorating state of a Germany and Hitler promise the Reich would endure for a thousand years. The two men walked to the makeshift kitchen. Mallory pointed to the two tin cups on the table.

"This coffee tastes like piss," said Mallory.

The Lieutenant picked up his cup and walked to the window and drew back the heavy tattered blackout drape. "It's tastes like defeat," said Pokel.

"Forget the coffee. I am concerned for the…" Mallory caught himself before he used the word "girl" or even the name Edith.

"Never mention her name on board," cautioned Pokel. "Let the child sleep. This morning I have to cut her hair and dress her in boy's clothes.

"Who are you Lieutenant? How did you get picked for this mission?"

"Oh, I assure you, I am Lieutenant Kurt Pokel. American? Yes. Why I was picked for this mission is complex. Perhaps one day we will have the opportunity to talk at length. Not this morning. I have other responsibilities."

The bedroom door slowly opened and a small head peeked out. The child was looking for Pokel. The Lieutenant beckoned to the youngster. She ran to the safety of his arms. Pokel bent over and scooped her up with a reassuring smile.

The orderly returned. "It's time, Sir. Captain Fromsdorf has a demanding schedule." The orderly handed Mallory a bulky grey overcoat.

"I expected Commander Hoff would be here this morning," said Mallory.

"I do not know, Sir."

Mallory was escorted across the yard to a secluded bunker connected to the U-boat pen where the U-853 was being outfitted. They had gone a short distance when shots rang out. The orderly looked straight ahead.

"What was that?" asked Mallory.

"Yesterday during the air raid the guards in front of your quarters ran for shelter. The base commander ordered their execution by firing squad. These are treacherous times, Sir."

When they arrived at the Captain's quarters the orderly knocked. An abrupt "Come" resounded from the inner room. Mallory entered the room. The orderly left. A uniformed German naval officer, with his back to Mallory, stood facing a large map dotted with U-boat silhouettes.

"The war is lost, Commander. You and I are about to embark on a journey from which I will not return." It was an odd but truthful introduction. The officer turned and addressed Mallory. Mallory was stunned by Fromsdorf's remarks.

Helmut Fromsdorf, the U-boat's captain, appeared to be no more than twenty-five years old. Fromsdorf's height overshadowed Mallory's five feet ten inch frame. Fromsdorf was about six feet eight inches tall. *He was exceptionally tall to be on a crowded U-boat. There are so many overhead obstructions to avoid. A U-boat was more compact than an American submarine. Could this be the man Admiral Dönitz selected for the Fuhrer's top-secret mission?*

"You look surprised Commander Mallory. Did my comment surprise you or is it my age?"

Fromsdorf's abruptness caught Mallory off guard. Before Mallory could respond, the orderly entered the room. "Lieutenant Pokel is waiting, Sir."

"Tell him to join us." Fromsdorf looked at his pocket watch. My Number One will be here in a few minutes, also."

"Yes Sir," said the orderly.

Pokel entered the room. "And now for some official introductions," said Fromsdorf.

Fromsdorf held Mallory's dossier. "Lieutenant Kurt Pokel, meet William Robert Mallory, code name Robert. Commander Mallory is a member of the American OSS. This is Commander Mallory's first mission."

Mallory attempted to disguise his surprise at Fromsdorf's continued candor.

" I find it difficult to believe, Captain."

"Believe what?" asked Mallory.

"You're well educated from an influential family. Certainly you could have been assigned to the Pentagon or posted as an aide-de-camp."

Mallory couldn't determine if Fromsdorf was probing or inquisitive.

"Does it surprise you we know so much?" Fromsdorf asked.

"You tortured the prisoner at Shell House," Mallory angrily replied.

"Oh no. The Gestapo's barbarian methods failed to get any information about you that we didn't already have. You see we have our own sources within the American intelligence community."

Mallory recalled when the entire city of Copenhagen went on strike. The Germans rushed hundreds of additional troops into the city. They cut off water and electricity. Later the resistance spread to other parts of Denmark. Hitler insisted the best way to deal with resistance was to "utterly crush it."

Mallory clenched his fists.

Fromsdorf acknowledged Mallory's anger. "Rest assured I do not agree with the desperate tactics of the Gestapo. I am not a Nazi. I am a patriot."

Mallory was perplexed. Fromsdorf displayed the confidence of a much older warrior. Perhaps his certitude reflected a hidden fear.

"I may be ambitious, Commander Mallory, but I am no monster."

Mallory said nothing. He turned his attention to the wall

map.

"An interesting map. Each silhouette represents a U-boat's last location before it was sunk. Truthfully, our flotilla has been nearly destroyed. Germany has paid a high price. The end is near. I still do not understand the reason for the mission. It is a calculated risk. I have already informed my family I don't expect to return." A brief frown flashed across the German's face.

"And what of Otto Bruns? I haven't had an opportunity to interrogate him. He may be an imposter," said Mallory.

"Bruns is being held under guard at the far end of the barracks. I don't know a thing about him. He must be a valuable commodity. I have read the Fuhrer's directive. I will do my best to deliver both of you to the American authorities. That's all I know."

Mallory believed Fromsdorf. Mallory turned toward Lieutenant Pokel. "Now for Lieutenant Pokel. Tell me, Pokel, who are you?"

Pokel's deportment changed as he responded.

❧

"My name is Kurt Pokel. I have no reason to deceive you, Commander Mallory. Unlike you, I have no code name. I was born in America. My mother is an American. She met my father in England while on a family vacation. We lived in in the states for a short time. Then we moved to Germany. There was no work. My mother's parents raised enough money for us to come to the States when I was a baby.

My father was a discontented bully. He supported the growing America first movement and eventually became a Nazis. Once again he wanted to return to Germany. One morning he took me aside. He was taking me on vacation. I never said goodbye to my mother or my friends." Pokel continued his story.

"When Germany invaded Poland, I was trapped in Berlin. Then I was conscripted into the German Army. The Germans didn't know what to do with me. I was sent to the eastern front during Operation Barbarossa. I was wounded during the initial German advance in June 1941 and returned to Berlin for surgery."

Mallory scratched his head. *I'm having a tough time believing his story.*

"My story really begins when I was transferred to the Beelitz-Keilstätten military hospital south west of the Berlin. I met and fell in love with a nurse, Ingrid Becker. Ingrid was a patriotic German. She joined the Nazi Party when she applied for her position at the hospital."

"Get on with it, Pokel. Tell Mallory how you got here," insisted Fromsdorf.

"It was a wartime affair. Yet I was determined to escape Germany. I planned to reach the Swiss border. To this day I still have my American passport. I planned to request asylum."

"You must have been desperate. You could have been shot," said Mallory. "And Ingrid?"

"At first she refused to go, but at the appointed time she left with me. We were captured at the border and returned to Berlin."

"You are very lucky, Pokel," said Fromsdorf. "The normal course of action would have been a firing squad. But the Abwehr had a better use for you."

Kurt Pokel's court martial trial lasted less than two hours. The tribunal's verdict surprised everyone. For some unexplained reason Private Kurt Pokel was sentenced to forced labor on the docks in Flensburg. In hindsight, a cursory explanation for the tribunal's leniency may have been Pokel's unique circumstances. Pokel's father was a deceased German combat soldier. Pokel retained his U.S. passport. Pokel dared to tell his interrogators on several occasions, "I want to return to the United States."

Upon arrival in Flensburg, Pokel was confined to barracks. He was soon assigned menial tasks working on the docks. One morning in1942 Pokel was summoned to the military intelligence unit (the Abwehr) in Flensburg. The Naval-Abwehr joint operations group was responsible for espionage within the United States.

The Abwehr was located in Building A, a heavily guarded

facility enclosed by a chainlink fence. Two men dressed in civilian clothes escorted Pokel through a series of rooms. The last room, a large lecture hall, was furnished with tables and chairs. Sliding wall maps and charts displayed regions of the United States.

One of the officers pointed to the map of Long Island. The two men then began to question Pokel about his travels on the Long Island Railroad.

Pokel responded, "I was a boy when my father took me to Yapank." The one interrogator kept pointing to the south shore of Long Island.

"Did your parents ever take you to Amagansett?" Again, the man pointed to a location where the waves of the Atlantic Ocean broke directly on the southeastern shore of Long Island. Pokel denied any knowledge of Amagansett. Pokel recounted his outings at Camp Siegfried and his brief stopovers in Patchogue, a Long Island village sixty miles from Manhattan.

The interrogation lasted approximately one hour. "You will be severely punished if you tell anyone about this meeting," one of the officers warned. "On the other hand, if you make an effort to cooperate in the future you will be rewarded,"

Pokel stood at attention. The two men gave the traditional Hitler salute. Pokel choose to return a military salute.

"One final question, Pokel."

"Yes Sir. What is it?"

"Your friend, Ingrid Becker. She is pregnant and a prisoner in Spandau. The SS have given permission for her to stay at a Lebensborn. Her release could be arranged," said the Abwehr officer.

"Yes. I would very much like her to join me here," Pokel replied.

The officer smiled at Pokel's audacity.

Pokel turned to leave. He took one last look at the Long Island wall map. In bold letters above Amagansett's location was a card labeled "Operation Pastorious." *It must be an espionage operation.*

One week later Kurt Pokel was reassigned to the communications division at the Flensburg Naval Academy with a rank of Second Lieutenant. All translators were junior officers.

Ingrid arrived in Flensburg several weeks later. Pokel petitioned to marry. Kurt and Ingrid were married in December 1942. The Pokels were assigned Spartan quarters. A few months later their son, Jürgen, was born.

∽

Mallory's attention returned to Captain Fromsdorf. "Is it accurate for me to conclude Lieutenant Pokel's reason for volunteering for this assignment is purely to return to the United States?" asked Mallory.

"I don't know the Lieutenant's intentions. Ask him," said Fromsdorf. "At this juncture I must focus on my orders to outfit the U-853."

"Sir, may I explain?" asked Pokel.

"Of course, Lieutenant."

"Commander Mallory, my wife and son are living in Flensburg." Pokel looked around the room as though searching for hidden listening devices. "The Third Reich is in chaos. I was presented with this opportunity to return to the States. The Abwehr has promised no harm will come to my family. There are no guarantees. But I do have a plan. Once I complete my mission, I'm on my own. I may be discovered and tried as a spy. Then again I may simply disappear."

"It's that simple?" asked Mallory.

"No. But it's my only chance to save my family." Pokel's next comment risked everything. "The war will be over by the summer or fall at the latest. The U-853 will never return to Germany. Germany will surrender. From my viewpoint that's what our mission is all about. We are the beginning of the end."

Neither Fromsdorf nor Mallory responded. They both knew Germany's surrender was inevitable. Then Fromsdorf said, "You are never to repeat your comments again, Lieutenant. I promised to keep my crew safe and return them to the Fatherland. Our mission depends on the crew's morale.

93

If the sense the war is lost, we are all lost."

"Yes, Captain Fromsdorf."

Helmut Fromsdorf's reaction to Pokels' comments went deeper than either Pokel or Mallory suspected. Earlier that month Fromsdorf had visited with Captain Helmut Sommers, the U-853's former skipper. Helmut Sommers was a war hero. Sommers was severely wounded on the U-853's last mission while risking his life to save several crewmembers.

"Take care of my crew. The war will soon be over. Don't allow your ambition to overrule your judgment. You have nothing to gain by sacrificing your life and the lives of your crew. They have served Germany with courage and distinction. Keep them safe."

Fromsdorf assured Sommers he would do his best to keep the crew from harm's way. Fromsdorf knew his crew's morale was low. His officers warned of rumblings among crewmembers. They lacked faith in the Captain. Some mumbled Fromsdorf was ambitious and wanted to prove himself before the war ended. His crew was young. They had survived missions and returned home alive thanks to Captain Sommers. Three was an unlucky number. They were not looking forward to a third mission. The German Navy never reported U-Boat losses, but the astronomical casualty numbers were evident. Still, young men continued to volunteer for the submarine service.

As Fromsdorf's first meeting with Pokel and Mallory was about to end, Henry Beck entered the room. "Gentlemen, this is my executive officer, Number One, Lieutenant Commander Henry Beck," said Fromsdorf.

"Yes. I have already met Commander Mallory. We were on board the U-853 when the British strafed our docks," said Beck.

"You're late. You look anxious. Is something wrong?"

"Sir, this package arrived for you just a few minutes ago. The courier was flown here from Flensburg."

"Please excuse us for a moment," Fromsdorf said to Mallory and Pokel.

Pokel and Mallory walked into the hallway. After a few minutes Beck emerged and told the two to go back inside.

Fromsdorf held a folder stamped top secret. "I have received another envelope. I have been directed not to open it until we are underway. I have three envelopes now. One contains a manifest of unidentified cargo already dockside. The shipment awaits Commander Mallory. You will mark and invoice each container. Two additional items have been delivered. Torpedo-size tubes. I have no idea what they contain. And now I have received a third envelope. The mystery builds gentlemen. We have our work to do. Commander Mallory, the orderly will escort you to the loading docks. Number One will be waiting. Be careful. The crew is already uneasy and I don't want their suspicions further aroused."

"I will," Mallory said.

"Beck believes one of our crew suspects you are an American or British agent."

"How did he learn that information?" asked Mallory.

"An anonymous note was left at the communication center. In turn, they contacted Beck."

"It's something to think about," said Mallory.

"Sabotage on a U-boat is unheard of. One out-of-control crewmember could spell disaster once we are underway. Each man has a critical assignment."

A troubled scowl crossed Mallory's face. "Perhaps it's best to have our party come on board just prior to departure. Confine the crew to quarters and have them report in work details until all our supplies are loaded."

"Be careful, Mallory. You are walking a tightrope," Fromsdorf cautioned.

Mallory looked directly into Fromsdorf's eyes and said, "That's odd Captain Fromsdorf. I understand the U-853 is called the Tightrope Walker. It has an uncanny ability to escape even under the most perilous conditions."

"Let's hope our luck continues," Fromsdorf replied.

Chapter Sixteen
Prepared to Depart

On February 25, 1945 the U-853 prepared to depart Stavanger, Norway. Unlike other departures there would be no band, flowers or family to bid farewell. The U-boat was moved to a new position for final outfitting. Beck and Fromsdorf stood on the bridge. The other officers and crew were below tending to their last minute duties. All of the provisions, ammunition and secret cargo were secured. One crewmember started a hilarious disturbance when he dropped a box near the galley storage cabinets. Several hundred condoms spilled on the galley floor. The last of the perishable foodstuffs were packed into one of the two toilet compartments near the galley. Every available space was used. Fresh water would have to be rationed. One of the fresh water tanks was filled with diesel fuel. Salt water would be used for bathing. Cologne was at the ready for suppressing body odor.

Mallory spent most of the previous day numbering the wooden boxes stacked against the shelter's wall. Eventually, the crew lined up. One by one the boxes were handed through the forward hatch and into the U-boat's belly.

The last of Mallory's shipment, two torpedo length aluminum cylinders, were lowered through the forward torpedo hatch.

Mallory overheard the mumbling amongst the crew. One crewman seemed to be leading the group. They wondered about the unusual cargo. Most of all they focused their attention on the man in odd uniform. He wore navy issued boots and fatigue pants. His grey overcoat and Greek fisherman's cap was totally out of place for a submariner.

One seaman whispered, "He may be a member of the Abwehr or Naval Intelligence. It could be dangerous to keep too close an eye on the stranger."

The seaman assigned to assist Mallory had reported to sickbay. The man's replacement was slow and uncooperative, and guarded. Mallory spoke with Beck.

"The man you assigned to help me is a malingerer. I've done most of his work."

"I'll look for a replacement, but we are already shorthanded."

"I don't trust him," said Mallory.

"I'll confine him to quarters and request a replacement."

"Get some rest. Be ready at 0500. We will have a brief ceremony with all hands on deck at 0800 and depart. I hope the British don't have an air raid planned."

Beck escorted Mallory to the barracks. When they arrived, Mallory looked for Pokel and the child. They were in the rear bedroom. Pokel was laying out the child's meager belongings. Her hair had been cut short. She cuddled a stuffed bear.

"The journey will be an awful experience. I can't imagine how the child will endure," said the Lieutenant.

"You may be right," said Beck. "But now I have my own duties to attend to. Until 0500 hours, gentlemen."

Shortly afterwards there was a knock on the door. The orderly brought a tray of cold rations and two tin cups of brandy. The kind orderly also brought a bowl warm gruel for the child.

"Quite an extravagance under the circumstances," said Mallory. Pokel agreed as he lifted his cup.

"Commander Fromsdorf's orders," replied the orderly.

Soon the time arrived to depart. The crew assembled on deck. Fromsdorf addressed his men on the importance of their mission without describing the objective.

"Our mission is to harass and destroy vessels in the American shipping lanes. This is a perilous assignment. Our nation demands our best and we will give it."

Fromsdorf turned to his Executive Officer. Beck raised

his hand and presented a traditional military salute, which Fromsdorf returned. Their action surprised the crew since on such occasions Admiral Dönitz had ordered the Hitler salute be used. Fromsdorf left the bridge. "Dismissed," shouted the Executive Officer. The men scrambled to their assigned positions.

As the U-853 was about to cast off Mallory arrived. Mallory was dressed in a standard drab grey uniform, three-quarter length leather U-boat battle coat, neckerchief, and duty cover (hat), minus insignia. He hurried across the gangplank and waited. Next came Lieutenant Pokel and Edith. Edith's cropped hair, short pants, dark shoes, long socks, and a wool shirt and jacket gave her the appearance of small boy. She pulled at the hat Pokel held on her head. Edith clung to Pokel.

Finally, four navy police officers escorted Otto Bruns to the gangplank. Bruns hesitated for a moment. Mallory watched from the bridge. One of Bruns' escorts stepped forward. He motioned for Bruns to get on board. Bruns continued to hesitate. The guard pointed toward the conning tower. Bruns froze. The escort shoved the frightened Bruns toward the gangplank. He looked up at Mallory and stepped forward. Bruns accepted his unknown fate. Bruns went below where he was kept under guard. Mallory would not speak with Bruns until the second day at sea.

The U-853's two improvised passenger compartments were finished just prior to departure. The odor of oil-based paint was stifling. The passengers had little choice but to tolerate the cramped quarters. Lieutenant Pokel and the child occupied the compartment adjacent to the forward torpedo room. Fromsdorf was especially concerned about his men's morale. The additional compartments decreased the crew's space. Even with improvised hammocks some crew would have to take turns sleeping on torpedoes. The second passenger compartment was smaller than the first. It held two suspended bunks, one over the other. Two small lights dimly illuminated the cubicle. The men had to move sideways with their backs pressed against the metal wall to reach their racks.

Lieutenant-Commander Beck followed Mallory to his compartment. "You will find the voyage rather confining," Beck said. "To further add to your discomfort the Captain has asked you remain amidships for now." They passed through the next bulkhead and Beck pointed to the galley. Beck turned and opened a closet door. This is the toilet. The only toilet." Beck laughed. He gestured for Mallory to turn around.

"The engine room is through that bulkhead," said Beck. "For now you must limit your movements to the galley and the toilet."

"And up there?" Mallory pointed to the control room and coning tower.

"The control room and radio room are off limits. Understood?"

"Understood," said Mallory.

"Let's hope for all our sakes, but especially the child..." he paused. He grimaced. "I hope the voyage is without incident. Now please return to your quarters."

Then Beck joined Fromsdorf in the control room. The two men climbed up and on to the bridge. Ever so slowly the U-853 maneuvered along the channel guided by a tugboat. Then it headed toward the open sea.

"Did you make note of the eleventh hour shipment?" Fromsdorf asked.

"No sir. Another envelope?" Beck's anticipation increased.

"I'm surprised it missed your eagle eyes. We received twelve cases of wine." Fromsdorf replied.

"Wine? The admiralty has standing orders - no alcohol on board," said Beck.

"I know the order, Henry."

"Yes sir," Beck replied sheepishly.

"It arrived on a flight from Flensburg. Oddly, the cases are marked with the Luftwaffe insignia. I opened one of the cases. I blew the dust off one of the bottles. It is a white Mosel."

"And the rest?" asked Beck.

"Six cases of Bordeaux - Chateau Lâfite Rothschild."

A look of disbelief crossed Beck's face.

"I couldn't believe it, either, Beck," said Fromsdorf with a smile. " Both wines were reputed to be the Air Marshall's favorites."

"I've heard Göring keeps his favorite wines in tunnels beneath his home at the Berghof," said Beck.

Fromsdorf paused. "Our precious cargo is safely stored on board, Beck." Fromsdorf understood the meaning of the gift. Göring's prized wine carried an unspoken final message from Flensburg: the U-853 would not be returning to Germany.

On the morning of February 25, 1945, the U-853 left Stavanger on its transatlantic mission.

Chapter Seventeen
Underway

Everyday life on a U-boat was strenuous. Life on board the U-853 was arduous, especially for the child. Edith was an innocent asset in a series of dramas. Now, on February 26, 1945, Edith was on the next part of her harrowing journey.

The U-853, like all U-boats, was constructed with an inner and outer shell. The two skins did not protect the crew from extremes of surrounding water temperatures. The North Atlantic waters were exceptionally cold in February, 1945. Water temperatures varied at different depths. The tight quarters and need for physical flexibility limited the layers of clothing.

Initially, Kurt Pokel vowed he would not become attached to the child. Of course, within days, he found himself hovering over little Edith. Pokel dressed the child in layers and covered her with a wool navy-issued blanket. Pokel and the child were restricted to their tiny quarters. Pokel sat on his bunk cuddling Edith. *Perhaps she will feel secure.* She clasped his hand tightly. *She must be afraid I will abandon her.* Edith was becoming withdrawn. She rarely spoke and when she did it was in a whisper.

Edith displayed little emotion. It was as though she was void of all feeling. At times Edith experienced trance-like states. Intensity filled her eyes. It was a powerful gaze as though the child was under a spell. Edith experienced night trauma, also. Edith would suddenly sit upright, eyes wide-open and scream.

Awakened by Edith's piercing cry, Mallory would leave his bunk and open the curtain to Pokel's compartment.

"The child looks horrified, Pokel."

"She flails so hard, I fear she may injure herself," said Pokel.

"I try to comfort her."

Pokel held Edith in his arms and walked the short distance to the galley. He could feel her heart pounding. Perspiration soaked her clothes.

"Your calm voice and the U-boat's occasional motion seem to calm the child."

Lieutenant Pokel was unaware of the child's history. The nearly three-year-old child's history amounted to emotional trauma. Taken from her Lebensborn mother by Manfred Bartel and his wife, Gertrude, Edith became a pawn in Eva Braun's futile scheme to garner Hitler's attention. Richard and Sonja Klein became the child's next surrogate parents. Sonja Klein refused to bond with Edith. None of these events matched the damage inflicted by Heinrich Franz's brain change research, the effects of which Pokel observed often. Lieutenant Pokel observed the effects of Franz's "brain change" research.

On the second day at sea Commander Fromsdorf came to the passenger cabins. Fromsdorf dismissed the ever-present sentry. The compartments didn't have doors. He called to Pokel.

"How is the child doing?" Fromsdorf asked. The young commander's gesture seemed quite sincere.

"It's the odor. I feel a bit nauseous," said Pokel. "Edith isn't sleeping."

"We are moving at a very slow but, steady pace," said Fromsdorf. "We must remain submerged as much as possible. The snorkel allows fresh air for the boat and the diesel engines. Even with the snorkel we could be detected. In a calm sea the periscope and the snorkel leave a feather wave. It can be seen from a distance." Fromsdorf stepped into the compartment. He glanced down at Edith.

"Does she ever speak? She is the quietest child I've come across," Fromsdorf said.

"Ah, you notice it, too. Strange. Isn't it? I'm afraid she is a bit nauseous, too," Pokel responded.

"Keep Beck informed. We have a crewmember with medical training. Beck has a supply of bottled water for the child. Dehydration is a submariner's enemy. You are now free to move around. Avoid the radio room and the conning tower. A sentry will remain nearby. It's more for your security and privacy. Avoid talking with the crew."

"Yes sir. And what of Bruns?" Pokel asked.

"He will be confined to quarters unless escorted to and from the galley and the toilet."

"Why is the toilet such a problem?" asked Pokel.

"Like everything else, the toilet is subject to water pressure. It takes a bit of training to operate. The sentry will take care of that aspect. Carelessness could cause the damn thing to back up. We could flood. Let the sentry handle it," he repeated.

Fromsdorf decided to check on Bruns. He pulled opened the curtain of the second compartment and found Bruns lying on his bunk. Bruns rolled out and wearily stood facing the commander.

"My name is Fromsdorf. I am this boat's commander."

It was the first conversation between the two men.

"I've been kidnapped with no explanation. I've been vomiting from the boat's motion and stench. I haven't showered in several days. I can't stand my body odor."

"Ah, Bruns. Don't look so forsaken. You may be the lucky one in this mysterious undertaking."

"I demand to be returned to Germany. I have powerful friends."

"Nonsense, Bruns. If you did you would not be in this predicament. But, you will soon have influential friends in high places when you reach port. You are performing a great service for the Fatherland."

"The Gestapo threatened to harm my parents and my pregnant wife. What great service?" Bruns asked.

Fromsdorf smirked. "We are about to find out."

Bruns looked confused.

"As you were," Fromsdorf said. He headed to the galley to find Mallory.

❦

"Well, Mallory, tired of sleeping on the Petty Officers' compartment floor? My men complain you give them no privacy."

"Yes. I plan to leave Bruns to his own demons before I interrogate him. Then I will sleep."

Fromsdorf shrugged. "It's your choice. Avoid the Petty Officers' quarters. They have little patience. Don't push Bruns too hard. He might catch you sleeping and kill you." Fromsdorf laughed.

Mallory found the commander's remark troubling. Nevertheless, he laughed.

"Have you opened the first envelope?" Mallory asked.

"No. I will in a few minutes when Beck completes his duties. I'll give you plenty of notice."

Mallory looked at his watch. I find it difficult to acclimate myself. Within the U-boat there is no day or night, just constant noise and the stench. "It's 0900 hours. It feels like midnight."

"Life becomes more intense as the days wear on. The absence of sunlight, the cramped quarters and the bland diet upset your bodily functions. Ask Beck for a few sleeping pills. Let's hope we don't encounter the enemy."

Mallory was about to leave when Beck arrived. He informed Fromsdorf all stations were manned and their speed was approximately seven knots.

"The snorkel will slow us down. Beck, come with me. Mallory, wait here."

The two men went to Fromsdorf's quarters. The commander unlocked his desk drawer and withdrew the first envelope. Inside was a three-page document titled "Operation Seahawk."

Fromsdorf removed his cover and scratched his head.

Operation Seahawk? How does the Admiralty come up with these names? A joke came to mind. He stopped in mid-thought. This was a serious matter. He read the order.

Fromsdorf was ordered to follow an indirect course. The heading dodged the usual sea-lanes. The U-853 was to remain submerged. *Surface only when you determine crew morale necessitates such a risk. Maintain radio silence.* The last page was explicit. In upper case letters under Admiral Dönitz's name a second directive was posted. "Avoid offensive contact with the enemy. Do not enter into shallow waters. Avoid depths of less than two hundred feet."

German naval intelligence suspected the British had broken the Enigma three-digit cypher. U-boat commanders were apprehensive and suspected the Americans and British might broadcast bogus radio messages. A vigilant Dönitz switched to a four-digit system. Fromsdorf was to alert his radio operators to listen for the code word "Rainbow." When the "rainbow signal" was given Fromsdorf would ready the U-853 to be scuttled. The four passengers must be protected at all costs.

Fromsdorf read the directive again. *I'm confused. Why scuttle the U-853 unless it is in imminent danger of capture? The Fuhrer's orders are deliver the passengers to America at all costs. How can I protect the passengers if I scuttle the U-853?*

The final paragraph of page three instructed Fromsdorf to open Envelope Two when the U-853 reached the mission's midpoint. The order listed a specific grid position. U-boats used grid charts. The numbered grid boxes avoided the use of latitude and longitude in fear the enemy would intercept the U-boat.

Fromsdorf looked perplexed. He handed the pages to Beck. When Beck finished reading the instructions Fromsdorf handed him a pen. "Sign the bottom of the page." Beck signed the acknowledgment. Fromsdorf initialed the first two pages and signed page three. He returned the envelope to his desk drawer. "Please have Mallory report to me."

While Beck was gone, Fromsdorf reached into a small compartment over his desk just beneath the ship's safe. He removed a leather-bound book. It was the U-853's war Diary or ship's log. Fromsdorf uncapped his fountain pen and made a brief entry. As the ink dried he pondered Dönitz's "Rainbow" directive. He placed the log back in his desk drawer.

Next he unlocked the bottom drawer of his desk. He slid his hand slightly to the right and felt for his pistol. FN Model 1910 was a recent acquisition. It was loaded. A second magazine remained in the drawer. Fromsdorf recognized the danger of firing a pistol inside a U-Boat.

Prior to departure Fromsdorf ordered his officers to secure their side arms in the boat's firearms locker. Beck carried the key to the locker. Fromsdorf made a second unusual precaution. The crew's sea bags were inspected for contraband. His junior officers alerted their commander of grumblings and discontent among several crewmembers. Fromsdorf decided to keep his personal sidearm nearby. Fromsdorf removed the holstered pistol. He checked the loaded magazine. He placed the holstered pistol back in the drawer. Rather than carry the key, he dropped it into a small compartment over the desk where he sometimes kept the log between entries.

Beck returned with Mallory. "Thank you, Beck. That will be all." Fromsdorf summarized his instructions. He emphasized the U-853 would be scuttled to avoid capture.

"And what will become of Bruns, Pokel, the child and me?" Mallory asked.

Fromsdorf grimaced, but remained silent.

Mallory recognized the strain and consternation on Fromsdorf's face. Obviously, the commander was withholding information. Mallory suspected the answer. Fromsdorf's passengers were expendable.

⁕

On the second day at sea Fromsdorf entered the control room. He looked about as he gathered his thoughts for an important announcement. The captain signaled for a general announcement. He waited for his complement of four officers, three chief petty officers, fourteen petty officers and thirty ratings responded.

"Is the crew assembled?" Fromsdorf asked. He looked about for the boatswain's mate. Fromsdorf grew impatient and asked again, "Is the crew assembled?"

"All but the boatswain's mate," Beck responded.

Fromsdorf could tell Beck wanted to explain, but this wasn't the time.

"This is the Captain speaking. I have some very important information for you about our mission and the passengers on board. We are on a Fuhrer-ordered mission. It is top secret. Even now there may be enemy vessels and planes searching for us."

He saw his officers' grim expression. "We must remain submerged as much as possible. This mission will push all of us beyond all other missions combined. Gossip and criticism will not be tolerated. Any man found rendering dissent or obstructing our mission will be severely punished. This is a mission of utmost importance to the Fatherland. It is imperative crewmembers avoid talking with our passengers. The forward compartments are off limits unless you have an assigned duty. You will follow our protocols. We are heavily loaded with critical supplies. Remain within your designated duty stations. That is all."

"Beck. Come to my quarters."

"Yes sir."

Beck and Fromsdorf stepped into the captain's compartment. Fromsdorf pulled the curtain closed. The radio operator heard the boatswain's mate's name as the curtain closed.

"Sir, Boatswain's Mate Arndt has been a problem since he joined the crew. His last assignment was with the Luftwaffe."

"How did we get him?"

"Arndt is an experienced gun captain."

"I questioned him this morning. He complained bitterly about his transfer. He is pessimistic about the outcome of the war. Arndt had a run-in with his petty officer, last evening.

"Check with Mallory. He told me one or two of the crew were loitering on deck. Warn Arndt. I will not tolerate insubordination. Keep Arndt confined. He may be unstable. We can't afford a loose cannon on this mission. Shackle him if you must."

"Yes, sir." As Beck opened the curtain he caught Blasse, the radio operator ducking back into the radio room. Beck stepped forward and admonished Blasse to remain at his post at all times. *Arndt and* Blasse *were friends. They are the source of the current unrest.* "Blasse, I warn you. No gossip. I will inform the captain."

Blasse looked at Beck, but didn't acknowledge him beyond a curt "Aye, Aye, Sir."

I don't like him. Now I have two culprits to keep on a tight leash.

∾

Days passed slowly on the U-853. With the exception of the radio operators, the crew worked a schedule of eight hours on and eight hour off. The five radio operators also shared duties with sonar detection. Each man worked fifteen to thirty minute shifts. The crews' safety depended on their vigilance. When the U-853 surfaced, four sharp-eyed crewmembers manned the bridge. They focused on the horizon. One failure could spell disaster as an Allied fighter or bomber began a strafing run. A delayed dive command might leave a crewman stranded on the deck as the conning tower compartment and deck hatches were closed.

Chapter Eighteen
Saving Otto Bruns

Day four found Mallory pacing. For the first four days Mallory slept in the chief's quarters. It was time to interrogate the man he knew as Otto Bruns. Mallory pulled back the canvas privacy curtain. Bruns was lying on his rack in a near-fetal position. The confined area smelled of vomit and urine. Brurns was suffering from seasickness compounded by severe dehydration. An empty water bottle rolled on the floor with the motion of the U-boat.

Mallory touched Brun's forehead with the back of his hand. The man had a fever.

"Look at me, man," said Mallory.

Bruns turned slightly. He appeared confused. His pupils were enlarged. "Listen to me, Bruns. You are very ill. I am going to speak with the Captain."

Bruns simply nodded and turned back to the compartment wall.

Mallory turned and walked a few paces to the captain's compartment. "Bruns needs immediate medical attention. I'm afraid he his going into shock."

Fromsdorf looked up from his desk and said, "I'll have Beck look at him. The man Arndt replaced had medical training. I have some, but Beck has some limited skill. I'll have him check Bruns."

Beck agreed with Mallory. Bruns needed to be sedated and hydrated. "I have some pills to help with the nausea." The two men removed Bruns' soiled clothes.

"Hold still," said Beck as he inserted an IV into Burn's arm. "I hope your man doesn't die before we reach our destination," said Beck.

Fromsdorf peered into the compartment. "My orders are to deliver these passengers. Keep Bruns alive. Once we reach our grid coordinate, we will rendezvous with the supply U-boat. I'll request additional medical supplies," said Fromsdorf.

"Sir, with your permission, I would like to send Arndt back to Norway for court martial," said Beck.

"I'll take it under advisement. Tend to Bruns. And, Beck, have an orderly clean this room and swab the deck. The stench is awful."

"Yes, sir."

❦

For the next two days Mallory and Beck took turns nursing Bruns. Finally, his fever broke. Beck found a worn jump suit and socks for Bruns. Soon only the stench from the bilge permeated the compartment.

When the U-853 reached its appointed grid location Fromsdorf ordered all hands to battle stations. He peered through the sky telescope. No fighters in sight. He scanned the calm Atlantic surface. No surface vessels. When Germany dominated the North Atlantic a U-boat commander could count on a supply vessel. A Type XIV U-boat was designed to re-supply other U-boats with fresh food, medical supplies, and torpedoes.

"Sir, what will we do if our supply vessels fails to show?" asked Beck.

"It won't curtail our mission, Beck. Take over the "con." I must speak with Mallory. "I am concerned we may not have adequate food and water if we do not connect with the supply U-boat."

"There has to be a contingency," said Mallory. "Have you opened the second envelope?"

"No, but I will." Fromsdorf entered his compartment and unlocked the drawer. He opened the second envelope. Inside Fromsdorf found his orders for the second segment of the mission. He unfolded another map to be placed under the grid on the chart table. The orders were specific. Maintain radio silence. In the event the rendezvous does not take place continue to the designated grid location. Attached to the orders was a note signed by Admiral Dönitz.

In the event the U-853 fails to be resupplied, the U-853 was to continue with the mission. Fromsdorf was to reach the third grid location. At that point he was to inform the crew 'the U-853 will not return to Germany.' It is imperative the U-853 not be captured with passengers and cargo. "

"The Fuhrer relies on the safe conduct of your passengers. Once your mission is complete you are free to conduct missions in accordance with the instructions in envelope three." Dönitz ended with a cryptic sentence. "Urgent to arrive at your final grid location no later than May 6, 1945." Signed, Dönitz, Commander-in-Chief of the German Navy. The document was stamped with the Admiral's official seal.

Fromsdorf returned to the conning tower control room where he placed the second map under the grid. While he and Beck measured the distance to the next point the U-853 radio operators worked in shifts listening to the British, American and German frequencies. Then an odd event occurred. Fromsdorf felt certain he would receive a signal from Germany or from one of the other U-boats dispatched from Norway to follow the U-853. There was shouting from below. "Captain." It was the chief radio operator. We have lost radio contact."

Fromsdorf rushed to the radio room. "Are you certain?"

"Yes sir. I've run several tests. The radios are functioning. It must be our antenna."

"Keep working. Assist the Chief Engineer. We must locate and fix the problem."

Fromsdorf called for Beck. They discussed the problem. Someone has either tampered with our radios or the antenna. "Not a word of this to the crew. I'll get to the bottom of this."

It had to be Blasse or Arndt. To be sure Fromsdorf ordered the Chief Engineer to complete inspection of the electrical system including the antenna systems. "We always have the emergency antenna buoy," said the Chief.

"The buoy will reveal our position. No. That won't do. Find the problem. Fix it."

"Aye, Aye, sir." The Chief and the radio operator headed to the aft of the U-boat.

The Chief turned and remarked, "We may have to surface for a repair, sir."

"Find the problem, Chief," Fromsdorf barked.

Beck approached Fromsdorf. "We must push on, Beck."

Mallory was dismayed when Fromsdorf told him the news.

'We need our communications," Mallory insisted.

"I agree," said Fromsdorf. "We will have to surface in the near future. The child, Lieutenant Pokel, and Bruns are all suffering from severe seasickness. The child is dehydrating. The rough seas on the surface will worsen their conditions."

"Is it possible to get the child to drink or eat?"

"The cook prepared a lukewarm potato soup, but she refused to taste it." Beck returned and called Pokel into the passageway.

"The child will have to be restrained. She trusts you. I'll give her an IV."

Pokel started to protest, but he knew there was no choice. He tore strips of a pillowcase and tied her wrists and ankles. Beck returned with the IV and some liquid medication. Within an hour Edith lay exhausted but calm from the sedation.

⚮

Arndt and Blasse sat in the galley playing chess. Arndt spotted the Chief Engineer inspecting the overhead valves in the passageway. A crewmember entered the galley and said, "Something's going on. The Chief is inspecting the valves and wiring. Why now?"

One of the two cooks preparing a coffee concoction turned and shrugged. "Best we leave it alone. It's not our business and the Captain isn't in the best mood."

Arndt added to the discord. "I told you Fromsdorf wasn't fit to be Captain."

"Shut up Arndt," shot the second cook. "You'll get us thrown in the brig."

"I'm done," Arndt said to Blasse. He left the galley and headed aft. He passed the Chief stepping from the entrance to the rear torpedo room.

"What are you doing back here Arndt? The Captain told you to remain in the galley and not wander the boat."

Arndt looked at the chief. "Are you going to report me?"

"Get back to the galley."

Arndt turned and headed back to the galley as the Chief and the radio operator began inspecting the cables from the torpedo room.

"There," shouted the Chief. He startled the radio operator. "Look. The cable has been cut just as it goes through the watertight seal through the conduit to the outside antenna." The two menb left and reported to the Captain.

The U-853 would have to surface in order to make the repair. The mystery remained. Who cut the cable and why?

Suddenly, the U-853 began to shift aft. "Sir we have flooding in the after battery."

"My god. What's happening?" called one of the two crewmen handling the two huge wheels that control the submarine's stability. Submarines rely on buoyancy for balance and maneuverability. With gold bullion stored below and extra supplies in the torpedo racks even the slightest additional weight could jeopardize the U-boat.

"Chief, are all hatches secured?" shouted Fromsdorf.

"Affirmative sir."

"Captain, this is the torpedo room. We are taking on water."

"Chief engineer, come with me." Fromsdorf and the Chief headed aft. The bow was beginning to tilt up a few degrees. The movement gave the sensation the U-boat was heading to the surface, but it was beginning to descend to a dangerous depth.

Once again Beck called out for the gauges to be checked. Now the U-853 began to list to the starboard side. "We continue to take on water," came the cry from the torpedo room.

The Chief had checked every accessible valve only hours before. The bow pointed further up. Fromsdorf ordered all available crewmembers to scramble forward. "We can't allow our batteries to flood. Hydrogen could escape and cause an explosion. Beck ordered the buoyancy tanks adjusted. The call came again. "Flooding in the aft battery." Suddenly the vessel shifted again.

The Chief called to Fromsdorf. "Sir the aft toilet. We have perishables stored there. The door was supposed to be locked. It is open." The Chief began tossing small wooden crates and boxes into the passageway. "I found the problem sir. The toilet valve is wide open."

"Damn it. We have a problem with the two-stage heads," the Chief called out to Fromsdorf.

Fromsdorf ordered one of the cooks to assist the Chief.

"What's wrong, Chief?"

"Before leaving Norway the U-853 was retrofitted with two new heads (toilets). The old heads required the crank flush with direct discharge into the sea. The cranking was noisy. The discharge might float to the surface and betray the U-boat's location."

"We were all trained how to flush the new two-stage heads. It is critical that only one valve was opened at a time in sequence. The first valve flushes the waste to a macerator tank. The valve is then closed. The second stage valve is opened to allow seawater to fill the tank."

"Yes, Chief. I understand. We were warned that the second stage valve had to be closed before the tank flooded," said the cook.

"Well, damn it. Someone has opened the stage-two valve."

"This was no accident," said the cook.

"Warn the captain. The fast-flowing seawater will flood the rear battery compartment," shouted the Chief.

Back in the control room and unaware of the Chief's discovery, Beck ordered the aft tanks be emptied to stabilize the boat. "Blow the after tanks first."

Suddenly the U-853 took a nosedive and created the sensation of sinking. Actually the U-boat was rising to the surface, but stern first. "Oh my god. I'm going to die," cried one of the young helmsmen.

It was the most frightening, yet exhilarating, feeling Beck had ever experienced. "Stay calm, man. Keep your wits about you. Hold steady." Anything and everything that wasn't tied down began to crash to the deck. Dishes flew through the galley. Several of the crew lay unconscious. "Hold on," Beck shouted.

Suddenly, the U-853 broke through the surface stern first. The huge whale vaulted into the air and crashed violently down. Never before had a U-boat experienced such impact. Beck couldn't believe he was still alive. Neither the Captain nor the chief had reported in. "Run the bilges. Damage reports," Beck shouted.

Chapter Nineteen
The Recovery

The chiefs and other officers scurried to inspect the interior, assess damage, and search for injured crew. The conning tower was now the damage control center.

Fromsdorf and the Chief struggled back to the conning tower. Fromsdorf suffered from a dislocated shoulder. The Chief received a severe blow to the head but was able to function.

"How bad is the damage?" Fromsdorf asked.

"We have two men with critical injuries, life threatening. Eight others have broken limbs, but no severe bleeding. There is one confirmed casualty."

"Who?" asked the captain.

"Arndt. His neck was broken. They found him on radio room floor. He damaged the transmitters and receivers. We have one functional radio the 40-watt back up. Without an antenna it's useless. Even the most powerful transmitter on land can't contact us."

"And the radar warning device?"

"Damaged, Sir."

"Find Blasse. He's had a hand in this," ordered Fromsdorf.

"I've ordered the injured triaged. We don't have enough morphine for all of them."

"Then break out the schnapps. Open the wine. Limit it to the injured. We need the crew sober."

Beck turned to carry out the order when Fromsdorf added, "Bring me the traitor, Blasse," Fromsdorf said again. Beck nodded and headed off to find Blasse.

Blasse was sprawled on the galley floor moaning in pain. Beck ordered two crewmen to carry him to the passage below the conning tower where Fromsdorf was waiting.

The two crewmen lifted Blasse to his feet and held him in front of the Captain. "You and Arndt have created havoc."

Blasse hesitated to speak. His eyes cast down. "What difference does it make? You are taking us on a suicide mission. Better to die now than betray the Fatherland."

A look of disgust crossed Fromsdorf's face. "You are the traitor, Blasse." Fromsdorf raised his arm and motioned to take Blasse away. "Wait. Toss him overboard," Fromsdorf ordered.

Blasse looked stunned, but then arrogantly laughed as though he accepted his fate. He struggled once as he was dragged on deck. Beck stood on the bridge. He gave the order and Blasse was shoved over the side. Blasse's head bobbed above the surface. He instinctively struggled. A wave washed him against the hull. Blasse disappeared.

Through the entire calamity Mallory and Bruns had been tossed around their compartment. A large vertical pipe on the compartment wall may have saved them from severe injury. There was enough space between the pipe and the wall for the two men to hold tight. Once the U-853 was stable Mallory crawled to Pokel's cubicle. He found an unconscious Pokel on the floor next to the child. All during the fiasco young Edith remained restrained to her cot. Mallory managed to pull himself up alongside the child. Huge welts appeared on her wrists and ankles from the restraints. Ironically, they had saved the child's life. The child moaned. The sedation was wearing off, but she was alive.

A heavy smell of diesel fuel drifted from the bilge. A ruptured fuel line added to the dilemma. The U-853 was in survival mode. The officers and crew understood the severity of their predicament. The U-boat was floating, helplessly exposed to an approaching Atlantic storm and the probability of being discovered by land-based search planes.

The anti-aircraft guns were manned. Four men were stationed as lookouts. All the hatches were opened. Once again fresh air flushed the fumes from the boat.

The two galley cooks began to sort through their supplies. Saving the perishables was a daunting task. The fresh fruits and vegetables stored in the aft toilet could not be salvaged. The crew would have to rely on canned goods. A diet of what the crew called "diesel food" would add to the physical and psychological damage the crew suffered. "At least we're alive," said one of the cooks.

The pace of the repairs increased as an Atlantic storm approached. Waves were beginning to wash across the bow. The hatches would have to be closed. The damage reports were ominous. The U-853 would have to rely on a number of redundant systems and the skill of the crew. After approximately six hours on the surface Fromsdorf ordered, "Prepare to dive, Mr. Beck. Coax her gently now."

The rear torpedo room reported a major leak in one of the cooling pipes, but it was soon controlled. The U-853 creaked and groaned as she leveled-off at 30.48 meters (100 feet).

"Steady as she goes, Beck," called Fromsdorf. His voice was growing week. His shoulder throbbed. The U-853 started to porpoise again. Fromsdorf calculated he needed to jettison weight for the U-853 to gain buoyancy. Before leaving Norway the torpedo compensating tanks were filled with fuel. This added an additional six tons. Now the fuel was approximately one third depleted. Each torpedo weighed 4.5 tons. After another calculation he decided to dump four torpedoes.

"We will still have fourteen torpedoes on board," he told Beck. Next, Fromsdorf and Beck calculated dismantling the 105 mm deck gun when next they surfaced.

"We are behind schedule, Beck. It's imperative we make up for lost time."

"Sir, according to my calculations we are no longer capable of a sustained underwater speed of eighteen knots. With the terrible pounding the hull took when we surfaced I feel certain a submerged speed over seven knots will surely destroy the boat."

"Very well, Beck. I agree. I haven't opened the third set of orders, yet. Nevertheless, I suspect our next orders will call for a mid-April arrival in the treacherous waters near the New England coast. The boat needed every bit of maneuverability it could muster."

Fromsdorf knew he faced a daunting decision. *Those damn crates of gold bullion. Our trim, speed and maneuverability are encumbered. We have to jettison the gold bullion, but not until we're in calmer waters.*

Satisfied with Beck's calculations, Fromsdorf placed his slide rule on the chart table, rubbed his eyes and left the bridge. He struggled down the ladder. Fromsdorf was determined that the U-853 would complete its mission

Chapter Twenty
Bruns' Admission

Once the U-853 was underway, Mallory was determined to interrogate Bruns further.

"Who told you I was a virologist?" asked Bruns.

"I memorized your dossier. I know every detail of your life. You've been working with the Japanese. Anthrax. You're a criminal. You have to be a valuable commodity to risk so many lives. If I had my way I'd shoot you."

"You know nothing," retorted Bruns.

"I negotiated your exchange with the Naval High Command."

"Nonsense," said an indignant Bruns. "The exchange was arranged at Hitler's direction. He is the Commander-in-Chief and wields absolute power. It had to be Hitler who ordered my abduction. The Fuhrer initiated this mission. Admiral Dönitz would never act on his own initiative. This mission is a desperate measure. Why risk a precious U-boat and crew to deliver a physicist?"

"Physicist?" asked a puzzled Mallory. "If you aren't Otto Bruns, who are you?" The name Otto Bruns will do. My parents…my wife, my son…they are under house arrest in Berlin. I've done nothing wrong."

"You're a Nazi scientist, a specialist in biological warfare."

"Listen to me, Mallory. I am a physicist. Your government knows it. Dönitz knows it. Your government needed a cover story, if the Gestapo captured you."

"Why are you telling me this?" asked Mallory.

"Does it matter? On the other hand, you saved my life. I owe you. In a way, I feel sorry for you, Mallory. We're pawns in a game. I doubt we will get out of this alive."

Mallory didn't know how to respond. "Game? This is no game."

"Believe me. I am a physicist, part of a research team station in Peenemunde.

I was in Berlin when the Navy Military Police took me into custady."

Mallory was astonished. Bruns talked on. "Have you ever heard of magnetic levitation?"

"No. Sounds like hypnosis or magic."

Bruns laughed. "Your government put your life on the line Mallory. You should know the truth. I led a secret team. I did work with the Japanese, but not inventing germs. We developed a prototype for a magnetic propulsion system for the V-2 rocket."

Mallory had no idea what Bruns was talking about. "Keep it simple, Bruns."

"The two torpedo size aluminum cylinders we are transporting don't contain germs or vaccines. The crew believes they contain diamonds or precious stones. They contain something far more valuable. That's why your government kidnapped me."

Bruns told Mallory the cylinders held the components for a prototype rocket launcher. "The model is a scaled-down V-2 rocket called the V-3A. What we have is a catapult, the power system and the schematics. The Peenemunde catapult superstructure was destroyed during a bombing raid. The smaller of the two cylinders holds the critical components, and my blueprints. The cylinder is insulated."

"Why insulate the canister?" Mallory asked.

"By the end of 1943 liquid oxygen propellant was growing scarce. I had been experimenting with magnetic force fields. The Luftwaffe needed an aircraft that could use an improvised runway. Göring wanted a vertical lift aircraft. Our experiments dealt with circular electro-magnetic force. It was my idea to develop a forward direction thruster."

"I still don't understand," said Mallory. *Bruns is fabricating this story. It's bullshit.*

Bruns sensed from Mallory's expression his captor didn't believe his story. "It's true. Magnets. The cylinder contains powerful magnets made from rare earth elements. We manufactured superconductor magnets and attached them to the underbelly of the V-3A rocket. With sufficient electricity, we generate enough thrust to use less liquid hydrogen and liquid oxygen to fuel the booster."

"Who knew about this?" Mallory asked.

"It was supposed to be a secret. Obviously we had a traitor in our midst or your government would never have known."

"I still don't believe you."

"There was an understanding between Himmler and Göring to keep the program secret. I know this."

"How?"

"The V-3A is designed to accommodate a modified Messerschmitt, ME-262. The ME-262 A1 fighter was modified to rest on a launching cradle. We designed a mobile launcher. The launch would exert tremendous G-force on a pilot. Göring conducted G-force experiments on prisoners. Few survived. Göring enlisted a squadron of Luftwaffe volunteers to participate in a so-called controlled experiment. I met the group instructor, an American. A psychologist name Heinrich Franz."

"This is bullshit. Are you telling me there was an American psychologist working for Göring? I don't believe it."

"Don't you understand, Mallory? It is a brilliant idea. My idea. I've discovered a way to harness a magnetic force into a forward thrust. The concept goes beyond the rocket launcher. Imagine the power of magnets replacing cannons on the battlefield. Your government wants the launcher. They want my knowledge. I was abducted before I could conclude the test. Now Göring will get the credit. The bastard." Bruns was beginning to sound like a madman.

All of a sudden the reality of Bruns' babbling overwhelmed Mallory. Mallory's mind started to wander. "What else?"

"You've already guessed the next step. Haven't you? I can

see it in your eyes," said Bruns.

"My god. Disregard the terrain. Imagine a mobile launch pad with an electro-magnetic force field. This whole damned submarine is one potential giant magnet. We have everything on board including the batteries."

"Exactly. Picture a submarine sitting off the Atlantic coast hundreds of miles from New York City." Bruns pounded his fist against the compartment wall and shouted "Boom!"

Then Bruns' expression darkened. "Our experiments depended upon conventional electricity. We needed rare magnets to complete the final magnetic levitation experiment. The elements are beyond our reach. They are refined from mining residue. Can you imagine waste being invaluable? The largest deposits of rare earth elements are in China. We gathered samples from Rhodesia, also. I suspect your government is already mining rare earth elements."

"What makes you so sure?" Mallory asked.

"Why would your government abduct me? They struck a deal with Hitler."

"What deal?" Mallory sneered. "You will tell me, Bruns. I'll get it out of you, one way or another."

"The child. There is something important about the child. I think I know the answer." Bruns smiled then grimaced. His lips stretched tight. The man Mallory knew as Otto Bruns harbored a key secret. "Your superiors lied. They've misled you, Mallory. Can't you tell by now?"

The frustrated Mallory grabbed Bruns and jerked him forward. "Tell me the truth, Bruns." Mallory pushed Bruns back against the steel wall.

Bruns was frightened. He began to answer when Lieutenant Pokel pulled open the compartment curtain.

"Damn it Pokel. Get out of here." Mallory turned back to Bruns.

Pokel interceded. "I'm sorry for the interruption. This is an emergency. The child."

Mallory gave Bruns a cold stare. "We'll continue this

conversation. You better not be lying."

It didn't matter. The brief interruption gave Bruns the opportunity to change his mind. Bruns had said enough. *Mallory will have to discover the truth for himself.*

"What's wrong with the child?" demanded Mallory.

"I don't think she will last another day. She's unresponsive. Her vital signs are stable, but she's traumatized. Look around, Mallory. The crew is in a bad state. They've been in combat before. How is a child to survive?"

"She's your responsibility, Lieutenant. Do your best. You are her only hope. My intuition tells me we are close to our destination."

"Where, Mallory? What more will go wrong?"

Chapter Twenty-One
Camp Upton,
Long Island, New York
Late Spring, 1945.

Camp Upton was established during World War I as a training and debarkation center for troop deployments to Europe. Camp Upton was unique, as it became the location of the US Army's Recruit Education Center. Illiterate American and foreign-born recruits were shipped to Camp Upton to learn English and eventually be suitable for induction into the US Army. The process of Americanization could lead to US citizenship after the completion of three years of military duty. Camp Upton was disbanded after World War One. Upon the United States' entry into the Second World War, Camp Upton was rebuilt to house thousands of illiterate and foreign-born recruits.

In late 1945 German prisoners of war arrived at Camp Upton. The registrations listed prisoners' date of capture and unit attachments. Among this group were troops affiliated with the SA (Nazi Brown Shirts), SS (Himmler's zealot Nazi Units), SD (the security service in charge of intelligence and espionage) and other military personnel. These high-priority prisoners were being processed for eventual repatriation to Germany.

A young US Army intelligence officer, Thomas Brady, was assigned the final prisoner-interrogation. Brady was given a Luftwaffe pilot for interrogation. Alfred Fischer was captured in January 1945. He was a passenger on a military transport plane evacuating Luftwaffe officers stationed along the German border with Belgium.

Brady was a doctoral candidate in psychology. He spoke fluent German.

"I am a psychologist. The Allied Command and our Justice Department have implemented an order requiring designated prisoners be interviewed to determine their state of mind," said Brady. "You are one of those prisoners."

"There is talk among my fellow prisoners that you are searching for war criminals. Is that why you are questioning me?" Fischer asked.

"No. You would have been placed in isolation by now." "You must have a record of my previous interrogations. I have no wish to discuss this further. I have my rights as a German officer."

"You do. But I have my job to do and it is in your best interests to cooperate," said Brady.

"And if I don't?"

"Perhaps word will leak to your camp leaders that you are revealing too much and anxious to receive special treatment."

A look of horror crossed Fischer's face. "I would be killed."

"Cooperate. And I promise to keep the information classified."

Fischer slumped into the wooden chair in front of Brady's desk. "What do you want to know?"

"What type of aircraft did you fly?" Brady asked. "I was trained to fly a Messerschmitt Me 262," Fischer replied. "I'm not a pilot," said Brady. "I'm much more comfortable with my feet on the ground. This final interrogation is routine, before you are transferred."

"Another transfer?" Fischer asked.

"I'm not asking about airplane specifications. This interrogation focuses on your frame of mind in preparation for eventual repatriation to Germany."

Fischer laughed. "Are you so sure the war is coming to an end?"

Brady avoided the question. "I'm interested in the special training you may have undergone while training to fly a special airplane."

The pilot looked surprised. "How do you know the plane

was special?" Fischer asked.

"You had to be involved with some type of special weapons project to merit being sent here," said Brady.

Fischer turned away to avert eye contact with Brady. "No one has asked me about my pilot training before," he said.

"Tell me about the the Messerschmitt Me 262."

Fischer smiled, but remained silent.

"Have you ever heard of behavioral psychology?" Brady asked.

"No." Fischer sounded annoyed. He nervously tapped his fingers on Brady's desk.

"Simply put, behavioral psychology is the study of how people behave. What makes them function? What is it that motivates a man to abandon the fear of death? It took courage for pilots to fly a new plane without flight time," said Brady.

"Many died," said Fischer. "We had to believe in ourselves and know we were making a great contribution to the Fatherland."

"Yes, of course. That's my point. Did you or your fellow pilots receive special training beyond what other Luftwaffe pilots received?"

Brady studied Fischer's intense facial expression. *He is highly focused.*

There was a prolonged silence. Then, Fischer began to talk about a program at Berlin University's Hermann Göring Aeronautical Institute. "They called it The Monarch Project. Early test flights had proven disastrous. It was a structured experiment to build confidence and focus in the pilots who would fly the Messerschmitt ME 262."

The American officer was fascinated. "And how did they increase confidence?"

"The researchers provided mind-altering drugs and hypnosis. We called the director of our project the Pied Piper," said Fischer. "At first he treated us like children. He humiliated us. Some pilots cursed our trainers under their breath. A number of pilots left the program. I remained. Each day the training intensified."

"Your description makes the training sound extremely

punishing," Brady said.

"We had already completed the high altitude training. The work at Berlin University focused on our ability to go beyond our endurance. We were trained to step outside of ourselves and focus completely on the mission," said Fischer.

Brady watched Fischer's posture become erect, almost tense, as he continued the interview. "Do you recall the name of the project leader?" Brady inquired.

"Yes. His name was Heinrich Franz. He was attached to Himmler's research division, but Göring became involved with the work. The ME-262 was Germany's final hope. I do know Göring planned to mount a ME 262 on a special launch called a sled. The sled catapulted the jet fighter into the air using electrical energy. It was a dangerous experiment. The sled was unique. It could be moved to different locations. Göring was anxious to put it to use. We all understood the risks. Franz was training pilots to overcome our fear. I personally saw several ME 262's crash and explode. It was horrible to see my comrades burned alive." Fischer slowly rubbed his eyes.

Brady paused to allow Fischer to regain his composure. Then he said, "Tell me about Franz."

"I had no proof, but I suspected Franz was an American. It was rumored he was also a high level officer in the Abwehr. Who knows? I heard him say the Abwehr employed five hundred psychologists and he was the best."

"Tell me more," Brady encouraged.

Fischer paused then said, "I have already told you too much."

"I need more detail," Brady replied.

"I was given drugs and subjected to hypnosis. I spent two nights in a padded cell. The lights were intense. The most difficult part was the voices shouting louder and louder until I screamed. Then there was silence. Then the cycle would start, again. It was torture. I can still feel the pain and the headaches."

"Headaches?"

"Yes." Fischer rubbed his forehead. Fischer cupped his hands and tapped his forehead several times as though to chase away the pain.

"Tell me more about the voices."

"I can't remember the details," said Fischer.

"OK then, tell me more about Heinrich Franz."

"He was a strange man. He appeared to enjoy watching me suffer." "But you told me you didn't do anything physical. It sounds very strenuous to me."

"The hardest part was taking the pills. In a few minutes I began seeing a kaleidoscope of colors. I would hear voices."

"What did the voices say?"

"I can't recall," said Fischer.

"Did you ever experience any electroshock treatments?"

"What do you mean?" asked Fischer.

"Were wires attached to your body? Was electric current shot through your body?"

"Many times. One of Franz's assistants attached the wires to a monitor. They measured my heart rate, afterwards."

As the interview continued Fischer complained, "I feel light-headed." Suddenly, Fischer became sullen. "That's all I know. I've already told you too much."

"I must complete the interrogation, but we can continue tomorrow," said Brady as he ended the interrogation.

Fischer pushed himself out of the chair and stood at attention. He did not give the Hitler salute as several of the other prisoners had done. The pilot, more than any other person he interviewed, intrigued Brady.

Even though the interrogation was incomplete, Brady felt compelled to forward a brief account of Fischer's interrogation.

Within hours of reading Brady's report an encrypted message was relayed to Muroc Army Air Filed, Muroc, California. Muroc was the location for highly-classified and unique aviation technology, the predecessor to Edwards Air Force Base. A general staff officer read Brady's notes.

"We better grab this ME 262 pilot before Naval Intelligence gets their hands on him," said the general's aide. And they did.

Brady was ordered to postpone questioning Fischer. Five

days later, three MP's and a staff officer from Muroc arrived at Camp Upton. Fischer was transported to California by train.

When word of Fischer's transfer arrived at OSS headquarters in Washington, several OSS officials were dispatched to Muroc to interview Fischer.

"What seems to be the problem?" asked the colonel in charge of Fischer's dossier.

"We received an alert from Camp Upton's intelligence unit. You snatched Alfred Fischer, a Luftwaffe pilot, without going through channels," said one of the OSS officers.

"And what channels would they be?" the colonel snorted.

"You can keep Fischer," retorted the OSS officer. "We want to question him about a secret project and an American working with the Nazis in Germany."

"He's all yours," said the colonel.

Who could imagine that Alfred Fischer was the first clue to an extraordinary experiment that would haunt the American military and intelligence communities for years to come?

Chapter Twenty-Two
The New England Coast.

The long and treacherous journey was coming to an end. The second week of April 1945 the crippled U-853 arrived off the New England Coast. It was time to open the final envelope. Fromsdorf summoned Beck and Mallory to his quarters.

"I wanted you here Mallory, because I am concerned for my crew." Fromsdorf handed him one of the three pages from the envelope.

Beck was surprised. He had not seen the order. *Why was the Captain handing the document to Mallory first?*

Fromsdorf's orders called for him to arrive at grid marker 75 off the Maine coast, no later than April 25, 1945. The U-853 was to meet a launch. Otto Bruns and the two aluminum tubes were to be transferred to the launch. Once the transfer was complete Fromsdorf was directed to grid location 83. Mallory handed the page to Beck. Beck left and returned a few minutes later.

"Sir. There has to be a mistake. The grid coordinates place us very close to the American submarine base. Grid location 83 will place us off the North Coast of Long Island in the Long Island Sound. Location 83 shows depths of less than two hundred feet. We are being sent into a graveyard."

"We have our orders, Beck."

Mallory looked perturbed. "What are the rest of the orders?"

"We are to return to grid marker 79 and await a radio dispatch from Germany."

"We have no radio," said Beck.

"I understand your concern, Beck. We've made it this far. We will complete the mission," Fromsdorf assured the two men. "Remember there are at least three other U-boats following a similar route. They are bound to discover us. "All isn't lost."

Mallory knew from Fromsdorf's expression the Captain doubted his own assurances.

Fromsdorf checked his charts. They dated back to 1939. The waters off the Atlantic coastline were treacherous, as the depths had certainly changed due to storms and currents.

On the evening of April 22, 1945, the U-853 arrived at grid location 75 a few miles from Portland Maine. It was a heavily-trafficked sea lane. Fromsdorf scowled. *They couldn't have picked a more deadly location for us. There has to be at least one other U-boat in the area.* The U-853 waited for 24 hours, but no launch arrived. At that point Fromsdorf made a critical decision.

The Captain ordered Beck to a new heading for grid marker 83. The boat proceeded at a slow pace. The American U-boat hunters were using new sonar equipment and aided by dirigibles from a base in New Jersey.

On the evening of April 24, not far from New London, Connecticut, the U-853 reached a halfway point to its destination. The Captain peered through the sky periscope. The evening sky was clear. The surface periscope revealed a puzzling picture. The night sky over the coastline was no longer blacked out. Fromsdorf called Beck to the conning tower.

"Here, look for yourself. There's no blackout. The entire coastline is a light as though the war was over."

"Could it be?" he asked Beck.

Fromsdorf left the conning tower. He awakened Mallory. "Come with me," he whispered. "Something is wrong. There's no coastline blackout. We'll wait until midnight and surface."

As midnight approached Beck became anxious. He returned to the conning tower. This would be the third time in an hour he had called out "up scope." This time the view was different. In the distance he saw the silhouette of a launch. "Awaken the Captain," he told the petty office standing by the chart table. When Fromsdorf arrived he confirmed Beck's observation.

The silhouetted vessel appeared to be the designated launch. It was time to transfer Otto Bruns and his precious cargo. The U-853 crept closer. The launch was equipped with sonar.

"They tracked us," said Fromsdorf. The Americans have

sophisticated equipment. The captain of the launch flashed the signal for the U-853 to surface.

Fromsdorf alerted the crew. "This is the Captain. All hands prepare for battle stations. We are about to surface. Gun crews on the ready. Be prepared for an emergency dive. Attention Forward Torpedo Room. Prepare to hoist the aluminum canisters. Stand by the forward hatch."

Otto Bruns was awakened by the commotion. Mallory prodded him to get ready. The disoriented Bruns searched for his leather case, his only possession not waterlogged when the U-853 nearly sank in the mid-Atlantic. His soiled civilian clothes were stowed along the aft passageway. He'd have to wear Beck's borrowed fatigues.

The U-boat surfaced. Gun crews rushed to their appointed positions. The large motorboat cautiously approached.

The craft appeared to be a PT boat. It was painted grey. It did not display any identifying numbers. The boat signaled one more time. The vessel's captain called out in German "Ahoy, U-853. Blue Dawn."

Fromsdorf watching through his binoculars turned to Beck, "Acknowledge."

"Blue Dawn," shouted Beck. Then Beck remarked, "An American for sure."

Fromsdorf chuckled at Beck's comment. "Order the canisters hoisted on deck."

The U-853's forward torpedo hatch was opened. Fromsdorf had not anticipated a transfer at sea. Torpedoes were already loaded into the forward tubes. This was a highly dangerous practice even without the triggering mechanisms set. Space was needed for the additional cargo. The crew struggled to hoist the two canisters forward and up.

Three crewmen raised the deck hoist. A line was tossed to the PT boat. A light chop splashed against the launch. The helmsman maneuvered the craft to maintain tension on the transfer rope. One of the PT crew reached too far and nearly fell overboard. The US Navy calls the procedure "underway replenishment." The PT boat held a steady course and speed alongside the U-853. It was a dangerous unpracticed maneuver for both captains. The U-853's rudder indicator had been damaged, adding to the danger and delicate nature of the maneuver.

Otto Bruns still didn't have his "sea legs." He was feeling nauseous. Bruns was frightened to be sure. He didn't know what to expect. Mallory didn't know either. Two crewmembers helped Bruns into a sling normally used to transfer an injured crewmember.

A gust of wind swept across the U-boat. A slight error by either vessel could cause a collision. The maneuver required Fromsdorf's undivided attention. Both captains watched the wave motion. The timing needed to be exact. A slack transfer rope or unexpected breakaway could spell death for Otto Bruns. Finally, the PT captain signaled. Bruns was transferred to the PT boat. Next the two cylinders with their precious contents were secured to the boat's port and starboard gunwale racks.

The PT boat signaled again. The stern swung slowly away, made a quick turn and moved cautiously away from the U-853. Then with all three engines pushed to full throttle the boat sped into the night. There was no time or need for farewells.

It was the last time Mallory ever saw Otto Bruns. *I wonder where they are taking Bruns. I wish I were headed for a safe harbor.* Mallory had no idea the significant role Otto Bruns would play in his future.

Fromsdorf issued the command, "Prepare to dive." The U-boat dive alarm sounded. In precision order the deck crew retreated below. The gun crews retrieved their boxes of ammunition and followed suit. Fromsdorf, Beck, and Mallory remained on the bridge as the PT boat disappeared into the night.

"Get below, Mallory," Fromsdorf said.

"OK," Mallory answered.

"Sir. I still don't understand how the American captain found us," said Beck. "We were told to anticipate three U-boats departing Norway. They have to be somewhere in the area by now. How did the American PT Captain know he was contacting the U-853 and not one of the other U-boats?" Beck's point was well taken.

Fromsdorf could tell Beck was puzzled. "Let's get below."

"Take her down to three hundred feet and level off," Fromsdorf instructed Beck. The U-853 began to dive. The noise within the U-853 was amplified by the diving horn, hatches closing, the engine noise and the commands shouted by the crew.

Once below and the hatches were secured Fromsdorf avoided Beck's question. Intuitively he sensed something was askew. There were two more critical parts to his orders. The Captain left the control room and headed to his quarters. He unlocked his desk. In his hands he held the U-853's log. The journal was damp and wrinkled. Fromsdorf attempted to separate some of the pages. The log needed to be handled with care. When the mid-ocean sabotage occurred the log fell beneath Fromsdorf's desk as seawater rushed forward and flooded the bilge and forward compartment floors. Fromsdorf discovered the soaked log when he returned to his quarters. It was too late. *It is my fault the log has been damaged.*

He placed strips of writing paper between the log's pages and hoped for the best. Each time he returned to his quarters Fromsdorf removed the log from the desk and placed it on his bunk to dry. It was the best he could do. (3)

Chapter Twenty-Three
New York City, April 1945
The Spy Revealed

On Monday, April 9, 1945, Sean Cummings received a mysterious call at work. The secretary handed Sean the message. "Please meet me in the Taft Hotel Lobby tonight at 6:30. Important we discuss impending contract. Edward Shaw."

Cummings was suspicious. He didn't know Edward Shaw. He searched the company's client list. He asked his secretary to check the vendors. Edward Shaw was not listed. Cummings' decided it might be an impromptu contact from one of Kappe's Manhattan operatives. Later the same afternoon Cummings secretary returned with a second message. The cryptic Mr. Shaw left a reminder. He added, "This is about the Paula Evans Account." Now Cummings was alarmed.

Cummings left his Madison Avenue office at five PM. He headed to the Hotel Taft and waited from a vantage point in the hotel lobby. At exactly 6:30 a bellboy walked into the lobby. He approached several men before reaching Cummings.

"Are you Mr. Sean Cummings?" the bellboy asked.

"I am," said Cummings.

The bellboy handed Cummings a note. He waited for a response and a tip while Cummings read the note.

"Thank you." Cummings crumpled the note and walked to the registration desk. A man approached Cummings.

"Mr. Cummings?" he asked.

"I'm Cummings."

"Let's step over there for a moment, please."

Cummings followed the man across the lobby to a bank of telephones.

"My name is Edward Shaw, FBI. I'm here to speak with

you about Miss Paula Evans."

Cummings tensed. He looked around for an escape route. *I'm trapped.*

"Relax, Mr. Cummings. Agents are guarding every exit. We want to avoid a scene. Listen carefully. Director Hoover has ordered a sweep of German operatives in the immediate New York Region," Shaw said.

"What do you want of me?" asked Cummings.

"The FBI round-up. Paula Evans was caught in the net. We have her."

"Paula Evans has done nothing wrong," Cummings insisted.

"She's been sleeping with you. She must have some idea of your work."

"I am an advertising agency account executive. We do printing and advertising for commercial and government work. You must know that."

"I know you are Sean Cummings a member of the IRA and Abwehr spy. I know our government electrocutes spies and saboteurs. I have evidence you participated in Operation Pastorious. You helped four German agents land in Amagansett. You involved Miss Evans. She is about to face severe justice for her part unless you follow my orders."

It was useless to feign ignorance. Agent Shaw had every detail down pat.

"What now? Where is Paula?"

"For now, Miss Evans is under FBI protection. I'm warning you. Navy Intelligence is looking for her. I can't protect her forever."

Cummings followed Shaw to an elevator. Two other men both dressed in blue suits and wearing grey fedoras followed. Shaw brought Cummings to a sixth floor suite. There were a number of agents sitting around a table. Several others moved about the suite. Shaw sat down at the far end of the table. He motioned to Cummings to take a seat. Two agents stood behind Cummings.

One man stood on the far side of the room opposite Cummings. He was thin. His epicene face was especially pale. He wore a blue business suit prescribed by Washington traditional culture. To the untrained eye there was nothing special to make the man stand out. Sean Cummings spotted him straightaway. *He's the man in charge.* Cummings encountered his kind back home in Ireland. *They order the execution, but never pull the trigger. They stand on the far side of the wire.*

The man was Erskin Young. Young remained silent his eyes fixed on Cummings' body language. A cynical smile crossed Young's face. Young relished never being clearly visible. He felt comfortable in the shadows.

Agent Shaw did most of the talking. He removed an envelope from his inside jacket pocket.

"I have two documents for you," said Shaw.

He slid the papers across the table to Cummings. Cummings refused to read them.

"OK, then. I'll read them to you."

The first page was Sean Cummings' confession, a full admission of his activities aiding the Amagansett saboteurs.

Shaw pushed the paper back to Cummings. Cummings refused to sign.

"Mind you, spies are tried in a secret military court. I don't need your confession."

One of the agents handed the confession back to Shaw. He signed Cummings' name and the agent witnessed the signature.

"You must be joking. You can't do that," said Cummings. Cummings turned a gold Claddagh ring around his finger.

"I've never seen a ring like that," said Shaw. "Is it a token or carry some meaning?"

"Token? I guess you could call it that. Loyalty. Yah, that's it. It's a sign of loyalty." Cummings sneered. "Are you guys loyal to one another?"

"No sense being incensed. We've got you."

Then Shaw read the second document. It was Paula Evans' confession to aiding a spy ring. "You know that is treason. We're at war. Miss Evans faces a harsh sentence. Probably not death, but life in prison."

"You're bluffing," said Cummings. Cummings began to

nervously tap his right foot on the carpeting.

Erskin Young watched Cummings. He motioned to Shaw. Both men entered the bedroom.

"Let me speak with Mr. Cummings alone," said Young.

Shaw walked back to the table. He gestured for Cummings to go into the bedroom.

"Mr. Cummings. I am Erskin Young."

"Of course you are," said an angry, cynical Cummings.

"You're right. My name doesn't matter. What matters is you are in trouble, and you've dragged your girlfriend with you, Cummings."

Cummings didn't respond. Cummings towered over the frail Young.

Young continued. "I'll level with you. First, we aren't the FBI. I represent a number of Federal agencies including the Navy. Have you heard of the Office of Strategic Services? The OSS is about to conclude an operation. I anticipate you will be a part of it."

"I never heard of the OSS and I don't know of any operation," said Cummings.

"True. You haven't received orders from Germany. I imagine they will be waiting for you at the Patchogue Post Office."

Cummings looked shocked.

"Your orders will direct you to assist with another U-boat landing. This time on the north shore of Long Island."

"And how do you know all this?" Cummings demanded.

"Because I planned it." Young stepped back. He placed his right hand under his chin and his left hand under the right elbow. He gazed at Cummings' shoes for several moments.

Cummings laughed then turned and walked to the bedroom window.

"It's a long way down, Mr. Cummings. There are other ways out of your predicament. I assure you, Miss Evans will be released unharmed, if you cooperate."

"Cooperate? How? And what assurance do I have Evans will be released safe and sound?"

"I anticipated your question," said Young. He handed

Cummings an envelope. "Open it."

"Another confession?" asked Cummings.

"Quite the contrary," replied Young.

Incredibly, the document was a letter signed by the US Attorney General granting Cummings immunity from prosecution. Cummings was dumbfounded.

"The other letter is for Paula Evans."

"She did nothing illegal," Cummings insisted.

"The country is in a uproar. Who knows what will happen?"

"Do I have your cooperation, Mr. Cummings? I assure you, this operation has the full backing of the President."

Young motioned for Cummings to return the two documents.

"And when do I get the documents?" asked Cummings.

"We will meet in Patchogue. You'll receive a call from Commander Shaw or me. Consider Shaw your 'handler'. Follow his orders. The password will be Blue Dawn. Listen to no one else, Cummings."

Cummings walked out of the bedroom to find Shaw sitting at the table. The other agents were gone.

"So, you are Commander Shaw, not FBI agent Shaw," said Cummings.

Shaw looked up at Cummings. "You know too much Cummings. I wouldn't want to be in your shoes if this operation fails. You may think you are a survivor. There's no place you can hide. Good luck. You'll need it."

Cummings gave Shaw a casual salute and walked into the deserted hotel corridor. *How could these guys know so much about me? I've been so careful. Paula is innocent. These guys know everything about me. I know nothing about them.*

Cummings' assessment was correct. He would be a dead man, if he underestimated Erskin Young. Young had no scruples. Somewhere on life's journey Young had misplaced his conscience.

⁓

"Looks like my befriending the two remaining Pastorious

spies has paid off," said Young.

Thanks in part to you, Dasch and his cohort, Burger, were spared the electric chair," said Shaw.

Unbeknownst to Director Hoover, Erskin Young's father had close personal ties with the Roosevelt family. Erskin convinced Roosevelt's advisors that George Dasch could be of assistance in tracking down Nazi spies. In turn, Erskin was given permission to visit Dasch. The warden and, in turn, the guards were given official-looking nondisclosure statements to sign.

"One word to anyone regarding my visits and you'll face charges. Not a word to Director Hoover. I'll have you doing time right here, Young threatened. "Understood?" Young enjoyed the intimidation.

The warden was first to sign. The others followed. Hoover remained baffled why the pair of spies was not executed.

Young befriended Dasch and listened to the man's ravings of mistreatment and betrayal by the FBI and J. Edgar Hoover.

Unlike Director Hoover, Erskin Young was the grandson of a Boston Brahman, J.J. Pickering. Hoover was feared and mistrusted by the DC powers. He was never accepted as part of the DC's inner circle.

Young, on the other hand, had access to some of the most powerful men in the United States. Erskin Young's father, a Boston financier, represented American corporations investing in Germany following World War One.

During the late 1940's and 1950's Erskin Young and William Robert Mallory would coordinate the enigmatic part of the Sunrise Project know as Operation Paperclip which directed the search for Nazis scientists after Germany's surrender. In turn these war criminals were brought to the United States to work for government agencies and corporations as the Cold War intensified.

Thanks to his carefully scripted relationship with the captured spy, George Dasch, Young gained insight into the German intelligence network within the United States. Young persuaded Dasch to reveal the name of German agents who assisted with Operation Pastorious. Sean Cummings' name topped the list. Dasch insisted Cummings was critical to his team's successful landing.

During a heated conversation with Young, Dasch divulged, "There is one crucial piece of information J. Edgar Hoover does not have."

"And what might that be?" asked Young coolly.

Dasch was annoyed by Young's attitude and made his revelation more dramatic.

"His name is Sean Cummings. Cummings helped with our landing. Later that week I discovered Cummings assisted an American to depart on board the U-boat that brought us here."

"What?" exclaimed Young.

"Yes. I don't know the name of the American who left on the submarine, but I'm positive he was bound for Berlin."

"You're certain about this. No bullshit. I'm warning you," said Young.

"I know the Abwehr planned the operation, nothing more. One of my comrades, Bruno, told me before he was executed." Dasch smiled. He was pleased with Young's reaction. "And now I want you to help me," demanded Dasch.

"How?"

"Hoover keeps me in solitary confinement for twenty-three hours a day. I am denied a book to read. I can't have a pencil or paper."

"I'll speak to the warden, but not a word to Hoover."

Dasch nodded in agreement.

⤸

Erskin Young did not share George Dasch's most recent revelation with his colleagues. Then, on a rainy Tuesday morning in 1944, he was summoned to the White House for a briefing. British Intelligence forwarded a document stamped "Top Secret – Eyes Only", meaning it was to be opened only by the President. Roosevelt was astounded by the message. The dispatch was authenticated. Martin Bormann wrote on behalf of the Fuhrer.

Hitler requested United States guarantee safe passage and

asylum for two individuals; a child identified as SS 1-3128 and an adult male guardian. In return, Hitler would surrender a physicist working on a revolutionary project.

On October 28, 1944 Roosevelt gave a campaign address at Soldier Field Stadium in Chicago. Erskin Young was with the group that accompanied the President. Young waited for Roosevelt to be helped back into his official limosine and then approached the President along with Roosevelt's wartime Attorney General Francis Biddle.

"We need your approval to proceed with Hitler's proposal, Mr. President," said Biddle. Biddle turned to Erskin Young. "Young, hand me the papers and a pen."

"You agree, Francis?"

"Yes, Mr. President," Biddle said.

The weary Roosevelt nodded and scrawled his signature across the bottom of the page. The secret plan the Americans called "Operation Seahawk" was put in motion. William Robert Mallory was selected to carry the operation to fruition.

It was now late April, 1945. William Robert Mallory stood on the bridge of the U-853. He watched as Nazi scientist, Otto Bruns, was spirited away on board an unmarked PT Boat. The final act of Operation Seahawk was about to begin.

Chapter Twenty-Four
The Eleventh Hour

Noontime, April 26, 1945, found Sean Cummings pacing his Madison Avenue office. Earlier in the day a courier delivered a package. It contained orders from Erskin Young. Young directed Cummings to arrive in Patchogue on Friday, April 27, 1945.

Cummings had no communications from Berlin. The New York papers were filled with stories of the Russian advance and Germany's imminent unconditional surrender. Vice President Harry Truman was sworn in as President following Roosevelt's death. Truman was briefed on Operation Seahawk. Truman's advisors questioned the efficacy of the project. It was too late to stop or change without abandoning William Mallory. Mallory and his charges were on a submarine someplace off the New England coast. The landing was set for the week of May 1, 1945.

It was 6:55 on Friday evening when Sean Cummings stepped from the train onto the platform of the Patchogue railroad station. It was his first visit to Patchogue since his meeting with Shaw and Young at the Hotel Taft. Following Young's orders Cummings had had no contact with Paula Evans. *She must think I've deserted her. I wonder what Erskin told Paula about me? It makes no difference.*

Cummings was unaware of Young's recent conversation with Attorney General Biddle. Biddle was adamant. " I need your assurance that your 'assets', Cummings and Evans, will not become 'liabilities'. Use your discretion to close their accounts once Operation Seahawk is terminated."

∾

The train from Manhattan to Patchogue was once again

filled with weekenders heading for Fire Island and Montauk. Sitting at the far end of the last car Sean Cummings watched the odd compilation of riders. Cummings was a people watcher. His life depended upon his intuitions and senses. He had been riding the train every other weekend since 1942.

Cummings mechanically followed his routine. He purchased his Lucky Strikes and the *Advance* and walked to the Patchogue Hotel. Cummings smiled as he looked up at the Rialto Theatre's marquee. This weekend's playbill at the Rialto was a double feature, Johnny Weissmuller in "Tarzan and the Amazons." Allan Jones in "Honeymoon Ahead" was the second movie.

The village appeared to be revitalized. In a small way Cummings felt like he was a resident.

Cummings' step livened as he arrived at the Patchogue Hotel. He longed for Paula Evans. He looked around. He didn't see her. He walked to the front desk and registered.

"You're new here," Cummings said to the desk clerk.

"Yes sir. Started a few days ago."

"And where is Miss Evans?"

"Not sure, sir. She was here earlier in the day. I know she's been busy with a new manager. He's been following her like a hawk."

Cummings sensed the so-called manager was a federal agent.

The clerk handed Cummings the room keys.

"Shall I inform Miss Evans you were asking about her?"

Cummings paused for a moment then said, "No thank you. I'll check back later." He picked up his overnight bag and headed for his second floor room.

Cummings sat in the leather chair near the front window of his room. He glanced at the Post Office and the traffic below. *It will be a busy evening. I have to follow the schedule precisely, as Young outlined.* He glanced at the front page of the *Advance* before he tossed the newspaper on the bed. The headline screamed – Adolf Hitler Is Dead.

Nazi Germany had a new leader. Allied prisoners of war were being liberated as the US troops advanced into Germany.

America's attention was increasingly focused on Japan and the Pacific. The annual meeting of the Patchogue school board drew little interest.

The phone rang. It was Paula. "We have to talk," she said in a whisper. "I am in deep trouble. A federal agent follows me everywhere. I'm scared, Sean."

"I'm coming downstairs," he said. He guessed the phone line was tapped.

He walked down the stairs rather than taking the elevator. For the first time he searched for a potential escape route should the need arise. Events were turning grim.

There behind the counter was the beautiful Paula Evans. Evans appeared agitated as she scanned the lobby.

"What's wrong, Paula?" he asked as though he didn't already know the answer.

"You must have some idea. Federal agents have questioned me. I was kidnapped for several hours. A woman and two men questioned me about your Nazi affiliations. They said you are a spy. Is that true, Sean?"

"Tonight," he assured Evans.

"I can't. They are following me everywhere," Paula said.

"I'll get them to call off your watchdog."

"How?" Paula was desperate.

"Trust me. I'll take care of it."

"I trusted you. And now I'm a suspected spy."

"Tonight," said Cummings.

Patchogue Hotel

The Bonnie Mart Restaurant stayed opened until nine on Friday evenings. Cummings walked through the revolving door and looked around and found Erskin Young sitting in a booth with a window view of South Ocean Avenue and Main Street. Commander Shaw sat across from Young. Young was sipping a Coke. Shaw was licking the last of a milkshake from a straw.

"Sit down, Sean," said Young.

"Sean is it? I'd rather have you keep it Cummings. What the hell are you doing to Paula Evans?"

"Miss Evans didn't hold up well under questioning," said Young.

"Call off your dogs, Young, if you want my cooperation."

"We have your cooperation, already, Sean. Now if you're looking for some privacy…a night of passion with the delicate Miss Evans…I'll concede." Young nodded his approval to Shaw. Shaw slid out of the both and walked to a phone booth in the rear of the restaurant.

Shaw returned several minutes latter. "It's done."

Young smiled. "Enjoy your romp, Sean. My compliments."

Cummings leaned across the table and scowled. "I don't like you, Young, and I resent your comments."

A surprised Young momentarily trembled. "The feeling is mutual Mr. Cummings," replied Young with a tinge of arrogance.

"So what's a big shot doing here in Patchogue? Shaw can't do the job?" Cummings asked. His attempt to antagonize Young didn't work.

"You are an important person Cummings with an important mission. Have you visited the Post Office?"

"No."

"The Post Office opens at eight tomorrow morning. An envelope is waiting for you. Everything is in order. Don't look so surly, Cummings. I have a surprise for you, but it can wait until we next meet."

Shaw looked directly at Young. It was obvious Shaw had no idea of the "surprise."

"I have to get going," said Young. "Please take care of the check, commander."

It was a brief meeting. At least Young had agreed to reduce Paula's surveillance. Cummings was anxious to return to the Hotel. Paula's shift ended at ten. Sean regretted his attachment to Evans. He recalled those early visits to Patchogue and the beginning of his entangled affair with Paula.

Patchogue Post Office

The sedate young Evans was barely twenty-one when she met Sean Cummings in 1942. Cummings was an older man. He was patient and attentive, but not overbearing. Evans anticipated the inevitable evening would arrive but she never expected the passion would be so addicting. And it was. Miss Evans and Sean Cummings would playfully wrestle on the newly-carpeted floor of room 201. As the relationship progressed Paula became serious and a bit possessive. Sean resisted her control.

Paula anxiously awaited Cummings' return from his meeting. The federal watchdog left the hotel after taking a brief telephone call. Her shift ended in forty minutes. A few minutes after ten Cummings heard a key turning in the lock to his hotel room. Paula closed the door and walked to Cummings.

"What is going to happen to me," Paula sobbed as she embraced Cummings.

"Everything will be all right. You must be cautious. These federal agents are dangerous. They aren't accountable to the usual authorities."

Suddenly, Paula pushed Cummings away and demanded to know, "Are you a Nazi spy?"

"Yes."

"My god, Sean. I love you. How could you deceive me?"

"Do you remember when we first slept together?"

Paula's face paled. She looked away. "What?"

"We agreed our relationship was simply for fun. I told you I was a salesman. I wanted no responsibilities, least of all, marriage."

Paula walked to the window and feigned interest in the street below.

"Don't deny it, Paula. You agreed. I'm sorry I lied to you. I never meant to hurt you. Everything will be all right in a few days. This whole damn thing will die like a bad dream."

"That's what Shaw told me," she said.

"Did he make any promises?"

"I think we can trust Shaw, if I stick to my agreement."

"What agreement?" Paula demanded.

"Didn't Cummings tell you it's top secret?"

"I told him my reputation is ruined," Paula said. "My life will never be the same. Patchogue is a small town. Rumors." she shouted. "Damn it. What will my family think once the story appears in the newspapers?"

"Shaw promised this was top secret."

"Yes. He told me the story would never appear in the newspapers. Shaw said he would relocate me if the story got out. Even find me a new job." Paula was confused.

Cummings stepped forward and touched her shoulders. "I am sorry I dragged you into this."

"I don't want to move. I want to be with you, Sean. We could run away. Surely there's someplace we can go where they can't find us."

"Listen to me, Paula. These guys can find us anywhere. Don't give them any cause to kill you."

Cummings' warning shocked Paula. She stepped back and fell on to the bed. Sean knelt at the bedside. "There's no time for this Paula."

"Is this the end, Sean?"

"It has to be for your sake," he said. "Go home. Get some rest. I'll be in touch."

"Is there someone else?" Her forced smile turned to a frown. Her pouty lips aroused Cummings.

"I have an important meeting. Just go home. You can't tell Shaw something you don't know. Let it be."

"We have time to make love," she said touching his face.

"No. No, we don't. Not tonight. It will complicate matters. Go home, Paula. I will call. I promise."

"And, no. I am not seeing someone else." Cummings had violated his own rule: Spies enjoy sexual détentes but never attachments.

"Whatever," Paula replied. She shrugged her shoulders.

Cummings felt angry. Their accommodation had never involved commitment. It was an agreement for simple pleasure. "I'll call you in the morning."

"Fine," Paula said. She stood in front of the bathroom mirror and frowned. *Look at me. I've aged ten years.*

After Paula left, Cummings withdrew a business envelope from the inside pocket of his suit jacket. He received the envelope from a nameless female courier as he entered Penn Station. He didn't tell Young or Shaw about the incident. Cummings never knew the names of other Nazi agents in Manhattan. One by one they were apprehended. Cummings was certain there was a turncoat or double agent in their midst. He felt it in his bones. *Only one Abwehr agent knew of my involvement. It has to be the missing Mr. Day, the man who never showed for our meeting in Manhattan.* Indeed, the man Cummings knew as Mr. Day was George Dasch, the Nazis spy and informant. *I'm trapped.*

Cummings removed a copy of Treasure Island from his overnight bag. The novel's pages held the secret to the encrypted message. It took nearly an hour to decipher the courier's dispatch.

Cummings was exhausted. He was uncertain whether or not the message was authentic. At some point the FBI would be on to him. If Young's team tracked him down, J. Edgar Hoover's men would be close behind. Perhaps it was an FBI trap. Cummings knew he had to cooperate with Erskin Young. *First things first.*

The courier's message directed Sean to go to the Post Office on Saturday morning and check the post office box. If the box held an envelope, Cummings should return to New York City. The writer suspected an FBI trap. If the box was empty Cummings was to follow the instructions he had just deciphered.

Cummings took one last drag on his cigarette before crushing it in the ashtray. He gave the butt an accentuated twist. I need to make a clean break. Paula Evans was the one complication. What will I do about Paula?

The next morning Cummings entered the Post Office lobby. A man stood at one of the two marble-topped counters. He appeared to be writing a note. Sean walked to the post office box. He looked through the tiny door window. The box was empty. It was time to proceed.

Cummings left the post office and walked down the narrow driveway next to the A&P. There were a few cars in the parking lot, but nothing seemed suspicious. He walked west toward South Ocean Avenue and continued his leisurely walk through the village to the Baker Street memorial near Patchogue High School.

To the east and west of the Civil War monument were two display cannons. A woman watched a young boy climb the cannon to his left. A man walking a dog approached the other cannon. The dog lifted its leg and urinated on the antique cannon's wheel.

Cummings waited patiently for the man to walk away. The woman and boy soon followed. Cummings casually walked to the cannon to his left and lit his last cigarette. He crumpled the empty pack and dropped it in a box on the cannon firewall. The task accomplished, he strolled along South Ocean Avenue toward Main Street. He stopped one last time at the stationary store to purchase Lucky Strikes. He stepped outside and looked around. This would be his last visit to Patchogue. He tamped the pack of cigarettes against his left palm before removing a smoke. Just then he felt a strange sensation as he took his first drag.

He was once again an Irish patriot rather than a Nazi

spy. *Be cautious, lad. Your job isn't complete.* He tossed the cigarette on the sidewalk and crushed it with his shoe. He held the pack of Lucky Strikes in his hand for a moment as though contemplating his future. Then he threw the crushed pack in the garbage barrel. Cummings longed to return to Ireland. He knew a homecoming would be many years away. But he rather enjoyed life in America. The spy business had its perks as well as its risks. Time would tell.

An elderly man watched Sean Cummings cross the railroad tracks and disappear along South Ocean Avenue. The man walked from shadows of Brookhaven Town Hall and crossed the street. A limp hampered his gait. He stepped to the sidewalk. He paused and rubbed his left knee then proceeded to the cannon on the left of the war memorial. He tamped his pipe on the huge spoke wheel of the artillery piece. Then he reached around the wheel and quickly recovered the crushed Lucky Strike pack.

Chapter Twenty-Five
A Hazardous Course
Thursday, May 3, 1945

After midnight on Thursday, May 3, 1945, Fromsdorf charted a hazardous course for the U-853. These were dangerous waters. Contrary to standing orders to U-boat commanders, Fromsdorf was ordered to set a course to a grid mark beyond Block Island into the Long Island Sound. The waters are shallow. In 1945 planes and ships constantly patrolled them. Destroyer escorts guided submarines in and out of the New London-Groton submarine base on the Connecticut side of the Long Island Sound. The destroyer escorts or DE's knew the route through the minefields and kept "friendlies" off the submarines' backs.

Fromsdorf knew the risk. His charts pre-dated the war.

"We have no choice," he told Beck. "Our orders direct us to a grid location not far from Port Jefferson."

Beck looked at the grid location. The Long Island Sound is approximately twenty-one miles wide and extends 110 miles from the East River to Block Island.

"The approach to Mount Sinai Harbor appears to have a number of dangerous shoals," Beck warned.

"Do we have a choice?" asked Fromsdorf.

Beck didn't respond. He placed his parallel rulers on the chart.

"This appears to be our safest approach," Beck finally said.

"I agree," said Fromsdorf as he left the conning tower control room to inspect the U-853's passageways. With the rear toilet out of order, the crew was forced to use the forward toilet. The stench was overwhelming at times. Fromsdorf gave orders not to use the macerator or the dump valve. Still with all they had endured the crew's morale was high. During the inspection,

Fromsdorf stopped to speak with the crew.

"Keep up the good work," he told the electricians who hustled to put all the U-boats batteries back on line. "We are almost at our destination," he re-assured his crew.

Next the Captain turned to the passengers' compartments. Fromsdorf told Mallory to meet Beck in the control room. "I suggest you review our charts." Fromsdorf sounded ominous.

"Yes. I should have some idea of the terrain."

"We'll be putting you ashore in a rubber boat. Pokel and the child will follow once you signal the coast is clear."

"The child seems to be doing better than Pokel."

"He is weak, but the adrenalin rush will keep him afloat. Once ashore Pokel has to lie low until your government finds a secure location for him."

"His wife and child are under Dönitz's protection, but there is only so much the Admiral will be able to do as the Allies close in…and they will."

Fromsdorf didn't know Admiral Dönitz's emissaries were negotiating surrender. German troops had surrendered in northern Germany and the Netherlands.

The U-853 had not received a radio signal since the mid-ocean sabotage. Blasse had managed to cut off the U-853 from the German high command. The most powerful transmitter is useless without an antenna and receiver.

"Up periscope," called Beck. Beck began to scan. The visibility was clear to the horizon. A waning moon provided partial illumination.

"If only we could wait another week we'd have darkness on our side. Mallory, look here," said Beck. Mallory peered through the periscope.

"What do you see?" asked Beck.

"The bluffs are high, but we can make it." Mallory slowly rotated the periscope.

Mallory was startled. "Beck, the Connecticut shore line is outlined in bright lights as though the war was over." He turned to Beck and gave a quizzical look.

"The far shoreline. There's no black-out," said Beck.

"Appears all clear. I'm uneasy," said Mallory.

Next Beck scanned the night sky.

Fromsdorf returned to the control room.

"Sir, we are ready to make the approach. One point." Beck signaled for the horizon scope to be raised. Fromsdorf viewed the Connecticut coastline.

"Strange. All those lights. Still, we have our orders, Beck. May third is the appointed night."

The U-853 began to thread the needle directly around Herod Point Shoal. The shallow water was dangerous. Beck calculated the tides and currents based upon eight-year-old charts. Unpredictable currents could raise havoc on a U-boat with a damaged rudder.

"Sir we have to surface soon. The crew is struggling to cope. We need fresh air and our batteries will have to be charged. I will have the Chief Engineer inspect our snorkel. Perhaps with a temporary repair we can get it in position."

"Steady, Beck," said Fromsdorf. "What is our location?"

"Beck checked his chart." He calculated they were midway between places called Wading River and Miller Place. Fromsdorf check the grid sheet.

Fromsdorf ordered all engines stopped. "Now we must wait for the signal from some point on the Long Island bluffs."

Mallory left the control room and went to check on Pokel and the child. "Are you ready, Lieutenant?" Mallory asked.

"What choice do I have? I am so sick. Yes, let's get off this damn U-boat."

At 023 hours Fromsdorf made his decision.

∽

The Patchogue Hotel
Thursday May 3, 1945

Sean Cumming sat near the partially opened window of his room in the Patchogue Hotel. He lit a Lucky and blew and watched the smoke drift away. He was a weekend smoker. He detested the smell of cigarettes on his business suits nearly as much as the smell of booze on a woman's breath.

A 1938 Dodge "humpback" panel truck coughed its way west on Silver Street. The carburetor needed work, but parts were scarce. "I'm tired of all the intrigue," the old man said aloud. No one was listening. He talked to himself a lot of late. He was constantly anxious and compulsive. The old man attributed his mental state to the death of his wife and the pressure of being a double agent. He despaired at ever having agreed to help the Navy spy on suspected Long Island Nazi sympathizers. But it was too late to turn back.

The truck's engine sputtered and nearly died. The old man disregarded the corner stop sign and rolled out on to Medford Avenue.

He chewed on his pipe. It was an appendage. A bum knee and arthritic hands intensified his worry. The old man was determined this was the last "favor" for his friend Kuhn. *Why risk getting caught after all these years? I've done my share. This is it.* It was nearly eleven PM. He eased the panel truck along East Main Street. He coaxed and cajoled until it stopped bucking. The pickup was timed for exactly eleven.

Back at the hotel, a restless Sean Cummings crushed his cigarette in the ashtray then dumped the remains in the toilet. He policed the hotel room for anything he may have overlooked. *It probably doesn't matter. Young and Shaw have me where they want me.*

Cummings tossed the room key on the bed and walked to the stairway exit. He had cased the exit earlier in the evening. He left the building through the self-closing door. He paused and looked back at the hotel. Thoughts of Paula Evans flashed through his mind. He knew Paula's destiny was in Erskin Young's hands. He lied to Paula. *No, things might not be all right. I never meant to harm her.* His reverie was brief.

Cummings slipped along a path behind a church. The path led through a clump of pines to a private driveway. Cummings pressed into a huge hedge separating the driveway from another residence. It was his only cover. He didn't wait long. The Dodge turned right onto Rose Ave. Cummings darted across the street opened the passenger door and climbed in.

Cummings did not know his contact's identity.

"I'm Bach," said the old man.

"Cummings." Cummings felt tightness in his chest.

"Is that your real name?" Bach asked.

"Is yours Bach?"

"Don't worry about it." The old man was gruff.

"What happened to my original Abwehr contact?" asked Cummings.

"You must be more aware of your surroundings, Cummings. Your Abwehr contact followed you to the drop."

"And?"

"I slit his throat. His body is in the bottom of a Dumpster behind Brookhaven Town Hall. I assure you, Cummings, I don't kill needlessly."

Cummings turned and studied Bach's face.

The conversation ended. Bach handed Cummings a crumpled road map. "Find the 'X,'" said Bach. "It marks our location off Route 25A. I have a load of vegetables and groceries in the back. They are scheduled for early morning delivery. Let me do the talking, if the cops stop us. The story is 'my truck broke down. I'm late on the delivery to the convent. You came along to keep me company in case the truck crapped-out again.' Go it?" Bach's truck was a familiar vehicle between Patchogue and Wading River.

Cummings looked at the map then nodded he understood.

"We're lucky," said Bach.

"Why?"

"It's forty degrees. You and me are going to be lying in the sand overlooking the Sound. If this drizzle keeps up no one will be walking the beach. Hardly any moon."

"Looks like we have the advantage," Cummings replied.

"Don't be so sure. They've got planes flying up and down both coastlines. There are binoculars under you seat. Remember to bring them along, " said Bach.

It took a while to reach the nearest crossroad off 25A. The

truck dropped into a rut as Bach turned on to a dirt road. At the second intersection he turned left. A row of summer cottages lined both side of the road.

They passed a car parked near a wooded lane. The passenger door swung open. Four legs flexed up and down.

Bach slowed the truck then stopped on the roadside. "They may have seen the truck. We don't need any witnesses," he growled. Before Cummings could react, Bach reached into his pocket.

"No Bach. Please, put the knife away. We don't need to kill them," Cummings protested. "They were too busy screwing. You told me before that you don't kill needlessly. Let them be. Besides, killing them could jeopardize our mission."

Bach waved the knife at Cummings. "For your sake, you better be right." Bach pulled back on to the winding road and drove another mile or so before turning onto a secluded yard. They parked in front of a summer cottage.

"This is it," said Bach. "We wait on the bluffs. They will bring our landing party here."

Bach left the truck and opened the rear door. He returned with a large flashlight. "Grab those binoculars. Let's go."

"Hey. You got a blanket or piece of canvas back there?" Cummings pointed to the truck. "I have underwear and socks in my sack, but these are my only clothes." Cummings felt the damp breeze.

"There's an old blanket in the back of the truck. Hurry. We have to get going. The wind is picking up. We better move along," said Bach. He had visited this site several times before. He decided it was the best location for a landing party. The locals used the path to get to the beach. The bluffs provided sufficient coverage, but they weren't as steep as the nearby terrain.

❧

On board the U-853 Fromsdorf decided to surface once the signal from shore was acknowledged. "I see it," shouted Beck. Fromsdorf looked through the horizon scope.

Fromsdorf smiled. "Down scope," he called. "Get ready, Beck."

At 023 hours Fromsdorf made the calculated decision to risk discovery by a hunter-killer flight. "Prepare to surface," Fromsdorf ordered.

The deck crew was tense. They anticipated the dreaded cry and alarm for an emergency dive as an American fighter swooped in spraying the deck with machine gun fire. But instead only the U-boat's muffled engines could be heard.

From the contours of the beach Bach spotted the U-853's conning tower emerge followed by the signaled acknowledgment. Bach nudged Cummings. "Over there," Bach whispered as he pointed his binoculars to his right.

A slight fog began to shroud the U-boat. With precision the U-853's deck crew inflated a rubber boat. Mallory turned to Fromsdorf and Beck. The American agent was now about to unwittingly change the course of American history.

"I'll go ashore and signal for the others to follow," he said to Fromsdorf. The wind speed was increasing. Mallory was jostled as he was helped on board the rubber raft. A long rope was tied to the end of the raft. Two eighteen-year-old crewmen paddled. Mallory wore coveralls over his suit. An American flag was pinned to his left sleeve. In the back of his mind Mallory's greatest fear was being shot or captured by a Coast Guard patrol. From his seat in the rubber craft the bluffs looked impossibly high.

The north shore of Long Island is rocky. The water's edge is pebbly. Mallory slipped and fell into the shallow cold water. He regained his foothold and scrambled for the cover. Pokel and Edith were next.

Pokel was nervous. "You must muster your courage and your health, Pokel," said Fromsdorf.

"I'll be glad to be off this boat. I've been sick for the entire crossing," Pokel replied. He was pale and nauseous.

"You must get the child ashore and into the hands of your contact," said Fromsdorf.

"I'm am worried about my family's safety," said Pokel. "I

hope they are safe in Flensburg."

"Focus on your mission. Your family will be safe. The Admiral gave his word."

Being cut-off from the outside world neither man knew Flensburg had not yet fallen into Allied hands.

Then Pokel asked the forbidden question. "Who is this child I call Edith?"

"I have no reason to know. Beck thinks that she is the child of someone within the Fuhrer's inner circle. The child has to be important. I hope she is worth the sacrifice my crew has been asked to make."

Pokel's expression changed. He looked alarmed. *What would be the ultimate cost of this mission?* Pokel sensed he knew the answer. He shuddered. *"I may never see my family again."*

"For such risks the child has to be special," answered Fromsdorf. Then he opened his coat and removed a dry bag."

"This packet contains the U-853's log. Some pages are illegible. Admiral Dönitz does not want U-boat logs to fall into enemy hands. I suspect the Americans want our mission to remain top secret. The log is priceless. Take it. Keep it safe. You may be able to use it as a bargaining chip, if you are captured. Destroy the log if the Americans try to double-cross you. It is your decision."

Pokel hesitated. "Without this log there is no record of our mission."

"Exactly," said the Captain. Pokel took the log and tucked it in the small of his back then buttoned his coat. Beck came up from below. He never saw Fromsdorf hand the log to Pokel.

"Sir. We are running out of time. We must take advantage of the flood tide."

Pokel saluted both men and hurried to the rubber boat. Edith was already in the arms of one of the returning crewmen. Pokel climbed into the boat. He stumbled forward. The boat pitched. Wind gusts forced several waves into the rubber inflatable. The child was drenched and frightened. Pokel took the child from the crewman. She clung to Pokel's lapels. She pressed her face into his chest. The craft cast off. The two crewmen struggled to keep on course.

Finally, they reached shore. Mallory ran from his hiding place to help Pokel with Edith. No sooner had all three reached the cover of the bluffs when Cummings appeared.

"This way. Follow me," he told them.

Mallory turned toward the shoreline. The rubber boat with its young paddlers vanished into a patch of fog.

Mallory and his party followed Cummings to the top of the bluff. Mallory stopped to look out over the Sound. He felt a twinge. *Had these last months been a bad dream? What happened to the man called Otto Bruns? Did Fromsdorf order the crates of bullion jettisoned to maintain the U-boat's buoyancy? What would become of Kurt Pokel? Who was this child I risked my life to smuggle into the United States? Did it matter? I have no record of this mission ever taking place. Then again wasn't that the plan?*

Mallory looked toward the distant shore. He glanced at his watch. At approximately 0330 hours William Robert Mallory watched the U-853 submerge into the depths of World War Two mythology.

Chapter Twenty-Six

Saturday, May 5,1945
A Summer Cottage on Long Island's North Shore

Cummings waited at the top of the bluffs while Bach led the landing party down the winding path to the summer cottage. Pokel was exhausted, but refused to allow Cummings to carry Edith. The intermittent rain turned into a brief downpour. Pokel and the child desperately needed shelter and dry clothes.

"What is this place?" Mallory asked.

"It belongs to a relative. We will be safe here," said Bach. The house was no more than a makeshift three-room shack. Nails pounded into exposed two by four lumber with suspended shelves. A small addition served as a storage area. Cots and several tables lined the largest of the three rooms. Bach walked into the storage room and returned with a satchel. An outhouse sat behind the building.

"Here you go he said. It's the best I could do without raising suspicion." He tossed the bag to Pokel. "The wife and me never had kids."

Pokel reached inside the satchel and pulled out a small bundle of clothes.

"They may not look great, but she'll be warm," said Bach. He tamped his pipe and started to light it.

Mallory asked, "Is everything in place?"

"Yes. You and the kid go first." Bach pointed to Pokel and Cummings. "You two will leave in the truck."

Pokel protested. "I should go with the child. Can't you see how frightened she is?" Edith looked pathetic in her oversized clothes. Bach spoke a little German. The men's conversations drifted from English to German and back.

"Kids are flexible. She'll get over it," said Bach.

Cummings slumped on one of the cots. "Enough. I need some rest. When will Mallory and the kid be picked up?"

"Sometime after dawn. If all goes well we'll be out of here before noon," Bach responded. "Let's try to get some sleep."

Mallory walked to the outhouse, but the stench further upset his already queasy stomach. He relieved himself on the side of the building. He walked back inside to find Pokel placing a package under his cot. He started to ask Pokel what the package contained, but thought it best to watch and wait. Mallory's clothes were wet from the mishap on the beach. He unbuckled his pants and hung them on a nail. His shoes were soaked. He wanted to start the wood stove, but worried it might draw attention.

Pokel muffled the sobs of the terrified child. Bach sat in one of the rattan chairs puffing on his pipe. Cummings mumbled then rolled on his side and covered his head with his coat.

∽

Sunrise
Saturday May 5, 1945

Bach pushed open the front door. He carried an armful of driftwood to the kitchen and dropped it on the floor. "Gonna be a nice day."

Cummings was first to roll out of his cot. He rubbed his eyes. "What the hell is going on Bach?"

Pokel hardly stirred but managed to ask, "Do you have any food for the child?"

"That's what I'm doing. And I have some coffee for us." Bach reached under the sink and found a few pieces of kindling.

"Better get a move on it. They'll be here soon. Cummings, you keep watch."

Bach lit the kindling then snapped a piece of driftwood into the stove.

The men folded their blankets and stacked them in the

storage closet.

"I'm worried for Edith," said Pokel. He walked the child to the outhouse, but she refused to relieve herself. Pokel returned. "Edith can't continue to live in these clothes. Her underwear is soiled. She has a terrible rash. She needs care I can't give her. And you, Bach? Your knew we would have a child with us."

"Not a sickly one," Bach snapped.

Cummings shook his head and shrugged. *Bach is a bitter old man.*

It was Saturday morning. Several cars drove past. By month's end the sleepy community would be bustling with traffic.

"I hear a car pulling off the road." Cummings pulled back the tattered curtain for a better look.

"A Buick sedan?" asked Bach.

"Yes," answered Cummings.

"OK. That's your ride Mallory. Pokel. Give this broth to the girl. She'll soon have fresh clothes and all the food she can eat."

As the black Buick sedan pulled next to the cottage, Mallory saw three people inside. The driver remained behind the wheel with the engine running. One of the two passengers got out and walked to the door. There was a knock on the door. Cummings opened the door and a woman entered. She was impeccably dressed in black. Her penetrating eyes and grimace shouted an intolerant personality.

The woman asked for Robert.

"I'm Robert." He stepped forward. "William Robert Mallory."

The woman stepped back. "Hmm. Yes of course you are. You look a bit ragged, Mallory. You've aged since your ID photo was taken."

Mallory scratched the back of his head. *What the hell is she talking about?*

"I am Sister Teresa. I understand you have a delivery for me."

Mallory looked to Pokel and then to Edith. Pokel held Edith's hand. He knew it was time for them to part.

"This lady is a friend," said Pokel. Edith squeezed her guardian's hand even tighter.

Sister Teresa walked toward Edith. The nun towered over the child. Sister Teresa poked her index finger under Edith's chin. "The child smells putrid. She needs a bath." "She smells like weeks of suffering on a U-boat," Pokel snapped.

The woman didn't respond. "Look at me child."

Edith circled behind Pokel. She hugged Pokel about the legs and cried.

"It's time to leave." Her severe command angered Pokel, but he coaxed Edith to stand in front of him.

"Bring her to the car," Sister Teresa ordered.

Mallory watched the interaction. *This woman is no nun. Another charade?* Mallory's instincts told him the woman was not a member of a religious order and surely not a friend. Sister Teresa had OSS written across her temple. Mallory knew her type from survival school. She was one of the official torturers who stretched pain to its limit and a bit more. He looked around at his traveling companions. *My god. Are any of us really who we claim to be?*

Pokel coaxed Edith to the waiting car. Mallory followed. The far side door opened. The other passenger stepped out.

Mallory was surprised. It was his long-time friend, and fellow OSS officer, Erskin Young. Oddly enough, Young said nothing. He gave Mallory a condescending smile and pointed to the path. Mallory followed him to the bluff over-looking the Sound. For a moment the two men remained silent. In one practiced motion Young withdrew a Camel from a silver case, lit the cigarette returned the affectation to his jacket pocket. He flicked the lid of his Zippo. He paused, glanced at Mallory then took a long drag.

"I don't like children. Most of all I can't stand the sound of that kid's squawking," said Young.

Mallory rushed at Young and grabbed his lapels. "You sonofabitch," Mallory snarled.

"Go easy William. For god's sake you'll push me over the edge," Young gasped, eyes wide-opened and body trembling.

"You bastard. That 'squawking kid' has endured a lifetime

of horror. She's covered with sores from days of lying in filthy clothing. We almost died out there. Grown men were constantly sick. The stench suffocated me. And you complain about a terrified child. You can go to hell." Mallory released the tension of weeks on board a U-boat.

"Grow up, man," Young replied. "This isn't Yale. We're in the real world. You had a job to do. It's you who has the problem. They taught us to remain distant. Don't become personally attached to our asset. Remember? It's your problem not mine."

"Bullshit. You live along the gray-line. You come out at sunset. Manipulate lives. You create chaos then step back and watch people perform at a distance."

Young's temples flared. He pushed back at Mallory. "Yes William. Exactly. And you, my dear friend, are the terminator, the killer. No one asked you to take on the mission. You volunteered."

"I risked my life for a bogus cover story. You lied. Two dedicated OSS officers died back in Copenhagen."

"Yes, good men died and there's more to come," said Young. "Oh, by the way. Your contact, Mikkelsen, was arrested shortly after your departure."

"What went wrong?"

"Not sure exactly. Hoffmann, the Gestapo Chief with a reputation for cruelty took an interest in Mikkelsen and a local partisan commander. We couldn't allow Hoffmann to torture Mikkelsen."

"So you ordered a mercy mission?" asked Mallory.

"Yes. What choice did I have? The British called it Operation Carthage, a daylight low altitude raid on Gestapo Headquarters. Twenty bombers and thirty fighters came in over the city. One of the low flying Mosquito fighters struck a lamppost. Damn thing flew out of control and crashed into a Catholic school. The other planes mistook the burning building for the target."

Mallory kicked the sand and looked away for a moment. "How many died?"

"A total of 125 Danish civilians were killed including 86

school children."

"And Gestapo headquarters?"

"Mikkelsen and seven Danish prisoners along with Gestapo personnel were killed," Young answered.

Mallory's eyes swelled with tears. "It all seems so easy for you, Erskin."

"It's reality, William. I don't have to like it, but I accept it."

"And Otto Bruns. Who the hell is he? Bruns broke. The stress. He nearly died while we were at sea. All he talked about was magnets and launchers. He's no virologist."

"Did he tell you his real name?"

Mallory didn't answer.

"No. I didn't think so. The pathetic creature was kidnapped. He fears for his family. His wife and child were being held by the Gestapo." Young paused then defiantly turned his back on his accuser.

"In '42 we captured a Japanese cruiser at the Battle of Midway. It was loaded with poison gas canisters. The Germans have the V-2 Rocket. We suspect a submarine is on its way from Germany to Japan with a rocket on board. Picture a V-2 rocket with poison gas launched from a submarine aimed at New York City? Can you envision the chaos and devastation? Of course you can't. You liberal bleeding hearts don't have the guts to wander there. Germany's finished. It's over."

"Fine. I can give all this up. Discover an authentic life." Mallory shouted.

"The war is just beginning, William. The man you know as Bruns is a priority package. At this moment Operation Sunrise is underway. We are scouring every city, town, every cave in Germany for biologists, chemists, and rocket scientists. I could go on and on. We need to gather them up before the Russians snatch them. We can't trust our allies. The world is changing, William. Listen to me. Something big is about to happen. We are about to annihilate Japan. That's all I can tell you. Believe me, William. We have new enemies to deal with. Germany's finished. It's over "

"Over?" asked a confused Mallory.

"Admiral Dönitz and his representatives have submitted to an unconditional surrender. Didn't you listen to Dönitz's broadcast? All submarine commanders were ordered to surface under a black flag. They were instructed not to scuttle their U-boats."

Mallory slumped. "The radios on board the U-853 were sabotaged." He walked to the edge of the bluffs and looked east. *How will the U-853 know the war is over?*

Young lit another cigarette. "Oh, one final word about Bruns. His wife and child have disappeared. We think the Russians have them. He mustn't know."

Young walked down the sandy path toward the waiting car. "We have a child to deliver." Young paused and turned. He smiled as though the prior conversation never existed. "So, William, welcome home." (6)

Chapter Twenty-Seven
"Oh, So Secret".

Sean Cummings sat on the front steps of the summer cottage and watched Mallory and the others drive off. Bach rested on a milk crate whittling a piece of driftwood.

"When are we getting back to Patchogue?" he asked.

"In due time, Cummings. Let the others get far enough ahead."

"I've a train to catch."

"Not in Patchogue you don't," Bach replied without looking at Cummings.

"They'll nab you for sure."

"Who? I thought Shaw arranged everything."

"He did. I'm driving you to Oakdale. Shaw suspects the FBI is on to you. He'll meet you there with a train ticket."

"And what about…?

"Miss Evans? I don't know. I do know this much. From what I gather both Young and Shaw view you as a valuable asset. You're safe my boy, just as long as they need you. Like a seesaw." Bach let his whittling project fall to the ground. He raised his arms and turned toward Cummings. "Look at me, son." Bach raised his arms and turned toward Cummings. "Up-and-down. Keep balanced and you stay alive." Bach laughed and returned to his whittling.

Inside the cottage Kurt Pokel lay on his cot. He turned on his side and pulled his legs into a fetal position.

"And what is to become of Pokel?" asked Cummings.

Bach got up and walked inside. "Pokel, look at me."

Pokel turned on to his back.

"Do you know a man named Jack Price?"

Pokel looked up at Bach. "A friend from Brooklyn."

"Erskin Young has arranged for you to stay with Price."

Pokel looked surprised, but fearful. "I haven't seen Jack in years."

"My orders are to take you and Cummings to a safe house. A man named Shaw, Lieutenant Commander Shaw, will meet you. Everything is arranged."

Pokel was alarmed. *Is this a trap? Are they planning to kill me? Mallory saw the package. Does he suspect it is the U-853's log?*

Pokel's head fell back on the pillow. He slept fitfully for another hour. When he woke Pokel walked into the kitchen area. All that remained from breakfast was cold coffee in a saucepan. He poured the remains into a chipped mug. The cottage door was ajar. He looked outside. Cummings and Bach were on their way to the overlook. He returned to his cot. Pokel swept his hand under his pillow and grasped the watertight bag. He opened the bag and withdrew the log. It smelled musty. Many pages were stuck together. He carefully leafed through the back of the book. On one of the last pages of the log Pokel found Fromsdorf's final entry.

(02/05/1945 0800 South of Point Judith, Rhode Island)
Will proceed to grid location 83. Once landing party ashore
Will return to grid location 79. Await radio dispatch.
Location: near Block Island, Rhode Island.
Approx. position: Latitude 41° 13.583' N Longitude 71° 25.119' W
Water depths: less than 200 feet.
Radios and Antenna damaged.
Insufficient fuel to return to safe haven. Must inform crew.
Admiral Dönitz has directed all U-boat commanders to safeguard the boat's log.
Will transfer log to Lieutenant Kurt Pokel for safekeeping.
Fromsdorf.

Pokel ran his fingers over the page. *They don't have a chance of reaching Germany. I wonder what Fromsdorf will do?* Just then he heard Cummings and Bach outside. Pokel returned the log to the pouch and tucked it inside his coat sleeve.

"Pokel. It's time to get out of here. Pack up. Pokel, damn it! Answer me."

"I heard you, Bach. I'm coming."

Chapter Twenty-Eight
Lake Ronkonkoma

Lake Ronkonkoma was a sleepy, rural, Long Island village on Sunday morning May 6, 1945. The driver of the black Buick sedan was well acquainted with the summer resort. His parents vacationed here nearly every summer until the beginning of the war. The car proceeded along Portion Road and then turned left. The lake, Long Island's largest, was on their right. The car slowed as it approached a winding driveway on the left. On a hill overlooking the Lake was a large Victorian home. A winding stairway led to the road and down to a boathouse on the lake. The home stood in contrast to the other cottages. The driver turned left and proceeded up the pebbled drive to an ornate wrought iron gate. A young man opened the pedestrian entrance and walked to the car.

The driver pointed to Sister Teresa. She rolled down the car window and spoke to the young man in whispered tones. He returned to his position and began to crank the gate open.

"Drive on," ordered Sister Teresa.

The driver maneuvered the sedan along the driveway. The car stopped. A small bronze plaque near the entrance read "Our Lady Of The Lake Retreat House."

A nun stepped from the porch to the driveway. Unlike Sister Teresa the woman wore a smile and waved.

"Good morning. My name is Sister Anne."

Mallory squirmed and looked at Young then the child.

"Good morning, Sister Anne. Mallory you wait here," said Young as he stepped from the car.

Sister Anne walked closer to the opened car door. "And who do we have here?" she asked.

The ominous looking Sister Teresa motioned to Young to move aside. "Come out child," said Sister Teresa. Edith clung to Mallory.

Sister Teresa reached across the seat and pulled Edith out. "Schnell!"

Edith screamed in terror.

The Sister Anne looked alarmed. "Now, now child. Everything will be fine." The sister spoke in gentle but firm German.

The unfolding scene troubled Mallory. *This is bizarre. Why don't they take the child inside? Why continue the drama here?* The disturbing scene stirred Mallory's conscience. *I have to keep a record. I don't like what's happening.*

It took a while for Edith to stop sobbing. Finally, Sister Anne asked, "What is your name child?"

Edith stared at the ground and answered "Edith."

"Your name is Katherine. Do you hear me child. You are mistaken. Your name is Katherine ." Sister Teresa turned to Young and Sister Anne. "This is a copy of Katherine 's birth certificate, just as you requested Sister Anne. The birth records are on file at Mather Memorial. The birth certificate is recorded with the Town of Brookhaven. The name of record is Katherine Grace Stone."

"I'm a bit dismayed. Mother Superior informed me of your anticipated arrival, but not the reason for the child's stay with us. I'm puzzled."

Young intervened. "Sister Anne, this is a matter of national security. I don't know the extent of your information about the child." Young interrupted his remarks to retrieve a small leather case from his inside pocket. He flashed his security clearance in front of Sister Anne and replaced it. "Sister Anne, have you heard of the War Secrecy Act?"

"No she replied," feeling a bit dumb-founded.

"If you reveal one word of our discussion today you could be punished along with the other sisters. I respect the contribution this retreat house is making to the war effort. You must never reveal our meeting."

Sister Anne looked frightened.

"We will send for Katherine in due time. Take care of her," said Young.

"From this point forward speak English to the child. No German. Understood?" demanded Sister Teresa.

Young turned toward the lake. He heard a car approaching along the driveway.

"My ride," said Sister Teresa.

Young and Sister Teresa walked toward the approaching vehicle. Mallory thought he heard Young tell Sister Teresa "Excellent work." The pair was too far away to hear more of their conversation.

The car pulled ahead of the Buick and turned around and drove away.

Mallory never encountered the so-called Sister Teresa again. The initials, "ST", were the first entry in his newly created journal. There would be many more notes and descriptive accounts for years to come.

Young followed Sister Anne and Edith, now known as Katherine , to the retreat house entrance. Young never went inside nor did he even say "good bye." He returned to the car and climbed into the back seat. "Ok Sergeant, let's go."

The driver pulled away from the retreat and headed south.

"Pull over," demanded Mallory. "What the hell is going on here?"

Raynor's Beach Pavilion was straight ahead. "Pull into the parking lot, Sergeant," said Young. "What is it now William?"

"Who the hell is Sister Teresa?"

"She's one of us. That's all you need to know, William."

"One of us? She abused that kid. And she's one of us?"

" Captain Murk is an OSS officer from the Farm. Again, that's all you need to know. But there is one person you haven't met."

"And who is that?"

"Our driver, Sergeant Jack Price. Sergeant, meet Commander William Robert Mallory."

The driver turned and gave a casual salute. "Pleased to meet you, Sir."

"We are fortunate to have Sergeant Price join us. He's a skilled driver." Young laughed. "We discovered the Sergeant while conducting a background search on Kurt Pokel. Sergeant Price is a military logistics specialist. He is officially unattached from the Army and assigned to the Sunrise Project. But more important…you tell him Sergeant."

"Yes sir. I am a childhood friend of Kurt Pokel. I knew him before his father took him to Germany."

"Sergeant Price has agreed to help us relocate Pokel and his family. The Navy has deployed a unit to enter Flensburg, Germany. Their mission is to located Pokel's wife and child. Officially, the Sunrise Unit no longer exists."

"It sounds spooky to me," said Mallory. "Black Operations, William. America needs men and woman willing to risk their lives in defense of liberty. We need your skills. The OSS is merging into the Central Intelligence Agency. Our project is a small segment of Special Operations. We are accountable directly to the President of the United States."

"You mean covert operations that can't be laid at somebody's door?" asked Mallory. His question was tainted with cynicism.

"This is neither the time nor the place to discuss our mission. Rest assured you will play an important role, if you join us. Sergeant Price will manage logistics."

"Welcome Sergeant. Do you have the pedigree?"

"I don't understand the question," Price replied.

"Haven't you informed Sergeant Price?" Mallory asked Erskin Young.

Young scowled.

"Our unit is a bit snobbish, Sergeant. Young has a tendency to recruit from the Ivy League schools. You know. The eastern establishment."

"No sir. That ain't me," said Price. Price turned to look straight ahead at the cars pulling into the pavilion parking lot. "Sir, I think we better move on," he said.

"Agreed Sergeant. It's time for us to meet the others in Oakdale."

⋘

May 6, 1945: The U-853 sunk near Block Island, Rhode Island.

Chapter Twenty-Nine
Long Island Cover Story

Tucked behind what was once the Vanderbilt Estate in Oakdale, Long Island is a little known community.

"Turn here, Sergeant." The Buick made a quick left turn and passed a small brick gatehouse.

"This is the former Vanderbilt summer estate," Young noted. "Over there to your right." Young pointed to a large mansion.

"So the establishment even controls the new CIA. You're snobs," said Mallory.

"Don't be ridiculous, William. Vanderbilt was periphery. He's talking nonsense. Don't pay attention to him Sergeant."

Price shrugged. The sedan continued along the narrow drive to the end of what is today Idle Hour Boulevard. Price paused in front of an archway and then drove on.

"That's interesting," said Mallory. He pointed to an ornate barn and it's tower. The clock probably worked at one time."

"The Sixteenth Amendment. Income taxes killed the old money," said Young.

"Nothing has changed," said Mallory. "Wars make the rich even richer. The money dynasty will always control the world's destiny."

"For god's sake, William. The eastern establishment's sons and daughters have always served and sacrificed for our nation. Your grandfather was a Boston Brahman."

Jack Price didn't know what the hell to make of their bantering.

"That's the cottage, Sergeant." Young pointed to a nearby bungalow.

Price pulled in front of a white cottage surrounded by a neglected picket fence. The blue bungalow door opened.

Lieutenant Commander Shaw walked to the car.

"Greetings Shaw," said Young. The three men followed Shaw inside.

"We're waiting for Bach to deliver Cummings and Pokel," said Shaw. He walked to one of the two bedrooms. "Commander Mallory there is a change of clothes on the bed for you. The shower is out back. Hot water is precious here, Mallory."

"Use all you want, William. You reek. Smells like low tide. Wouldn't you agree Shaw?" asked Young.

Shaw disregarded Young and walked to the kitchen. "Is everything arranged?" he asked Young.

The ever-vigilant Mallory walked through the house.

"Relax, William," said Young. "Go get changed."

At that moment a woman entered the living room from the smaller of the two bedrooms. It was Paula Evans.

Shaw introduced Evans to the men.

The group waited for another hour.

Young began his speech. "I must remind everyone our mission is top secret. You will be scheduled for detailed debriefings with Shaw. You were instructed not to keep a journal or notes. From this point forward do not rehash anything with your teammates. With the exception of Miss Evans everyone has signed the Secrecy Act's nondisclosure form. Regrettably, there will be no accolades for your accomplishments."

Shaw handed Evans forms to sign. "Don't bother reading it. Just a lot of gibberish. Doesn't matter. One slip of the tongue and …"

"Just sign the damn thing, Paula," Shaw urged. *I know someone will be lurking in the shadows ready to execute her without a thought.*

"Of course we have your gracious thanks, Erskin," said Mallory. "You sat on your ass while we took the risks. Now we are beholding to you for our safety."

"Please William. Let's not go there. You all know too much. Shaw, break out that bottle of Irish whiskey. I know you keep one for special occasions. I believe Commander Mallory would benefit from a splash."

Before Shaw could pour Mallory's whiskey, the sound of

Bach's sputtering truck alerted the group. The three men got out and walked to the cottage. Shaw stepped outside to greet the arrivals.

Paula Evans grew increasingly nervous, not knowing what to expect. She got up and walked to the door. Young stopped her. "Wait for them to come inside," he cautioned.

Cummings was last to enter. Paula ran to him.

"What the hell? What's going on?" Cummings demanded.

"Aren't you happy to see me?" asked Paula.

"Yes, but there is too much happening all at once."

Kurt Pokel stopped and stared at the man on the far side of the room. "Jack Price?" he asked.

Price smiled, but restrained an emotional response. He walked across the room and shook hands with Pokel. "We'll have time to talk later, Kurt. We are behind schedule. It's dangerous to have too much traffic in the colony."

Young waited for a few minutes. The room was filled with a sense of anticipation and anxiety. "Listen up people," Young said. "We have a number of critical points to cover. Shaw will present the scenario."

"It's complicated. I want to make it simple." Shaw continued. "First, I must tell you a U-boat has been cornered off Block Island. I suspect it is the U-853. News reports are intentionally sketchy. It's government policy. I know this. The German High Command ordered all German U-boats to surface and surrender. A Coast Guard frigate and two destroyers are in pursuit."

"Admiral Dönitz sent other U-boats to New England. Fromsdorf was certain they were near-by, but he had no way of contacting them," said Pokel.

"The British were tracking several U-boats. The Coast Guard and Navy have intercepts from two, the U-857 and the U-858. As of yesterday, the Coast Guard reported the U-857 might have been sunk two weeks ago off Cape Cod. They have been unable to confirm the kill. No wreckage has been found. So it's possible the U-858 is our culprit."

Young told Shaw to leave the radio turned on. WNBC was

interrupting its regularly scheduled program with up-dates. Two Navy zeppelins were dispatched from Lakehurst, New Jersey to join the chase. "Things are heating up," Shaw insisted.

Young interrupted Shaw. "That's why it's critical you folks remain out of sight. Understand? We can't have you connected with the U-853."

"In other words, the U-853 is expendable," said Mallory.

"You all knew what you were getting into when you volunteered."

Shaw continued. "Tonight we will split up. Pokel and Price will leave with Bach. I will leave with Young and Mallory. Cummings and Miss Evans will remain here."

Paula Evans looked at Cummings and blushed.

"I will talk with Bach's group before we leave. Cummings and Evans step into the kitchen with me," said Shaw. "Mallory, you might as well be in on this, too."

Shaw instructed the couple not to leave the colony for any reason. "You are not to contact the others. No telephone calls. Operators eavesdrop on party lines." Arrangements were in place for the pair to stay in the cottage until sometime in late July or early August. "We need time for things to cool down. Hopefully, you will be overlooked in the pandemonium once victory in Europe is declared."

"And how will we shop or contact you?" asked Cummings. Shaw caught Cummings twisting his Claddagh ring as he had done when they first met. "I see you still have your good luck token."

Mallory caught Cummings shoot a sharp look at Shaw. Mallory's father owned a similar ring, but never wore it. "Let's get on with it," said Mallory to Shaw.

"Bach distributes vegetables and staples to small groceries and restaurants. He'll be your contact." Shaw handed Cummings a map of the area. "Check the place out. I am sure it won't be difficult to pretend you are honeymooners."

"My parents will be worried. My boss will notify the police," said Paula Evans.

"I have it covered. As we speak a note is being delivered to the

Patchogue Hotel. You've eloped with our dear Mr. Cummings. The note asks the manager to call your parents."

"They will be upset," Paula Evans replied.

"Not as upset as they would be to read you have been arrested by the FBI for spying."

"I understand," said Paula. Her eyes were downcast.

"I'm sure you'll find enough to keep busy. In case you get bored there's paint and brushes in the shed out back. Start with the fence. That'll keep you occupied." Shaw winked.

Shaw left the kitchen and opened the front door. He walked outside. Bach, Price and Pokel followed. "Bach will drop you in Sayville. Pokel, you must follow Price's instructions. Young prepared a cover story for you along with important documents. Do not vary from Price's orders. Memorize every detail until the lie becomes truth."

"What has happened to my family? Once Germany has surrendered and Flensburg is occupied we will search for them. Young will live up to his assurances."

Pokel was angry at Shaw's answer. He started to reply, but Shaw cut him off.

"Listen carefully. If you are captured by the FBI you will be electrocuted."

"I'm an American citizen. It was my intention to escape Germany and return home."

"No one will believe you. Treason is punishable by death. The war with Germany is over. We are still at war with Japan. No, Pokel. You are wrong. Erskin Young is your only hope to reunite with your family."

Bach walked away from the group and climbed into his truck. This time the old Dodge started without hesitation. "Let's get going," Bach called.

Shaw wished them good luck. "Stay out of sight until you hear from me." Shaw watched the truck pull away. Young was standing on the front porch. Both men agreed Pokel was a problem. "He's all yours, Young," said Shaw. "My hands are full with the others."

Mallory walked outside and stood next to Shaw and Young.

"Tomorrow is May seventh. A plane will be waiting for us in Farmingdale. We are headed to the Farm. The Director is anxious to get your first hand report. Let's hope this business with the U-853 is over before we reach Washington."

"Over? What do you mean?" asked Mallory.

"Two destroyers and a frigate are hunting a U-boat. Several other destroyers and two blimps with advanced sonar are entering the fray."

"All that fire power for one U-boat. Why?" asked Mallory?

"The U-853 is doomed, Mallory." Young's emphatic demeanor sent a clear message. The U-853 was destined to disaster since the day it left Norway.

∽

May 7, 1945: German general, Alfred Jodl, signed the formal surrender documents in Reims, France. Nazi Germany unconditionally surrenders to the Allies. VE Day.

May 7, 1945: U.S. Navy divers find the wreck of the U-853 in 130 feet of water. All fifty-five crewmembers lost.

May 14, 1945: A week after Admiral Dönitz's order the U-858 surfaced and surrendered off the coast of New Jersey.

Chapter Thirty
Summer In The Colony

Sean Cummings and Paula Evans spent the greater part of Monday making love. They had a brief quarrel over Sean's smoking in the bedroom. Sean smothered the Lucky like an admonished schoolboy. Then in the next moment he rolled over and passionately caressed Paula. After years of clandestine nights in Sean's hotel room, they felt a sense of unleashed freedom and desire.

By mid-afternoon they dressed and walked outside. A nearby path led to patchwork of canals that drained the wetland into the Great South Bay. They found a secluded dry spot. Sean pulled Paula to the crushed grass. Paula cuddled close. Sean looked at the clouds. His mind wandered to Limerick. *Will I ever see Ireland again?*

"What's to become of us?" asked Paula.

"What do you mean?"

"Oh, come on Sean. You know damn well what I mean. Some secret government organization is hiding us from the FBI. This is crazy. I feel hopeless. I feel like I have no future without you. Are you going to abandon me?"

"No Paula, but I'm a German spy. I'm a man without a country. Our lives are in the hands of Erskin Young."

"Young is an evil man. I feel it." Paula moved closer and squeezed Sean's hand.

"I'm frightened, Sean."

"We'll work something out. Let's get back to the cottage before someone discovers us."

When they returned to the cottage Paula turned on the radio. Sean found Shaw's bottle of Irish whiskey. He poured the last few ounces into a coffee mug and walked into the living room. Paula swayed to the music from the radio.

"Who's singing?"

"Why that's Doris Day."

Paula continued to move gently toward Sean. "Put down the mug and dance with me."

"I don't dance," said Sean.

She took the mug and placed it on the end table.

They embraced. "Dancing is easy," she said looking up at Sean's frown. "Oh come on. Relax."

She took the lead and pulled Sean into her. He slid his hand down her back and across her buttocks. "Now I feel safe he whispered. I may not have a country, but I have you." Sean was on the verge of unzipping Paula's dress when the music stopped.

"We interrupt this Columbia Broadcasting System program with an important radio relay from London. Please stand by." After a long period of silence a new voice was heard.

"This is Edward R. Murrow speaking to you from London. On May 4,1945 I announced the surrender of German troops to General Montgomery. Tonight America the war in Europe is over. The Germans have signed an unconditional surrender." Murrow's voice was covered by static. A few minutes later CBS returned to the music of Les Brown and his orchestra.

Sean walked to the fireplace. He pressed his hand against the mantel's edge. His shoulders sagged. "Our fate belongs to Erskin Young."

Paula began to cry and walked into the bedroom. "Oh god, what have I done?"

⚶

Spring slipped into summer. Sean painted the fence. "Do you do odd jobs?" the stranger asked without introducing himself. "I need a room painted. I live in the Mews.

Sean started to say "No," then changed his mind. "Let me have a look."

"I'll stop by tomorrow," the man answered. "That's an

interesting accent. Are you Irish?"

"Yes," Sean said.

"Lived here long? I mean here at the colony."

Sean recalled Shaw's cover story. " I'm living permanently here in the states. My wife's relatives live in Buffalo. We needed time alone."

"I'm single," said the man. I caught a glimpse you and your wife the other day. Quite a catch." He turned and walked back toward the Mews. Sean painted the artists living room. Word spread. He took on several jobs. Handy men were scarce.

Life was uncomplicated in the colony. Sean and Paula didn't fit into the social life. It didn't matter. Young had warned them about anonymity. Several times each week Bach delivered groceries and a block of ice. Bach brought some clean but tattered clothes for Sean. Bach surprised Paula.

"It's one of my deceased wife's dresses." Paula thanked Bach.

Cummings took Bach aside and expressed concern. Shaw had not returned as promised.

Then one afternoon in mid-July Bach arrived unexpectedly. He told the couple to be ready to leave Oakdale on July 26. He carried two small suitcases. "Here are train tickets and fresh clothes. I'll return to drive you to the station. Rooms have been reserved for you at the Roosevelt Hotel near Penn Station." Bach assured the couple Shaw would meet them in Manhattan.

They arrived at the Roosevelt Hotel around three in the afternoon. Shaw greeted them in the lobby. "No need to register. We have several hotel suites in Manhattan for Company business. This is one of them."

Shaw unlocked the door to a fourth floor suite. "You'll be comfortable here," Shaw said. "Enjoy New York. Central Park is beautiful. Rent a row boat." Shaw handed Sean an envelope. "Inside you'll find some cash. There are several forms you both need to sign. Bring everything with you on Saturday morning. Meet me on the seventy-ninth floor of the Empire State Building. Nine o'clock sharp. You are moving to a small town near Buffalo."

"What?" Sean didn't like the sound of Shaw's proposal.

"Do you want to stay out of prison, buddy boy? We promised

to keep you and Miss Evans safe. The FBI is running out of spies. Hoover has turned his attention back to the West Coast. It's time to relocate. Everything is set. There's an aircraft plant not far from where you'll be living. You'll leave by train Saturday afternoon."

"A defense plant? How the hell did you arrange that?"

"It's not difficult to put you on a government contract job. I'll have your new identifications and a letter of introduction when we meet on Saturday. Please do not contact your relatives, Miss Evans."

Sean and Paula dined at the Hotel Taft on Thursday evening.

"Can we afford this extravagance?" Paula asked.

Sean smiled. The waiter arrived with a bottle of champagne.

"To you, Paula." They clinked their champagne flutes in an unspoken toast.

Vincent Lopez and his orchestra were about to perform.

"There's something I want to tell you."

Paula was bewildered.

Sean nervously twisted his Claddagh ring off his finger. He gently held Paula's hand. "I want you to have this," he said placing the ring near the tip of her finger.

"Why Sean Cummings, what's this all about?"

"I've fallen in love with you Paula. I didn't want to, but I have."

Paula tilted her head to one side then turned away.

"What's wrong?" Sean asked.

"I didn't want you to see me crying. I love you, too."

"Will you accept this as a token of my love?"

"Damn it, Sean. Stop being so corny."

Sean slipped the ring on her finger.

It was the evening Paula always imagined since meeting Sean. Back at their hotel room the couple made love with intense passion.

They spent Friday walking the city's streets and window-shopping. On Friday evening they ate at a small delicatessen not far from their hotel. They were both apprehensive about a move to Buffalo."

Their wake-up call came at 6:30 Saturday morning. Sean looked out the hotel window. "Can't see a damn thing. The city is covered in fog."

They dressed and packed. At 8:15 the hotel doorman hailed a cab for the brief ride to the Empire State Building. They took the elevator to the seventy-ninth floor to meet Shaw.

The elevator operator was puzzled. "Did you say the seventy-nine floor?"

"Yes," Sean said.

"That's odd. You know it's Saturday. I doubt anyone will be there."

Sean and Paula exchange glances.

"When they stepped out of the elevator Sean expressed surprise. The lobby was empty.

"Wait here," he told Paula. "I'll look around."

"Shaw said nine sharp. It's 8:55," Paula replied. "He'll be here."

Unbeknownst to the couple Shaw was delayed on Long Island. He drove as far as Garden City. The deep fog was a problem. He parked his car at the railroad station and took the next Manhattan-bound train. He had no way of contacting Sean.

The OSS domestic unit occupied a suite of offices on the 79th floor. The non-descript building directory read "New York State War Council Office of Gas Consultant." The clandestine unit formulated scenarios to protect the US against the possibility of a V-2 rocket gas attack. The unit was in the process of closing down. The staff labored around the clock packing boxes of classified material marked "Destroy." They were rewarded with the entire weekend off.

Shaw's train arrived in Penn Station at nine o'clock. He rushed upstairs. He pushed ahead of two women waiting in line and jumped into the Checker cab. "Empire State Building, pronto."

"Listen mister. Ain't no tip going get me to bull my way through this fog," said the Yellow Cab driver.

"This is important man," Shaw insisted.

When they arrived at the Empire State Building, Shaw handed the driver a five-dollar bill and ran for the elevator.

"Seventy-ninth floor," he told the elevator operator.

"Hey. Are you the guy that couple on 79 is waiting for?"

"I might be," said Shaw.

Lieutenant Commander Edward Shaw, United States Naval Reserve, stepped from the elevator on the north side of the building at 9:39 AM. Shaw turned to find Sean and Paula seated at the far side of the lobby.

"Hi folks. I apologize…" Shaw never finished his sentence.

At 9:40 AM, on July 28, 1945, a B-25 Mitchel bomber flew into the 79th floor of the Empire State Building. The pilot became disoriented in the fog.

Sunday's Daily News headline read "B-25 bomber crashes into Empire State Building killing at least 14 people. Twenty-four additional injured."

Chapter Thirty-One
They Never Existed

On Saturday evening, Erskin Young placed a call to Bach. "The commander hasn't checked in. Any idea?"

"They left for the city on schedule," Bach answered. Bach and Young avoided names while talking over the phone.

"What was the itinerary?"

"Stay at a hotel. Pick up their documents at the ESB. Leave for the new location. That's all I needed to know." The crusty Bach was tired. "Listen. I just want out." The phone went silent. "Are you still there?"

"The Empire State Building?" Young asked.

"Yes, I'm sure of it."

"Where have you been Bach? Don't you listen to the radio?"

"No."

"A B-25 flew into the Empire State Building this morning. The authorities are still looking for victims. I have to go." Young dropped the phone onto its cradle.

Young turned to Mallory. "Shaw had a meeting scheduled today at the Empire State Building. Get there. I'll arrange for a flight to New York. Assess the damage. There were survivors. I want every detail covered. Be careful. The place will be crawling with FBI agents. One of our teams is already in place. Don't get involved. Find Shaw. My god, the 79th floor."

Mallory landed in New York after midnight. After a brief rest at the Algonquin he headed directly to the fire marshal's command post on Forty-Second Street. The initial report showed eleven dead. The survivors were at Bellevue. Later in the day the death toll reached fourteen including the plane's crew. Mallory telephoned Young.

"The Medical Examiner's Office is inundated with phone

calls from relatives," Mallory reported. "Some of the victims are burned beyond recognition."

"Stay in the background. Tell them you're a relative. Keep at it. We can't allow any connection between them and our unit."

Mallory gave it his best shot, but the ruse didn't work. He knew if he waited longer the military would soon intervene. Finally, he approached one of the deputies working the Medical Examiners' office. "I'm here on official business." Mallory presented his ID.

"Three people, two men and a woman, were on the 79th floor when the plane hit."

"How do you know?"

"My contact's name is Shaw. Shaw failed to meet me. He's a Lieutenant Commander."

The deputy's expression changed. He gasped. "A man's torso was found on the 72nd floor parapet."

"It may be your missing Shaw," said the deputy. He handed Mallory a military identification card.

"I'm afraid it's my man."

It was Shaw's ID. Mallory pocketed the ID.

"I need the ID," insisted the deputy.

"I can't leave it with you. Shaw was working on a case. Top secret. I'm warning you. Do not discuss our encounter or release his name. You will go to jail. I'm serious."

The deputy lowered his head. "I understand," he mumbled.

Mallory scribbled two names on a pad and handed it to the deputy. These two never existed."

"For your sake keep all three names off any lists."

The deputy nodded agreement. Mallory tore the page from the pad, crumpled it and placed it in his pocket.

"There are body parts scattered all over. We've located fingers with rings. Clothing fragments. We're still looking for victims beyond the building's perimeter. Realistically, we may never identify some. You haven't seen the carnage up there. The plane hit the building with such force that one of the engines landed on a nearby penthouse."

"This is important, man. Do you have other articles that

might identify a victim?"

"Yes. We have wallets, pocket books, and jewelry."

"Show them to me."

The aide led Mallory along a hallway to one of the temporary morgues. "There. On the far table," said the aide.

The stench of burned flesh nearly overwhelmed Mallory. He forced himself to continue. He took a fountain pen from his coat pocket and used it to sort through the jewelry. *I can't touch the stuff.*

There it is... Cummings' gold Claddagh ring. Mallory remembered the ring from his conversation with Cummings, Paula, and Shaw back at Idle Hour. Mallory turned his head in both directions. No one was watching. He pocketed the ring. Mallory walked over to the aide. He was inspecting a tagged victim.

"I'm sorry to be tough on you. We are still at war, you know." Mallory left the room and headed toward the street. He walked a short distance.

Exhausted, Mallory slumped on to a bench. He felt faint. He hadn't eaten all day. He hardly knew the three victims. Still he felt an eerie kinship. He called Young from the Algonquin late that evening. "I need to fill you in."

Mallory anticipated Young's response.

"I'll request the Navy send a telegram to Shaw's sister. His parents are deceased."

"What will you tell her?" Mallory asked as though he didn't know the answer.

"A plane went down off Key West Naval Station. Shaw was a passenger. Shaw is missing. The Navy has called off the search."

"As simple as that?"

"I keep telling you, William. We are at war."

"What about Cummings and Evans?" Mallory needn't have asked.

"They were always expendable. You knew that. They're gone. I'll pull their dossiers." Young's response was cold and disciplined. "I want you back here tomorrow, William. We have work to do." Somewhere in his journey Erskin Young misplaced his conscience.

Book Two

Chapter Thirty-Two
Mid August, 1945

A light drizzle covered the windshield of William Mallory's car. Droplets of water fell on his elbow from the open window. He didn't notice. The thunder within his mind was louder than the distant booms of the intensifying storm. A number of issues troubled Mallory. The loss of Cummings, Evans and Shaw on July 28 kept reoccurring in his sleep. Perhaps he tried too hard to forget.

On August 6 and again on August 9 the United States dropped atomic bombs on Hiroshima and Nagasaki. There was indescribable devastation. Mallory sensed the world was about to enter a new era.

Mallory turned on the car radio. Nothing happened. He slammed the dashboard a few times to no avail. The old Ford needed repair. His OSS monthly salary barely supported his Alexandria apartment. He relied largely on the inheritance his grandfather left him. The money was safeguarded in a blind trust. Initially, the OSS had strict regulations regarding the finances of its personnel. Mallory was allowed to receive trust drawdowns of not more than ten per cent of his monthly salary excluding hazardous duty pay. Mallory had been offered a position with a prestigious banking firm. Many of his former colleagues were leaving government service for lucrative careers. *Perhaps it's time for me to leave government service?*

The rain intensified. The sound and motion of the windshield wipers were hypnotic. *Damn it. I should have stopped at that general store. I could use a candy bar and a cup of coffee.* Mallory suspected he was still suffering from the insufficient diet on board the U-853. He had not been able to sleep more than three or four hours at a clip. Mallory began projecting. For sure, nothing good would evolve from his scheduled meeting at Camp Perry. Since his return from Germany, Erskin Young and Mallory debated his role within the evolving organization. Mallory felt his career had become all-consuming. There was more to life.

In June Mallory returned home for a brief visit with his mother. His father had died in 1940. He was in the first year of graduate school when the Japanese attacked Pearl Harbor. Mallory told his advisor, "I plan to join the Navy." Several days later his advisor presented an alternative plan. The OSS was quietly recruiting on campus. No sooner had he finalized his plans than Mallory met Margaret Collins.

Erskin Young's parents owned a summer estate on the Cape Cod. Doctor Frederick Collins, a wealthy pediatric surgeon, owned a smaller, but nevertheless substantial, summer retreat.

Mallory and Young were sailing all afternoon. Mallory got his first glimpse of Margaret as he walked from the boathouse. The vivacious woman chatting with Young's sister and friends captivated Mallory. The Young's Irish maid filled the women's flutes with champagne. Margaret looked up to find Mallory gaping at her.

"Who is that odd looking fellow?" she asked.

"Oh, that's William Mallory, one of Erskin's chums. Quite the ladies' man."

Margaret smiled. *Now there was a summer challenge.* Margaret turned her back on her admirer and walked inside.

A week or so later Erskin received an invitation to the Collins' home for tennis and cocktails. "And bring your friend along," Margaret said.

"If you mean Mallory, forget him. He doesn't play tennis and he's about to enlist. Doesn't want any commitments," Erskin responded.

"Neither do I. Then again, you might be making the whole thing up, Erskin. I know you want me to yourself." She laughed.

It was true. Erskin had always admired Margaret since they were kids. She knew it.

"Be a good boy, Erskin. Bring Mr. Mallory with you."

And that's how the romance began. Their first few dates were casual. Margaret was as opinionated as she was gorgeous. She wore her skirts too short for the times. Margaret enjoyed her Scotch on the rocks, perhaps a bit too much. She never finished her cigarette.

One evening after a dinner topped off with a bit too much to drink, Margaret suggested they drive to a secluded spot along the beach. Mallory drove about a half mile along the sandy, bumpy road. He dimmed the headlights, but left the engine running. He leaned over and caressed Margaret's neck.

Margaret shifted her body. She pulled her blouse out of her skirt and said, "Unsnap my bra."

Mallory hesitated. All evening he had thought of little else but sex with Margaret.

"Wait. I have a better idea," said Margaret. She slowly unbuttoned her blouse then turned to Mallory. "Let's go for a swim," she dared Mallory.

It was simply too much to resist. Still, he protested. "Somebody is bound to discover us."

"Nonsense darling. I've been here before."

Mallory didn't know how to take her answer. He shrugged. "OK." *I guess you have.*

Margaret got out of the car and undressed. She meticulously placed her clothes over the back of the front passenger seat.

"What are you doing?" Mallory asked.

"Can't go home with a wrinkled skirt." My father would kill you if he discovered you took me for a midnight swim…and naked at that. She turned and ran off into the dunes. "Grab the blanket," she called.

Mallory looked around. There were no passing automobile headlights. He was perplexed. *Margaret's been here before. Does it matter? This is no time for an examination of conscience.* He took one last look around. The evening was still. Unlike Margaret, Mallory stripped and tossed his clothes across the front seat and headed for the beach. In the building heat of excitement Mallory forgot the blanket. As he reached the top of the sand dune he spotted Margaret. It was low tide. She was standing in the shallow water. The moonlight outlined her body. He walked into the water and on to the sandbar.

Margaret turned and pulled him into her. He pulled her down. They playfully touched one another. The water lapped over them.

"Not here," she said. Margaret took his hand and slid it along her body. "Let's go back to the car."

Mallory stood. He reached out and pulled her up. Her body glistened. When they got back to the car, Mallory opened the rear passenger door.

"After you," Margaret said pointing to the back seat. She playfully pushed Mallory on to the back seat and slid on top of him. "I love you," she said.

Mallory didn't say a word. *I love you, too.*

"Come on top of me." she said. Mallory rolled to one side and he and Margaret effortlessly exchanged positions. "Go slow," she murmured.

It was nearly two in the morning when Mallory awoke. "Hey. Wake up. Shit. We're going to be in a lot of trouble with your father."

"Screw him," she said.

Mallory started to slide off Margaret when she pulled him back.

"One more time." It was a forceful request. She dug her nails into his back.

He began thrusting. "Harder," she demanded.

Mallory didn't react.

Suddenly she stopped. "Get off me." She began to cry.

He embraced her.

"Don't touch me."

Confused, Mallory replied, "I'll take you home."

Margaret's neatly folded clothes were scattered on the car floor. She shook them. "Damn, what a mess," she said to herself. They dressed.

Mallory tried to talk with Margaret. She would have none of it.

As Mallory approached the Collins' home he turned off the engine and let the old Ford glide the last few feet along the driveway. The side entrance light was on. Margaret looked disheveled. Her beautiful hair was a messy tangle. Something had gone wrong. He had no idea what it was. He started to open the driver's side door.

"Don't bother getting out. " Margaret slammed the car door and disappeared through the side entrance. She never looked back.

A week passed. Mallory left several messages, but Margaret never returned his calls. Mallory decided not to share his experience with Erskin. Mallory detected what he dared not ask Erskin, "Are you interested in Margaret, too?" *I wonder if her father discovered our escapade. Was it love or sex? With Cheryl Lee it was sex.* But that was another story. He pushed the thought away. *One last call.* Mallory picked up the phone, but changed his mind. He would soon regret that decision.

Over a year had passed and Mallory was still preoccupied with the thought of Margaret Collins. He was guilt-ridden. *Why?* The thunderstorm intensified. A flash of lightening followed by thunder startled Mallory. He over-reacted and lost control of the car. The Ford swerved into the oncoming lane. The tread-worn tires lost traction. The car spun around. It halted just in front of a drainage ditch. *For god's sake, man. What's wrong with you?* He knew the answer.

⤢

The sign read Camp Perry Naval Reservation. Mallory was

perturbed. *This meeting could have taken place in Washington. Why all the mystery? Had their usual watering hole on F Street become passé? Things were changing.*

Marines guarded the front gate. Mallory presented his identification.

"Sir, please be sure to get your ID upgraded before you leave," said the Corporal as he returned Mallory's OSS credential.

The thunderstorm passed. Men in gray uniforms worked along the road. Marine guards supervised the work. Mallory learned the work crew was comprised of German prisoners waiting for repatriation. These were no ordinary prisoners. They were captured U-boat crews. The German high command believed these men were lost at sea. They were held incommunicado in violation of the Geneva Convention. There was no way the US intelligence community wanted Berlin to know the U-boat logs and codebooks were in American hands.

Mallory drove on. The concrete road ended at a large barrier marked "Road Closed." A penciled map was tucked into the overhead visor. Mallory checked it. *This must be it, the edge of the existing CB base.* He drove around the barrier and followed the crushed stone road. Erskin Young's directions were impeccable. Directly ahead was another Marine guard post.

"Mr. Young is expecting you Commander. Proceed." Mallory returned the Sergeant's salute.

Young's temporary headquarters was a classic brick three-story turn-of-the-century structure he unofficially dubbed Lovell House. Young admired OSS espionage agent Stanly Lovell. Young frequently quoted Lovell's premise: "It was my policy to consider anything whatever that might aid the war, however unorthodox or untried."

A man dressed in a dark gray business suit greeted Mallory. His blonde hair was turning gray about the temples. He spoke with a heavy German accent.

"William Mallory for Erskin Young."

"Mr. Young is expecting you. Please have a seat in the library." Before Mallory could be seated Young called out with his usual Brahman affect, "William, old boy. Come on in."

"For god's sake Erskin. It's me, not one of your subordinates."

Young stared at Mallory for a few seconds to process Mallory's remark. "You're correct, William."

Mallory knew from Young's accentuated frown his former fraternity brother felt otherwise.

"Quite a place you have, Erskin."

"Not my place, but it is quite conducive to work. In addition to the offices, the CB's have renovated the home. Upstairs we have private living quarters including a kitchen and five bedrooms."

"What's your mission?"

"On the surface it's repatriation."

"And?"

"A number of these prisoners have applied to remain in the United States. We have a messy situation since the German's listed these individuals as missing at sea," said Young as he began pacing the room. Mallory sensed Young was about to reveal something important.

Young stopped, turned and braced behind a leather chair. "Next month President Truman will sign an executive order 9621. The OSS will be terminated."

"Terminated? Sounds like an execution," said Mallory.

"Call it what you will. Our duties will be split. You and I will be reassigned."

"Just like that?" Mallory asked.

"Anyone getting sacked?" Mallory asked.

"On the contrary. With folks returning to civilian life the organization will be recruiting."

"What's the bottom line, Erskin?" Mallory pressed Young.

"You and I are going to continue the work we finished. I'll be assigned to the State Department. You'll be with Justice. Once the dust settles everything will fall into place."

"What does that mean?"

"William, I'm sending you back to Germany. Frankfort. You will receive your orders in a few days. Did you ever purchase a uniform?"

"No," said Mallory.

"It's time. Your cover story will be Navy Intelligence. Compared with your last mission you will be bored."

"How so?"

"We need to locate Heinrich Franz, an American psychologist. He was spirited into Nazi Germany. The Navy is certain he's still there."

"What's so important about Franz?" Mallory asked.

"Franz left the US in 1942. He helped train test pilots. He's a wizard when it comes to getting people to do things they ordinarily would fear. That's all I know."

"And my base. The military has a repository of Nazi records at Frankfurt. You'll have an office in the shadows of the Hindenburg's hangar."

"That's a bad omen."

"I doubt you'll be spending much time on your ass. We need you to find Franz ASAP. Get him back here before the Nuremberg Commission finds him."

"He's a war criminal, right?"

"Correct, but that's not your concern. We are part of an incredible process.   Our code name is Operation Paperclip. Your immediate task; find Franz. Jack Price will handle the logistics. We have an initial list, 750 scientists to be extricated. You'll be in charge of a combined intelligence unit. We have to find Franz and the others before the Russians."

"And the child from the U-boat?"

"Leave the child to me."

Young walked to the sidebar and poured a whiskey.

"Want one?"

Mallory shook his head "No."

"Cheers." He gulped the whiskey. "By the way Mallory, you need not fret. Franz has an executive pardon. We need him."

"Is my new task related to the U-853?" Mallory asked.

Young walked to the window. "Hmm. I sense a hesitation. Are you still on board, William?"

"I'm thinking about resigning. Finishing graduate school. I

might want to settle down."

"It's Margaret Collins. Isn't it? You can't let go of her. She's gone, William. You had your opportunity."

"What do you know about Margaret?"

"I know she got knocked up. Always thought you were the culprit, William. Then again, Margaret is more than you can handle, especially in bed."

Mallory's color blanched. He looked away.

"You bastard. You got laid," said Young. His faced twisted in anger.

"It wasn't like that," Mallory answered.

"Bullshit. I don't believe it." Young began to pace again. He turned to Mallory and said, "She kept the baby, a girl. Old man Collins sent Margaret to some place in New Hampshire. That's all I know." Young kept repeating, "You bastard. You screwed her." Young walked out of the office still mumbling "You bastard."

A few minutes later the German internee returned. "Sir, allow me to show you to you quarters. Mr. Young has retired for the evening."

Chapter Thirty-Three
Frankfurt, Germany
1946

William Mallory disliked the converted Luftwaffe barracks. He didn't like Frankfurt, Germany either. Mallory regretted his decision to join Young on his search for Nazi scientists. Prior to his departure for Germany, Mallory spent two months searching for Margaret Collins. Old man Collins lay dying in Massachusetts General. Alcoholism and his belligerent temper left him abandoned by his wife and friends. He would be dead before Mallory arrived at the hospital.

"I'm sorry, Mr. Mallory. Doctor Collins died yesterday. Mrs. Collins arranged for the cremation. I understand there will be no memorial service. Doctor Collins must have been hated," said the hospital administrator.

"I'm sure he was," Mallory agreed. He called the Collins home on the Cape. The housekeeper told him she was closing the home. It was for sale. Mrs. Collins was living on Long Island. The housekeeper wouldn't reveal the Long Island address.

"I will tell Mrs. Collins you inquired, in the event she calls here. Honestly, she's not well and I don't want to burden her unnecessarily."

Mallory asked Young's parents to help. "I want to locate Margaret. I'll be leaving for a new assignment. It is important we talk."

"I'm sorry, William. We would help if we could. We don't know where Margaret is. I do know Dr. Collins had a young sister or cousin living in Huntington, Long Island. That's the best I can do."

Mrs. Young's tip was all Mallory needed. Mallory called a former OSS member who subsequently joined the FBI. A few days later Mallory arrived in the village of

Huntington on the north shore of Long Island. Huntington was a relatively sleepy community surrounded by farms to the south and the Long Island Sound to the north. The railroad came to Huntington back at the turn of the century. Commercialization was just beginning.

The Collins' home sat on a small hill overlooking the harbor. Dr. Collins was the highest paid physician at Massachusetts General Hospital in 1944. He purchased the Long Island home for his spinster sister.

Dr. Collins was a simple man. Sadly, his discretionary funds were spent on a mistress. The rest went to cigars and alcohol. The home in Huntington was all that remained once Doctor Collins' accounts were settled. Clara, the old man's sister, lived in the simple home for years. Now she shared the residence with her sister-in-law, Beth, Margaret, her unmarried niece and her illegitimate daughter. Suddenly the house was too small and chaotic. Clara resented the intrusion. After all the years of living alone, Clara felt by right the home was hers.

It was Clara who caught the first glance of the stranger approaching the front door. She who answered the doorbell.

"What is it?" she asked Mallory.

"Is Miss Margaret Collins at home?"

"And what business is it of yours? And how do you know she lives here?" demanded Clara in her normal fashion.

"I'm a friend, William Mallory. I'm leaving for Germany in a few weeks and I wanted to say goodbye."

"She's never mentioned you," snapped Clara.

"Ah. So she does reside here."

From down the long hallway came a voice. "Is everything all right Auntie?"

"There's some man here to see you Margaret."

Margaret stepped out of the hallway shadows and approached the door.

"William?"

"Margaret, I had to come."

"For god's sake William. I don't need any more complications in my life."

"Please, let's talk."

"Not here. I'll fetch my coat. We can walk to the harbor."

Margaret returned with a light jacket over her shoulders. Mallory waited on the sidewalk. He gazed up at Margaret as she walked down the steps. At that moment he knew for certain he loved her.

"So William, where have you been these past months? I thought for certain I would hear from you. Perhaps a letter."

"I've been everywhere and nowhere."

"Ah. You can't tell me. Erskin is very guarded when he calls."

"He knew where you were?"

"Of course. Didn't he tell you?"

"No. The bastard told me he had no idea where your father sent you."

"Sent me?"

"An embarrassment. I was pregnant. We have a daughter. My father raged. He didn't send me away. I left. No man controls me, least of all a drunk."

"Hey. Could we start over again?" asked Mallory.

For the next hour the couple sat on a bench at the harbor side. Margaret lit a cigarette and began an awful confession. The conversation focused on her father. Mallory listened. He was anxious to learn about the child. Yes, Margaret was certain Eleanor was Mallory's daughter. The words rolled off Margaret's tongue with a staccato anger.

"I got pregnant to punish my father. I wanted him to feel the pain and anguish he brought on me. All I did was injure myself and now look at me." Margaret stifled the tears and lowered her voice. She turned toward William and said, "I'm so sorry. I've made such a mess of things. Please just go away."

William put his arm around her shoulders. He could smell alcohol on her breath as they kissed.

"Now what?" asked a bewildered Margaret.

 "May I meet my daughter?"

"Do you want to?"

"Let's stop playing games. I'm here for two reasons. I want to meet my daughter."

"And?"

"It's complicated, but I want you to marry me."

"Just like that? William. It will take time."

"I must leave for Germany. I might be able to postpone my departure until February. I want you and Eleanor to come with me."

"You're being impetuous. You have no idea what you are getting into."

"I've thought of nothing else but…"

"I can't give you an answer, right now."

When William and Margaret returned to the house, Aunt Clara and Mrs. Collins were about to walk into the village with Eleanor in her carriage.

"Well, William. This is a surprise," said Mrs. Collins. She looked at Margaret as though to ask, "What's going on?"

Margaret released Mallory's arm and stepped to her mother's side. Margaret whispered, "He wants to marry me."

Mrs. Collins stepped back and announced, "That's ridiculous, Margaret."

"Clara. He wants to marry her." Both women laughed in disbelief. Clara began mocking the idea of marriage. "You hardly know the man."

All during their bantering Mallory was bending over Eleanor bundled up for the chilly afternoon breeze. "She's adorable," he remarked. He picked Eleanor up and moved closer to Margaret.

Margaret looked at Mallory and Eleanor then back at her mother and aunt.

"Of course I'll marry you, William. The sooner the better."

"Surely, you're joking," said Clara.

"William, you can't be serious. The marriage is doomed to fail."

"Nonsense, mother," said Margaret as she huddled closer to William. "We intend to marry as soon as possible."

Two weeks later a Presbyterian minister married the couple.

❧

The night of his proposal to Margaret, Mallory telephone Erskin Young. Young sounded surprised and angry. The conversation quickly turned into small talk as Young struggled to control his fury. *Mallory might be my friend, but I deserve Margaret.*

"I'll need a new booking to Europe. I want to go by passenger ship rather than fly," Mallory said.

"I'll see what I can arrange. The taskforce isn't paying for your new family."

"I didn't think so. Nevertheless, the voyage will give us time to get to know one another."

"It's your choice," said Young. "I have an update for you. The Department of Justice, State Department and the Navy have committed to Operation Paperclip. That's all I can tell you over the phone."

"I know Paperclip is important, Erskin, but for now, just get us on a ship to Germany. I'm willing to go to Portugal, if all else fails."

"Fine, but most of those passenger vessels are a mess from transporting troops." "I have a suggestion," Mallory said. "Maybe the Queen Mary."

"I'll get back to you. He dropped the phone into its cradle."

❦

On February 6, 1946, The Mallory's left for Europe on board the MS. Gripsholm, a Swedish American liner.

"The Navy is paying for your family, too," said Young.⊠

"Nothing is free. What's the catch?"

"The Immigrations Service made an agreement with Governor Dewey. Lucky Luciano is being deported. He's in Sing-Sing Prison. He is booked on the Gripsholm, too. Keep an eye on him. I don't trust INS."

"OK, but why do I have to mix business with pleasure? It's our honeymoon."

"Fine. Then you pay for the voyage," said Young.

Fortunately, Charles "Lucky" Luciano did not sail on the Gripsholm. His deportation procedure was delayed. Luciano departed Pier 7 at the Brooklyn Terminal on Friday, February tenth.

The ten-day voyage to Gothenburg proved uneventful. The

newlyweds did have the opportunity to get to know one another. Mallory was deeply in love. Nevertheless, he was troubled by Margaret's afternoon drinking. When she drank her personality changed. *One Manhattan is never enough.* She enjoyed a Manhattan before dinner and several glasses of red wine with dinner. On those evenings Margaret's behavior turned dark. Mallory was able to soothe her. On two occasions they could not go to dinner. Margaret was so drunk he sat near her bedside fearing she might choke on her own vomit. The next morning she would profusely apologize. Mallory attributed her behavior to stress. *She couldn't be an alcoholic.*

Many German ports suffered severe damage from the Allied bombings. The Allies struggled to regain control of strategic areas from roaming gangs of thugs and rogue Nazis. The Mallorys made the two-day journey from Gothenburg to Frankfurt by train.

Mallory was stationed at the US Army's installation at Frankfort Airport. The Justice Department arranged for housing, a two bedroom poorly furnished flat, nearby. He was a month late and was expected to start work the very day after his arrival.

Mallory's primary task involved the search for Heinrich Franz, the American psychologist. Franz had disappeared. There were rumors he was in South America, perhaps Argentina. The key to Franz's whereabouts was former Navy Lieutenant Walter Kappe, Franz's former Abwehr control. Kappe planned several sabotage operations in the United States. Kappe arranged Heinrich Franz's journey to Nazi Germany in 1942.

A catalog of identification cards and other Nazis personnel records were classified and stored in a Luftwaffe barracks on the Frankfurt installation. There were thousands of cards and huge piles of dossiers, but nothing on Kappe or Franz. Day after day Mallory would remove ID cards from the catalog chest and begin reviewing them. It was a tedious task. There was another problem. Just prior to surrender, Himmler ordered all records of SS personnel destroyed. A number of municipalities did not follow the order. The Allies seized those records. The temporary German government and the State Department denied the catalog existed.

As Mallory worked his way through the ID cards he discovered other people were accessing the information. Many of the cards were marked with either a green or red dot. When he inquired as to their significance he was told the symbols were classified. Mallory discovered a pattern. The marked cards identified German scientists.

Mallory recalled a conversation with Erskin Young. Young told Mallory Operation Paperclip was searching for Nazi rocket scientists, chemists and biologists. About two weeks into his work Mallory sent a dispatch to Young informing him of the pattern. Young called Frankfurt and spoke with Mallory.

"Locate Franz. Then find out who else is searching the files. The records are classified. Access is limited. Check all the logs. Who's reading those files? They better have a clearance."

Mallory returned to his search for Franz, but he couldn't let go of the idea an unauthorized person was into classified files. Why? He doubled the sign-in procedure for all the intelligence communities, including the Navy.

About a month into his search Mallory received a tip. The spymaster, Walter Kappe, was working for the United States Army not far from Check Point Charlie in Berlin's American zone. Kappe was a former Abwehr Officer in charge of the German spies in Manhattan. Kappe was Sean Cummings' controller. Mallory notified the Judge Advocates unit in Nuremberg. Kappe was arrested. Oddly enough he was soon released. Was it a mistake?

Mallory suspected the contrary. *Someone inside our military intelligence arranged for Kappe's release.* Mallory surmised it wouldn't take much pressure before Kappe gave up a number of wanted war criminals including Heinrich Franz.

Mallory telephoned Erskin Young. "Kappe has disappeared."

Young responded indifferently. "Kappe is someone else's problem now."

"That's all you can say?" Mallory protested.

Young is not telling me the whole story.

"William, forget about Kappe. Find Franz before he disappears, also."

Chapter Thirty-Four
The Search Intensifies

Young mailed Mallory a camera to photograph documents that might provide a clue to Franz's whereabouts. There were hundreds of documents to read. Mallory sat surrounded by piles of folders. His desk like his mind was cluttered with too much information. There was a knock at the door. It was Sergeant Stent. The Army's clerical pool assigned Stent to manage Mallory's office.

"Sir. A Mr. Jack Price asks to speak with you," said Stent.

"Show him in, Sergeant," said Mallory. He got up and walked to the door and greeted Price. "Sergeant. Glad to see you."

Price walked through the door and the two men shook hands. "No more Sergeant. I'm Captain Price. It's unusual. Officially I am a civilian with military rank assigned to Department of Commerce."

"Commerce?"

"I have no idea who made the arrangement. I'm attached to the Field Information Agency, Technical of the Military Government of Germany."

"I'll be handling logistics for you, but not here at Rheine-Main Air Base."

"Where are you located?"

"The IG Farben Building in Hoechst. Young thinks German companies are hiding industrial secrets they were supposed to surrender. Young thinks the industrialists are sharing technical data with their affiliates. Young may be on to something. IG Farben is our target. I'm a bit skeptical. They are just too cooperative."

"I need you here, Price. I'm surrounded with mountains of paper," said Mallory.

"I can see that. Young told me you brought your family with you. How did you find adequate housing?"

"It's not. We are housed in a dilapidated apartment building assigned to US personnel. It's awful. Hopefully, once base accommodations are finished we'll move in."

Price scratched his head and said, "Frankfurt's center is a mess. Allied bombings destroyed a lot of the city. Hoechst is relatively untouched. To my surprise, the IG Farben building, in Hoechst, is one of the largest building complexes in Germany. It's relatively untouched. I just can't figure it out."

"Look at this." Mallory motioned for Price to walk behind his desk. "I'm photographing a series of documents." The page on Mallory's desk read, " Zyklon B labels from Dachau concentration camp will be used as evidence at the Nuremberg trials."

"What's Zyklon B?" asked Price.

"It's a chemical used in the gas chambers."

"No wonder Young wanted our team to go after IG Farben."

"There's more to it. There has to be," said Mallory.

"Hey. We were talking about your family."

"I'm sorry I brought them to this god-forsaken place. The crime is high. Gangs roam the streets extorting money and food. Families with children have received extra food ration stamps, but it is below subsistence."

"I saw the sign at the entrance. US personnel are forbidden to talk with the German civilians. It's a strict policy, but a laugh. A woman can be bought for a pack of cigarettes or chewing gum. Prostitution is rampant."

"I understand why you are worried for your family. Young told me you had a daughter. Just between the both of us, Young sounded bitter and sarcastic. I won't go into the details, but it wasn't pleasant," said Price.

Mallory shrugged and struggled to change the subject. "You are not married."

"No." Price answered quickly. "I have no intention of ever settling down. Can't see myself involved in an ordinary desk job. No wife would be able to tolerate my schedule."

"Let's get back to our discussion of locating Franz," said Mallory. "This may sound strange, but I think some powerful German officials are sheltering Franz."

"You may be right," Price answered. "It's strange how he's

been able to elude us. He may be hiding right out in the open, if only we knew where to look."

It was nearly 4 PM when their meeting ended. Price borrowed a jeep from the motor pool and it was due back that evening. He still had a few stops.

Mallory decided to leave with Price. Price dropped him on the corner near the apartment complex. Mallory looked at his surroundings. *This was no place for my family. If I can't get adequate housing, they should return home to Long Island.*

Mallory arrived at his apartment building and climbed the stairs to their second floor apartment. The elevator like most of the building was unsafe. He unlocked the door and walked down the short corridor to the small living room. Eleanor was sitting in her playpen. Margaret was asleep on the couch. He looked around the apartment. There was little he could do to make the place comfortable. *Officers' housing won't be ready for at least another month.*

He leaned over to kiss Margaret when he caught the smell of alcohol. *Margaret must have been drinking. She wasn't taking a nap. She'd passed out.* Mallory was angry. He walked into the kitchen and opened the cabinet beneath the kitchen sink. *Margaret finished the gin.*

Mallory carried Eleanor into their bedroom and placed her in the crib. She had been sleeping in their room since they arrived. The apartment was cold since the heating system still wasn't fully functional. The neighborhoods around the air base enjoyed constant electricity. Even the toilets flushed, but not where they were living. Even the drinking water needed to be boiled. *Is it any wonder Margaret struggled to adjust to living in Germany?*

Mallory put another blanket over Eleanor and returned to the living room. It was barely 5:30. Margaret was restless. He pulled a chair across the room and sat looking at the woman he loved.

"What have I done?" he said aloud. Mallory blamed himself for the predicament. Eleanor began to cry. He walked back into the bedroom. *What kind of a father am I?* He placed Eleanor over his shoulder. Mallory fumbled at lighting the stovetop. He frantically searched the cabinets for the baby formula. A dish crashed to the floor.

"Hi." Margaret stood in the doorway. "I'm sorry, William."

Mallory didn't answer. He struggled to suppress his anger. He didn't want an argument.

"I said 'I was sorry.'"

"I know you are. We have to deal with this, but let's wait until the morning."

"I'll make it up to you. I was tired. I fell asleep." Margaret pressed against Mallory.

"You had too much to drink. It has to stop."

Mallory's comment angered Margaret. "I'm not a drunk."

"I didn't say you were. There's something wrong. I had no idea this place would be so awful. I'm to blame, not you. The marriage, the move…it all happened too fast. You needed more time. I was wrong. I should have listened to you."

"I knew what I was getting into. Stop trying to protect me. Do you enjoy making me feel inadequate?" Margaret protested.

"Margaret, I love you very much. The experience of living here with the food shortages, the cold and most of all the absence of friends hasn't helped you or our marriage."

Margaret cast a forlorn look at her husband. "This goddamned building feels like it will collapse every time a door slams or a truck goes by. Dust pieces of plaster, mice…the whole thing is outrageous."

Mallory avoided eye contact. Eleanor began to cry. Mallory paced the tiny kitchen. He wanted to hide.

"Please sit down, William. You're making me dizzy. Yes, I do hate it here. I'm trapped in this apartment all day. There are just so many conversations I can have with a child. The other wives have no children. They leave each day for work on the base. I have no one to talk with. You're deep into your work."

"Is that why you're drinking so much?" Mallory's voice lowered to a whisper as though someone might be listening. "One drink and you become melancholy. Two drinks and you are."

"Grow up, William. I drink because I enjoy it. I'm not an

alcoholic. You didn't protest when I was screwing you on the back seat of your car."

"You had to be drunk?" Mallory slammed a cabinet door. His face was turning red. He finished stirring hot water into a bowl of cereal. "Maybe we are both in denial," he said and left the room. Sadness and recrimination engulfed the Mallorys.

A confused Mallory tried to sleep on the couch. He never meant to argue with Margaret. *What options do I have?* All sorts of crazy thoughts ran through his mind. *Will she divorce me if she returns to Long Island? Have an affair?* He began to project his worst fears. His head ached. He began to cry. "What a mess," he sobbed. He buried his face in a pillow.

Mallory awoke determined Margaret should return home before she drank herself to death. *If she wants a divorce so be it.* He loved Margaret too much to watch her grow out of control.

Mallory didn't report to work the next morning. The building's telephone service needed repair. Around 9:30 someone knocked at the door. It was Sergeant Stent.

"I'm sorry to trouble you Sir. I was worried when you didn't turn up for work." Stent told Mallory.

"Stent, I need your help. Please check into flights leaving here next week."

"And the destination Sir?

"The United States. Please get a schedule of both military and civilian departures. Mrs. Mallory will be returning home with our daughter."

"Yes Sir," said Sergeant Stent. Stent looked worried. "If I can help in any other way, please…"

"Thank you Stent. Life in Germany is too difficult at this point," said Mallory. Stent left. Mallory walked back to the couch. He quietly approached the bedroom. Eleanor had slept through most of the night. Now she cuddled next to her mother beneath a pile of blankets. Frost covered the inside of the windows. He scraped a smile on the pane and sighed. The silence of the momentary truce was a relief. *The separation might be good for us. I need time, also.*

Stent made all the arrangements. Margaret and Eleanor

departed the following week. The couple barely spoke. Margaret was torn with guilt and anger.

"I don't have to go, William. I'll stop drinking. This entire business is your idea not mine," she protested and pleaded.

Mallory was determined. "We're both depressed. The pressure has been too great. I want a healthy wife not a drunken lover. I'm sorry."

To the other passengers Mallory, Margaret and baby Eleanor looked like a family, but they weren't, really, now.

Margaret asked, "Aren't you going to kiss me goodbye?"

Mallory tilted his head. "Oh, Margaret. Everything happened too fast. He kissed Eleanor. Margaret looked up at her husband. They kissed, but it was bittersweet."

Mallory turned and motioned toward the departure gate. He felt tears on his cheek.

"Damn it William. Don't cry. Men aren't supposed to cry," Margaret sobbed. "This doesn't have to be."

"Please don't make this any harder for us, Margaret."

Margaret forced a smile.

Mallory watched the plane take off. The scene played over and over again in his mind for days.

After several weeks of unanswered letters, he called Margaret. Clara answered.

"What did you say? I can hardly hear you. We have an awful connection."

"Is Margaret home?"

"I'm sorry William, Margaret isn't home. Try calling in the morning. When are you coming home? You have responsibilities here not in that awful place."

Not even a 'How are you?' Oh, well, that's Clara. "Please tell Margaret I called." There was no response. "The old goat must have hung up on me," he said and shrugged.

Months passed before he received a brief note from Margaret. "We are well. Eleanor is outgrowing all of her clothes. Aunt Clara has been under the weather. Mother keeps asking when you will return home. I spoke with Erskin several days ago. Could you give him a call? He suggested we arrange to have a portion of your monthly check mailed to me. I would appreciate you assistance. Love, Margaret."

৵

Over the next months Mallory threw himself into his work. He closed the apartment and moved on base. It didn't matter. Most nights he slept on the office couch. He kept a fresh change of clothes in the bathroom closet along with his Navy uniform he never wore. Mallory was totally consumed with finding Heinrich Franz and getting the hell out of Germany.

Mallory and Price met frequently to plan strategy. Unlike Mallory, Price the self-proclaimed bachelor, loved Germany. He exploited the women and relished the ability to walk into IG Farben, flash an ID, and have the CEO at his backend call.

One afternoon, Prices' phone rang. "Jack, Erskin Young called a few hours ago. He's getting impatient with our search for Franz," said Mallory.

"We have several leads. I have a surprise for you. I think we have him. It was pure luck." Price said with a smile.

While paging through the CEO's personal journal, Price discovered a note scribbled in the margins: "Voucher: Liechtenauer to Franz." Franz was a common German name, but who was Liechtenauer? Price began the search. Price called the American archivist assigned to compiling an inventory of Farben documents. The young man responded immediately. Walther Liechtenauer was a former company director.

"How do I contact him?" Price asked.

The archivist laughed. "Easy. Try Spandau Prison." But, he wasn't in prison.

Walther Liechtenauer was tried for war crimes. There was an irony in the verdict. The judge sentenced Liechtenauer to five years in prison. He served less than two for a very good reason. Liechtenauer was the darling of the occupying Allied military. In particular he had unlimited access to the Americans. They viewed the former director as a liaison to top corporate management. In turn, Liechtenauer used every opportunity to ingratiate himself with US Army logistics sources. Behind the scenes, and at the direction of the financial giants meeting in Italy, Liechtenauer was piecing together a new cartel to replace IG Farben's subsidiaries now banned from operating in the Allied nations.

Walther Liechtenauer had never married. During the last days of World War II a boy wandered on to Liechtenauer's estate. The estate manager and his wife cared for the boy. The Russians occupied the estate killing the manager and kidnapping his wife. They burned the estate. The boy, Ansgar hid from the rampaging soldiers. A few days later he was found by an American patrol. They assumed he was related to Liechtenauer. Liechtenauer reluctantly agreed to be the Ansgar's guardian.

"How are Franz and Liechtenauer connected?" asked an impatient Mallory.

Price continued. "Seems Franz was on IG Farben's payroll. We've found records he worked with a research team at the Hermann Göring Institute. Franz was experimenting with a combination of hypnosis and drugs to improve Luftwaffe pilot-performance. But, get this."

"What?"

"Franz was also getting funding from two other sources, the Abwehr and Martin Bormann."

"Bormann?"

"IG Farben was supplying drugs to Hitler's personal physician. They were also shipping some crazy shit to Franz, both at the same address – Bormann's estate in Berchtesgaden."

"What the hell was Franz doing?"

"The archivist found two reports from Franz to Liechtenauer. He was experimenting with improving the behavior of children. Seems one was living on Bormann's estate. But the estate has been bombed and the other buildings dynamited. So that's out."

"And?"

"My guess is Franz is living some place near Liechtenauer's estate. I sent two team members to Liechtenauer's. The place was devastated except for a nearby cottage. Someone's been living there. Maybe two or even three people. They searched the place, but were careful not to leave any signs that anyone had been there."

"Let's get back there," insisted Mallory.

Price agreed but insisted they wait until he could assemble a larger detail to surround the parameter. "I have the place under surveillance. I'll know when Franz returns."

"If it is Franz," said Mallory.

Price and Mallory would later learn that just prior to going to prison Walther Liechtenauer entrusted his ward, Ansgar, to Heinrich Franz. Ansgar soon became the prize subject of Franz's new mind control study.

It didn't take long for the surveillance team to call in. "The cottage was occupied. There are three people, a man and two teenagers."

"I wonder what that bastard has in mind?" remarked one of the two men watching the cottage.

His partner shrugged.

Price and Mallory headed south. They arrived just as Franz and the teenagers were leaving with their suitcases.

Franz was taken into custody. "List him under a false name. I don't want Army intelligence getting wind of our success. He belongs to the joint taskforce. Not a word, not even the Navy."

Price took Franz to an unoccupied house in a severely damaged section of Frankfurt. The psychologist remained there for nearly two weeks. He was quiet and apparently unfazed by his imprisonment. As long as he remained silent he was not in danger. Several days into his interrogation Price met with Franz.

"It's useless."

"What?" asked Price.

"I'm not going to reveal any secret information. I have nothing to divulge. You think you are a master at getting people to talk. No. You are wrong. I am the master of the mind."

Price laughed. "We know of your work at the Göring Institute. What the hell were you doing with the drugs while staying on Bormann's estate?"

"Oh that was a simple favor I was doing for Bormann. Bormann denied he was footing the bill. The estate manager and his wife were caring for a very withdrawn child. The manager's wife didn't like the child, but she liked me." Franz snickered.

"Get on with your story," ordered Price.

"That's all I have to say."

The atmosphere changed immediately when Price announced Franz was headed back to the United States. Franz faced a number of charges. The most imperiling one was treason by directly aiding the enemy.

"The death penalty? Isn't that a bit much?" Franz coolly asked. "I'm much more useful to you alive and I suspect you have no intention of killing me."

"Don't be so sure," Price answered.

"You would have turned me over to the military police or one of the military intelligence agencies by now if I were going to be tried. Oh no. You have something else in mind."

"The Navy is interested in your work at the Göring Institute. However, my employer is fascinated with a research project they believe you initiated at Dachau," replied Price.

"In turn, I have two questions. Who is your employer? What project are you talking about?" asked Franz.

"My employer is the United States government. We want you and the research you conducted on the Monarch Project."

Franz laughed. "You aren't going to turn me over to the Nuremberg unit. Strange twist, isn't it? Of course I will return to the United States. I love my country. I love children. I will help you in any way I can." He laughed again. Franz's regained his confidence.

Mallory contacted Erskin Young with news of Franz's capture. Franz was going home. Price handled the logistics. Young didn't return the dispatch for several days. Mallory needed specific documents for Franz to be interned on a military reservation. Price and Mallory were surprised by Young's return dispatch. The orders included a document issued on official Department of Justice stationary and stamped "classified."

In return for his cooperation with the infant Operation Paperclip, Franz was promised a Presidential pardon. Franz's file would be expunged. He would be placed on the government payroll.

Neither man could believe what they were reading. Mallory examined the document several times. On the bottom of the page was a place for two signatures. Erskin Young's signature appeared over the DOJ endorsement. Mallory was instructed to sign and date the required signature on behalf of the Immigration and Naturalization Service.

"What the hell is this? I don't work for INS." He pointed to the blank line for his signature.

"Looks like you do now," Price said. He watched Mallory reluctantly sign the visa forms. This would be the first of more than one thousand endorsement certificates needed for a valid entry visa. Later these same documents would provide a path to US citizenship.

"Damn it, Price. Franz is a war criminal and a traitor. Are we so desperate?"

Price remained silent. He was amazed by Mallory's overt display of moral indignity. Then he said, "What the hell. Greater minds than mine are at work. Who knows what they intend to do with Franz and the others."

"The others?"

"Yes. I imagine we have seven hundred or more names of 'potentials'. We still have to sort them out. From where I stand, it looks like you will have plenty of documents to sign. One thing troubles me."

"What's that?"

"Are the documents you must sign legal? Is INS cooperating with us? And who the hell are we? You keep referring to Operation Paperclip. I don't know a damn thing about the overall task."

"You must be joking, Price. Our task? Find valuable Nazis scientists and clear them for entry into the US. You know that. What more do you need to know?"

"I guess you're right. Hear no evil. See no evil. Speak no evil. Just get the job done."

"Yes, but what happened to 'And the truth shall set you free?'"

With that, Mallory signed the documents. Two weeks later Heinrich Franz was at his new home, the US Army installation at Camp Upton on Long Island.

Chapter Thirty-Five
Frankfurt-Mannheim Airbase
Spring 1946

The winter of 1946 was marked by fuel and food shortages. Spring was slow to arrive in Frankfurt. A fifty-degree day was welcomed. Mallory appreciated the break in the weather. He took frequent long walks around the base. He thought often of Margaret and Eleanor, but his task dominated his being. Work on the passenger terminal continued. The Air Force occupied the south side of the huge installation. Each week, base activity and personnel increased. It was the center for arrivals and departures of US forces.

Mallory was satisfied with the pace of his mission. Price traveled throughout Germany validating his list of Nazis scientists. The base was bustling with various intelligence agents searching the catalog of Nazis registration cards.

The Nuremberg Tribunal that started in November of 1945 would continue through October 1946. Mallory and Price had to dodge Nuremberg investigators. Mallory knew the Russians suspected American intentions to scarf up prime Nazis. Stalin was infuriated by American refusal to share atom bomb technology. The French and British were uneasy too. American counterintelligence units suspected the Russians, French and British were on their own pursuits. Animosity was high. Tensions among the war allies increased.

After one of his long walks Mallory returned to his office. Stent was waiting with an urgent message.

"Sir. You're mother-in-law called a few minutes ago. She said it was an emergency."

Mallory looked at his wristwatch. "It's evening in the United States. I wonder what the emergency could be, Stent?"

"She didn't say, but she sounded frantic," Stent replied.

Mallory attempted to call, but the overseas circuits were busy. The exchange couldn't handle the traffic efficiently. He kept trying and finally, he got through.

"William, it is time for you to come home, before it's too late." Mrs. Collins was short of breath.

"What's wrong?"

"Margaret wants a divorce. Haven't you received the papers?"

"A divorce?"

"Yes. It's Erskin. He's living in Patchogue, not far from here. He's become a fixture around here. The two of them are out all night. I've become Eleanor's surrogate mother. I'm going crazy and Clara is no help. I'm ashamed of my daughter's behavior. Get home right away, if you want to save your marriage.

"I'll do my best Mrs. Collins."

❧

Flights to the states took days, sometimes weeks to arrange. Sergeant Stent cut a few corners and Mallory was on a flight via an overnight stop in Iceland.

After landing in New York, Mallory took the train to Huntington. He took a cab to the Collins' home, but stood outside for several minutes. Finally, he climbed the porch steps and rang the doorbell.

Clara opened the front door. She skipped the "welcome home" and small talk. "You're too late," was all she could say as Margaret came down the stairs.

"William, what are you doing here?"

"Your mother called. She said you wanted a divorce. I had no warning, nothing."

Margaret led Mallory into the living room. "William you're making this so hard," Margaret said. She sat on the edge of the couch. Mallory sat next do her. Margaret moved away. Mallory tried to touch the back of her hand. "Please don't do that," she said.

"We can work this out," he said.

"Seriously? I've only written once. You've sent dozens of letters. Most are unopened in that drawer." She pointed to a small table. "William, I don't deserve you," she said. Margaret's face was drawn. She struggled for words. "Don't you see? In the end I will hurt you. Let me have an amicable divorce. These things take time. They are complicated." Margaret looked away. "We have Eleanor to consider."

"I'll never stop loving you, Margaret. It doesn't have to end like this. Money isn't an issue. I'll resign tomorrow."

"But it must be this way." Margaret whispered. "Please William. You must leave. I was not expecting you. Erskin will be here any minute. I don't want a scene."

"This isn't you. It's the alcohol."

"That's your answer to everything, William. The alcohol."

Margaret got up and walked to the front window. "I thought I heard a car. Damn it. Erskin is here. William you are such a fool."

Mallory walked to the window and pulled the curtain aside. Erskin Young walked along the front sidewalk.

"I'll talk with Young," said an angry Mallory. He rushed onto the front porch.

"Well, William. I didn't expect you here, at least not so soon."

"You screwed me Erskin."

"No William. You screwed yourself. Actually, I'm doing you a favor." Young stepped back. He expected Mallory to start a brawl.

"You sent me to Germany to get me out of the country. You knew Margaret would be unhappy."

"You never should have married her. I tried to stop you. I'm doing you a favor. Margaret doesn't love you."

Mallory stepped forward about to grab Young. "Let's step outside and discuss this," said Mallory as he opened the front door.

"Listen to me," Young continued as both men stepped out onto the front porch. "I've known that since we were kids. Margaret doesn't love herself. How can she love anyone else? I can deal with her. You can't. Give it up, William."

"You son of a bitch," was all Mallory could muster. He felt betrayed by his wife and his friend. "Maybe you're right Erskin, but I will never forgive you." Mallory walked down the sidewalk. He stopped and looked back toward the house. Margaret was standing by the window. She closed the curtain.

"You'll thank me one day," said Young. "Give her a divorce and get on with it."

"And Eleanor?"

"I never wanted children. Still don't. I'm sure the attorneys will find in your favor. As far as I'm concerned, you can have full custody of Eleanor. She only reminds me of you."

❧

Mallory never stopped loving Margaret, but he accepted the futility of forcing her to love him. Several months passed before Mallory reluctantly agreed to the divorce with a provision for joint custody of Eleanor. He returned to Germany to finish the final details of Operation Paperclip. Jack Price eventually took charge of the European unit. At the same time another unique event took place.

In late spring of 1946, Price's childhood friend, Kurt Pokel, mysteriously appeared on the Justice Department payroll. His dossier was stamped top secret. Kurt Pokel moved into Mallory's headquarters on the airbase. Ingrid Pokel and their son, Jürgen, remained behind in Sarasota, Florida. Pokel arrived at a critical time. Renegade Nazis still roamed Germany, including Frankfurt. They intimidated German nationals and threatened Allied personnel. Price and Pokel carried concealed pistols to thwart any assassination attempts.

Tensions among the former World War II allies reached a point when the Soviets threatened to stop all access through the zone they controlled. These machinations overwhelmed Mallory for months to come. Then one morning over coffee he confided in Jack Price and Sargent Stent, "It's time for me to go home. I've had enough." Mallory was determined to leave Frankfurt and return Washington, DC. It took months for

Mallory's transfer to be approved. In February 1947 Mallory's uncontested divorce became final. Several weeks later Erskin Young married Margaret. The couple, along with Eleanor, moved to Centerport, a secluded community on Long Island's North Shore.

⁂

The circumstances surrounding Mallory's divorce wounded him. Just as he had done in Germany, Mallory threw himself into his work. Surrounded by hundreds of files Mallory found an excuse to isolate himself in a Department of Justice office. The sign on his door read "Records and Documentation – Access Restricted".

Amid the House Un-American Activities Committee's hearings rumors circulated about a secret government program to give Nazi war criminals sanctuary in the United States. Fear suppressed official inquiries into the validity of the rumors. The US needed to do everything necessary to combat international Communism and weed out traitors.

Mallory and Young were responsible for the newly arrived Nazis. The very nature of their work forced Mallory and Young to seek deeper cover and anonymity. Allegations the US government was sheltering Nazi war criminals were denied. Accusers were discredited. A dangerous atmosphere prevailed.

Mallory grew increasingly distant. He didn't trust people. He locked his feelings in a desk drawer: an inexpensive marble notebook titled "Volume Two". Mallory started the journal when he returned from the Flensburg mission. The journal was Mallory's connection with his humanity. He struggled to put the evolving events into perspective. The anger subsided but the bitterness remained.

Erskin Young returned to the shadows. From time to time their work required Young and Mallory to meet. Mallory was tasked with documentation and placement of Nazi recruits. The arrivals received a hospitable orientation and informal interrogation at several secret locations. Unlike the Nuremburg prisoners these detainees were allowed to mingle in a country club type atmosphere.

The assertive Young was promoted to taskforce coordinator. Young was especially interested in the Nazis research into mind control and behavior modification. The original Nazi project was called "Monarch". Initially the joint CIA-military umbrella research project was given the name MKULTRA. (1)

Without official sanction, Erskin Young formed a special research unit to investigate the effects of drugs on personality change. The research soon took a bizarre turn with a spin-off program named Operation Pied Piper.

Chapter Thirty-Six
Camp Upton, Long Island
1945-1946

Between the fall of 1945 and the winter of 1946 most German prisoners were repatriated to Germany.

In May 1945, Otto Bruns was transported from the U-853 to the New London submarine base. He was immediately flown to a small airstrip on Plum Island. On May 8, 1945 Bruns was confined at Camp Upton, Long Island and interned with other German prisoners. Bruns, the only civilian intern in the camp. By the summer of 1945, Otto Bruns was relocated to Fort Bliss, Texas, the designated assembly point for one hundred or more Nazi Scientists who accompanied rocket scientist Wernher von Braun. Even though Bruns had previously worked with the Peenemünde Team, he didn't seem to fit in.

One evening in January 1947, Erskin Young received a call from Colonel William Hawkins, the Army Intelligence liaison to the Department of Justice.

"I'm sorry to dump this in your lap Young, but your man, Bruns, has to go," said Hawkins.

"This is not a secured line Colonel. No names."

"I understand," Hawkins responded. He sounded put off.

"You've created a problem. I'm uncertain what direction to take," Young replied.

"I want him out of here. We are expanding our mission. A number of large corporations plan to locate research facilities near-by. Army Air Force research will be a vital part of the new US Air Force. We can't afford some reporter discovering we have an undocumented Nazi on board."

"I'd be careful with your housecleaning, Colonel. Bruns may

be undocumented but you have more than one Nazis recruit on your research team, Colonel," Young shot back.

"Young, you just told me this was an unsecured line," Hawkins scolded.

"I'm not getting into a pissing contest with you, Colonel. I'll telephone Justice. Hold tight."

"Forty-eight hours, Mr. Young."

"Then what?"

"I assure you, it won't be pleasant for your package or for you."

Young slammed the phone on its cradle.

Two days later on a dirt road near the air base, Otto Bruns became the unwelcomed responsibility of the United States Department of Justice. Bruns was a kidnapped German citizen detained in the United States. The DOJ faced a predicament. Bruns needed official documents.

On at least two occasions Erskin Young presented Bruns with the possibility of repatriation with financial assistance. Young even threatened deportation to South America. Bruns wouldn't budge. Bruns enjoyed a special advantage. His name did not appear on the Nuremberg Tribunal search list. He threatened to go public.

Authorities at the Immigration and Naturalization initially cooperated with Operation Paperclip. Erskin Young's team was now directing the program. As the number of Nazi scientists increased the INS bureaucrats became fearful their participation might be a violation of President Truman's executive order to screen applicants. INS officials refused to endorse Bruns. They wanted out of the loop.

Young created a sanitized dossier for the physicist including a fraudulent Social Security number and top-secret security clearances. The ball was now in Mallory's court.

"From my perspective it's time to phase-out Operation Paperclip. We've gone beyond the directive," Mallory protested.

"Fair enough, William. Find a way to cut Bruns loose. Until then Bruns is your asset," Young insisted. "There was one caveat. Army Intelligence considers one aspect of Bruns' work to be of value to the 101st Signal Battalion. They are fascinated in the potential of electromagnetism to disrupt communications."

"I've sketched a scheme for Bruns to transition to a classified research and development position." Several days later Mallory initiated his plan.

Bruns was taken to a safe house in Montauk on the tip of Long Island's south shore. Bruns along with two field agents lived in Montauk for several months. The agents were briefing specialists. Bruns needed a new identity. Initially he cooperated, but balked at two details. He insisted on keeping the alias Otto Bruns.

"You've assured me the name "Otto Bruns" is not on the Nuremberg list," Bruns argued.

"That could change," Mallory insisted.

"Well, I will keep the name Bruns. I suspect Young is the only one who my know my true identity." Bruns smiled.

"What else?" Mallory asked.

"I want your word you will continue to search for my family." Mallory cast his eyes at the ground.

"What's wrong?" demanded Bruns.

"We have no information about your family. I am being honest."

"Still, I want your word you and Young will continue the search."

Mallory reluctantly agreed. He suspected the rumor from Germany was true. Bruns' family could not be located. They were either dead or captured by the Russians. It was a predicament Young would have to handle. Mallory continued to make periodic visits. Each time Bruns demanded news of his family.

After a while Mallory simply turned his head and gestured "No news."

The agents worked with Bruns to alter his appearance. His hair was cropped short. He kept his beard neatly trimmed to camouflage an ugly facial scar. He was inclined to a simple wardrobe. His usual attire was a tweed sport coat, white shirt, kaki pants, and laced shoes. His one extravagance was a collection of bow ties Mallory purchased at Swezey and Newins, a department store in Patchogue. His tortoise shell glass frames appeared to overwhelm his face. Bruns never regained the nearly twenty-five pounds lost during his captivity and the transatlantic U-boat voyage. He suffered from aggravated colitis.

Toward the end of the Montauk episode Mallory directed the Paperclip team to compile a new government file for Bruns minus any specific references to the Nazi Party. By late spring 1947 Professor Otto Bruns returned to Camp Upton, the newly created Atomic Energy Commission research facility.

Bruns' work at Brookhaven National Laboratory focused on electrical systems that are especially sensitive to power surges. The magnets Bruns originally incorporated into his research proved inadequate. Nevertheless Bruns continued to work on the venture he called the "magnetic generator." Bruns was considered a key player in the development of what has come to be known as rare earth neodymium magnets or super magnets. Bruns continued to work at Brookhaven Laboratory until early 1970 when several newspaper articles raised concern about Nazis war criminals working in the United States. Then one morning he failed to report to work. Bruns vanished.

Otto Bruns first met Heinrich Franz, the behavioral psychologist, at the Göring Institute. Heinrich Franz was among the last of the Operation Paperclip newcomers. Building 33 was an upgraded barracks the two shared while new buildings were constructed for the infant Brookhaven National Laboratory. Bruns recalled Franz was the psychologist who worked with Alfred Fischer, the Luftwaffe aviator, at the Göring Institute. At first the two men were reluctant to discuss their current placements at Camp Upton. Nonetheless, as they began to trust each other the pair engaged in long private conversations. They had much in common. Franz had arrived in Germany via a U-Boat. Bruns' spoke briefly of his U-Boat experience. Eventually they realized they shared over-lapping research interests. Franz was intrigued by one of Bruns' work, the effect of electromagnetism on the brain and behavior.

"After all, electromagnetic forces influence atomic structure in any form," Bruns suggested. "Then why not the brain and in turn the entire human nervous system?"

"The concept isn't new," Franz replied.

"Agreed. However, my technique would be revolutionary, especially on children. Sound waves can be used to strike the brain without leaving any external bruises or loss of hair."

"You may have hit upon a brilliant idea, Bruns. We discovered direct electronic stimulation on certain parts of the brain seriously damaged tissue. Resonant cavitation may cause serious concussion. However, the brain of a child is so compliant."

"The child's mind is malleable," Franz replied.

Franz's eyes widened in recognition of an "aha" moment. It was a unique instant of discovery for both men.

"I worked with children in Germany to alter their behavior. Hypnosis. I sometimes used drugs. A pharmacist concocted a solution to cause amnesia in my patients. It worked with adults as well. There were other more punitive measures, too."

"And your experiment with the pilots?" Bruns asked.

"I employed similar but more stringent and invasive techniques with Luftwaffe pilots at the Göring Institute," Franz told Bruns.

"Fascinating," Bruns smiled. *Finally, a colleague who appreciates my value.*

Over the ensuing months Bruns and Franz developed a unique collegial relationship.

❦

In July 1951 Erskin Young telephoned Franz. He suggested a meeting to discuss a research project. Franz was unaware the CIA and Navy Intelligence were behind the scheme. "We need you to transfer your work from test pilots to prisoner interrogation," said Young.

"Now that's quite a leap," Franz replied.

"Not really. We know the Chinese and the North Koreans are using drugs, sleep deprivation and who knows what to interrogate American prisoners."

"Would you be interested in a contract with a research laboratory in Texas?" Young asked. "The salary is quite generous and we would provide a number of financial incentives."

"I may sound ungrateful, but I have no wish to move again. However, allow me to counter your offer," Franz answered. Franz elaborated on his conversations with Otto Bruns.

"I've put enough money together to move to Bay Grove."

"Why Long Island?" asked Young.

"My practice will focus on children with special needs. I sense Long Island and Bay Grove offer enormous opportunity."

"I feel certain you may maintain your practice," Young replied. He disliked bargaining with a man he considered a traitor.

Franz sensed Young's disdain. "And what is in it for me?"

"You could face a death sentence for treason," Young countered.

"I doubt it. Not now."

"What will it take?"

"A lot," Franz responded. "Let's begin with your promise of an executive pardon…a full pardon."

"I'll do my best."

"You'll manage. Tell me about your agency's new endeavors," said Franz.

"I'm not sure we are on the same page. What you call the agency was a war effort. We are operating in an entirely different arena."

"Your explanations tend to be convoluted, Mr. Young. Always so guarded. You talk like a spy." Franz simply smiled.

Young refused the psychologist's beguilement. To reveal one worked for the CIA was taboo. "Must there always be a simple answer? In this instance no answer is preferable for your safety and mine."

Franz frowned.

"All right. If it suits you refer to your work as Project MK Artichoke."

"My god, Young. Can't you come up with something a bit more colorful?"

Young scowled. "The letters 'MK' stand for our technical division. That's all you need to know. "Let's move on to business."

The ever-devious Franz withheld an important piece from Young. Franz learned his former patron, Dr. Walther Liechtenauer, was living in the United States. Dr. Liechtenauer was the Board Chairman and CEO for Trinity PharmoDynamics' US operations. In a letter to Liechtenauer, Franz outlined a proposal to study the effects of psychotropic drugs on children. Franz offered to share his work with Liechtenauer. Soon they began exchanging brief letters.

Liechtenauer wrote: "Your research proposal intrigues me. I can envision a number of opportunities for pediatric pharmaceuticals. I'm most fascinated with your proposal to alter the personalities of children. Is it possible these changes would have a long-term effect…say a carryover into their adult lives?"

Franz wrote back: "My previous research focused on short term effects. There was a wide range of behavior. Some subjects suffered from mild disorders while others were underscored by violent social behavior. I have a colleague who proposes the use of electromagnetism as opposed to electroshock therapy. In short, I can only speculate on the outcome."

A few weeks later Liechtenauer inquired about schizophrenia.

"Could Franz induce schizophrenia into a normal personality? If so, could the procedure be reversed?"

It was a peculiar question. Why schizophrenia? Liechtenauer's query changed the course of Franz's research. The depth of Liechtenauer's inquiry obsessed the psychologist. His first challenge would be to cause his subject to suffer a "mental breakdown". Franz's explanation went beyond a short-term or time-limited psychiatric disorder where the patient demonstrated an inability to function on a daily basis.

Franz responded a few months later. "I am struggling with a plan to mold a unique personality. I suspect my agency patrons will be pleased. Such hypocrites. They encourage my research but demand distance and the luxury of "denial". My main concern is the financial support. I feel certain it is possible to create a long-term disorder to encompass a disassociation between the subject's thoughts, emotions and behavior. Under such circumstances the subject would withdraw from reality and normal social interaction. "Could the process be reversed?" Franz answered his own question.

"I am like an instructor teaching a student to take off and fly, but not to land the plane. Only time will tell. Nevertheless I doubt a sociopathic personality can be reversed. The damage is done. The fantasy and delusion are too strong."

"Liechtenauer posed one final question. Would your subjects need a lifetime of after care?"

Franz never answered the question, thereby answering it.

Liechtenauer provided funds for Franz to establish a practice in Bay Grove. Franz never told either Young or Mallory of Trinity PharmoDynamics' involvement.

Franz insisted, "Bay Grove is an ideal location for a research study. I've spent days gathering demographics. I've established a credible rapport with influential community leaders including principals of three elementary schools. Bay Grove is ideal." Franz persuaded Young to be patient. I will gather my children, but first I have to assemble a staff."

"Why?" Young asked.

"I'll need assistants to do the foot work. There are teachers and families to be interviewed.

"Let me be clear. You're working on interrogation techniques with children?" asked Young.

"Not at all. I am working on what some call brainwashing. I refer to my work as 'brain changing'. In other words, I want to change the personality of these children. It's related to an unproven theory of "dissociative identity disorder."

"I don't know if your suggestion will fly with my superiors, especially since children are involved. Messing with kids' heads sounds creepy. Even worse, does it have to involve Otto Bruns? Between you and me Bruns might prove a problem. I can't go into it."

"Yes, Bruns is invaluable. It won't take him away from his work at the lab."

"Like I said, I'll present your idea to my superiors. I'll caution you. Bruns' last efficiency report noted he shows signs of depression."

"He's instrumental to my work," repeated Franz.

Young understood depression. His marriage was toxic. The CIA discouraged divorce. Only the pall of homophobia hung heavier over the agency. A discrete affair was tolerated. Margaret's alcoholism and risky sexual dalliances did not go unnoticed.

"One last question?" asked Franz.

"Shoot."

"Will I be working with you?"

"No. But I have someone in mind," Young said. A faint smile crossed his face. *William Mallory.*

"I'm still not comfortable promoting your project, Franz." Young had a habit of pacing a room when confronted with a difficult decision. Suddenly he stopped and said, "I'll be in touch. I caution you Franz. Not a word about our conversation with anyone."

Chapter Thirty-Seven
The Approval

It took Young several days to arrange a meeting in Washington. Finally he met with the Deputy Director for Scientific Research – Central Intelligence Agency, Gary Owens.

"Have you read this report?" asked Owens.

"Of course," said Young.

"This fellow, Franz, is creepy. A bit insane. I haven't completed the entire jacket, but can you imagine the potential his work gives us during interrogations."

Young laughed.

"What's so funny?"

"Sir, Franz's tests are unethical. His research subjects will be unsuspecting children and their families. I suspect Franz violated all aspects of decent human conduct and morality on his victims in Germany. The proposal you're holding may violate the new Nuremberg Code."

"And?"

"With all respect Sir, Franz's prior work may have created a bunch of walking time bombs."

"I'm sure Franz is exaggerating," said Owens.

"His work was primarily conducted on prisoners. Read his conclusions. Franz asserts he could bend a subject's mind. He can turn the docile into an enraged killer."

"It's all this mumbo-jumbo, Young." Owens handed the file to Young. "Now read the part about spiritualists."

Young read the last paragraph.

"Read it aloud, man. I want to hear it again to make sense of it all," demanded Owens.

Young read: *My recent studies support a capability to create an iatrogenic dissociative identity I can produce a personality as a spiritualist conjures the dead. Such a latent and enduring psychiatric disorder may be called upon through the application of a stimulus or triggered phrase. I successfully programmed four subjects to kill innocent victims. The whispered phrase "blue dawn" was just such a trigger. Franz's subjects killed without a memory of the event. I am certain such triggers when expertly implanted could also be activated visually in photographs or imbedded into letters.*

"Sounds like a goddamned religious cult to me," Owens said. "A bunch of science fiction. Let me put the question out there. Can we use Franz to our advantage?"

"Perhaps. According to our sources Franz trained German test pilots to fly under near-suicidal circumstances. He has an extensive research background with psychotropic drugs."

"What the hell are psychotropic drugs?"

"Franz called them mind control drugs," Young responded. "I have no doubt we need a cover story for this kind of work. We can't afford some reporter catching wind of this operation."

"Get to it then. I'm a little suspicious of the relationship between Franz and Otto Bruns. Franz is too insistent on Bruns' participation. You don't suspect Franz is a queer, do you? I won't tolerate a faggot.

The question caught Young by surprise. "No Sir."

"The agency is under enough scrutiny by Congressional oversight committees. One day it's commies. The next it's Nazis. It's like living under a magnifying glass. This is supposed to be a secret organization. Under no circumstances can Franz be traced to the company. Is that understood?"

Young nodded in agreement. "We can funnel the funding through several university accounts. Naturally, they'll want something in return," said Young.

"They always do. Do whatever it takes, but don't let it blow back on us."

It didn't take long for Young to get back to Franz. Magically, Franz received a grant to study the effects of behavioral-cognitive techniques on elementary school children.

"Who will be funding my research?" Franz asked.

"Does it matter?" Young asked.

Franz didn't respond.

"From now on we will refer to your research as Operation Pied Piper. Your contact will be William Mallory." (2)

"Ah, yes. The same Mallory who worked with Price in Germany?"

"None other. Now he's nearby. He'll contact you," said Young

ॐ

William Mallory's clandestine office was relocated to the second floor of the United States Department of Justice on Chambers Street. Not that Mallory needed an office. For the past months there was little for him to do. Unopened letters accumulated on a small table next to the mail drop slot in the office door. Once a week he a requested a temp from the secretarial pool to sorted the correspondence. He tossed most of it in the trash. The rest was shredded.

"Excuse me, Mr. Mallory," the temp said nervously. Mallory had earned a reputation among the women in the typing pool. "The guy is a grump." They all agreed.

"What?" asked Mallory. He turned his swivel chair to face the young woman. "A courier left this envelope." She handed it to Mallory and returned to her work. For a moment Mallory forgot the packet and focused on the temps' rhythmic motion. Her dress was tight and accentuated an athletic figure. His mind drifted back to the first time he made love with Margaret. The temp must have felt his stare. She briefly turned her head then sheepishly smiled. Mallory grinned, too. Then he opened the envelope.

Mallory was surprised.

"Meet me at Smith and Wollensky's. Use the Grill entrance, not the restaurant. You'll find it crowded, and loud. It's ideal for our meeting. We'll both be forced to behave like gentlemen." The note was unsigned, but clearly from Erskin Young. Mallory's nemesis had once again entered in his life.

Now what? The bitter feelings Mallory suppressed for many years flooded his mind and body. Mallory accepted the new assignment and transfer from Washington to the DOJ's

Manhattan office to get out from under Young. *I don't want to deal with the guy. Our conversation will drift from business to places I don't want to go.* Denial had its compensation. *I don't want to know about my ex-wife. I close my eyes and see her screwing Young.*

At noon the following day William Mallory reluctantly entered the Grille. The obedient soldier was led up a rise opposite the bar. He scanned the room for his archrival.

"Mr. Young phoned a few minutes ago," said the maître d.

Just like Young. His way of showing he is the boss.

Mallory felt uneasy. Young was right. The Grille was crowded and noisy. *I've been cloistered in my office too long. Not a woman in the joint.* Men wearing blue and grey suits, Manhattan's business uniform, elbowed into tight spaces between bar stools. *Standing room only.* Martini glasses littered the bar. *Lawyers and stockbrokers unofficially quit work at noon on Friday.*

Mallory ordered coffee, black. He watched the entrance. Finally Young arrived. Young slowly approached the table as though he, too, was reluctant to have this meeting. His grey suit and leather attaché case blended well with the other patrons. Mallory could tell that something was wrong.

Young's youthful athletic features had vanished. Young extended his hand to offer a greeting. Mallory declined.

"No handshake for an old friend, William?"

"Sit down, Erskin. We work for the same employer. We aren't friends."

Young slid his leather attaché case next to his chair.

Mallory was about to make a foolishly rehearsed comment when the waiter stopped at their table.

"I'll have a Martini, straight up, and a tall water with lemon. No rush. We'll be here a while," Young told the waiter.

"My god, Erskin. You look awful. What are you doing to yourself?"

"Thank you, William."

The waiter returned with Young's water and Martini with two olives. He lifted his glass. "First of the day," Young said sipping the elixir. "A pick-me-up." He ate one olive then gazed into the glass. He swirled the remaining olive. He appeared deep in thought.

Mallory withheld empathy. Erskin was a master of deceit. Finally he said, "You look awful. What's happened to you?"

Young ran his finger over his balding scalp. Dark rings under his eyes betrayed sleepless nights. "What's happened? Where should I begin?" Young tightened his jaw.

"Please don't go there, Erskin. We aren't here to talk about Margaret. And don't bring Eleanor into the conversation."

"You asked the question, old boy. I'll answer it."

Mallory signaled to the waiter and pointed to his empty coffee cup.

"Have you ever loved an alcoholic? I do." Young's Martini splashed from the glass. His hand trembled. He ground his teeth.

"From where I sit you could be talking about either you or your wife."

"I admire you, William. You look fit and still have a full head of hair." Young calmed himself enough to sip his drink. A year ago I began asking myself 'What do I call a drunk?' I keep getting the same answer. I call her 'someone I love.'"

"Goddamn you, Mallory. I've put myself in a fine fix. I've inherited what should have been yours."

Mallory suppressed a bitter comment.

The waiter returned. "Ready to order?"

"Not yet, but bring the gentleman another round," said Mallory.

Young's sunken eyes reminded Mallory of the weary distant look of German prisoners he interviewed. They longed for their families and a life they could never reclaim.

The waiter returned. He placed the frosted glass on the table. Young swallowed the last drops of gin.

"Get to the point, Erskin. What's going on?"

"It's Margaret. She's driving me insane. And now this Pied Piper thing."

"Pied Piper?"

"We'll get to it." Young was distressed.

"I can't believe what I'm hearing. Aren't you the one who told me to get tough? You warned me 'We're living in a new era.'"

"You're right. I need to freshen-up." Young excused himself

and walked to the men's room. He splashed water on his face. *I look awful. Get hold of yourself.*

A few minutes passed before Young returned. "Now let's start over," said Mallory.

Young cleared his throat. His voice revealed a hesitation. "Margaret is out of control. If it wasn't for Margaret's mother your daughter would be a mess."

"Don't go there. It's been too long...I wouldn't recognize Eleanor."

"I never wanted children. Not in our line of work. Eleanor came with the marriage. You never exercised your visitation rights. Why?"

Mallory eyes focused on his coffee cup. "Too painful. I figure Eleanor will remind me of your betrayal." Mallory felt an uncertain revulsion. "Can't you get Margaret to a doctor or a sanatorium? You have the money."

"Money isn't the issue. She refuses help. Margaret is killing herself. I try to talk with her when she's sober. She uses me as an excuse for drinking. The cops brought her home a few times. She has blackouts." Then Young dropped the bomb.

"She's whoring it up and it's getting close to home. The Deputy Director cautioned me several months ago. He suggested I have her committed. My god, William, I love the woman."

Mallory understood the implications. *The Agency is sensitive to embarrassing liaisons. Blackmail turned more than one employee into a double agent.*

"And you? Tell me you aren't sleeping around. You're a womanizer," Mallory replied with satisfaction.

"I realize Margaret would never totally love me, but I thought we could have a degree of affection. At times there was lust, but no intimacy."

Young looked away. "She loves you, if she is capable of loving anyone."

"What about your affairs?" Mallory demanded.

"Please, William. Keep your voice down. I have my needs, too. When Margaret rejected me, I turned to someone else."

"Just one?"

"Yes. Having a mistress took the pressure off my marriage. The fighting subsided. From my point of view Margaret is easier to live with when she's drunk. I'm telling you, she's going to kill herself."

"I'm sorry for you, Erskin. Better get yourself some help. Eleanor is the one I'm worried about."

Young's complexion turned pale, clammy and drawn. He finished his drink and gestured for another. "Slow down, man. We haven't talked business."

"Yes, but one last thing."

Mallory fidgeted a spoon against the coffee cup saucer. "What is it?"

"Beth Collins is ailing. I'm afraid the day is coming when Beth won't be able to look after Eleanor. She'll need to be placed in a boarding school."

Mallory drew a long breath. He measured his words. "When the time comes we'll talk about it. Now let's get on with the business at hand."

Young appeared stung by Mallory's remark. "Yes of course." Young reached for his attaché case and removed a large brown envelope. "This is for you." He pushed the packet along the table edge. It was stamped "classified."

"Open it," Young said.

Mallory removed the contents. A business envelope was paper clipped to the file.

"The receipt is inside the envelope. Sign it. Give me the receipt."

Mallory browsed the file's contents and signed the receipt.

"You have the original document. The only copy."

"Isn't this quite unusual?" asked Mallory.

"You'll understand once you've read the material. Lock the file in your office safe. I have the combination."

Mallory looked shocked. *The son of a bitch has been prowling my office.*

"The project is beginning to snowball. I need you to be on top of it before it gets out of control."

"Did I glimpse Heinrich Franz's name on the jacket?"

"You did. And your friend Otto Bruns is involved. Marginally, but he deserves surveillance."

"Project Pied Piper? How do you boys come up with these operational names?"

"Never mind," said Young. "I don't have time for your sarcasm."

Mallory slid the folder into the envelope. "Let me guess. Franz is working with test pilots once again."

"Far from it," said Young. He looked stern. "Our resident psychologist is working with children."

"Children?"

Young turned his head back and forth as though a spy might be near. "Mad science," Young whispered. His left hand cupped his mouth.

"Erskin put your hand down. Who the hell could be listening? Now tell me again."

"Mad science," Young repeated. "Franz calls it brain change. Elementary school kids, seven of them, I think."

"You think? So it's a hand-off to me. Erskin, you can't be serious. We're talking about children. Do their parents know? We'll need consent."

"Study the folder. It's a proposal. Franz has the details. Make sure you are on top of it. Franz is weird."

"Why get involved?" Mallory asked.

Then Young outright lied. "I don't know the details," but of course, he did.

"I'm tasked with convincing a number of reputable universities to cooperate. Listen to me William. Pied Piper is part of a far-reaching enterprise the Agency calls MKULTRA. The situation could change in an instant. Franz is your responsibility now."

"What are you getting me into, Erskin?" Mallory clenched both sides of the table.

Young abruptly pushed away from the table, and reached for his attaché case. He looked down at Mallory. "I'll skip lunch. I feel a bit unsettled. Enjoy your lunch, William. I'll tell the maître d to charge it to my tab."

It would be months before the two men would meet again.

Chapter Thirty-Eight
December 1951

The Dunns were the last family to be interviewed by Heinrich Franz. He drove passed the Dunns' home earlier in the day. He hoped to catch a glimpse of Andrew at play, but to no avail. Andrew's file reflected a brilliant student with deep psychological problems. From Franz's perspective, Andrew was a prized subject, perhaps the second most valuable child for his study.

The Dunns' home on Brigantine Street was a simple cottage style dwelling, a reflection of its occupants' journey through life, conservative, traditional, unpretentious. The interior was simply decorated with the exception of Mrs. Dunn's chachkas. Doris Dunn assured Andrew each piece represented a family memory, which she never revealed. Appearance and propriety were the underpinnings of their generation. In those days family secrets were closely guarded. Family dysfunction was a key element in Franz's research.

It was an unusually cold, damp, December day in Bay Grove. Third grader, Andrew Dunn, spent most of the day on the living room rug reading and tinkering with random pieces of an Erector set.

"What do you have there?" asked Uncle Fred

"It's a crane. I need to find a few more nuts and bolts." The precocious inventor turned the box upside down spilling the remaining pieces between his legs. Andrew never paused even while answering Fred's question.

"Andrew. Look at me. Andrew!"

Andrew sensed Uncle Fred was annoyed. He gave Fred a quick glance then continued to thread a piece of string through the top of his invention.

Fred really wasn't Andrew's uncle. He was a retired seaman who lived with the Dunns ever since Andrew could remember.

Uncle Fred was a lodger in Nellie Brady's home. Nellie was Doris Dunn's grandmother. Doris' mother died during a diphtheria epidemic. Doris was dispatched to her grandmother's chicken farm on rural Long Island. Uncle Fred was a tenant, nothing more, nothing less. Nellie died two years after Doris married Ken. Fred had nowhere to go. Ken invited Fred to live with them.

Fred was a godsend. Ken Dunn never asked Fred for a penny, but Fred pitched in to pay for the food. Fred was the neighborhood handyman. He painted and accepted any odd job to supplement his meager pension. Fred's specialty was lawn mowing. Neighbors laughed watching young Andrew run after Fred as he steered his riding mower on route to a neighbor's yard. Andrew adored Uncle Fred.

Ken and Doris Dunn both worked. Ken's retail business failed in early 1951. Now he worked three part-time jobs. He was rarely at home. Money was tight. The country was on the verge of a recession. Doris worked six days a week for a small legal firm in Sayville. She left home early in the morning and returned around six. The retired seaman was Andrew's surrogate parent and understood the boy better than his parents.

Fred proved to be a blessing in other ways. He served as Andrew's protector on those occasions when Doris was overcome by her demons.

Uncle Fred and Andrew shared an attic bedroom heated by a floor register cut through the kitchen ceiling. There were times when Andrew was home alone. The moaning of a winter wind or summer thunderstorm frightened the boy. He feared the house was haunted. Uncle Fred assured Andrew there were no apparitions. Nevertheless, as young children often do, Andrew saw what he believed.

Uncle Fred often asked himself, *Has Andrew inherited his mother's demons?*

Over the years, Fred watched Doris grow into a beautiful and intelligent, young woman, marry and begin to raise a family.

The commitments of married life were a burden for Doris. With each year, Doris' demons grew. Her mood-swings intensified. Her feelings of loneliness and depression overshadowed her marriage. Ken dealt with Doris' behavior by absenting himself from their home. Eventually, Fred and Andrew were her sole companions.

Sometime in the late 1980's psychologists began to categorize bipolar disorder. Uncle Fred wasn't a psychologist, but he grew increasingly concerned for the young woman he had come to love as the daughter he never had.

Uncle Fred knew the most intense time of the day for Doris and the family was when she returned home from work. He anxiously watched Doris enter the house. Something peculiar always happened and he knew what to expect – the unexpected. There were days when Doris raged and flew into a fury.

"Why are these dishes in the sink? I work all day only to come home and face dirty coffee cups," she screamed. Fred never knew what would trigger Doris' "episodes."

As Doris's illness slowly worsened, her episodes became more frequent and severe. The cycles were shorter. At times Doris spoke in disjointed sentences. A glass of wine seemed to help settle her. She came to believe kosher red wine possessed mystical medicinal properties. Manhattans and whiskey sours worked, too.

Fred tried to comfort Doris, but to no avail. By Christmas 1951 the cycles between Doris' bursts of mania and depression were longer in duration.

The arguments between Ken and Doris increased as her untreated illness intensified.

"I'm doing the best that I can," she would scream at Ken. "You're always gone."

"Listen. You act crazy. I don't want a divorce. I want peace and quite."

"I struggled to suppress my demons at work. It's exhausting," she confessed to Fred. Uncle Fred feared for Doris. *Sometimes she seems suicidal. I'm so afraid she will hurt herself.*

Fred feared for his precious Andrew. Doris' rages increased, but the violence was yet to come. In time it was young Andrew who bore the brunt of his mother's illness. No mater how hard he tried, Uncle Fred's interventions failed.

One night after an argument Ken threw a glass across the room. "I'm sick of this place," he shouted. "I'm getting out of here before I do something stupid."

Andrew ran after him. "Please Dad, don't go. I'm scared," he pleaded. He struggled to hold on to his father's leg.

"Go back inside kid. Everything will be all right."

"No. Don't go," he cried looking up at his father.

Ken bent over and lifted Andrew into the air. "Hey, it's going to be fine. Now get inside." He turned Andrew toward the back door and watched him go inside. Once again Ken abandoned his son to a hysterical and potentially dangerous wife and mother, an innocent in her own right.

Doris viewed the exchange between father and son from the bedroom window. When Andrew returned to the kitchen, Doris began to scream and strike out.

"Your father is evil," Doris screeched as Andrew ran upstairs. She hurried to the dining room sideboard and opened a drawer. Hidden among the table cloths were photographs and letters.

"Here, read these. I'm not crazy!" she howled. Doris tossed the papers into the air. They scattered and fell on the stairs. Andrew peeked down at his tormented mother. Exhausted and unhinged Doris collapsed. She clawed her face. Her nails drew blood. She shrieked, "Why?" Suddenly, Doris' face contorted and from deep within his mother's twisted body came the rumble of an androgynous horrifying voice. *"I am what you will be."*

Confused and terrified, the six-year-old ran to the safety of his hideout beneath the eaves.

⁓

Andrew's third grade teacher, Miss Parker, was troubled by his drawings and short writing assignments. Miss Parker recognized a reality beyond a boy's vivid imagination.

"Andrew's stories are stunning and sometimes dark," she told Principal Carter.

"His test scores are exceptional," Carter added.

The district superintendent asked Principal Carter to compile a list of twelve exceptional children. Private funds were available for a pilot program for seven children.

"I will add Andrew's name. No guarantees. I must limit the selection to six," Carter assured Miss Parker.

"Didn't you say there would be seven children?" Miss Parker timidly asked as to not offend Carter.

"I did say seven children. We select six. I have no idea why only six."

"Perhaps the seventh child has already been selected," Miss Parker added.

"This is a wonderful opportunity of our children and our school, Mrs. Parker. The children will benefit. I'm told there will be various enrichment experiences. There families will receive a small stipend. Most of all, Andrew and some of the others will receive emotional help."

"Lord knows Andrew needs support," replied Miss Parker. She shook her head in disbelief. *How could such awful conditions exist among families in Bay Grove?*

Principal Carter was troubled by an emerging problem among children in his school.

"We have so many men without work. Bay Grove has no industry. Unemployment is increasing. Eisenhower promises to end the war in Korea once he becomes President. Closing our defense plants will increase unemployment. I've heard orders at the Lace Mill have dwindled. So many of our veterans are disillusioned."

Too many veterans suffered from prolonged fighting and untreated stress. Alcoholism and spousal abuse seemed to increase. Young children were left unattended during the day while parents worked.

"These are tough times for Bay Grove. I'm happy a few kids will benefit from an enrichment program. I only wish there could be more," Carter said. He added Andrew Dunn to the list of potencional candidates. Several days later he made his final selections.

Carter reviewed the list. He placed Andrew's file in the top drawer of his filing cabinet with the records of the other five finalists. Principal Carter did not realize he had just altered the course of six lives.

∾

Heinrich Franz and his associate intern, Linda Wilson discussed the upcoming interview as they drove along Brigantine Street in Bay Grove. It began to snow.

"The Dunns are our final interview. I want to complete the selection process and get on with our work by mid January."

"You still haven't met with the entire staff. I think it is important we all know the full extent of the study," Linda Wilson said. She was a bright doctoral candidate at Columbia. She was Franz's intern, but he was suspicious of her intuitive depth, her inquisitive mind.

"We've been over this before. Once I've selected the children I will meet with staff. A few points need to be fine-tuned. Let's leave it at that," he insisted.

Wilson looked out the side window. *Franz doesn't like to be questioned. I sense he feels I'm challenging his authority.* This was the final part of her doctoral thesis. She had too much time and borrowed money invested in her career. She needed to begin repaying her parents and the bank. *Graduate and move on. Don't screw up now.*

It was just before suppertime. Ken Dunn paced the kitchen of his Cleveland Street home. The kitchen was the busiest room in the house. On most evenings Ken sat at the oval table reading his paper while Doris scurried between the stove and table. Her usual assuring smile was distinctly absent this evening. Andrew sensed his mother was troubled. Fred took his usual place and sipped coffee from his cherished chipped mug, a retirement gift from his former employer. Ken, the conservative and Fred, the liberal usually debated some inane issues, but not this evening.

"Andrew."

"Yes, Dad."

"Head upstairs and put on your school clothes."

"But Dad, it is Christmas vacation. I didn't wear school clothes today.

"Well, figure it out, then get down here. "We have two visitors coming after supper," Ken shouted as Andrew bounded up the stairs to his attic room.

"We are eating early tonight." Doris added.

"I don't understand why you made the appointment right at our dinner time," Doris scolded. "Everything is in a dither."

Dinner wasn't quite finished when the front door bell rang. While Ken answered the door, Doris hurriedly cleared the dishes. "Ken, I need some help," she said.

"Where's Andrew?" Ken asked.

"He's upstairs with Uncle Fred.

The attic room, as always, was cold. A floor register cut in the kitchen ceiling heated upstairs. From his vantage point, Andrew peeked through the floor register's checkered vents at the family below. He watched as his father ushered two into the kitchen. His mother took their coats. Coffee boiled on the stove.

"I apologize about the mess," said Doris. "I work until five. We just finished eating."

"Your home is lovely, Mrs. Dunn. I feel we are the intruders. Franz turned toward his assistant. "This is Miss Wilson." Linda Wilson smiled. "Miss Wilson will be assisting me with the children in our study.

Ken pointed to the kitchen chairs and invited the pair to sit down. Franz did all the talking. Miss Wilson placed her clipboard on the table and prepared to take notes.

"Andrew, get down here," called Ken.

Andrew bounded down the stairs to find his parents intently listening to Doctor Franz. He knew better than to interrupt when an adult was speaking.

"This is a consent form," said Franz. "You are giving permission for Andrew to participate in our enrichment program. It is a routine document. Nothing serious. I will leave you a copy along with a short survey. Take your time. Here is a stamped envelope."

"Come over here, Andrew. I want you to meet Dr. Franz and his assistant, Miss Wilson." Andrew smiled.

"Miss Wilson and I hope to be meeting with your parents and you, Andrew, on a regular basis," said Franz. "Allow me to tell you about out very special 'enrichment' program," Franz continued. He described the plan in vague terms.

The Dunns listened patiently. They never asked for details nor did they question Franz's professional qualifications. After all, Franz was a doctor.

"Take a seat, Andrew," said Ken. Andrew sat on the edge of his chair. He fidgeted.

"Sit still, Andrew," Ken said.

It took nearly two hours for Franz and Miss Wilson to complete the interview.

While Franz met with the Dunn's in the kitchen, Linda Wilson and Andrew moved to the dining room table.

"Let's play a game, Andrew." She placed two photographs on the table in front of the boy.

"Here is the game. I want you to draw each of the pictures as neatly and carefully as you can before the sand in the upper part of this timer runs out."

"On your mark. Get set. Go." Andrew had five minutes.

"Stop. Very nice, Andrew. You are a talented boy."

Andrew smiled. He liked Linda Wilson. He sensed Miss Wilson could be trusted. Miss Wilson brought Andrew's drawings to Franz. They were nearly perfect in perspective and detail.

"Excellent," said Franz.

Franz retrieved a coupon from his briefcase and handed it to Ken.

"Mail this coupon to the address on top of the page. In about two weeks you will receive several boxes containing an encyclopedia and dictionary. There will be a binder, also. It will be the family's first set of guidelines for helping Andrew prepare for college."

Franz smiled and said, "This is a family project. We are all in this together. Several other families will be joining us. It will be a wonderful opportunity. Trust me. We are going to become a special group, a family."

For a moment Ken thought he saw a quizzical expression cross Linda Wilson's face. He let it pass.

Doris was elated. "We are excited to begin."

"We will contact you. I'm certain Andrew will play an outstanding role in our program. His teacher and principal are so enthused. But, I have one concern," said Dr. Franz.

"What's that?" asked Doris.

"Andrew's success depends on you and Ken. We need your full cooperation and participation. Otherwise we are wasting your time and ours."

"You'll have it," said Ken.

"This program is bound to assure Andrew will get into college. Maybe he'll get a scholarship."

"Ken smiled. He shook hands with Dr. Franz and bid goodnight to Miss Wilson. Doris returned to the task at hand, the pile of unwashed dishes in the sink.

"That's it?" Doris asked.

"I guess." Ken shrugged.

Just before bedtime Andrew asked, "Dad, what kind of a doctor is he?"

"Why Andrew, he's a regular doctor. He just works with kids like you."

"Dad, what's a consent form?"

"Dr. Franz has our permission to help you get good grades."

"Dr. Franz gave us a bunch of papers to read. Once the box of books arrives, Dr. Franz will meet with you on Thursday afternoons and all of us will meet one Saturday each month. Now, that does sound too difficult. Does it? You're a lucky boy Andrew," Ken said.

"Why, Dad?"

"I want you to have opportunities your mother and I never had. College Andrew. I want you to go to college. Maybe you'll be a teacher or a doctor. Maybe a lawyer. But you have to go to college. That's what these classes are all about." "Doctor Franz assured me these enrichment classes are going to be exciting for you. They are bound to help you do well in school."

"But I'm doing pretty good now, Dad"

"*Well*, Andrew. Pretty *well*, son. Not *good*. And you *are* doing *well*, I agree," Ken said with a pride of knowing the difference between well and good. "Just imagine how much better you will do with Dr. Franz's help."

"I'd really like to be a policeman or a soldier, Dad," Andrew said.

"He's a third grader, Ken. Andrew doesn't have the slightest idea what you are talking about," Doris insisted.

"It's all right Mom. Maybe I'll be a principal like Mr. Carter."

"Maybe you will, son," she agreed.

Upstairs in the attic bedroom, Uncle Fred slid his chair away from the floor register. He didn't like what he overheard.

Chapter Thirty-Nine
The Introductions

Mallory drove from Manhattan on January 21, 1952. He regretted the drive. The previous evening he had gone to the movies alone something he still felt uncomfortable doing. The film, "Blondie Goes To College," with Penny Singleton was a relief from reading Heinrich Franz's research proposal. He needed to break away from the repetitive obsession with Project Pied Piper.

Mallory preferred riding the Long Island Rail Road to Patchogue. Today was different. He didn't want to take a taxi to Bay Grove. *Taxi drivers ask too many questions.*

"Keep your distance from Franz and his project," Young warned. "We don't want blowback. This project is volatile."

It was a clear morning with the promise of temperatures in the low forties. Traffic was heavy as he approached the merge on to the Southern State Parkway. After reading the Pied Piper file a number of times, Mallory was puzzled. *Why children? Have the parents been informed? Have parents given consent to the research?* He was more than concerned. His initial reaction was to call Young. Instead, he decided to wait. He wanted to observe Franz and his colleagues working with the children. He needed to be convinced this wasn't a carry-over of a mindless concentration camp experiment.

As usual, the children arrived at Franz's Bay Grove clinic for their Saturday program. Their parents arrived later in the morning. The parent session opened with an informal coffee and cake social gathering. Linda Wilson joined the parents as a prelude to Franz's appearance.

"Good morning, everyone," said Franz. "Before you head off to your sessions I want to introduce the latest and last family to join us." Franz turned and acknowledged Mr. and Mrs. Stone, Stephen and Virginia. Mr. Stone nodded and said hello. Mrs. Stone followed suit. But, neither smiled nor frowned. Even to a casual observer, the Stones appeared a bit aloof, different from the other parents. Unlike the others, Stephen and Virginia Stone resided in nearby Patchogue. Their daughter, Katherine, was a year older than the other children.

Franz continued, "Katherine is a gifted girl. We welcome the Stones to our program."

"One of the children, Ray Wood, turned to another and said, "Guess we know who the 'brown nose' is."

Several of the parents were concerned, too.

"I've read something about Mr. Stone in the *Advance*, not long ago," Ken Dunn whispered to Doris. "I think he's in the export business. Something about the Lace Mill."

"I've heard the Lace Mill might be closing," Doris answered.

By the end of the morning word spread among the parents that Stone held a controlling interest in the Lace Mill, which of course, wasn't true.

Franz mingled with the parents for a few minutes and departed with the Stones. Miss Wilson turned their attention to a schedule she had written on a blackboard.

Mallory arrived at the clinic several minutes later. The marble floor and richly paneled waiting area was empty. The parents were actively involved in their conference. Mallory entered the main clinic. It appeared to be divided into three wings. To his left were a series of rooms each with a windowed observation door. The sound of children's laughter drew Mallory down the corridor. He stood, unnoticed, watching an odd scene. Four boys and two girls hilariously laughed.

Mallory watched the clown's antics. *My god! It's Franz.*

Sure enough the bubbly magical clown was Heinrich Franz. Franz's face was covered with meticulously applied grease paint. No circus clown could have looked more professional. He watched Franz's antics for a minute or two. But, Mallory was puzzled. *There should be seven children. One of the boys is absent. I wonder where he is.* Mallory turned and walked down the long hallway. Had Mallory remained he would have seen Franz' favorite performance.

Franz had seated the children in a special order. Katherine Stone sat at the head of the group. Andrew Dunn sat next to Katherine 's right. Mary Taylor, the least animated of the children sat to Katherine 's left.

Ray Wood, Ed Jablonski, and Bill Hess sat in a semi-circle behind the others. One at a time, Franz called each child to the front of the room. Andrew Dunn was the first to go. Franz removed a penny whistle from his bag of tricks. Franz played a high-pitched tone on the whistle. Andrew came to attention.

"Sit down, Andrew." Andrew sat in the upholstered chair. His legs didn't touch the ground. Franz was about to demonstrate the power of hypnosis.

"Andrew when you hear the whistle you will be a cowboy. When the whistle sounds again you will stand up and climb on your pony and circle the room. Then you will return to the chair." Andrew appeared to be sleeping when Franz blew the whistle. On cue, Andrew left the chair and galloped around the room on his imaginary pony. He appeared to be unaware of his classmates. Back on the chair, Andrew's head and body slumped a bit.

"Now, Andrew, I will count from one to ten. On ten you will wake up feeling refreshed with no memory of the last few minutes."

Franz counted then snapped his fingers. Andrew's eyes opened. He jumped out of the chair. The weeks of prior conditioning had paid off. The high pitch tone was the trigger. Andrew responded exactly as Franz had predicted. The children shouted with delight.

"Very nice, Andrew. Who would like to be next?"

"Me. Me. Me," came the cries of the excited group.

Franz paused. This was his theater. His stage.

"Ah, Katherine. Yes of course. Come on up." What ever suspicions the other children had that Katherine Grace Stone were confirmed. Katherine was Franz's favorite. At some point Ray Wood, the group's deadpan wiseass, mumbled "Katherine

Grace. Sounds more like K.G. should stand for 'cagey.'"

Franz heard Ray's comment. He walked to Ray's side and whispered. "You will be punished Raymond." The other children pretended not to pay attention. Nevertheless Katherine's disparaging nickname – "Cagey" - stuck.

While Franz entertained the six children, Mallory wandered into a wing of the building marked "restricted." Mallory walked a few yards down this corridor where he discovered a room with a large window. Mallory could view the room's interior.

Mallory was startled. *What's going on?*

A boy lay on what appeared to be a surgical table. He was partially covered with a blanket. Two restraints held him to the table. Several intravenous lines were inserted into his left arm. A man dressed in a long while lab coat placed a helmet on the boy's head. The helmet resembled a diver's hardhat. Two aides, a man and a woman assisted the man. The man monitored a blood pressure cuff. The woman checked the IV lines. On the nearside of the table was a rolling cart with a large device. Mallory could see the man in the lab coat turning dials.

It can't be. What is Otto Bruns doing here?

At that moment Bruns moved a lever on the side of the box. The clinic's lights dimmed for an instant.

The boy's body quaked. Two tight restraints held him to the table. One aide placed a stethoscope and monitored the youngster's heart rhythm and breathing. The aide nodded and a second dose of what appeared to be electroshock was applied. The lights dimmed again, but this time a bit longer. The boy's body shuddered.

Mallory pushed opened the door and rushed into the lab. "Stop this immediately!"

A startled and confused Bruns turned.

"What are you doing here, Mallory? Get out. You will do more damage than you can imagine. The treatment must be completed."

"Treatment? You are shocking this kid. He could die. You're mad. Are you doing this to all the children?" Mallory and Bruns went face to face.

"Nonsense. The helmet is noninvasive. It regulates the magnetic field flux concentrated in a given area. I control the flux density. The medications I administer assure the boy feels no pain and guarantees total amnesia. Now out! Leave here immediately. I will talk with you when I am finished here."

Bruns' two frightened and confused aides hovered in a corner.

"Harm the boy? Get out of here now, Mallory. You have jeopardized this child's health."

Mallory glanced at the aides and then the boy. Mallory was furious, slowly backed out of the room. He didn't want to harm the boy. "I'll be waiting for you Bruns."

I have to speak with Franz. Bruns has to be stopped. Mallory rushed to find Franz.

The children's parents were leaving the facility. A few remained in the lobby. Mallory passed among them unnoticed. When Mallory returned to Franz's classroom he found the children sitting motionless in their seats. *They seem to be in a trance.* No longer dressed in his clown costume, Franz passed among the children. The Pied Piper stopped in front of the blonde-haired girl. Franz touched the blonde-haired girl on the top of her head with his index finger. Her eyes opened. She stretched, yawned and rubbed her eyes as though emerging from a night's sleep. Franz continued until each of the children responded.

Mallory removed an envelope from his suit jacket. He unfolded the list of family and children's names he had copied the previous night. He checked the list. Mallory was certain the girl identified as Katherine Stone was SS-1-3128, Edith, the child from the U-853. *Why wasn't I informed?* Katherine 's true identity was known to a select few, the new keepers of the secret. *Why didn't Young inform me, the child was part of this research project? Erskin withheld Katherine 's identity to protect the Agency, not me. He intends to provide them a degree of deniability. In the end I am expendable.*

Until the ill-fated Saturday, Mallory was unaware of Pied Piper's details. Otto Brun's experiments on the boy were outrageous. Mallory did not suspect that a sleep-inducing agent had been concealed in the cookies and milk at snack time. The children were thirsty rats in Franz's human experiment.

Mallory glanced at his watch. Mallory realized he needed to return to the clinic's lab. *I must talk with Bruns. I've got to get to the bottom of this research project.*

He rushed back, but the room was empty. He was about to leave when Otto Bruns entered.

"I told you I would meet you after the session was complete. Weren't you briefed on the nature of our work?"

"I read Franz' initial proposal. There was not mention of your work. This is craziness, Bruns. Do the boy's parents know what you are doing?" Mallory demanded.

"Which boys?"

"Are you telling me you have performed procedures on all the boys? The girls, too?"

"The boy in this morning's procedure is Walter Katz. And yes. Mrs. Katz knows. All the parents have signed consent forms. Walter's parents are divorced. She is enthused about my work. Granted, she hasn't seen the procedure," said Bruns.

"Why Katz? Why separate him from the others?" Mallory asked.

"The boy suffers from a malady that makes him appear emotionally and intellectually impaired. On the contrary, he is extremely gifted. His intelligence borders on genius. His potential in mathematics is limitless. I will cure his illness. I will be his patron."

"You are living an illusion, Bruns."

"Does Franz know you are here?"

"He was told I would be observing the project today. I arrived late."

"I am anxious to see his reaction when I tell him how you behaved. He will be furious."

"I am the project supervisor," Mallory responded.

"Not for long, Mallory. Once Franz speaks with your superiors, you'll be removed."

Mallory felt Franz had the upper hand. As for Bruns, the tables had turned since the days on the U-853.

Mallory sneered at Bruns. "We'll see."

Mallory returned to the main lobby. The children were in line. Linda Wilson escorted them to the waiting van. Mallory waited for her to return.

"My name is William Mallory. I am the project supervisor."

"I'm Linda Wilson. I wasn't aware. Dr. Franz didn't inform me. How may I help you, Mr. Mallory?"

"You're Dr. Franz's assistant. I've read your personnel file."

"Yes, I work with the parents."

"Is there some place we might talk in private? Perhaps a nearby restaurant."

"I'm perplexed, Mr. Mallory. Let me get this straight. You want me to meet with you to discuss our research? Without Dr. Franz being present?"

"Yes. It is quite important."

"No. That isn't possible." Wilson started to leave.

Mallory handed Linda Wilson his card. "This is my telephone number. Please call if you change your mind. Again, it's important," said Mallory.

Franz arrived as Wilson and Mallory were ending their conversation. "Mallory, may I speak with you privately?"

The two men walked to the rear of the reception room.

"I just finished speaking with Bruns," said Franz. "You had no business getting involved with his procedure. You've agitated him. He is a sensitive man and vital to this project." With that Franz turned and walked over to Linda Wilson.

Franz trembled with anger. "Stay away from Mr. Mallory. He's a troublemaker. We don't need him meddling in our work."

"I have no plan to meet with Mr. Mallory without your permission, Dr. Franz. However, I am concerned about our work with the children. Why is it necessary for us to be administering sodium pentothal and other medications to these children? We have not informed their parents. What would happen if one of the children becomes ill or worse?"

"Your responsibility is to work with the parents. I will take care of the medical implications."

"Our research is all-consuming. Early on you said we would be increasing our staff."

"I'm afraid that won't be possible for the present moment. Let's proceed one step at a time."

Otto Bruns waited in the hallway. Once he saw Mallory leave the building, Bruns approached Franz. Linda Wilson returned to her office.

"And how did it go with Mallory? Who will deal with him?" Bruns asked.

"Mallory is my responsibility," said Franz.

"Don't under estimate the man," Bruns' voice resonated a fearfulness he experienced on board the U-853. "I know…"

Franz raised his hand. "Enough! Are you insane, Bruns? Never mention the U-853 again. And I warn you, Linda Wilson knows nothing of the U-853 episode."

"I apologize."

"Our research is federally sponsored. It is ethical. We have nothing to fear from Mr. William Mallory. I'll telephone Erskin Young."

❧

Mallory had anticipated heavy traffic for his return trip to Manhattan and was stop and go all the way. Mallory was troubled by his experience at the Bay Grove Children's Clinic. He turned on the radio. He needed a distraction. He felt outrage and shame. He encountered these feelings before. His mind flashed back to his reunion with Erskin Young on the bluffs overlooking the Long Island Sound. Young was so casual about the deaths of the OSS agents in Copenhagen. *Young is turning into a monster.*

How much longer can I tolerate watching Otto Bruns torture young Katz and the others. What will become of the children when this program ends? Who am I to judge? National defense outweighs the lives of a few children. Mallory's anxiety increased as he tried to rationalize what he had just experienced.

He looked at himself in the rear-view mirror. *I played a role in bringing nuts like Franz here. They may be geniuses and maybe our national defense may depend on them, but I*

257

don't like what's happening.

Mallory recalled Erskin Young's admonishment. "We are in a new kind of war, William. The rules, the standards, have changed. What you call abhorrent is necessary for our nation's survival. You always have a choice. Stay or go. But you can't erase the past. Your so-called conscience is your worst enemy."

Mallory was in turmoil. *Can I support an operation that exploits these innocent assets?*

Mallory's hands perspired. He rubbed his palms along the creases of his pants. He grasped the steering wheel tighter than before as though his grip controlled a daunting conscience.

Suddenly, he tasted the bitter rush of stomach bile rise into his mouth. He drove onto the shoulder of the road, opened the door, turned sideways in time to avoid vomiting on the inside door panel. The scene was repeated, again. Mallory pulled a handkerchief from his rear pocket and wiped his mouth. His eyes burned. His nostrils flared from the wretched stench.

He pushed himself up and closed the door.

Am I becoming one of them? My god, I am.

Mallory loosened his tie. He took long, deep breaths. After a few minutes he drove away.

Chapter Forty
Apprehensions

Mallory telephoned Erskin Young at home on Sunday morning.

"William, is this an emergency?" asked young, when he picked up.

"I'm afraid it is," Mallory said. "We need to meet. I'm troubled by what I saw at the clinic yesterday."

"More pangs of conscience, William?"

Young's sarcasm annoyed Mallory. "This is too sensitive to discuss over the phone."

"Tomorrow morning, 11 o'clock. Meet me at the Museum of Natural History, the gift shop. I'll mix among the crowd. I have a two o'clock so let's meet around noon. There's something else. I should have told you sooner."

"I received a call. Margaret's health has deteriorated. She's still drinking."

"I don't want to talk about her," Mallory shot back. "Tomorrow's meeting is all business. Agreed?"

"Agreed," said Young reluctantly and hung up. He stretched on the bed.

"What was that all about?" asked Young's current conquest as she lit her first cigarette of the day. She paid no attention to the sound of a tumbler of whiskey crashing on the floor as she reached for an ashtray.

"Put that thing out and roll over here," barked Young.

"You sleep. I'm going to my place." She carefully stepped around the broken glass and walked to the bathroom. The morning light accentuated her naked figure.

She showered and dressed. The foul odor of tobacco smoke

permeated her dress from the prior evening's antics. She opened the bedroom door and looked back at Young and sneered.

He laughed.

She left Young's apartment and hurriedly walked to the elevator. Her husband's train was due at Penn Station in a few hours.

Young wanted to stop her, but he didn't. A hung over and tired Erskin Young was preoccupied. He suspected Mallory now surmised the potential illegal aspects of Pied Piper. *Not good for our line of work.* William Mallory, his one time friend, had become a personal and professional quandary. Young's dilemma would be amplified as Mallory became aware of the big picture.

✧

As usual Mallory was first to arrive at the Museum. He paid the cab driver and climbed the steps into the grand lobby. The gift shop was crowded. Mallory walked to the bookshelves and browsed the Egyptology section. A tap on the shoulder caught Mallory by surprise. Young was uncharacteristically on time.

"I'll meet you in the back of the cafeteria. Take your time," said Young. He turned and headed for the staircase. The cafeteria was on the lower level directly across from the subway entrance. Mallory waited until Young disappeared in the bustling crowd of teachers and school children then he headed downstairs. Young already had had a cup of coffee in hand and sat in the far corner of the cafeteria. Young spread the *Times* on the table. Mallory paid for his coffee and worked his way among the visitors.

Young looked up from the paper and said, "Now, what's so important?"

"No beating around the bush with you, Erskin."

"I'm concerned for you, William. I caught an uneasy urgency in your voice. Another attack of conscience?"

"I visited Franz's clinic. I briefly observed Franz and Bruns at work with the children. It's dangerous business, Erskin."

"What's dangerous?"

"The research. You must have some idea what's going on."

"A bit. I'm really not interested in the specifics."

"I spoke with Franz's assistant. She's a doctoral candidate at Columbia. Nice kid, but in way over her head."

"You didn't frighten her did you?" asked Young. "The last thing we need is a panicked graduate student. This project is classified."

"I'm not certain. I know she'll go running back to Franz," Mallory said.

"What possessed you to talk with her?"

"I needed an insider. I watched Bruns experimenting with a young boy."

"His project is authorized," Young insisted.

"Erskin, I know you have no love for children, but you don't hate them."

"Hate them? No. Indifferent? Perhaps. I've told you, we have a job to do."

The conversation turned somber when Mallory said, "I'll finish my commitment to Pied Piper, but I need you to be honest, for once."

"About what?"

"For starters, one of the children, a young girl Katherine Stone. How did Franz come to select the Stone Family?" Mallory asked.

"Ask Franz. He's your responsibility."

"For god's sake Erskin, why is Katherine Stone in this study? It was never part of any agreement. Can you imagine the controversy if Stone's real identity is revealed? We guaranteed Admiral Dönitz anonymity."

"Perhaps you did, William. SS-1-3128 was your negotiation, not mine."

"Who else knows?" Mallory demanded.

"Calm down, William. Franz knows, naturally. It was his idea to bring her on board. Bruns knew. He was on the U-boat with you. Remember?"

"This isn't a time for sarcasm. You know damn well what

could happen if the project goes sour. You already assured the Congressional Intelligence Oversight Committee our task force has no connection with Nazis."

"Denial, William. Who would believe you provided safe passage to a mad scientist and a Lebensborn child? It's too fantastic. Don't even go there." Young frowned. "Are you thinking about bailing out…leaving the project?"

"I will carry through with my commitment. Then I deserve a transfer."

"Any preference?"

"Back to Washington. There's still work to be done with Operation Paperclip."

"I'll see what I can arrange. Be careful, William. The combined Agency task force is investing a lot of money and personnel into MKULTRA. Leaving your current assignment will take finesse. You can't just walk away."

"You sound ominous."

"Be realistic. There's no easy way out. You know too much."

"I haven't betrayed any secrets."

"And the Agency will be sure you won't. You'll be constantly looking over your shoulder. You have your daughter to consider."

"The wouldn't harm Eleanor."

Young didn't respond. His silence underscored the answer. Mallory returned to the service bar to refill his coffee cup. Two children ran behind him. They were hiding from their classmates.

"Oops. I'm sorry," he said. He was thankful coffee didn't spill on the errant girls. They ran to their friends. One had light red hair and appeared to be the same age as Mallory's daughter. Mallory looked back at the sullen-faced Young. *Young's right. I have to find another way out of this mess. They won't let me walk away.* They'll make an example of Eleanor. He returned to the table and said, "So Erskin, what would you do if you were in my position?"

"I'm not, but there's something else."

Mallory was wary.

"Mrs. Collins died over the weekend. She was Eleanor's gatekeeper," said Young.

"Why didn't you tell me yesterday?"

"I found out early this morning."

"How is Margaret taking it?"

"How else…on the rocks with a splash of water," said Young. He looked despondent.

Margaret continued to reside in the Centerport home she owned with Young. They had never legally divorced. "Uncle Rick," Margaret's latest boyfriend moved in several weeks after they met. Rick was a freelance writer and photographer with a scarce cash flow. Margaret's inheritance and Young's support payments kept their heads above water. Without her grandmother's care, Eleanor's life would be chaotic.

"Eleanor needs structure," Young said.

"I thought you didn't like kids," Mallory replied.

"I don't, but I'm not all bad."

Mallory's smile revealed he didn't agree with Young.

"I'll be in Canada for several months. You'll have to get involved," Young insisted.

"I'm afraid it's too late."

"I have an idea. You remain with the Pied Piper project on Long Island. Meet with Margaret. Convince her Eleanor needs a boarding school. I'll work with the Deputy Director. I'll tell her you need more time to be with your daughter. I'll suggest the Paperclip records restoration project in Washington."

"What?" responded a puzzled Mallory.

"Operation Paperclip accumulated thousand of files. They need to be reviewed, sanitized and archived. A boring job, but it's a possibility."

"Who is in charge? Right now you have no need to know."

"Sure," replied Mallory.

"Why the sudden change?"

"It's not for you, William. We both want to help Margaret."

The following weekend Mallory drove to Centerport. The once-elegant waterfront home appeared neglected. The lawn needed mowing. Several newspapers were scattered on the front lawn. Mallory rang the doorbell. He waited several minutes before the door opened. A face covered with shaving cream peered at Mallory.

"What's up?" he asked.

Mallory was taken aback. *This guy could pass for my younger brother.* "I'm Mallory."

"I'm Rick. Come in." Rick was wearing a pair of boxer shorts. "Just got out of the shower. You're early"

"Margaret, get your ass down here. Your 'ex' is here," Rick shouted. He winked and whispered, "Tough broad."

"I'm coming," came the reply from the second floor balcony.

Mallory looked up. He didn't see Margaret, but there, peeking through the rail balusters was Eleanor.

"Good morning, William," Margaret called from the top of the winding staircase.

Mallory gave a casual wave and smiled. Margaret slowly, carefully, maneuvered the stairs. She wore a silk blue dressing gown. As she reached the bottom step Mallory was shocked. Margaret was gaunt. Dark circles underscored her yellowed eyes. Her beautiful long hair had lost its luster.

Margaret greeted Mallory. "Oh don't look so woeful. You caught me off guard. You said you would be arriving this afternoon."

"It's after one, Margaret."

Margaret raised a trembling hand as though to brush away Mallory's comment.

Rick awkwardly backed away and headed upstairs without a word.

"Rick's a writer. We attend lots of social engagements. He needs contacts. He must find work. We're just about broke."

"How have you been," Mallory asked. He struggled for something to say.

"I'm sure Erskin has filled you in. I'm ill, William. I dread the thought of Rick dumping me. Alcohol does this, you know."

"It doesn't have to be this way."

Margaret turned and walked into the library. She looked out the window. "Ah, but it does. Too late, I'm afraid. Hepatitis. They can't remove the infection. Early stage cirrhosis." There was a tone of acceptance in her voice.

"And Eleanor?"

"Eleanor come down here and greet your father."

Eleanor didn't respond.

"Eleanor, damn it, get down here."

"Was that necessary? Are you provoking me Margaret? I've done nothing wrong."

"Always the gentleman. Always trying to fix me. Where the hell have you been for the last ten years?"

"You locked me out of your life," Mallory whispered. "Please don't upset Eleanor."

"And now what are you proposing?"

"I am sorry to learn of your mother's death. I was surprised. No funeral service?"

"No."

"Hey. You'd get a lot more from the child if you'd be a bit more gentle," called Rick from the top of the stair. He urged Eleanor to go to her mother.

Eleanor slowly moved toward her mother. "I'm sorry I yelled," said Margaret.

Eleanor clung to safety of her mother's dressing gown.

"Give your father a hug."

Eleanor stiffened, then turned and ran back upstairs.

"Let her go," said Mallory. "One day at a time."

"There isn't much time."

"Does Rick understand your circumstances?"

"Of course he does. I'm surprised he is still here. He'll take me to a party and pretend nothing is wrong. I'll sit in the corner sipping a Martini. I have to admit the sex was good while it lasted."

A pained expression crossed Mallory's face. An uncomfortable silence filled the room. They looked at each other for several minutes.

"Oh, don't look so doleful. Get on with your admonishment," Margaret said.

Malory fixed on Margaret's eyes. "Do you have a will?"

"No. Look around. Do I need one? I've sold father's paintings. I barely had enough to purchase the cemetery plot. The rest belongs to Erskin. You have joint custody of Eleanor. What else is there?"

"I've located a boarding school near Manassas, Virginia. I own a small farm on Linton Hall Road. A neighbor looks after it. There's a girls' boarding school a few miles away. It's run by a Catholic order."

"You know I despise Catholics. She'll grow up to be a bad girl. All those rules and guilt." Margaret sneered.

"Be reasonable. Please. We have few alternatives."

Rick entered the room. "Hey you two. I hate to interrupt, but Margaret has to finish dressing. We have a social engagement."

"That's Rick's cue. You have to leave, now. I'll think about the school."

Chapter Forty-One
Forebodings

Margaret died several months later. Rick remained with her until the end.

"Margaret didn't want you to see her at the end," Rick told Mallory. "I honored her request. Please don't be offended. I don't believe Margaret was trying to punish you. It was her way."

Mallory confessed, "I'm angry. I never had a chance to say good bye."

Erskin Young was despondent. "I started out loving her. I ended up hating her. And now I'm just numb. I couldn't wait until she died. Late at night I would gaze into a tumbler of Scotch and imagine Margaret's casket being lowered into the ground."

"I'm sorry, Young," said Rick.

Young's passion for Margaret was his greatest weakness. He despised himself for it. He would never put himself in such a position again.

Young left for Canada two weeks later to recruit two respected psychologists at a prominent university.

Mallory's initial request for a transfer to DC was denied. Nevertheless he enrolled Eleanor at the Chestnut School in Manassas. He commuted to Manassas several times a month. Mother Superior requested a conference.

"Your daughter is bewildered by the loss of her mother and grandmother. She is very fragile. Sister Kathryn comforts her."

"She is safe here."

"How long will Eleanor be with us?"

"I'm uncertain. There is no alternative. I'll do my best."

∾

Erskin Young did everything possible to deny grief. His work was all consuming. He neglected the Pied Piper project. That was Mallory's responsibility. He knew Mallory's transfer request was denied. It didn't matter. From Young's perspective Operation Pied Piper was an insignificant study.

"We need you to remain with Pied Piper, William."

Young rubbed his chin for an instant and said, "I'm now supervising a number of MKULTRA research projects.

"William, you won't believe the discretionary funds I control." Young smiled. *Neither ethics nor morality get in the way of institutional funding. Money. It's all about the money. Eventually the powerful commercial interests will want a piece of MKULTRA'S research findings.*

Unbeknownst to Erskin Young or Mallory, Pied Piper was a growing priority for Walther Liechtenauer, the chief director of Trinity PharmoDynamics. Dr. Liechtenauer was a survivor with a keen ability to recognize political trends.

"The United States is in turmoil," he told his superiors at a Lake Como meeting of the powerful Circle of Twelve. Truman's popularity is at a new low. Only twenty-two per cent of the people think he's doing a good job. There's a growing frenzy in Congress."

"What do you propose Walther?" asked one of the Twelve.

"I suggest we take advantage of several opportunities. First, we purchase a number of licensed pharmaceutical companies, small ones. One step at a time we pursue friends in regulatory agencies. I'm certain with the right leverage I will be able to establish Trinity PharmoDynamics into a pivotal position."

"Exactly what is the goal, Walther?"

"I'm very interested in the long-range profits from pharmaceuticals. Several agencies within the US intelligence community are experimenting with mind altering psychotropic drugs. The program is called MKULTRA. We have an excellent opportunity to form an alliance within the government."

"Are you sure about this?" asked another member.

Liechtenauer smiled. "Yes. I have a particular interest in one of MKULATR's research studies called Pied Piper. I believe we have come across an important investment. Right now a secret US task force provides the funding. It won't last. Once the government funding ends, Trinity will be in a position to transition the research to our laboratory facilities here in the US rather than Argentina. Our friends in key government positions will be useful in acquiring patents."

"Well done, Walther. One caution – the Circle of Twelve must not be implicated."

"I understand." Liechtenauer closed his folder, pushed away from the huge conference table and left the room. *Trinity PharmoDynamics, USA was now a reality.*

Dr. Liechtenauer respected and feared the Circle's power. There were more than twelve financial giants involved. Even Liechtenauer did not know their identities. He suspected they created and controlled the Davos arrangement, the World Bank, and the Federal Reserve System. He felt certain the Circle of Twelve controlled the most powerful financial institution on earth. So powerful its name was only whispered, the Bank of International Settlements.

Dr. Liechtenauer patiently collaborated with Heinrich Franz. Liechtenauer envisioned the research held great potential. He wanted to exploit the clinical research. Liechtenauer arranged for several thousand dollars to be deposited in Franz' personal bank account in Patchogue. In return, Liechtenauer requested a series of experiments involving the children.

Specifically, Trinity's staff concocted several sodium "A" and "P" drug formulas. Trinity's preliminary experiments with adult subjects indicated memories could be altered. Researchers theorized an individual's personality and behavior could be sculpted and controlled, if new memories could be instilled during early childhood development. Pied Piper's children were the first test subjects.

❧

Mallory arrived in Sayville on the eleven o'clock train. It was raining. He stepped from under the station's canopy for a moment. Linda Wilson was late. Perhaps she wouldn't show. Mallory was confounded by her call. A Chevrolet sedan pulled in front of the platform. Mallory recognized Wilson.

"Good morning," Mallory said. He tossed his soaked fedora on the rear seat. "This is a surprise."

"I apologize for the messy car. A graduate student has little time or money to spend."

Mallory ignored her remark. "Thanks for meeting me Miss Wilson. I know you are taking a risk."

"I'm amazed myself. Hopefully, no one will recognize us."

"There's always the possibility. We can stop now. I will understand."

"No. I need to talk with you."

"There's a diner on Main Street. The place will be crowded. I'll go in first. Once I have a booth I'll wave from the entrance."

A few minutes later they were seated in the rear of the diner.

"I'm bothered by your inquiry the other day. Am I involved in something illegal?"

"Tell me your concerns, Miss Wilson."

"It's Linda. All right. First, I feel as though I am betraying Dr. Franz's confidence by meeting you."

"In a way you are. You might jeopardize your work at Columbia. I read you are nearly finished with your dissertation."

"Is there anything about me you don't know?" she asked.

Mallory smiled. "Go on, Linda. I will not report this meeting to my superiors."

"My knowledge of the research project is confined to my work with the parents. The children come from difficult situations. You missed the opening session at our last Saturday meeting. On the surface the families appear what most people would call normal. Sadly, alcoholism, spousal abuse, unemployment, mental illness permeate the children's lives."

"There seems to be a profile," said Mallory.

Linda nodded agreement. "I informed Dr. Franz you approached me about our work. Dr. Franz became agitated by the mention of your name."

"What did Franz say?"

"He didn't pursue it. Did you know Franz is not a licensed physician or physiatrist?" Linda inquired.

"What does that have to do with it?"

"The drugs. Franz is administering drugs to the children. We have an inventory. Many of the bottles are numerically coded," she noted.

"Any ampules?"

"No, just liquids and pills." Linda looked directly at Mallory with intensity. "Mr. Mallory, you observed Franz with the six children. I knew he used hypnosis. I suspect he is using drugs to control the children."

"I watched Franz end the session by touching each child on the top of the head."

"Why did he do that?"

"It's a trigger. Franz strives to control their post-hypnotic behavior using a series of prompts, a shrill tone, a word, and a touch. We call them triggers. They stimulate preconditioned response."

"Will the subject be under Franz's control?" asked Mallory.

"It's not that simple. At first we believed an individual could not be directed to perform an act in opposition to the subject's moral convictions. Assault, perhaps murder or suicide seemed to be out of the question. I suspect Franz is attempting to change the children's overt behavior to coincide with their latent subconscious."

"Are you suggesting some form of behavior or mind change? I don't follow you, Linda."

"Imagine if Franz is successful in changing personality. The longer he works with the children the deeper into their subconscious he will delve."

"And?"

"Don't you see? Years from now when they are adults Franz or someone with knowledge of the specific triggers might be able to control the children's behavior."

"My god! Potential ticking time bombs," gasped Mallory.

"The implications are serious. Each child is identified by different personality traits. Until recently Franz explored their behaviors using non-invasive techniques including hypnotism. The children leave each session with vague recollections but no specific memories. The three boys have become disruptive at times. Their narcissistic traits disturb me."

"Did you discuss their behavior with Franz?"

Linda hesitated. Mallory's grim look was foreboding. "Yes. At the next session, Dr. Franz mixed several milligrams of an experimental drug into the three boy's orange juice."

"What do you mean an experimental drug?" Mallory asked.

"Dr. Franz receives a substantial grant from a pharmaceutical company. Didn't you know that?"

"There's no record of any pharmaceutical company participating in the research. Are you certain?"

"Yes. Franz told me the medication is an anti-depressant. He said the pharmaceutical company planned to seek a patent to market the drug."

"Are the three boys' parents aware?"

"I've interviewed their families. I never asked them, if they knew their children were receiving medications." Linda paused. "No, they are not aware. Although, they did sign consent forms giving Franz a wide latitude."

"And the other children?"

"We treat each child individually, Linda said. For example, Andrew Dunn is passive. He trusts Franz beyond question. I'm not sure about Mary Taylor. Walter Katz rarely attends group sessions. Bruns asserts Walter is not ready."

"What do you know about Katherine Stone and her family?" Mallory asked.

"You raise an interesting point. I never met the Stones until a few days before Katherine entered the program. The Stones seem austere. Katherine is bright and charming. Still, there is something unusual about the girl. Franz completed the Stone intake interview. I never read his notes. He keeps the files in a locked cabinet. I had an odd feeling when Franz introduced me to Stones. Franz is secretive when it comes to the Stones,"

"Odd feeling?"

"Yes. I sensed they had a prior connection."

"And the girl?"

"Yes, Katherine, also. Does that interest you?"

Mallory didn't respond. *Of course it interests me. Linda is highly intuitive. Her insight could prove to be a liability for her. The Agency has too much invested in Pied Piper to risk exposure.*

"Listen to me very carefully, Linda. Do not share you suspicions with anyone. Not your family or your closest friend. Above all, do not confront Franz. You could be in grave danger."

"Why would anyone want to harm me?"

"Please take my warning seriously. I can't tell you more."

"What will happen to Walter Katz?"

"I don't know."

"Bruns protects the child as though he was his son. The boy suffers from mood swings and depression. Walter is exceptionally bright. After your last visit, I met Mrs. Katz at the clinic. She subsequently signed a complex consent form. Mrs. Katz trusts Bruns," said Linda.

The waitress interrupted their conversation. "Excuse me. I don't mean to be impolite, but you have been here quite a while. You haven't ordered. It's lunchtime. Folks want the booth."

"I'll have a coffee, black," said Linda.

"Same," Mallory agreed.

"That's it?"

"Don't worry, we'll be ordering. It's a business meeting," Mallory said.

The waitress returned with two mugs and the coffee.

"Thanks," Mallory said. Clearly agitated, she walked away in a huff.

Mallory continued. "Could we return to our discussion about the drugs?"

"Sure. I told you I haven't seen invoices. The labels are coded."

"Linda, I think you're withholding something. What is it?"

"Franz left the dispensary cabinet unlocked. Taped to the back of the door was a list of the corresponding codes. He is always very cautious, but not this time."

Linda reached into her purse and removed a folded sheet of

paper. She started to hand Mallory the paper.

"Wait. Don't give that to me."

"Why?"

"Even though Franz has government support for his research, he may be breaking the law. In turn, all of us connected with the research could face criminal charges. It's a two edged sword. If we reveal illegal drugs to the authorities we could be charged with violating the secrets act. We signed non-disclosure agreements."

"I'm confused," said Linda.

"Linda, you are part of a shadow operation directed by an invisible agency. My superiors shield themselves. They are just as culpable as Franz, perhaps more. Your salary is funneled through a myriad of bank accounts. This is how the world works."

Linda glanced at the paper and placed it on the table. "I have to go. I'm due at the Clinic for a staff meeting. You've been very informative Mr. Mallory."

Mallory rose and said, "For your sake find a plausible way to get out of this project." *Linda Wilson's attempt to appear nonchalant isn't working. I know she's bright enough to realize the consequences of telling Franz about our meeting. Her hands are shaking.* Mallory reached out to shake her hand. "Be careful, Linda."

She tilted her head to one side, smiled and replied, "And you as well. Don't forget the list."

Mallory had made a professional blunder. At times during their meeting, he had used her first name. Mallory had dropped his guard and personalized the conversation. *Last names only for business interactions. First names are for other intentions.*

Mallory watched Linda walk to her car. He returned to the booth and ordered a second cup of coffee. "Anything else, honey?" the waitress sarcastically asked.

"A refill." Mallory pointed to the empty cup.

Mallory reluctantly read Linda Wilson's list. The first drug was scopolamine. Franz used it in small doses to induce drowsiness in the children. Franz discovered it produced amnesia, also. The risk of addiction was low. Mallory's OSS training familiarized him with scopolamine, a main ingredient in a favored poison, belladonna. Mallory recognized several of the other drugs. He didn't recognize the last drug, lysergic acid diethylamide. He faintly pronounced the name several times – lysergic acid diethylamide. The tongue twister had a diabolical ring to it.

Mallory finished his coffee. He read the list one last time. Mallory tore the paper into small pieces. He walked to the cashier and paid his bill. Then he carefully discarded some of the pieces into a small garbage can behind the counter. The remaining pieces he placed in his jacket pocket.

The mid-afternoon train to Penn Station departed Sayville at 3:05. There was ample time to walk to the station. He passed an elementary school. Children were at play. Their laughter reminded him of his daughter. Suddenly he was overcome with a sense of foreboding. He thought of the seven special children, the innocent assets, and Franz's guinea pigs. *There had to be a way to intervene.*

It was too late to stop the Pied Piper research project. MKULTRA soon encompassed more than one hundred satellite studies. Young recruited dozens of hospitals and universities with research clinics. They were hungry for income. A number of mind- altering experiments were conducted at a renowned Canadian university. MKULTRA had extended into nursing homes, orphanages, even prisons.

As he boarded the 3:05 train Mallory scattered the remaining shreds of Linda Wilson's list. In retrospect he felt ambivalent about destroying the list. Tightness grasped his chest as he reflected on his conversation with Linda Wilson. Mallory stared intently out the train window.

Brain change. Mind control. I've been co-opted. Heinrich Franz didn't do it. The Agency governs every aspect of my life. I did it to myself. I'm as guilty as the Agency, Young, and Franz. And I have no way to stop the project.

Chapter Forty-Two
The Discovery

Linda Wilson was late for Franz's scheduled staff meeting. Franz had grown increasingly compulsive about staff meetings. Linda hoped the doctor wouldn't demand an explanation for her tardiness. There was another problem. Her advisor at Columbia requested a conference the following Thursday. It conflicted with her clinic schedule. The advisor planned to retire and encouraged Linda to finish her thesis. A new advisor might complicate matters or even delay Linda's orals. Franz promised to enlarge the research staff. He hadn't. Yet, Franz demanded more of Linda.

I'm spending too much time on simple clerical tasks. Linda concluded Franz was becoming obsessed with secrecy and what he called "a need to know basis."

Linda parked her car and rushed into the clinic.

"Hi," Linda said to the receptionist. "I'm late for the staff meeting."

"The meeting has been cancelled. I tried calling you," said the receptionist.

"Thanks. I can use the time to clear my paperwork."

Linda finished her family reports a little before five o'clock. The receptionist had left for the day. *I'll leave these files on Franz's desk. This place has an eerie feeling when no one is around.* Linda's peculiar reaction increased as she walked into Franz's office. She placed her bundle of folders on Franz's desk next to a folder labeled "Personality Traits".

Franz was compulsive when it came to leaving a clear desktop at the end of his workday. Franz's files and reports were meticulously locked in two grey filing cabinets on the far side of the office. Linda opened the file. It contained notes and a seating chart for his sessions with the Special Seven group. Under each name was a corresponding number. Franz had written a legend on the inside of the file jacket. On the margins of the seating chart Franz had scribbled brief anecdotes. The random notes clearly revealed Franz's next experiments were focused on each child's personality traits. Linda became increasingly troubled by what she read.

The doctor grouped the children by what he called the intensity of their "shadow side". Franz noted:

"All the children are creative and astutely attuned to their family circumstances. I note Walter Katz for his critical thinking but the boy lacks superior communication skills. All the children suffer from emotional trauma, a key ingredient in our research profile."

A few pages on, Franz wrote: "The three boys- Ray Wood, Ed Jablonski, and Bill Hess - struggle to control their "shadow side." Fear of parental reprisal seems to keep them under control. All three have underlying narcissistic personalities. They are popular with their schoolmates and within the research group. It must be emotionally exhausting for the boys to suppress anger. Preliminary tests revealed their dark side could be manipulated when they are tired or stressed. Eventually, they could rage."

On the margin Franz underlined a cryptic note. "I must acquire a way to manipulate their rage."

Franz's notes convinced Linda Wilson Franz was planning to gain complete control over the children and their families. Franz reinforced fear in the children's minds. Ironically, the children adored Franz and the parents enthusiastically participated in the formation sessions. Franz's notes stunned Linda. She placed the folder on the doctor's desk and slumped in a chair next to the desk. She was baffled. *Did Franz intentionally leave the file on his desk? Was it a test of her loyalty? Now what?*

Linda left the clinic and drove to her apartment in Patchogue. She was torn. *If I remain, I am perpetuating a hideous research project. Maybe I will be able to persuade Franz to abandon the research. What do I owe the children? My career may be damaged.*

By the next morning Linda Wilson' decided on a course of action. Linda drove to the clinic to speak with Franz. The receptionist informed Linda the doctor was at a meeting with Otto

Bruns in Patchogue.

That's a relief. I won't have to meet with Franz. Linda hurriedly gathered her personal items and notes for her dissertation. Then, she walked to the doctor's office and placed her notebooks containing the family intake interviews on Franz's desk.

By two o'clock Thursday afternoon, Linda Wilson departed for her parent's farm in Perry, New York. Ironically, the file she read in Franz's office was not left intentionally. It was not a test. Franz had neglected to secure his notes. Linda would never know.

Nevertheless, Linda felt certain it was time to leave the project. It was clear all seven families would accept Franz's invitation to continue in his "enrichment" study.

Linda stopped in Patchogue to telephone Mallory. She wasn't sure why she should, but she did. "I've resigned from the project."

"Why? Don't you need the research to complete your dissertation?"

"Hypnosis, drugs, electro-magnetic treatments. They may be legitimate when applied under a carefully scrutinized study, but not on children. It's insane."

"I can't believe my superiors would intentionally harm children or anyone."

"I'd like to believe you. You're fooling yourself Mr. Mallory. The children and their families deserve better."

"Linda…" Mallory hesitated. "The project is classified. Don't go public. Tell no one, not even your parents."

"I wouldn't want anyone to know I've been harming children," she replied.

"There's more to it. Forget our conversation. Call Franz and apologize for your quick departure."

"I can't do that. How do you live with yourself, Mallory?"

"Don't worry about me. Believe me, Linda. Tell no one. Fade away. You could put yourself in grave danger. I can't say more."

"Goodbye, Mr. Mallory." She didn't want to believe Mallory's warnings, but she felt he was being honest. She was frightened. After a few minutes she gathered her courage and left the phone booth.

Chapter Forty-Three
The Apostles

The project took on a new intensity after Linda Wilson's departure. Franz invited the parents to a meeting. He told them the first part of the research was completed. His study would soon enter a new phase. He invited the families to continue. Just as he predicted all the families consented. Franz made them believe that they were part of an extended family group. They would be his disciples. Ken and Doris Dunn were Franz's strongest apostles.

All of the children used dissociative patterns to survive repressive home lives. Their intuitiveness, intelligence and imagination make them excellent liars, a key to guarding family secrets. Andrew Dunn was an outstanding example of dissociative behavior. Andrew Dunn's parents constantly battled. His mother was a manic-depressive. His father lived in denial. Ken sought refuge outside the home leaving Andrew to face the brunt of his mother's hysteria. When Doris raged she would drag Andrew into the bathroom. Her screams and admonishments echoed off the tiled walls. At the peak of her frenzy Doris became disoriented. Suddenly, she was shouting her husband's name. Andrew became his surrogate.

Once Franz discovered Doris' rage he offered a new tactic.

"Mrs. Dunn, I'm very concerned about Andrew's emotional state. He is afraid of you. He asked me to intervene. You have to change your tactic with your son."

Doris Dunn suddenly looked doleful.

"Mrs. Dunn, you could hurt Andrew during one of your rages."

"You have to seek professional help for your condition."

Doris Dunn began to weep.

Franz continued. "I've completed some research into

alternative disciplinary methods. I've been reading about a practice a group of Russian psychiatrists are using with great success. What I am about to propose may help you deal with Andrew."

"Please tell me more," she said.

Franz urged Doris to use enemas as a behavior modification tool for dealing with Andrew.

"Enemas? That seems outrageous."

"They must be used with restraint," Franz insisted.

"I know you are a professional, Dr. Franz, but I don't like the sound of it."

Nevertheless, Doris purchased a red rubber enema bag at the corner pharmacy. Then Andrew's predicament worsened. Any provocation or complaint could launch an enema inquisition.

Doris placed a towel on the bed linen. She ordered young Andrew to remove his pants and underwear and lay on the towel. She would leave the room and a few minutes later return with the enema bag filled with warm soapy water. A tube smeared with petroleum jelly was inserted into Andrew's rectum. Doris released the metal clip and water rushed into Andrew. He ached with pain fearing he would defecate on the bed or floor before his mother allowed him to run to the nearby toilet. Andrew never grew accustomed to the enemas, but he learned to disconnect from the experience almost to the point where he no longer felt pain or experienced fear. It was a psychological escape.

The frequency of enemas increased and so did Andrew's coping skills. He would bury his face in a pillow as his mother inserted the hard plastic tube. The click of the metal water release clamp triggered the miracle. Andrew visualized leaving his tortured body. Andrew's emancipated "self" stood behind his mother and watched.

Andrew scoffed his mother. Doris reminded him of a ridiculous Statue of Liberty. Her right hand held the enema bag nearly as high as her right earlobe. "Be still, Andrew," she said as she released the punishing water.

As hard as he tried, Andrew could tolerate the pain only so long before he pleaded, "Please, mother. No more."

Doris would remove the tube. Andrew squeezed his buttocks and rushed to the toilet. The soapy water gushed and burned. There was a distinctive odor Andrew never forgot. In a way, the enemas worked. As he grew older Andrew acquired numerous behaviors aimed at avoiding his mother's rage and the inevitable red enema bag.

Franz suspected Doris might use the enemas far beyond his recommendation. Franz called Andrew aside after each group session. He questioned the boy about his parents' behavior. Andrew revealed nothing. When pressured, Andrew embellished or lied. The boy knew better than to reveal family secrets.

Franz was pleased. The routine continued until Andrew entered ninth grade. Then one afternoon Andrew confided in Franz, "My mother is hurting me."

"How?" Franz asked.

"Enemas. I hate them."

"I'll speak with her," said Franz. He placed his index finger on Andrew's head, just as he had done hundreds of times before.

The boy became silent and motionless.

"When I remove my finger you will forget we talked. You are safe, Andrew. Trust me."

The enemas stopped, but the recollections lingered as a trigger for Andrew's adult dissociative behavior.

✦

Over the next seven years Franz spent an increasing amount of time with Katherine Stone and her parents. After all, Katherine was the project's keystone. The Stones were an enigma to the folks in Bay Grove. They perplexed the residents of Patchogue. Rumors of the Mill's closing circulated for more than a year. Ken Dunn, Andrew's father, was convinced Stephen Stone was some type of efficiency expert compiling data for the Mill owners in far-away New England. Eventually the textile business began to decline and the Lace Mill closed, but it wasn't due to Stephen Stone. Local folks still blamed Stone.

Stephen and Virginia Stone's reclusive lifestyle reinforced the commonly held opinion they were people to be avoided and feared. In reality, Stephen was a retired War Department accountant. The Stones were one of a hundred or more couples screened by the special task

The Stones were a childless couple living in Milwaukee, Wisconsin when two task force agents knocked on their door. Six weeks later the Stones were living in a cottage on a remote Camp Perry reserve in Virginia. They met with Erskin Young on several occasions between November 1945 and January 1946. Young's briefing dealt with an unwanted foster child. The child, a girl, was born out of wedlock. During their original interviews the Stones stated they wanted to foster a child. The intake office was skeptical. She felt the Stones were too old. "The couple's age was a negative. Raising a child will be taxing." A younger couple was selected, but they, for undisclosed reasons, withdrew from consideration.

Erskin Young was the case officer. Young turned to his alternate choice, the Stones. While the Stones knew they were undertaking a clandestine assignment for an unidentified government Agency, George Stone anticipated the task would be financially rewarding. It was.

The Stones were told the child was born on Long Island.

"Do you expect us to move to Long Island," asked Virginia.

"It will be easier for you. Your Milwaukee neighbors will be inquisitive. We have two moves for you. Your first will be Brooklyn. Then at the appropriate time you will relocate to Long Island. The transitions will relieve the pressure and risk of exposure.

"There is an imperative. No one must know of our arrangement," said Young. There was no mistaking the sense of terror this man Young projected. In return, the Stones were assured their names would not be included in Agency files. However, records released in 2009 list a George P. and Virginia A. Stone on a document related to MKULTRA.

In April 1951 the task force purchased a home in Patchogue. The Stones received a sizeable living expense for the child. In late May or early June the Stones drove to Port Jefferson. They waited near the ferry dock. At an appointed time Erskin Young arrived accompanied by a nurse and an infant. The meeting lasted about thirty minutes.

"The child's name is Katherine," Young told them. This is her embossed birth certificate and a number of notarized documents. File them away. Young and the nurse returned to his car and drove away. The Stones did not encounter Young again for several years. When Young next appeared it was to instruct the Stones to participate in a study being conducted by child psychologist Heinrich Franz at the Bay Grove Children's Clinic.

Both Franz and Otto Bruns knew Katherine 's true identity. The information was kept from William Mallory even though Mallory was the project supervisor.

"Mallory will find out soon enough," Young told Franz. And he did.

When Linda Wilson left the Pied Piper project Young and Franz decided to withhold select information from Mallory. Young considered Mallory vulnerable to bouts of conscience. To Young's chagrin Franz was a greater security risk.

A Navy intelligence officer sent a dispatch to Young. The documents included several mail intercepts between Franz and the Director of Trinity PharmoDynamics, a fledgling pharmaceutical company. Young was furious.

"Who is Liechtenauer?" Young demanded as if he did know.

Franz admitted his long-time association with Walther Liechtenauer.

"Did you reveal Katherine Stone's identity?"

"No. I swear I didn't," Franz lied. He revealed the Berchtesgaden episode.

In 1952 Allen Dulles appointed former OSS Captain, Theresa Murk, Deputy Director for MKULTRA. Murk was one of the youngest project directors and the first woman to hold the position. Murk continued in that position until her death in 1965.

Murk was the tyrannical OSS agent, disguised as a nun, who

took charge of Katherine Stone in May 1945. Young despised Murk and envied her rapid rise within the new Agency.

When Young discovered Franz's secret collaboration with Trinity PharmoDynamics he notified Theresa Murk. She recalled Young to Washington. Murk was furious.

"At some point Franz will be punished," she ranted.

"Not now. We are too far into the research study," Young protested.

"This could mean trouble for us, Erskin. It is a poor reflection of your judgment."

"My judgment. You're the one who gave the green light for funding the project."

"Is there a paper trail?" asked Murk.

Young insisted that Lebensborn records had been destroyed.

"Wrong again. The Steinheoring records of births between 1934 and 1945 exist."

"How do you know?" asked Young.

"It's my job and yours as well." Murk insisted.

"The Soviets have hundreds of certificates."

"And the West Germans?" Young was puzzled.

"We know the records were kept in Heidelberg. I suspect a certificate for SS-1-3128 is included."

"Someone would have to have known Katherine's mother's maiden name," said Young.

"We have to eliminate any connection between Katherine and the Third Reich."

"How would any one other than the present keepers of the secret know Katherine's connection to the Nazis?" Young demanded.

"You're insane, Erskin. Mallory, Franz, Bruns and Pokel all know. Now Walther Liechtenauer has entered the picture. He's a dangerous man. We need to get this fiasco under control."

"Liechtenauer?"

"I've had two conversations with the good doctor."

"You went behind my back?" asked a dismayed Young.

"Your report suggested the Agency's ability to protect Operation Pied Piper has been compromised. We have six individuals. Five are in possession of classified information that connects the U-853 with Pied Piper."

"They are all cleared employees."

Murk got up and walked around her desk and confronted Young. Young started to get up.

"Don't get out of that chair. Our ability to safeguard classified information has been compromised."

Young laughed.

"This isn't a joke, Erskin." Murk clasped her hands and scorned. "The Agency is closing Pied Piper immediately."

"What?"

"The Director wants it shut down."

"That doesn't solve your concerns about the personnel."

"The personnel are your problem. I'm bringing Mallory back to Washington. The Director agreed to your proposal. Mallory will fit in at the Justice Department."

"And the others?"

"Pokel and Price are in Frankfurt. They were part of the U-853 episode but not Pied Piper. I spoke with Liechtenauer. He'll accommodate Pokel. The Director suggests the Agency might benefit from Price's logistic skills. We've recently purchased a fleet of planes to ferry personnel and supplies in South East Asia. Price fits."

"So that leaves Franz and Bruns," said Young.

"I want them separated. We'll keep Franz on the payroll."

"But Pied Piper is a sub-project." Young asked.

"Dr. Liechtenauer offered an interesting proposal. Trinity PharmoDynamics will assume Operation Pied Piper. At that point Franz goes to Trinity."

"And Bruns?"

"He can remain at the Long Island lab or be assigned to a research program in Texas."

"And the seven children?" Mallory asked.

"Children? They are teenagers, Erskin. The Agency has been financing Pied Piper for years. Cut them loose." Murk returned to her desk.

"Abandon them and their families?"

"Abandonment is a strong word, Erskin, especially coming from you. Have you grown soft?"

Young coughed and then cleared his throat. "No, of course not. I'm looking out for the Agency's interests."

"Their futures rest with Trinity PharmoDynamics," said Murk. "I've been called to testify before the Congressional Oversight Committee. Do you see all these files? I have to destroy them, today, so I can confirm we have no records of a program called Pied Piper."

"How long do I have to complete my end of the shut-down?" Young asked.

"One week. Shred everything. Close the clinic. Not a trace of Pied Piper."

"And if one of our players doesn't cooperate?"

"Take care of it, Erskin," Murk responded.

Chapter Forty-Four

An Abrupt Shift
The White House Living Quarters.
Washington, DC
Sometime after January, 2016

It was Carol Dean's turn to cover the White House night shift. Dean was the senior Secret Service agent on duty. A recent shooting near the White House West Wing alarmed Carol Dean. The latest incident involved a bogus anthrax letter mailed to the President's husband, Andrew Dunn. President Stone insisted her detail be moved from its assigned post on the second floor to the residence.

Agent Carol Dean served on Katherine Stone's Vice Presidential security team. Carol Dean was Katherine Stone's first choice to lead her Secret Service Presidential detail.

"You're making the wrong choice, Madame President," Stone's Chief of Staff cautioned. He wasn't alone. Rumors circulated that others were opposed. The Secret Service was under scrutiny by the press and members of Congress. The Secret Service Director wanted to avoid negative public perceptions. "We need a strong male image," he argued.

Agent Dean demonstrated a professional loyalty to the President. Above all Dean was devoted to her sworn oath to protect the President. Nevertheless, Carol Dean inherited a number of internal political problems. The bad press began sometime back in 2009. Confirmed reports of pure negligence and dereliction of duty leaked to several journalists. A number of prominent Congressmen used the issues as talking points on morning talk shows. Officially, the Secret Service culture did not condone drinking and promiscuity. However, within the agency an atmosphere of agents "taking care" of their own was part of the culture. Stone was convinced those shared beliefs and values fostered negative perceptions.

One Washington paper published a story about an incident involving hookers and alcohol. Agents had brought prostitutes to their rooms. The most serious revelation involved the Presidential Protective Division (PPS), the so-called "Jump Team."

After a series of failed attempts at reform and two transitional Directors, President Stone began to micro manage the White House detail. She pressured the Department of Homeland Security and the Director of the Secret Service to reform its tarnished image.

"I want Carol Dean placed in charge of my personal detail," Katherine told the Secret Service Director during a telephone conference. "The internal culture within the Secret Service troubles me. Stories about complacency and racial slurs aimed at President Obama disturbed me. I demand loyalty to the institution of the Presidency. How can I place my life in the hands of agents who resent a woman President?" Stone sensed that John Norman, the Secret Service Director, resisted her request.

President Stone frequently raged. On this occasion it was during a meeting in the Oval Office with Homeland Secretary, Oscar Cooper and Director Norman. Both men assured President Stone her detail was above reproach.

"Bullshit," she ranted. "I'll be damned if some nut with a butcher knife is going to wander into the White House kitchen or get into our living quarters. Never again! Do you two idiots understand me?"

"I won't stand to be treated this way," the Secretary barked. "I'm no idiot. You have my assurance the matter is under control."

The Director nodded in agreement, but remained silent.

"I'm unaccustomed to be spoken to in this way, Secretary Copper. I'll let it pass, *this time*. As for you, Director Norman, get the Secret Service on a short leash," Stone retorted. I won't accept a machismo tolerance for misconduct. I want Carol Dean placed in charge of my security detail."

President Stone swiveled her chair and turned her back on

the pair. She looked out the Oval Office window. Then with her back to both men she said, "That's it, gentlemen. Forgive me if I've been too passionate on this subject. I apologize." *They despise a strong woman.* The two couldn't see the smirk cross President Stone's face.

Confused by President Stone's sudden mode swing Cooper said, "We'll get right on it, Madame President." He left in a huff. Norman followed close behind.

"That woman is a bitch," said the Director as the pair left the White House. "What's wrong with her?"

"She's playing us," Cooper responded. The humiliated Secretary simply shrugged. He regretted resigning his secure Senate seat. "I can't believe she's President. She was elected to a small town position years ago. She knows nothing about national security. Politics…" Cooper said with a shrug of acceptance.

"You should know, Oscar. You gave the nod when Anderson said he wanted her for his Vice President."

"And I regret it with each sunrise," Cooper replied.

"Calm down, Oscar."

"I can't believe she became Governor of New York by default. And now she's President of the United States."

"Circumstances," said Norman.

"Anderson should never have run. He was too old. The party would never have backed him if they knew his health was failing."

"It's too late."

"I couldn't believe he has resigned. Never consulted with his cabinet," said Cooper.

"That was his wife's influence," Norman added.

Then Cooper chuckled. "What so funny?" Norman asked.

"Stone is a manipulator. She plucked Ives Venal, her loudest critic, right out of Congress and made him Vice President."

"You're right. She put the screws to Venal," Norman agreed.

"Once he became Vice President, she confined him to the Observatory. Is there a better way to silence your chief rival? He does little more than read and drink Martinis. The bastard deserves it." Cooper laughed.

"It's a mystery why President Stone kept Drew Lindstrom on as Chief of Staff."

"It no mystery to me. She needs him to run the place. My sources tell me Lindstrom was reporting to Stone months before Anderson resigned," Cooper added. "Let's get this nasty business out of the way. You handle Carol Dean," Secretary Cooper said as he climbed into his waiting limousine.

Several hours later the White House Chief of Staff received a call from the Director. "Move Carol Dean into her new slot at the White House. ASAP."

◈

Carol Dean immediately began an overhaul of White House security. She transferred a number of agents to distant field offices and recruited others from a short list. Next she changed all the security passwords and response procedures.

"The call sign "Flagship" will be White House central security coordination. I have revised the security procedure manual," she told her staff. Next Dean met with the President and Mr. Dunn. "These are our new procedures. One of the agents will review them step by step." Dean smiled with a sense of satisfaction. "The respective code names for you, President Stone and for you Mr. Dunn are 'Sandpiper' and 'Sparrow.'" The names reflected Deans' insight into the Presidential marriage. *Female Sandpipers are the dominant sex of the specie. Male sparrows tend to be less dominant.*

◈

The sound of a gunshot from inside the President's master suite startled Carol Dean. Dean sprang to her feet. "Help! Someone help please," President Katherine Stone screamed. President Stone rushed into the hallway. She was covered with blood.

"Andrew. It's Andrew. He's been shot." The President was hysterical. "Carol, help him."

A second Secret Service agent, Helen Scott, stationed on the

290

opposite side of the corridor instinctively drew her side arm, swept the corridor for intruders and cautiously moved toward the terrified President.

The President collapsed. Agent Dean knelt next to the President she had sworn to protect. *Stay calm. The President's life depends on my judgment. I have contingencies.*

Dean called over her radio. "21 to Flagship."

"Go ahead 21."

"Flagship, we have a Code Red in the Presidential living quarters…the Master Bedroom. I repeat a Code Red. Sandpiper covered. I repeat Sandpiper covered. Send medical aid forthwith. Clear all radio channels."

The Code Red signaled a security breach with violence involved. Code Red alerted the President's security detail and the Uniformed Secret Service personnel guarding the North Wing.

"I repeat. Flagship lock us down," Dean ordered.

"Roger 21."

"Attention all personnel. This is Flagship. Initiate lock-down."

The UD (Unit Director), call sign 'Flagship', managed the lock-down. No one was allowed in or out until the White House was secured. Only then was an "all clear" order given. Landlines were shut down. High tech monitoring devices alerted the UD when mobile phones were activated.

A uniformed armed combat-ready team wearing bulletproof vests began a room-to-room sweep of the White House.

Upstairs in the Presidential residence Agent Scott remained vigilant. She waited for Dean's direction. Dean looked toward Scott and pointed toward the bedroom threshold.

"Helen. Be careful," ordered Dean. "Back-up is on the way."

"No time to wait for backup." Scott pointed to the master bedroom threshold.

Scott stepped forward. Her training kicked in. She paused. Took a deep breath then stepped into the room. *Sweep the room for perpetrators. Check for cover. You're no help to the President, if you get shot.* Scott turned toward the far wall.

"Holy Shit!" she gasped. President Stone's husband, Andrew Dunn, was sprawled across a loveseat. Dunn's body quivered.

Scott called into her radio, "18 to 21. The room is clear. Sparrow down. I repeat - Sparrow down. Send medical aid forthwith."

The rapid response team including two agents with paramedic training rushed to Dunn. The agents began to assess Dunn's injury. They rolled his limp torso on to the floor. The lead paramedic attempted to stabilize Dunn's head. The patient's right temple was shattered. Then in one involuntary response Dunn's body quaked.

"He's gone," said the lead paramedic.

"Bring him back," demanded Scott.

Agent Scott called into her headset. "21 this is 18. Sparrow. Code Blue. Repeat- code blue." The monitor continued to flat line as the two paramedics "packaged" Andrew Dunn for rapid transport.

"Repeat 18," Dean called into her radio.

"The paramedics are ready to transport. We have a Code Blue."

There was a momentary disbelief and sense of chaos. The Secret Service Agents were overwhelmed. Agents are trained to expect the unexpected. Nevertheless, who would have expected a shooting inside the President's bedroom?

"Take charge of the President," Dean ordered the attending agents. Multi tasking was Dean's forte. *Response time is critical.* Dean was responsible for the entire scene.

Helen Scott responded, "Affirmative." She quickly turned to check the paramedics. The other two agents checked the far side exits to the dressing room and private entry. Unexpectedly, there was a third agent. The agent was sweeping the room for telltale evidence. Scott called out "Goodman, check in."

The agent turned and walked to Scott. Before Scott could ask, Goodman said, "I was with Flagship and responded to the Code Red."

"You broke procedure."

"It's OK, Scott. I'm cool. Haven't touched a thing. Just snapped several photos. They will be useful. They'll give Forensics a jump start," Goodman responded imprudently.

Scott experienced Goodman's hostile behavior on another

occasion, in Paris. Goodman supervised one of the advanced jump teams. Goodman's team secured the President's suite and the hotel accommodation's at the Georges Cinq. Upon the President Stone's arrival Carol Dean met with the jump team. "Where's Goodman?"

The other teams members were silent. "Where's Agent Goodman. Is Flagship-mobile secure?"

Goodman's deputy finally said, "He needed a break and went to dinner."

Scott informed Dean of the protocol breach. Dean was furious, but repressed her anger. She was well aware the Jump Team resented her authority. Dean confronted Goodman the next morning. "Look, I needed a break. I went to dinner, had a few drinks and turned in." He was indifferent to their respective roles.

A call came over Scott's radio. "Flagship to 21. Is the package ready?" Helen Scott glared at Goodman. *No time for a pissing contest. I'll talk with Carol later.*

"Flagship this is 21." Scott evaluated the situation. She asked the agent-paramedics "Is Dunn ready to go?"

"It's your call, Scott," the lead paramedic responded.

Scott grimaced. "Flagship. The package is ready." Scott turned to the medics. "For the President's sake let's make it look good."

The paramedics looked at each other and nodded in agreement. The triage team arrived and Dunn was placed on a gurney. Let's roll," shouted Scott.

Following procedure Agent Scott made the call. She opened channel one. Medical Unit One this is 21. Meet my team on ground floor."

"Affirmative 21." Scott made the second call. "GWU this is Blue Storm. Be advised we are en route to you with a Priority One, 1600 Pennsylvania Avenue, male patient. Code Blue. Respond with the affirmative code."

"Blue Storm. Affirmative. GWU acknowledges with code 1953. GWU out." George Washington University Hospital was the closest trauma center.

"Where are they taking Andrew?" the President pleaded.

"Please, President Stone. I need you to remain calm." Dean paused then said, "Mr. Dunn is being evacuated to George Washington University Hospital. Agent Scott is with him."

"Not Walter Reed?"

"No." Members of the White House medical team are with Mr. Dunn. The attending physician is being paged. Everything is locked-down," responded Dean.

One of the agents attending to the President moved closer to Dean and whispered, "The President is covered with blood, but I can't find any wound. I have to remove her night gown… do a full body scan."

"No apparent injuries? Are you sure? It's your call. Do what you have to do," Carol Dean answered. "We have to protect the President."

One or more perpetrators may be at large within the White House. With all the new security measures how did this happen? "Let's get President Stone the hell out of here."

Dean called into her radio, "Bring in Marine One. Contingency Three"

Flagship relayed the call. "Marine One. This is Flagship. We have a Contingency Three. Flagship will clear you for landing on the White House pad."

"Flagship, this is Marine One. Repeat in sequence."

"Roger, affirmative Marine One. Contingency Three. Sandpiper."

"Affirmative Flagship."

Several Secret Service agents rolled out the interlocking parts of Marine One's portable landing pad on the South Lawn. The pad was coated with a material to provide visual contrast. Then they took positions in front of the President's gurney to shield her from the helicopter's turbulence.

Dean listened to the progress of the security units taking their positions.

"21 to Flagship."

"Flagship."

"Is the South Lawn secured?"

"Affirmative 21. An additional special weapons unit has been dispatched to cover you."

Dean anxiously waited for the sound of the approaching helicopter.

Within minutes came the roar of Marine One. It was dispatched from the Naval Support Facility at Anacostia.

Dean turned and walked back to the gurney. She double-checked the gurney's retaining straps. *President Stone is so distraught; it's best to keep her on the gurney.*

The President of the United States was secured. A million security checks ran through Dean's mind. Nevertheless, she was shocked to find Kevin Goodman standing near the head of the gurney. *What is he doing here? He is assigned to Flagship.* Dean gave Helen Scott a bewildered look. "Scott, return to the residence. Coordinate with forensics. I'll join you after departure. Goodman, report to Flagship." There was no misinterpreting her anger."

"Affirmative."

"Let's move," Dean shouted. No one could mistake Dean's determined expression. The agents rolled the gurney on to the South Lawn.

Marine One began its landing approach. The Marine pilot performed this maneuver many times, but never with the urgency for evacuating the President. Marine One landed with its crew at the ready.

On her signal Carol Dean led four Secret Service agents across the White House lawn. Marine One's crew quickly maneuvered the gurney and locked it in place. They signaled an "A-OK" to Dean.

"21 to Flagship. Sandpiper on board."

The security detail climbed aboard and departed with President Stone. Their destination was Camp David.

An exhausted and perplexed Carol Dean watched from a distance. *What the hell is happening?*

Chapter Forty-Five
The Letter

Dean returned to the White House residence. The master bedroom was a secured crime scene. Forensics was already on the scene.

"Damn it! I want the entire residence sealed off not just the master bedroom. We'll narrow our perimeter," Dean called to the forensic unit. This was Dean's first test. She wasn't going to tolerate insubordination or recklessness on the part of her staff; especially several male agents she knew opposed her leadership.

"Dean look at this," called one of the team. He pointed to the carpet behind the love seat where Agent Scott found Andrew Dunn.

Dean was stunned. *A pistol? A twenty-two.*

"I'll bag it," said the agent.

Dean knew the neither the President nor her husband were cleared for any personal firearms.

"Listen up. I want every speck in this room examined. Every detailed is classified. I don't want one piece of evidence discarded or thrown out. Is that understood?" *This situation is growing more bizarre by the minute. I have to let the team do its job. I can't micro manage this crisis.*

"Dean, I've found something under the love seat." The agent carefully removed a crumpled piece of paper. It was covered with blood.

"Did you change your gloves?" asked Dean. Just then Kevin Goodman entered the master bedroom. The forensic team member looked at Goodman then Carol Dean. Instinctively out of submissiveness he responded, "Yes mam. I know better than cross contaminate evidence. I've been doing this longer than you have."

"I didn't ask you for a resume," snapped Dean. "Goodman, I ordered you to Flagship."

Goodman acknowledged her command with a begrudged casual salute. "All yours, Dean."

Dean slipped on a fresh set of surgical gloves before touching the letter. "Please hand me an evidence bag." Dean measured her words. She carefully pulled the crumbled paper from its far corners. It was a copy of an email. The address was partially smudged, but the sender was Andrew Dunn.

It took nearly fifteen hours for the initial boundaries to be cleared. Every piece of evidence was labeled and inventoried. The FBI wanted access to the scene and the evidence. "It's classified," Dean told them. "You'll get your chance in due time." Dean wanted to be the first to read the bloodied email. She recalled the evidence controversy surrounding President Kennedy's assassination. *Nothing is going to disappear on my watch.*

Resentment and envy for Dean's scrupulous intensity reverberated through the Secret Service establishment. "Who the hell does that broad think she is?"

After five cups of black coffee, Dean's head ached. She was tired, irritable and feeling a bit paranoid. "I want you to double-check all entrances are sealed and one of our people is posted at each location along with the uniformed security. "

"Yes ma'am," said one of the agents. He began relaying Dean's instructions over his radio.

"Be sure you're on the secured channel," said Dean.

"Yes 'ma'am.'"

Dean looked askance. She disliked his use of "ma'am", but this wasn't the time for a reprimand.

Once she was alone Dean walked to the portable table on which the evidence from the room was placed. Dean double-checked the evidence inventory list against the number on the bag. She opened the evidence bag containing the crumbled bloodstained paper. Dean slipped on a fresh set of latex cloves. She carefully spread a sheet of waxed paper on the table and then laid the evidence on top of it. The bloodstained paper appeared to be an email. Dean unfolded a small magnifying glass she carried in her jacket. There were bloody smudged fingerprints on the right upper corner of the document.

The email stamped "WH Postmaster" was a National Security Agency (NSA) intercept" for the President's eye's only. Stone was paranoid about anonymous White House leaks. She distrusted several advisors including the Joint Chiefs. Stone ordered NSA to review all emails, phone calls and digital communications to and from the White House and the Executive Office Building. The so-called "Family and Friends Communications Intercepts" were classified. The Secret Service knew of its existence, but not the names on the list.

⌘

Dean held the bloodied document near the desk lamp. *It can't be. Oh my god. President Stone was intercepting her husband's email. Why her husband?*

Dean flattened the letter on the table. She was determined to read it. Dean was shocked. The email was addressed to David Clayton, Dunn's former administrative assistant.

Dear David:

About a year ago, I began to have severe, vivid nightmares. As the frequency and intensity of my dreams grew, I became alarmed. I secretly consulted a therapist. We met weekly for nearly seven months. I agreed to the use of sodium panthenol and hypnosis during these sessions.

Under hypnosis I described two visitors to my family home on Brigantine Drive during Christmas vacation in 1951. I was offered an opportunity to attend a special enrichment program. My parents were assured the sessions would improve my grades and enhance my opportunity to attend college. Several weeks later my parents received a box of study guides.

The so-called enrichment classes began in the winter

of 1952 and continued through my junior year in high school. The project director was Dr. Heinrich Franz. Dr. Franz was a wonderful teacher and so were his assistants. He jokingly called himself the Pied Piper. We were his special seven. There were five boys and two girls in the program.   We met once a week after school. On the second and third Saturdays of each month we were transported by van to a clinic in Bay Grove. That's where I met Katherine. After high school I lost track of the other participants except for Katherine.

Over the last months I've discovered a number of disturbing facts about my fellow participants. Three are incarcerated for murder. Another went insane. Recently, a member of the group surfaced. He worked for an intelligence contractor. He has stolen thousands of classified files and is a wanted man.

I fear I may have such latent sociopathic tendencies. I need your help. You are the only one I trust.

Andrew

Chapter Forty-Six

Vice President's Residence
US Naval Observatory
Washington, D.C.
Prior to Katherine Grace Stone Becoming
President of the United States.

David Clayton was no stranger to the White House West Wing. He had served on Congresswoman Elizabeth Harrington's staff. In October 1977 David rejoined the New York Delegation after a debacle at the General Accounting Office ended in a massacre of sorts. The Special Investigation Unit's hunt for Nazi War Criminals was shut down and classified. The unit was dismantled.

Several weeks after he returned to the New York delegation, Congresswoman Harrington turned to David for a new assignment. Robert Doyle, David's antagonist and colleague on the delegation, resigned.

"David, I need you to assume Bob Doyle's assignment. Doyle was my watch dog on the Level Two Oversight Committee."

Harrington's request surprised David. "With all due respect, I know very little about Immigration and Naturalization." "Oh, no, David. Not the Immigration and Naturalization Service. I'm asking you to consider the National Security Agency."

"I know even less about the NSA and spies."

"Exactly. Don't rush into it. Next week will be fine. I have a few folders I want you to read. It's only a Level Two oversight. I attend the NSA's top-secret briefings." Harrington pointed to a stack of files on the corner of her mahogany desk.

David took the folders and was about to leave. The Congresswoman added a final request. "Oh, one last thing. Stay in touch with your contacts at the General Accounting Office. You're still my liaison, even though Sam Beverly and Jack Thompson are gone. Any contact with them of late?"

"No. None."

"Well, keep me informed."

David sensed Congresswoman Harrington was considering the upcoming Senatorial race. Harrington garnered seniority in Washington and was becoming a powerful political figure. Harrington lost the Senatorial run. Nineteen seventy-seven was now history.

From David's perspective, politics had gotten downright nasty. Perhaps it always was. The cost of congressional elections ran into the millions. A presidential run demanded a billion dollars. Political action groups and the lobbyists on K STREET controlled Washington. David appreciated the reach of the world's financial powers. They controlled the world's resources including the halls of Congress. David suspected Trinity's Director, Ashton Pickering, pressured someone in the Administration to terminate the GAO's 1977 inquiry into Nazis on US government payrolls.

⬿

Clayton worked for a number of politicians following Congresswoman Harrington's departure from Washington. Then one afternoon, David received a call from the Vice President's personal secretary. David was offered a position on Vice President Stone's staff. Clayton moved into Number One Observatory Circle, the official residence of the Vice President of the United States.

"My husband respects you, Mr. Clayton. He tends to be reclusive. He needs a speechwriter and personal advisor. I believe you are the perfect alter ego so to speak."

The Vice President's offer surprised Clayton. *Why me?*

Andrew Dunn, Vice President Stone's husband, avoided media attention. The gossip columnists labeled Dunn "aloof." Clayton and Dunn first met at a golf outing. Clayton was a last minute replacement for Congresswoman Harrington's husband, Al. As usual the paparazzi were in Dunn's face. Dunn smiled. The Secret Service and Prince William police cordoned swaths of the fairways. At first Dunn appeared tolerant. He waved. A few even referred to Dunn as the "First Husband." It was awkward. There were no precedents. Katherine Stone was the first woman Vice President, soon to be President

The event was jam-packed at every tee box. Hecklers worked their way among the fans. They taunted Dunn calling him "Hubby". The situation reached a point when the caddies ordered the crowds to behave. The eighteenth hole couldn't have arrived soon enough. The Secret Service sheltered Dunn as his foursome maneuvered to the locker room. Dunn and the head of his detail had a brief conversation. The agent walked over to Clayton and said, "Mr. Dunn is feeling a bit under the weather. He will skip the festivities. Mr. Dunn would like you to accompany him on the ride to the Observatory. We'll take care of your car. Clayton agreed.

The return trip to the Observatory unnerved Andrew Dunn. "I hate these security motorcades. The outing was exhausting and now this ruckus. Thanks for coming along." With that Dunn began an unusual conversation between two men who were strangers.

"Married David?"

"No sir."

"Please. I'd be comfortable if you called me Andrew."

"No. I've thought about marriage. Now I'm a confirmed bachelor. I can't imagine the pressure you and the Vice President must feel. It could be quite a strain on your relationship."

"It is. I'm Mr. Stone." Andrew chuckled. David detected a dry cynicism.

"I read your recent interview with the *Post*. It didn't delve into your early personal life. You and the Vice President have been married forever. How did you come to be a couple?"

"Officially?" Andrew chuckled again.

"I apologize. I shouldn't have asked."

Andrew turned and gazed out the window. He leaned

forward and pressed a button on the console. A partition now afforded them privacy.

Andrew continued to gaze out the SUV's window. "Trust is a limited commodity in DC. There are always strings attached. Confidentialities betrayed. Honesty is suppressed. Something tells me I can trust you David." Andrew became moody.

David remained silent. He felt awkward.

Andrew turned and looked at David. "So, how did we become a couple? Truthfully I'm not certain, David. It seems we've been together most of our lives…at least since third grade."

"I don't remember exactly. No, I can't. Strange. Isn't it?" Andrew clasped his hands "Sometimes love is that way."

David noticed Andrew's neck was a blotchy red.

"Yes. I was in third grade when it all began," said Andrew rather fancifully, as though he was relating a dream. "It's a long story."

There conversation was interrupted by the intercom.

"Mr. Dunn. We are approaching the Observatory."

The two men shook hands. "I hope to see you again, David."

Until 1974 the Observatory had been the home of the Chief of Naval Operations. The first Vice President to occupy the residence was Nelson Rockefeller. The Rockefellers used the house for parties and official entertaining. Rockefeller, the former Governor, owned a luxury home in DC. The Observatory wasn't quite up to par. Security was the chief reason for relocating to the Naval Observatory. It is reported Rockefeller spent over a million dollars of his personal money on furnishings and upgrades to the house. Vice President Mondale was the first of the succeeding Vice Presidents to live there. The mansion was refurbished and security heightened when Vice President Katherine Stone and her husband Andrew Dunn occupied the mansion. After a brief debate and protest by the National Historical Society, Congress funded the construction of a number of cottages to accommodate the Secret Service and Vice

President Stone's entourage. According to DC gossip the cottages were a cover for clandestine construction of underground safe rooms, a contingency for a terrorist attack.

David Clayton's role on Andrew Dunn's staff was underscored when he occupied one of the newly constructed cottages.

Clayton held an official title of personal assistant on Andrew Dunn's staff.

Clayton departed when Katherine Stone moved into the White House.

"I'll rent an apartment until I find a permanent residence near Manassas," David told Dunn following Katherine Stone's inauguration.

"Take your time, David. We appreciate your contribution. I respect your dedication. Stay here until you relocate. Don't rush. Vice President Venal's Chief of Staff agrees. Be careful. He may trick you into working for him."

"I don't think so. I'm ready for relaxation and golf." Clayton laughed. President Stone smiled. It was time. Katherine Stone was an ambitious woman who dominated her husband. David experienced enough of her micro management. It was time to relax. Then the unexpected happened.

At 5:00 AM a call awakened David.

"Mr. Clayton, Don Jacobs, Drew Lindstrom's assistant, here."

This guy is perky for 5:00 AM.

The Chief of Staff requests a meeting this evening. Will you be able to be at his office by seven this evening or would eight be better?"

"It's five in the morning Mr. Jacobs. I'll have to get back to you."

"I'm afraid that won't do Mr. Clayton. This is quite important."

David paused. Rubbed his eyes and asked, "If it's so damn important why at night?"

"Best at night. Fewer staffers around. We'd like to keep it off the record," Jacobs responded.

"Seven? Make it eight. Can you give me a heads-up?" asked Clayton.

"I'm sure Mr. Lindstrom will brief you. Please follow NSA protocol, Mr. Clayton." *Interesting. Do not place the scheduled event on your Internet calendar.*

David Clayton had been summoned to Drew Lindstrom's office. *Why did the President's Chief of Staff want to see me? NSA business? This meeting is unofficial, yet classified. I doubt it. Why me?*

David walked into the kitchen and brewed a cup of coffee. Since Andrew Dunn's death, sleep eluded David. He couldn't accept Dunn's death was a suicide. It was a personal feeling he kept to himself. There were times when Andrew was sullen, but his mood reflected his marriage. Dunn was human, but he was in over his head. Dunn lived in Katherine 's shadow.

David Clayton had an insider's perspective of Katherine Stone. He kept it to himself. Katherine was rude and controlling as though she was raised to be self-possessed. Katherine was beautiful, but cold. She was a narcissist. Life was a performance before an audience she despised. David was confused by their relationship.

Andrew Dunn's life was circumscribed by Katherine's regimented day-to-day routine. Intimacy had all but disappeared. Was there more to Katherine Stone's growing distance?

The national elections were always a pivotal consideration. Though she publically denied she would run for President, Katherine was obsessed with opinion polls. Katherine was convinced the day would come. She was destined to be a powerful leader. Her first opportunity came when President Anderson was hospitalized. The most recent emergency involved heart surgery. Both times Vice President Stone waited near the so-called "red phone" in the White House Situation Room nervously awaiting hourly briefings on the President's condition. Then after consulting with his physicians and feeling pressure from his wife, Anderson resigned.

Katherine Grace Stone was President of the United States.

❦

At 7:15 PM David arrived at the entrance to the White House grounds. David displayed his pass to the White House guard and proceeded to a second checkpoint where he was directed to park. A number of government limousines were exiting. *The must have been an important conference judging from all these limos.*

Clayton felt uneasy about his call from the Chief of Staff. He recalled his final days at the GAO in 1977. *I'm certain Trinity's tentacles grasped the White House as well as Congress. It had to be Ashton Pickering and the "old-boy" network.*

David repressed his conjectures as he approached the security checkpoint near the entrance to the White House West Wing. One thought prevailed. *After all these years why the unexpected summons to the White House?*

Since 9-11 a wall of secrecy surrounded the President and in turn his Constitutional successors. *It had to be significant. Few occasions called for the President, his Cabinet and top advisors to meet.*

David spotted Lou-Ann Stokes. *What's Lou-Ann doing here? I haven't seen her in ages. What's this meeting all about?*

David slipped the ID lanyard over his head. A young intern directed David to a West Wing anteroom where he found Lou-Ann sipping coffee. "I thought you were preferred tea."

"David. It's great to see you and yes, coffee became a nasty habit I picked up while working with Jack."

David started to pour a cup of coffee, when Lindstrom's secretary entered the room.

"Too late for coffee, Mr. Clayton. Mr. Lindstrom is waiting."

"He's got you working late. I hope he's in a good mood," said Clayton.

"Yes, I'm working late. I'm used to it. And no he's not at his best, but don't tell him I said so."

"Thanks." David flashed one of his schoolboy smiles and winked.

"For god's sake, David. She's young enough to be your granddaughter," Lou-Ann whispered, as the attractive secretary pointed the way.

Drew Lindstrom's office was down the corridor from the Oval Office. Lindstrom was President Stone's chief advisor. His duties reached beyond the White House. He managed an array of assistants in the West Wing and the Eisenhower Executive Office Building.

"It appears they're running out of space," David chuckled.

"Rumor has President Stone is moving staff to the New Executive Office Building on 17th Street NW," Lou-Ann responded. "I consulted for her about a year ago. I met with staff. The building is ugly."

"President Stone is partial to privacy. She demands ambiance. Nixon did most of his day-to-day work at the Eisenhower building. President Stone held most of her meetings there, too."

"You have a unique insight into President Stone's personal life," said Lou-Ann.

"I did. Our relationship ended when Katherine Stone became President."

Chapter Forty-Seven
The White House Meeting
 Office of the Chief of Staff
Several Months After Andrew Dunn's Death

The taller of the two men paced between the map on his office wall and his desk. "Damn it. Where the hell are they?"

"Settle down. They'll be here." The second man walked to the bookcase slid open a compartment and asked: "Scotch, Drew?"

"No. And what the hell? Do you always help yourself to someone's booze without asking?" demanded Drew Lindstrom, President Stones' Chief of Staff.

"Most of the time. No ice?" Charles Best, the President's Chief Counsel felt perturbed. A Scotch on top of Best's late afternoon martini exacerbated the unpleasantness.

"Are you serious? That's it on the alcohol. I anticipate a tough meeting."

"And how did the Cabinet Meeting go?" asked Best.

"Not well. You can imagine the immediate reaction. They were shocked," said Lindstrom. They weren't anticipating the President's obsession with Zimbabwe. A potential Ebola outbreak in Uganda seems to be the concern. Does President Stone know Uganda is 3,000 miles away from Zimbabwe? "

""The President met with me this morning. We reviewed her authority to issue the executive order. Where is this sudden interest coming from?" Best asked.

"Her talking points project a need to defend America. Stop Ebola in Zimbabwe before it infects Americans. During the last Ebola crisis Zimbabwe lost millions of dollars in tourism. Their economy is faltering. Zimbabwe is ripe for major civil unrest. Maybe a civil war," Lindstrom responded.

"We can't police the entire world with a volunteer military.

We are already over extended. Stone has a limited knowledge of geopolitics, but she's shrewd. I questioned her plan to activate the Selective Service," Best replied.

"Someone has put a lot of thought into this. It's beyond Katherine Stone's imagination. Somebody is orchestrating the plan. Each day the CIA Presidential briefings focus on Zimbabwe with one interesting twist. She has a peculiar obsession with rare earth elements. China holds the monopoly."

"I still contend the President looks bad for cancelling the press conference, especially after today's tumultuous cabinet meeting with the Joint Chiefs. Her plan will leak to the press," said Best.

"You're wrong. The President had to circle the wagons first. Listen to me, Charles. The President has ordered a low profile assessment team inserted into northern Zimbabwe."

"Doctors?"

"No. A Delta team."

"The President has scheduled a television address for tomorrow afternoon. No press conference. Ironically, Charles, you started the wheels turning."

"Me?"

"You recommended an incremental activation of the Selective Service. You cautioned her to avoid the words conscription and draft. Lindstrom walked to a sideboard and poured a cup of coffee.

Best sensed Lindstrom's body language foretold a disclosure.

"Tomorrow, the President will reinstitute the Nixon lottery with an historic change. The Selective Service is antiquated. The President has signed an executive order to overhaul the entire program. One month from tomorrow women will be required to register." Lindstrom laughed. "Nice work Charles.

"All I said was women hold front line positions in the volunteer military. It's a woman's right and duty to serve. It's time for them to exercise their right to register."

"Then she'll put the nation on notice." Lindstrom's comment boded an evil thought. "Requiring woman to register for the draft will be controversial. The press will have a heyday. It will draw their attention from our plans for Zimbabwe."

"Don't attribute an invasion of Zimbabwe to me, Drew."

"Charles, a war in Africa could last as long as our involvement in Afghanistan and Iraq. Without a draft…oops…the Selective Service, we can't sustain a commitment."

Lindstrom turned and looked around the room as though someone might be eaves- dropping. "Between us, someone hasn't done their homework. We're in for another Iraq. We'll destroy whatever balance of power exists on the African continent. What's the motivation? Who is behind this?"

"Let's get off the subject Charles.   We have a different agenda this evening."

"Come on. You know better. I have a vested interest in the President's success. " Best gulped the Scotch. "Katherine Stone has a hidden agenda. Admit it. You're afraid of her."

"Not exactly," Lindstrom retorted. "It's her mood swings. It's beyond me why the Governor of New York selected her for his running mate for Lieutenant Governor," said Lindstrom.

"The poor bastard died in bed having sex with an intern." Best laughed. "Stone became Governor Stone."

"President Anderson needed a diverse ticket. Bingo. He picks Stone." Drew added.

"I just can't figure it out. "I wonder if President Anderson imagined what he was in for when he picked Stone for Vice President?" asked Best.

"You're going brain dead from the Scotch, Charles. Where there's money to be made rules are easily broken. Stone may lack diplomatic experience, but that broad is savvy and a survivor. Look how she handled Ives Venal. She's President."

Best stopped pacing. He loosened his tie and unbuttoned his shirt collar. Droplets of perspiration fogged his glasses. "In my opinion this place is frenetic. I smell something going sour."

Lindstrom pushed away from his desk. "I'm disturbed by the whole atmosphere. Negotiations with China and Zimbabwe are a smoke screen. The President has too much on her plate."

"She may appear to be all business, but don't you think it strange the President refused my advice to take time to deal with her husbands death?" asked Best.

"It was a suicide. We don't commemorate suicides in this country. It isn't Japan. The flags were lowered for seven days."

"Strange. Katherine Stone is the most powerful person in the world. Nevertheless, from where I'm sitting the President doesn't make a move without calling Ashton Pickering at Trinity PharmoDynamics. She seems mesmerized by Pickering," Best admitted.

"I don't want to know about their relationship, Charles. You handle it. What I don't know can't hurt me," Drew replied.

"I'm afraid it isn't as simple as burying your head in the sand. Pickering called me earlier today," Best retorted.

Drew paled.

"His tone was ominous. He cautioned me. Trinity wants to be kept in the loop," Best replied.

"I agree. Pickering and Trinity have a tremendous hold on President Stone. Did you ever watch the President when she finishes a phone conversation with Pickering? It's like she's in another world when she talks with him."

"Maybe they have something going," said Best.

"There's more to it. I can't explain. It's like she's a puppet or a robot."

"Powerful people stand to make a fortune on a Zimbabwe scenario," Best added.

"She's cunning. She wants to be re-elected.," said Lindstrom.

Best raised the tumbler of Scotch. "Well, here's to the first female President of these United States. So where does that leave us?"

"She is treacherous. Stop the bullshit, Charles. I won't be hung out to dry. Your job is to make sure I've covered the President's ass and mine too."

"Correction. We are all in over our heads. And don't forget it. Trinity has us by the short hairs. Tough serving two masters." Best placed his empty tumbler on the shelf and closed the bookcase doors."

"That's it. End of discussion. Tonight's meeting is our priority," said Lindstrom.

Lindstrom's secretary entered the office. "Sir, Ms. Stokes and

Mr. Clayton are outside."

"Thank you. Give us a moment. I'll greet them. Charles, button your collar and fix your tie. You're disheveled."

"I'm feeling a bit under the weather," Best replied.

"Honestly? You look like shit."

⁖

Lindstrom walked into the outer office. "Ms. Stokes and Mr. Clayton. Thanks for coming." Lindstrom had an innate compulsion to glad-hand visitors as though he was campaigning.

Best walked across the room to greet David and Lou-Ann. Lindstrom directed them to the large walnut conference table.

"May I offer you something to drink?" Lindstrom asked.

David and Lou-Ann declined.

"Then, let's get right to business. It's a bit complicated."

"What we are about to discuss is totally off the record. When you leave, this meeting never took place," interjected Best.

"I've heard that before," David snickered. "In other words, your office recording system is off and your calendar notes show you at a meeting cross town?"

"I'd advise you to remember with whom you are speaking," said Best.

"Actually, we aren't speaking to *anyone* from your perspective."

"Touché. Now you've vented, shall we get on with the matter at hand?" asked Lindstrom.

"Excuse me, Mr. Lindstrom." The Chief of Staff's secretary escorted a man into the room.

"Foxx, where the hell have you been? The meeting has already started."

The man didn't seem fazed by Lindstrom's admonishment. He tossed several books and his brief case on the conference table as though he owned the place.

"Ms. Stokes. Mr. Clayton. This is Alan Foxx from the Justice Department. He is directing a General Accountability Office investigation. I believe you have already met, Mr. Clayton."

Foxx smiled. "Only by reputation."

"Mr. Best's authorization counter-signed by the Inspector General officially places me in charge of the current inquiry."

Foxx turned back to David. "Let's hope the unit has more success under my direction than Sam Beverly."

Clayton tensed. *That's an insult fired right at me. Foxx is a son of a bitch. He knows I was working with Sam Beverly.* "Congratulations, on your appointment, Foxx." *I'm sure you'll continue to be a back stabber.* "Keep in mind, Lindstrom and Best assured us that this meeting is completely off the record."

A puzzled Foxx looked at Lindstrom and said, "Agreed."

"Foxx needs your cooperation in a nasty bit of business," said Lindstrom. "Foxx, please bring us up to date."

"Yes sir. What I'm about to share carries a top-secret classification. Folks at the National Security Agency, FBI, and CIA are feeling a bit uncomfortable."

"Damn right! Who wouldn't be?" Charles Best started to walk to the bar.

"Sit down Charles. You are making me nervous and we haven't gotten to the crux of the problem."

"What does that mean?" asked David.

Lindstrom slid two documents across the table. "It means if you share any of this or leak it, you are violating the National Secrets Act. That's treason. Sign these."

Lou-Ann and David read the documents. "We've signed these before, but someone always leaks the information."

Best looked directly at David. "Foxx has concerns about your relationship with the author, Dakota Putnam."

"Her first novel. It should have been cleared by the Inspector General and the Justice Department," Foxx claimed.

"I had this discussion with the FBI years ago. I did not give documents or classified information to Dakota Putnam. She told me about her manuscript days before it was accepted by her publisher."

"You were obsessed with Dakota Putnam. Don't deny it. I've spent days reviewing everyone's personnel files."

"Gentlemen, please. Let's get on with this," Lindstrom insisted. "Foxx. Stop badgering Clayton. You boys have a problem, settle it someplace else."

"When I was at the GAO we were ordered to determine if Nazi war criminals were on US government payrolls," David responded.

"We found them and more," Lou-Ann added. "But isn't it odd?"

"What?" asked Best.

"Odd. The former Deputy Inspector General headed the investigation. Why isn't Sam Beverly at this meeting?"

"Listen to me. I don't give a shit about Sam Beverly returning to Washington. He's too old. I was opposed to seeking your involvement, but I need your knowledge."

This guy is an arrogant bastard. David looked at Lou-Ann. Then he leaned back in his chair waiting for Foxx's pronouncement.

"I'm interested in Operation Paper Clip and MKNaomi," said Foxx.

Lou-Ann's posture stiffened.

The others appeared caught off guard by Foxx's question.

Foxx took off his suit jacket and placed it over his chair. Then he walked around the table and stared down at Lou-Ann.

"Back off Mr. Foxx. You've invaded my space," Lou-Ann snarled.

Foxx didn't move.

"Foxx, what's going on? Your-overstepping your boundaries," cautioned Lindstrom. "This isn't your show."

Best got up. He slid open the library cabinet doors and poured a Scotch.

"You need to talk with the other team members," Lou-Ann insisted.

"Bullshit. Your team fell apart. You had a chance to identify Operation Paper Clip and you didn't." Foxx was merciless.

David stood up and approached Foxx. "For a little man, you sure have a large ego."

Foxx took a step toward David, and then hesitated.

"Mr. Foxx's accusations are untrue. We were officially closed."

"Are you calling me a liar?"

"Erskin Young dismantled the investigation and seized all our documents just before he died."

"Do the names Otto Bruns and Heinrich Franz ring a bell with either of you?"

"Bruns. Otto Bruns?" asked Lou-Ann. "Of course. He was

the mystery man we could never locate. I concluded he was smuggled into the US and assigned to some type of defense project. We found two passports in his name among the personal papers of Karl Peter Koch, a Nazi virologist."

"I don't recognize the name Heinrich Franz."

"Wait a minute, Foxx. You've had access to the Sunrise File, Erskine Young's pet project."

"That's not important at this point. Are you sure Heinrich Franz's name never came up during your investigation?"

Across the table Best sipped Scotch and scribbled notes.

"Again. Are you positive you never discovered Franz's name?" Foxx persisted.

"Yes, I'm sure." David looked surprised. *I'm certain Foxx accessed the Sunrise Files. How else would he acquire this information?*

'We believe there is a link between Heinrich Franz and Otto Bruns. Franz died on a canoe trip years ago."

"Our sources speculate Bruns was a Paper Clip asset. He was never cleared for a citizenship. Otto Bruns was out in the cold. No passport. Documents point to Erskine Young and another intelligence agent. Paper Clip recruits were placed in defense plants and research facilities."

"The GAO Special Investigations Unit was on the verge of publishing a preliminary report when we were closed down. Some one didn't want that report to see the light of day," Lou-Ann answered.

Foxx laughed.

"From your perspective we've lost our credibility?" Lou-Ann asked.

David's quick temper flared. He was about to lunge at Foxx.

"Foxx may have a point," remarked Best to Lindstrom.

"Be careful, Mr. Clayton. From where I'm sitting you and Ms. Stokes are tenuous characters in a huge intrigue."

David ran his fingers through his thinning grey hair. *What the hell am I doing here?*

Just then Lindstrom's secretary returned with a lockbox.

David was distracted by her striking profile.

Lou-Ann caught David's glance and kicked his ankle.

Lindstrom unlocked the box and removed the contents. "These are classified 'top secret.'"

"And?" asked Lou-Ann.

Next Lindstrom placed five photographs on the table in front of Lou-Ann and David. "These photos were taken in the 1950's. The five children were part of a research project to improve academic achievement."

"We don't know anything about this," David said.

David caught the quizzical expression on Lou-Ann's face.

"We have established a link between these five children and Heinrich Franz. Surely you came across Franz's name."

"No," Lou-Ann insisted.

"Franz was a Paperclip asset...an American traitor. He worked for the Nazis in Berlin. Franz was returned to the United States and granted a Presidential pardon."

"Can't help you," said David.

"Franz was an associate of Otto Bruns," Foxx said.

"Yes. We discovered two passports purportedly issued to Bruns, but we never could locate him."

"The project Franz headed was code named Pied Piper. An interagency task force financed it. These five were the subjects." Lindstrom reached between Lou-Ann and David. He sorted the five photographs, four boys and a girl. *If Clayton and Stokes only knew there were seven.*

Best looked surprised at Lindstrom's assertion. *Five subjects? Lindstrom knows there were seven children. He's withholding two names.*

Lindstrom continued. "I'll put these three photos aside for a moment. I've accounted for them." Next he placed two photos next to one another. "Meet Mary Taylor and Walter Katz."

"Up until two weeks ago Katz worked for the Defense Department Logistics Agency. He monitored asset acquisitions and distribution," said Lindstrom.

"What happened two weeks ago?" asked Lou-Ann.

"That's why you're here," said Best.

"There have been a number of attacks on DOD computer systems not unlike the recent sabotage a number of private corporations experienced. Katz was a key player for tracking those intrusions. He's disappeared."

"And Taylor?" asked Lou-Ann.

"Taylor died several years ago." Lindstrom's staccato response led Lou-Ann to believe was withholding information.

"Who vetted the guy? Do you have his dossier?"

Lindstrom hesitated as though he was carefully planning his response. "Katz was hired during Desert Storm. A no-bid contract awarded to the Trinity International's subsidiary, PharmoDynamics. DOD purchased tons of material through Trinity. Inventory was scattered from here to Alaska. No central inventory. No catalogue. DOD couldn't account for purchases."

"When the DOD consolidated, Katz remained as part of a renewed contract with Trinity," said Best.

Foxx looked befuddled as though he hadn't been briefed.

Best took the last swallow of Scotch and said, "Katz walked away with thousands of classified files."

"How did you discover the security breach?" asked David.

"We didn't. Katz sent an e-mail to General Vereen, the Executive Director of the Defense Logistics Agency."

"What?"

"Another Edward Snowden exposé? My god he's the world's most wanted man."

"He was," Best's cryptic comment troubled Lou-Ann and David.

"Are you telling us Walter Katz has taken files crucial to national security?" David shook his head in disbelief.

" Katz hasn't revealed his grievances. No threats. General Vereen notified the Secretary of Defense and the Joint Chiefs."

"He hasn't gone public?" asked Lou-Ann.

"No. The President wants Katz located before he does. We want him to come in. The President guarantees his safety. President Stone wants to avoid the media frenzy Obama experienced. There was a lot of collateral damage. Snowden's files embarrassed our government."

"Yes. The more the administration tried to discredit Snowden the more files he released."

"What else do you know Mr. Foxx?"

It was clear Foxx knew little about the present revelations. He remained silent.

Lindstrom picked up Mary Taylor's photo to move it to the discard pile.

"Hold on. Taylor may be an important clue to finding Katz."

"She's dead. I told you." Lindstrom wanted to move on.

"No I get the picture. You want us to be the intermediaries and contact Katz," said Lou-Ann.

"In other words, we take the fall if something goes wrong."

"Nice, Mr. Clayton. Still, I'd advise you again to remember with whom you are speaking." Lindstrom resented being challenged.

"The conversation never existed," replied Lou-Ann.

"Can we return to the subject at hand?" Lindstrom walked to the office door. It's time," he said to someone standing outside.

"Just bring in Katz. We'll take it from there" Foxx piped-up with bravado as the three left the room.

Lindstrom interrupted. "Enough Foxx!" said Lindstrom. He led Lou-Ann and David to a small room guarded by a Secret Service agent. "I want you to read these files. No notes. The door is alarmed. If you need something there's a call button on the wall.

✍

Lou-Ann and David spent the next two hours reading classified documents. "This is a tremendous amount of information for us to read in a few hours."

"I agree. A great way to stifle an inquiry is to give the investigator a flood of paper work. Information overload. What the hell are we looking for, Lou-Ann?"

Lou-Ann skimmed the documents. "David I found a partially redacted invoice payable to the Trinity Corporation." She leafed through several more pages. "Look at this. The name Pied Piper scribbled at the bottom of a receipt."

"I don't understand. The CIA destroyed records. We never confirmed the connection to Trinity International. Their name is printed on these documents. They connect Trinity to MKULTRA. Check the initials these initials, 'HF'."

"Do you think it's a reference to Heinrich Franz? Hey hold on. Look at this one." David handed the document to Lou-Ann. "Check these initials, WL."

"Walther Liechtenauer?"

"Why not? It's a receipt for a shipment of pharmaceuticals to a children's clinic in Bay Grove."

"This is information overload. It's nearly midnight." Lou-Ann was exhausted.

"You're right. Let's call it quits. Did you see the baffled expression on Foxx's face when Lindstrom handed me Mary Taylor's file? He didn't want us to read it."

"From my perspective Taylor is the key to finding Katz."

David pressed the call button and the Secret Service agent unlocked the door. As they walked into the corridor David spotted Foxx asleep in a chair. The agent walked to Foxx and said, "Mr. Foxx, I'm closing this restricted area. You'll have to leave."

Foxx was startled. He looked down the corridor and saw David and Lou-Ann leaving. "Hey wait a minute." Foxx was agitated. "What did you find out? "Don't hide information pertinent to my investigation," he warned.

"We won't be browbeaten," Lou-Ann responded. Foxx's bravado faded.

"I'm not bullying you. I'm telling you straight-out. I want to know everything you discover. I'm convinced there is a relationship between Heinrich Franz and Trinity."

"Tell me, Foxx. Why isn't the Defense Logistics Agency involved? Katz worked for them. The DLA has its own investigation unit."

"Conflict of interest. The President didn't want an agency investigating itself."

"It seems President Stone has a vested interest. What is it? Don't you find that unusual?"

"She wants Walter Katz," Foxx replied.

"There was a preliminary GAO investigation," said Lou-Ann.

"Did the GAO determine whether the DOD faces any supply chain vulnerability?" David asked.

"What do you mean?" Foxx looked puzzled.

"National security issues. Are there any threats to our national security because of the current rare earth issues?" David persisted.

Foxx paused and then replied, "GAO's appraisal perplexed me. They fell back on a letter from the Secretary of Defense."

"Come on Foxx, you know more than you are telling us," insisted Lou-Ann."

"The DOD was going through its own internal evaluation."

"In other words, the DOD identified a national security risk, but is reluctant to admit is has not taken any steps to address possible material shortages."

"For god's sake, Foxx. You knew this all along. Our nation's security is at risk because we rely on China for rare earth elements, but no one will come out and say it." David's face turned red. "You guys are a bunch of assholes. And you hold the destiny of our nation in your hands?"

"Excuse me gentlemen," said Lou-Ann trying to dampen the tension. "David, I'm headed home."

"I apologize Lou-Ann. I need rest, too."

"Find Walter Katz. He holds the answers." David turned and walked down the corridor. Foxx walked in the opposite direction.

As they left the White House Lou-Ann paused. "David, are you OK?"

"Yes, of course. I'm a bit tired. The meeting was intense."

"Why?"

"Foxx got under your skin when he questioned your relationship with Dakota Putnam. You haven't seen her of late?"

"No. Not since the eighties. I've followed her career, but that's it."

"You two should have been a couple. Her marriage to Doyle was a disaster."

"It's all in the past, Lou-Ann. I'm just a bit tired. I don't relish this Katz affair. Oh, well as long as you are on the team something positive will come out of it. Thanks for caring."

"Sure thing. Let's talk tomorrow."

Chapter Forty-Eight
The White House Master Bedroom

Drew Lindstrom was a frequent evening visitor to the White House residence. As he approached the restricted threshold, Agent Kevin Goodman greeted the Chief of Staff. Goodman was the recently appointed head of President Stone's re-organized Secret Service detail. Goodman's reputation for valor and discretion placed him at the top of the Chief's short list. Goodman wasn't one for small talk. He rarely spoke. Carole Dean wrote the one negative anecdote in Goodman's personnel file. "Goodman has no respect for women, especially those in command."

"Good evening Mr. Lindstrom."

"Agent Goodman."

"The President is expecting you."

"I see the apparatus has been installed."

"Yes sir. It is the highest resolution body scanner on the market. Please step through."

Goodman held out his hand. "Not the briefcase. I know it's yours sir, but regulations are regulations. Please place it on the table."

Lindstrom grimaced, set the canvas briefcase on the table. Lindstrom looked through the briefcase as Lindstrom stepped through the scanner.

"Thank you, sir."

Lindstrom nodded, reached for his briefcase and walked toward the winding grand staircase. President Stone was waiting on the landing.

"Well, how did it go?" she asked.

"Want the good news or the bad?"

"You know I resent bad news, Drew. Let's have a nightcap. Lindstrom followed Stone along the west corridor toward the private sitting room. She paused. "Not tonight. I'm pressed for time." She led him into the President's master bedroom.

"Like it?" She turned and tilted her head. Her untied silk Chinese robe fell open.

Drew smiled with satisfaction.

She followed his eyes drifting down her body. "I'm talking about the suite. It's been totally redecorated," she said tying her robe closed.

Lindstrom knew The President was teasing him. *Business before pleasure.*

"I moved a few pieces back to the Lincoln bedroom and replaced them with several from storage." Katherine pointed to the window. "Jackie Kennedy purchased the writing table just before Dallas."

Drew looked around the room.

"Sit down, Drew." Katherine walked to a small cabinet. She poured two snifters of brandy. "Cheers. How did it go?" she asked.

"Charlie Best is a nervous wreck. Alan Foxx appears clueless. He could be a liability. I'm certain the Inspector General recommend Foxx just to get rid of him."

"How did David Clayton and Lou-Ann Stokes react?"

"I can't figure them out. I need time."

"You followed the plan. Correct?"

"Yes. But let's get back to Foxx."

"Did you assign a tail?"

"Foxx has been under surveillance. I read the log. He made three visits to a government storage facility in Maryland. It is a little used Justice Department achieve. Few people have signed the log in the last year. Records from the 70's."

"Is that significant?"

"I'm uncertain, but Clayton picked up on something. He accused Foxx of accessing the so-called Sunrise Files. Apparently Clayton's team attempted to subpoena them in '77 with no success."

"Never heard of the Sunrise Files. Watch Foxx. We don't need more trouble."

"Foxx is covered twenty-four-seven. I told the them to call me immediately if he returns to the archives."

"And the bad news?"

"I gather neither Clayton nor Stokes is enamored with you. But they respect you."

"Respect or fear?"

"Your choice. Stokes and Clayton appear loyal to one another."

Katherine sipped her brandy. "I'm concerned about Dakota Putnam. She's on to something. She's been snooping through Social Security records, again. She embarrassed the Obama administration. She is persistent."

"I'm convinced David Clayton is not her source. I do know she's pulling her columns from an unpublished manuscript. We've been following her e-mails."

"Drew, tell security to void her press credential. She's barred from the White House."

Katherine placed her glass on the nightstand. "Come over here," she said.

Lindstrom pushed himself out of the chair.

Katherine moved closer.

Lindstrom flushed.

"After all this time and you still look shy," she teased.

Lindstrom stood motionless. He anticipated her next gesture. Katherine always led.

"Have you told your wife about us?"

"No."

"Good."

Katherine untied her rob and let it fall. She pressed against Lindstrom. His jacket fell to the floor. Next she unbuckled his belt. "You're putting on weight, my dear," she chuckled. She pushed Lindstrom and he fell back into the chair. "I only have a few minutes," she whispered.

Lindstrom attempted to unbutton his shirt.

"Darling, I told you. There's little time."

With one gesture she slid out of her robe.

Lindstrom reached to caress her.

"Not yet. Let me." Her hand moved along his leg searching for his excitement. "Close your legs." It was a gentle but assertive command. Lindstrom obeyed. Then she slithered on top of him. Lindstrom's facial expression puzzled Katherine. "What's wrong?"

"Nothing."

"Of course there is."

"Passion. There's never any passion."

She laughed. "Passion? Drew I'm nearly fifteen years older than you. For you it may be passion. For me it's lust and rejuvenation. Now stop talking and get on with it. I'm expecting a priority call in less than thirty minutes."

Chapter Forty-Nine
Manassas
1:30 AM

David had grown accustomed to a bachelor's life; perhaps too comfortable. When he arrived home he poured a Jameson and grabbed the paper. He enjoyed living away from Number One Observatory Circle. The ambiance of a free cottage wasn't worth the personal sacrifices a Vice President's assistant must make. The decision to move was final when President Stone selected House Speaker, Ives Venal, as her Vice President. David vividly remembered the circumstances.

At the time, Venal was the most despised man in Congress. He raised David's ire with a series of television interviews immediately after Andrew Dunn's death. Venal held Agent Dean responsible. He demanded a complete Secret Service overhaul.

President Stone asked David to hold an informal meeting between Speaker Venal and Carol Dean. Venal's impromptu remarks embarrassed the President. The President dispute ended. The meeting turned into a fracas. David would come to regret his role.

"She put the President in danger," Venal growled and pointed at Dean.

"The investigation is still open," said David.

"It's closed," replied Venal.

"Mr. Clayton, I agreed to this meeting, but not an inquisition," Dean rebutted.

"The other agents don't respect you," Venal retorted.

"Agents are supposed to set politics and bias aside. Simply put – I'm a woman. The old boy network doesn't want a woman in charge."

Venal spoke with a slight lisp. It became a pronounced

"hiss" when he was excited. Consequently, and predictably, his enemies called Venal "the snake."

"I read your initial report, Dean. You continue to question the official medical examiner's report. Andrew Dunn's death was a suicide." Venal waved the two-page summary at Dean.

"I'm disputing my pending transfer for refusing to sign off on the final report. You're behind it, Venal."

"I'm not answerable to you, Agent Dean. Clayton, this meeting is a waste of my time." Venal looked at his cell phone and said, "I have another appointment." He walked out in a huff.

Once David and Dean were alone the conversation took a turn.

"David, I loyally served President Stone for years. Venal never wanted today's meeting. It's all show. For some reason I'm being tossed to the wolves."

"We worked together. I know the President trusts you. I don't understand this beef with Venal," David answered.

"From my perspective there's some kind of a cover-up. Why?"

"What?"

"I requested a private meeting with Drew Lindstrom. He kept putting me off," said Dean.

"What happened?"

"Finally, Lindstrom met with me. He was nervous. Rushed the conversation. Kept finishing my sentences."

"Tell me the crux of the meeting."

"I supervised the forensic unit. I told Lindstrom there was a concentration of blood on the master bedroom carpet proximate to the love seat where Dunn was discovered. Oddly, there were microscopic smatterings of blood on the desk."

"There was a desk?"

"Absolutely. Laura Bush redecorated the Lincoln Bedroom. Private donations were used to purchase authentic pieces. A pigeonhole writing desk was included with the furnishings. It was period correct, but never in the White House when Mary Todd Lincoln was First Lady. President Stone admired the piece and had it moved to the President's bedroom."

"The blood on the desk matched Dunn's blood type.

Furthermore, Forensics suggested the piece might have been wiped down."

"Have you re-examined the desk?"

"Look at this." Dean tapped her cell phone screen and pointed to a photo. "The desk was returned to its original location near the window of the Lincoln Bedroom."

"Here's something significant. The President was covered in blood. The paramedics thought she was wounded."

"What's the point?"

"The lab report came back. The only blood was Dunn's. There should have been traces on furniture other than the desk and the immediate scene."

"That's it?"

Dean hesitated. "The bullet exited Dunn's temple on the right side."

"And that troubled you?"

"Yes. You and I know Andrew Dunn was right handed."

"How could the medical examiner or your forensic unit miss that?"

"And the gun?"

"The prints on the gun were smudged."

"I traced the serial numbers on the pistol, a twenty-two semi auto. It was purchased at a gun show about a year ago."

"By whom?

"Secret Service Agent Kevin Goodman, my replacement on the President's security detail."

"Goodman had access to target pistols from the Secret Service armory. I suspect he circumvented regulations to furnish an unregistered pistol to someone in the White House."

"Andrew Dunn?"

"It's a mystery. We may never know. There were nine rounds left in the pistol magazine. I searched every crevice in the residence. I couldn't locate additional ammunition."

"Is that important?"

"Goodman never brought that pistol upstairs to the White House residence. He didn't have access at the time. Someone else did."

"And Goodman?"

"Leave him alone, David. This is getting messy. You could be in jeopardy. I've told you everything."

"Aren't you in danger?"

"No. I've told my story to a number of White House players. Lou-Ann Stokes knows, also. Who ever is behind this has a vested interest in keeping me alive. Kill me and Congress will demand an independent investigation."

"I told Drew Lindstrom the report was incomplete. He pooh-poohed me. He implied I was prone to a conspiracy theory."

"Conspiracy theory?"

"David, believe me. There were powder burns on Dunn's left temple. I became suspicious when the initial lab report found no traces of gun powder on Dunn's fingers."

"Are you saying it wasn't a suicide?"

"I'm telling you the report was inconclusive.

"There's one thing I didn't tell Lindstrom. He has to know it. The letter."

"What letter?"

"The President intercepted an email from Dunn. David it was addressed to you."

"Are you certain?"

"He revealed the contents of several therapy sessions."

"I knew he was seeing a psychologist. He complained about headaches and lack of sleep. Nothing else."

"In the e-mail Dunn claims several of his classmates are murderers. He was frightened about his own behavior."

"Where is the letter? Did you make a copy?"

"No. Now here's the kicker. The report has been sealed along with all the evidence." Dean's scowl reflected disappointment. "I trusted Drew Lindstrom. I believed in President Stone."

David didn't respond.

"You don't have to say a thing, David. I've been placed on leave pending a new assignment. Helen Scott, my deputy on the detail, was transferred to Thailand."

"Carol, you're pointing to a criminal conspiracy."

Chapter Fifty
Complexities

Washington has an interesting way of dealing with complexity. In the end Venal badgered the Secret Service to reorganize. President Stone acquiesced to Venal's doggedness.

David sent a summary to Lindstrom. David sympathized with Dean. She'd been treated unfairly. Lindstrom telephoned David a few days later.

"It's sour grapes. Carol Dean should be grateful. The President pulled some strings to save Dean's career."

"What's left of it," David replied.

"There's nothing to Dean's suspicions. You did your part. Trust the President's decision on this. There's no cover up. The report was sealed to protect a grieving President from the usual media passion to create a story from nothing."

"And Venal?"

"Where I come from hardcore snakes are kept in plastic cages. Venal is a snake. What better place to contain him than the grounds of the Naval Observatory? The President put Venal on notice. 'Keep your mouth shut.'"

"That's it?"

"Put it to rest David. Hey buddy, I have another call. Keep in touch."

Lindstrom's prediction seemed to hold. Carol Dean was reassigned to an administrative position with the Department of Homeland Defense.

Weeks passed and the Dean-Venal controversy faded. David supposed Stone selected Ives Venal for Vice President to isolate him from his power base. In accordance with the 25th Amendment, Venal's House and Senate approvals were the fastest on record. Consequently, it seemed that Venal was now on a short leash.

Nevertheless, something irked David. He couldn't comprehend Andrew Dunn committing suicide. David finished his drink and pushed back in his Lazy Boy.

I regret attending this evening's White House meeting. He tried pushing the Dean-Venal controversy to the back of his mind. He sensed it was the beginning of many thankless days and sleepless nights.

§

Sunlight broke through the patio doors. David pulled a pillow over his head. He'd tossed and turned since his three AM bathroom visit. It was no use. He couldn't sleep. Finally, he convinced himself it was time to face the inevitable. The hall clock chimed eight. He carefully rolled out of bed and slowly stretched. The ritual seemed to help with his chronic back pain. *I've got to get back to yoga class.*

He walked into the bathroom. Lately he stared into the sink to avoid his mirrored image while brushing his teeth. He was definitely challenged, if not confounded by age-related issues. *Would Viagra be next? Did it matter?* He hadn't been with a woman in months. He splashed water on his face then tossed the damp towel on the floor. Next he wandered into the kitchen. The Keurig light was flashing. He'd forgotten to fill the water reservoir. "Damn it." *The coffee isn't ready.* "Shit! Is this how the day will go?"

He glanced at his iPhone still connected to the charger. Lately, e-mail tempted him away from morning meditation. Ever so slowly he was drawn from the serenity of listening to his own thoughts and responding to his instincts. He was preoccupied with other people's priorities and neglecting the peace he sought in retirement. He needed to clear his mind and prepare for the day. A worn linen wingback chair faced a floor to ceiling bookshelf in the opposite corner of the room. On the fourth shelf from the bottom David had placed a number of items. These were his personal meditation icons. His favorite, a miniature brass sailboat, held promise of a yet-to-be fulfilled adventure. David inhaled deeply and with a slow exhale affirmed, *I need to return to my morning routine.*

The meditation was short-lived. David neglected his sidekick, Dusty, a mini Schnauzer. She recognized David's moods better than anyone, David included.

"Sorry, buddy. Come on. I've been so damn busy; I haven't been giving you enough attention. Let's head outside."

Dusty ran from the room and scratched the door leading to the small yard. For a change it wasn't raining. *Perhaps my feelings of impending crisis will diminish as the weather clears.* Back inside he fed Dusty. His phone rang almost in sync with an e-mail notification.

"Hello."

"Clayton, have you read this morning's Post?"

"No. I'm trying to avoid bad news. What's so important?"

"I don't know what the hell that means, but you better read your girlfriend's column."

"My girlfriend?"

"Don't hang up on me Clayton. This is important. Dakota Putnam is on her Nazi kick again. She claims the Social Security administration denied a recent Freedom of Information Request."

"Ridiculous. Dakota finished that score with the Obama administration. President Obama signed the executive order prohibiting Social Security benefits for Nazis."

"Maybe so, but the government never released the names of thirty-eight potential war criminals still receiving payments. They're classified."

"So?"

"Someone is drawing Putnam back into the mix."

"How do I know you're not the culprit, Foxx? A friend at the Bureau told me you and Bob Doyle are linked?"

"Bullshit!"

"It's going to surface. Come clean Foxx."

There was a long silence.

"Listen. Doyle was married to my sister for six years. I know him. He dislikes most people. He detests you. Blames you for his divorce from Putnam. I run into him from time to time."

"Doyle has no conscience, Foxx. He's an abusive alcoholic,"

said David.

"That's why my sister left," Foxx answered.

"Trinity doesn't have its hooks into you?"

"No I swear. Shut up and listen to me, Clayton. Putnam is on to our search for Walter Katz. Her Freedom of Information Inquiry specifically listed Otto Bruns."

"Hold on. Could someone on the inside have tipped Putnam? Maybe they figured Dakota might shake the bushes better than we could? One of her readers might have a tip."

"There's something far more important. I discovered a photograph."

"Where?"

"There's a DOJ warehouse just out side of DC in Maryland. I discovered files from the fifties and sixties."

"Damn you, Foxx. You *do* have access to Erskin Young's Sunrise Files."

"It doesn't matter. I need to show you a photograph. It's going to blow your mind. It's frightening. We need to meet."

"Can't it wait?"

"No. It's ten o'clock. I'll meet you this afternoon, 3PM. L'Enfant Plaza. The lower level. Yellow line."

"Foxx, that's the start of rush hour."

"Exactly. We have to avoid being seen together."

"Sounds a bit paranoid."

"You'll understand when you see the photograph."

"All right. I'll meet you. This better be good. Agreed?"

"Agreed."

David sipped his now lukewarm coffee and read the e-mail notification. It was from Lou-Ann. "David: Check today's *Post.*"

He opened the Post app and scrolled to Top Stories. "US Searches For Lost Nazi." *What the hell? No wonder Foxx was agitated.* David skimmed the story and called Lou-Ann.

"David what's going on? Has Dakota lost her mind?"

"I skimmed the story. The *Post* would never publish the article unless it was credible."

"They've done it before. Reporters fabricate anonymous sources," Lou-Ann replied.

"But what's the connection between Bruns and DOD

acquisitions? Doesn't she realize Otto Bruns is nearly ninety-five years old if he's even alive? Who is feeding her this stuff?" David asked.

"Dakota's source claims Bruns developed applications for permanent magnetic materials in US weapon systems. The government has been working on the technology for years. The magnets and electronic components contain rare earth elements. I Googled the topic. For god's sake David, twenty pounds of the stuff goes into one Toyota Prius battery. There are millions of hybrids. It's in all our electrical components."

"Dakota must have spent months on the research," said David.

"Scroll down. There's more."

"She's setting herself up for a bitter battle," David insisted.

" Dakota claims there is a crisis within the Defense Department. The DOD's computer systems are flawed and opened to intrusions. Her source asserts the Chinese have been monitoring DOD's computer systems for years. The Chinese Liberation Army runs the operation. Our intelligence tracked down a unit called Putter Panda. They operate out of a building in Shanghai."

"The Chinese have a monopoly on rare earth materials. We buy the stuff from them. They monitor our allocations. *Shazam!* They regulate the markets," David exclaimed.

"And she claims Putter Panda monitors the Eastern Distribution Center. It's the DOD's largest automated warehouse."

"Has Dakota tried to contact you?" David asked.

"David, I would have told you."

"I feel certain she will reach out to you, Lou-Ann. Find a place for us to meet and get back to me. I'm meeting Foxx. The weasel claims he has something important. I'll call you later."

"Hold on. The news ticker just posted the DOD's response to Dakota Putnam's story. I'll read it to you. "In response to the *Post* story the Secretary of Defense has requested an internal assessment to identify any national security risks. The Secretary assured the President that he will take all necessary steps to deal with potential material shortages."

"I have to go, Lou-Ann. I suspect Dakota's source may be Walter Katz. You've got to talk with her."

Chapter Fifty-One
Stratum Monitoring Center
A Location Near Dulles Airport.

A tiny blue light on Drew Lindstrom's watch began to flash. He pressed the crown twice. The numeral "1" appeared. Lindstrom carried two mobile phones. Both lines were scrambled, but the phone in the blue case was for one use only. It was Lindstrom's link to a signal intelligence collection unit. Lindstrom and Best created the unit at President Stone's direction. She told Lindstrom "I want it so shrouded in secrecy no one can prove it's existence."

Lindstrom excused himself from the meeting and quickly walked to his office.

"This is Lindstrom."

"Sir, we monitored a conversation between Alan Foxx and David Clayton. Based on the number of key words the computers prioritized the intercept."

"Summarize it for me, Ambrose."

"Yes sir. Alan Foxx discovered a photograph he plans to show David Clayton. They have established a rendezvous time and location. Sir, as you ordered, our surveillance unit tracked Foxx earlier in the day."

"Where was he?"

"He traveled to the DOJ achieves in Maryland. Spent twenty-seven minutes inside. He returned to his Washington office and called Clayton at 10 PM."

"Ambrose, I want you to order your team to interdict."

"Sir?"

"Stop the meeting and retrieve the photograph and other documents."

"The location is a heavily traveled transit station, L'Enfant."

"I don't care. Just get it done." Lindstrom ended the call.

&

David drove from Manassas to Vienna. He intended to ride the Metro into DC. At the last minute he changed his mind and continued by the station. The traffic was heavy, but he didn't anticipate the unusual delays. Foxx demanded a 3:00 PM meeting at the L'Enfant station. David's distrust of Foxx motivated the lengthy drive. He decided to stop at the Department of Justice building before meeting Foxx. It was nearly two o'clock when he pulled into a public parking facility a short distance from the DOJ.

As David entered the building memories of the 1977 inquiry flashed back. He waited in the lobby. David searched for a familiar face, but realized the futility. He approached the information desk.

"Excuse me."

"Yes, sir." The employee was young enough to be David's grandson.

"I worked here for a brief time years ago. I wanted to take a look around for old times sake. Do you happen to know Captain Bob McBride?"

"Never met him sir. The Personnel Office is on the second floor. You might try there."

"Mac was in charge of security. I spent hours in the basement archives back then. He'd bring me a coffee from time to time."

"The archives are gone, sir. Moved all the hard copies to microfiche. Then we computerized."

"Everything is gone?" David looked puzzled.

"Moved records to a storage facility across the river in Maryland."

"Well, thank you."

"It's a coincidence," replied the receptionist.

"What?"

"I don't suppose it matters, but another gentleman inquired

about the archives a few weeks ago. I think he was a writer. No, that was the woman. This man was from the GAO. I can't tell you anything specific. Hope you find what you're looking for."

David's wide-eyed expression alarmed the man.

Foxx was telling the truth.

"Sir, are you all right?"

David didn't answer. He turned and sprinted to the sidewalk. He furiously hailed a cab. "L'Enfant Station"

"Heavy traffic, mister. The usual six minute drive might take twenty or more."

David glanced at his watch. *Nearly three.*

The driver answered his cell phone. "That was my dispatcher. There's some kind of a problem at L'Enfant. Seems like the station is plagued with problems."

The driver increased the volume on the satellite radio. The metro station was being evacuated. There was smoke billowing from the Yellow line platform.

"Mister, this is close enough. If I get caught in the maze, I'll never get out of here."

David handed the driver a ten. "Keep the change."

Fire equipment, ambulances, medical personnel replaced the usual gathering of street musicians and peddlers and huge yellow tarps spread at points along the street.

David's cell phone vibrated. "Hello."

"David, are you OK? WJCA just broadcast a live report from the L'Enfant."

"The place is in a panic. Something about a smoke filled tunnel."

"Did you meet Foxx?"

"No. And I doubt I will."

"Too much confusion. People are terrified. Saw one city bus take some folks away.

Their faces were covered in soot."

"CNN just broadcast there's a possible gang fight on the Yellow line."

"I can smell smoke on the street. My god, it must be a lot of smoke to fill that one big waffled domed bubble."

A metro cop began motioning for David to move back from the triage area.

"Hey, I have to get out of the way."

David called Lou-Ann. "I parked my car near the Justice Building. I'll walk there."

As he left the parking garage he called Lou-Ann again.

"Has Foxx contacted you?"

"No. Please call the nearby hospitals."

"David, I've called several. There's no record of Alan Foxx."

"Call the White House. Get Lindstrom. Tell him what happened."

"I did. He seemed nonplussed."

"What?"

"Like he kind of expected it. He said, "Don't worry. Foxx will turn up.""

"David, I'm starting to rethink our involvement in this investigation. I miss Jack. I'm sick of my hotel room."

"Let's talk later. Please wait. I'll search for Foxx."

It required two days for the Metro authority to release a preliminary report to the media. It was brief. Dozens of passengers on the Yellow line suffered smoke inhalation. Rescue efforts were delayed when a body was discovered on the tracks. A joint DC – federal task force was viewing hours of video while others were searching for clues on the lower level of L'Enfant. Within hours they pieced together a number of isolated discoveries. A picture was emerging.

At approximately 2:45 PM a man meeting Foxx's description entered L'Enfant station. The security videos don't tell the entire story, but they shed light on the incident. Mr. Foxx purchased a pass and proceeded directly to the Yellow line platform. Two men approached. The two men appeared to argue with one another. A fight broke out and Mr. Foxx, an innocent bystander, was struck. He fell to the tracks. The victim's body caused an enormous electrical arch. In turn the fire generated heavy smoke. The victim's body was burned beyond recognition.

The next forty-eight hours marked a turning point in the search for Alan Foxx.

A spokesperson for the DC-Federal task force announced their conclusions.

"The fire was caused when a Yellow line patron was shoved on to the tracks during an altercation. The victim's name was Alan Foxx, an attorney at the GAO. Metro police continue to search for two men who may have inadvertently shoved Mr. Foxx to his death."

A series of still photographs flashed across the TV screen. "I call your attention to the two men passing through the toll headed in the direction of the Yellow line." The platform photos were distorted. "Please call the hot-line number on your screen if you have information to aid with this investigation."

Chapter Fifty-Two
The Encounter

A week passed and the Metropolitan Police did not receive a single tip. The two men in the surveillance video remained their prime suspects. A pile of documents awaited Lou-Ann and David at the West Wing. David left home at 5:30 that morning to beat the traffic on Route 66. Along the way he picked up two surprises for Lou-Ann, a Starbucks venti and a bag of doughnuts. Lou-Ann was late. He finally called her cell phone. She didn't answer. David was unaware of his partner's predicament.

Lou-Ann was running late. She left her room at the Hampton Inn. She grabbed a to-go bag at the reception desk and walked directly to her car. She unlocked and opened the driver's side door and tossed the bag lunch on the passenger seat. Lou-Ann was about to start the engine. The sound of a semi-automatic pistol being cycled sent a chill through her body.

"Don't turn around Ms. Stokes."

"Who are you? What do you want?"

Lou-Ann felt the cold barrel of a pistol against her neck.

"Drive to 495. Take the Mount Vernon exit."

"Lou-Ann started the car. She caught the perpetrator's image in the rear view mirror."

"Mount Vernon?"

"Shut up and drive."

They turned onto Route One. At Groveton the man said, "Take the next exit. Then turn left. There's a group of apartment buildings ahead. The next exit on your right. Turn into that parking lot."

Lou-Ann complied. As the car turned into the parking lot she said, "You can't be too smart."

"Why?"

"It's broad daylight. Someone is bound to see us."

"Look around Ms. Stokes. The parking lot is nearly empty. I assure you. No one will bother us."

The man exited the rear door and ordered Lou-Ann, "Hold your hands out the window." He slid a plastic wire tie over her wrists and pulled it tight.

Lou-Ann winced.

"Now get out. Walk just in front of me. By the way, I know you were an FBI agent. You can't react faster than my nine millimeter." Katz pointed to a first floor corner apartment. "On your left. One step at a time, Ms. Stokes."

For the first time Lou-Ann was able to fully gauge her abductor. His trim physique and closely cropped hair shouted ex-military.

An electronic card lock secured the apartment door. Lou-Ann watched the man as pulled a card from his pocket. "These locks are so easy to open." He slipped a keycard into the lock and the opened the door. Lou-Ann looked beyond the building. A garbage truck was unloading a Dumpster. Lou-Ann made a desperate move. She elbowed her adversary. He grabbed her arm and dragged her inside.

"Walk down the hallway."

Lou-Ann instinctively began to search for avenues of escape.

"Sit down over there."

Lou-Ann sat on a sofa. The only other way out was onto the raised patio beyond the sliding glass doors. *There's probably another set of doors off the bedroom. Why is this guy doing this to me?* Lou-Ann scanned the living room furniture and walls for a clue to her kidnapper's identity. On the near wall was a large framed military citation presented to Lieutenant Colonel James K. Clark, United States Army. Donald Rumsfeld, Secretary of Defense, signed it.

The man caught Lou-Ann's glimpse and said, "Clark's a nice guy. My supervisor at DLA. He is on vacation in Amsterdam for ten days. He doesn't know we're here."

The man walked to the kitchenette. Lou-Ann watched him release the magazine from his pistol. He cycled the chambered round into his hand.

" I have no intention of harming you Ms. Stokes." He stepped forward. "Hold out your hands." He cut the wire tie.

"I don't believe it. You're Walter Katz. The FBI is after you."

Katz appeared to be brooding. "It's far more ominous. I'm a throwaway, Ms. Stokes. I'm expendable."

"You're a traitor. You've stolen top-secret files. If you come in now you will be treated fairly."

"It's remarkable, Ms. Stokes, how quickly I went from being an asset to expendable."

"Why are you doing this?"

"A number of reasons. None patriotic. Payback. That's it – payback."

"Revenge?"

"For lives lost."

"Does this have anything to do with a woman named Mary Taylor?"

"Precisely." Katz began to nervously pace. "We lived a life of lies."

Lou-Ann began to speak in calmer tones as she regained her composure. *This guy didn't bring me here to kill me. He has a story to tell. I have to engage him. Establish a rapport.* "Walter, listen. It may be painful, but tell me why you took the DLA files."

Katz went into the kitchenette and filled a glass with water. "Diazepam. My nerves are shot." He swallowed the pill. He took a deep breath. Then he returned to the living room and sat on a chair facing Lou-Ann. "You're right. Mary Taylor is an important reason behind my actions. Andrew Dunn is part of it. All six of us were betrayed."

"I'm your captive audience, Walter. This is your chance. Tell me about it."

"I visited Mary on Long Island. She was a patient at Central Islip Psychiatric Center. The place was little more than a prison housing people."We were classmates in Bay Grove Elementary School. I had a crush on her from second grade. "I was so happy when I realized Mary was part of the special program at Dr. Franz's clinic. She was so much fun."

"Over the years Mary's personality slowly changed. Although

I was part of the program I didn't attend all their sessions. My tutor was Dr. Otto Bruns. He wasn't a psychologist."

"What was he?"

"A kind man. I was depressed. My mother was a single parent and we didn't have much compared to the rest of the kids in the group. The one thing we had in common was a troubled family life. We'd talk about it."

"When did you last see Mary?"

"Several years ago, around 2012."

"How did you locate her?"

"I didn't. She contacted me. A note. She asked me to meet her on the grounds of Kings Park Hospital, near the Long Island Sound. Oh…" Katz turned away for a minute to regain his composure.

"She was living in one of the abandoned buildings. Looked and smelled awful."

"I said, 'Come home to my house. Let me get you out of here.'"

As they walked the deserted grounds of the "Psych Center" Mary shared an incredible story.

"I still find it hard to believe, but now I know it's true," Katz spoke softly as though someone might be listening. "Then we entered one of the buildings."

"What was it like?"

"No electricity, no running water. The place smelled of excrement."

Mary told Katz she had been committed to a number of group homes until 1996. All they did was keep her drugged. She talked about voices and felt people were controlling her.

"The Mary Taylor I remembered was beautiful, vivacious and bright," said Katz.

"And then?"

"Physical abuse. She claimed the doctors were intentionally controlling her. Called it "driving." She felt worthless."

"There had to be more to it," Lou-Ann insisted. What happened to all the years after high school?"

"I lost track of everyone. They made us loners. Franz controlled my social life."

"Then you kept in contract with Bruns?"

"Yes, but rarely. After Franz died we were on our own. I don't know about the others."

"Our sources tell us Otto Bruns may have died. Can you give us a clue?"

"No, but even if I knew I wouldn't reveal his location. Otto helped pay for my education. My mother died in 1969. I had no one. As I grew older, Otto became my surrogate father. Looking back I recall times when he didn't allow me to participate in Franz's group activities."

Katz continued, "When I finished my undergraduate work Otto arranged a job for me with The Bland Data."

"Bland?" Lou-Ann asked.

"Bland is the computer processing division of Trinity International."

"I'm starting to get the picture. Trinity moved you from Bland to the DOD when they received the no-bid pharmaceutical award," Lou-Ann responded.

"Exactly."

"And you never heard from Mary again?"

Katz was slow to answer. His eyes glazed.

"Please continue," Lou-Ann gently urged. *He appears tired and confused.*

"I thought Mary had died, but she was living in an outpatient facility.

Mary's roommate had sent me a letter and a small carton of Mary's personal effects. Mary kept a diary. In it described the excruciating headaches we all suffered. The headaches were frequently followed by rage and then depression. During the episodes she screamed and screeched like an owl defending her nest. The attending physician prescribed chlorpromazine. The medication gave her an uncontrollable twitch."

Katz began to pace the room. His hands quivered as he grew increasing agitated.

"I corresponded several times with the roommate. She wrote that Mary was briefly re-admitted to a psychiatric hospital. The roommate recalled one visit. She found Mary sitting in a chair near the nurse's station. The head nurse was very kind. She calmed Mary by feeding her raspberry ice cream from a paper cup. Mary cuddled a Teddy Bear as though it was a child. In another letter, the roommate said Mary told her a story about a baby. The child was born at one of Long Island psychiatric facilities and taken from her at birth. The roommate believed her story."

"The poor woman suffered," said Lou-Ann.

"Mary was a brilliant woman. I have her medical record. She was shifted from one hospital to another. No one really cared. And, finally, after New York's welfare reorganization, she was dumped in an out-patient group home."

"Thank God Mary had a caring roommate or you would never have known what happened to her," Lou-Ann remarked.

"I still don't know the whole story. We were abandoned without any medical follow up. We were expendable rats in a puzzling maze."

"You had to know Bruns and Franz messed with your brain. You worked for Trinity. You were hacking into DOD systems. Walter. You were one of them."

"No. They turned me into an automaton. I'm simply a machine that performs a function according to a predetermined set of coded instructions. I'm a marginal man capable only of programmed responses. We were children. None of us gave our consent. I have awful dreams."

"Walter, don't run," Lou-Ann pleaded. "You still have your humanity." *Katz is melting down.*

'When I was a young boy, I was told 'Don't feel'. I wasn't allowed to express my feelings. I stuffed them."

"Walter. Listen to me. We can help you. It's not too late. You haven't published the DOD files. Come in."

"If only I could. Mary visits me at night while I'm asleep. Sometimes she appears as a grotesque, old woman or the gorgeous young girl I remember. She begs for help. The dream always ends with her mourning scream, "They're coming for you, Walter."

Suddenly Katz's jaw clamped shut. He grimaced and bent

over holding his head between his hands. "Oh, the headaches," he cried out.

Lou-Ann was startled.

"Walter. What's wrong?"

"The headache. It's starting."

Katz recalled one meeting. "Franz called them 'family gatherings'. Ray Wood, Ed Jablonski, and Bill Hess were playing half-court basketball. A dispute broke out among the three. They were screaming at one another. Ed began to rage. He was built like a brick shithouse. Ed grabbed Ray by the throat, lifted him off the ground and threw him. Ray looked like a rag doll when his head hit the concrete."

"Didn't anyone try to stop them?"

"Not at first. I was scared. I turned to Hess. Bill grinned. He relished the whole damn thing. If Franz hadn't intervened, Jablonski would have killed Wood. I don't remember what Franz said. The two stopped fighting, got off the ground and returned to the game as though the confrontation never occurred."

"Was this a common occurrence?"

"On occasion. Otto told me the seven of us were selected for a number of reasons. We were creative. I was the only one with limited communication skills. We could manipulate others. But, Otto warned me, 'You all possess a shadow side. Ray, Ed, and Bill had to work to control it.' I swear I feel like I could kill when I get stressed."

Katz stopped pacing. Lou-Ann saw Katz's sad facial expression as he looked out the patio doors.

"I don't fully understand what happened to the seven of us. Maybe it was the drugs, the shock treatments, or the hypnosis. Who knows? We were innocent children. And now..." Katz paused.

"And now what?" Lou-Ann asked.

"And now Mary and Andrew are dead. Ray Wood, Ed Jablonski, and Bill Hess are convicted murderers. I'm a wanted felon."

"We need to find Otto Bruns. He holds the answer. Where is he?" Lou-Ann demanded. "What about the others?"

Katz's eyes glazed and rolled upward. He looked at Lou-

Ann and buckled. He fell. His head hit on the wooden floor. His muscles contracted. He began to shake.

"Can't you see? I am the last of Franz's special seven. All six of us have had our lives destroyed," Katz mumbled.

"You said seven. Did you mean six? Which is it, six or seven?" Lou-Ann demanded. She knelt near Katz to support his head. Soon the episode subsided. Katz couldn't recall a thing. He was confused.

What did Franz and Bruns do to these people? Lou-Ann helped Katz crawl to the nearby couch. Nearly an hour passed before he recovered. Katz went into the bathroom.

The apartment doorbell sounded. "Mr. Clark. It's Bill, the superintendent. Are you in there?"

"Wait," warned Katz. "I'll duck into the bedroom. Tell him your Clark's sister. She lives in Wisconsin. Clark's been injured in Europe and you're waiting for him to return."

Lou-Ann spoke with the superintendent. She could tell from his incredulous expression he did not believe her. "He's on his way to call the cops."

"Katz returned to the kitchenette. He reloaded his pistol. "You wait here for the police. Tell them I kidnapped you. I've stolen your car." With that he grabbed his backpack and retrieved a mobile phone. "Here!" He tossed it to Lou-Ann. "It looks like a an ordinary cell phone. It's not. Hide it. I'll contact you."

"You shouldn't drive. You had a seizure." Lou-Ann rushed into the hallway to stop Katz. "Walter, was there a seventh member of the group?"

"I'll contact you. I've got to get out of here now."

He pushed Lou-Ann aside. Walter Katz was wily. He abandoned Lou-Ann's car about seven miles away in a Giant Grocery parking lot. The previous day he had parked his own car there with stolen license plates. A surveillance camera filmed the car driving away. Katz vanished.

Chapter Fifty-Three
The Zimbabwe Connection

It took a while for the recent encounter with Walter Katz to sink in before Lou-Ann's anger turned to determination. Katz was armed and dangerous. Nevertheless, he hadn't tried to harm her. Katz wanted to be heard.

Lou-Ann texted David. "We need to meet with Lindstrom and Best. Either we missed something in Katz's file or it was sanitized."

David sent back, "Called Lindstrom. He can't meet us today."

Lou-Ann – "Hold off with Best until I meet you."

Lou-Ann needed time to plan a contingency. Her plan included purchasing two new cell phones at Wal-Mart. *I'll give one to David. The NSA might be tracking our phones.* Perhaps, NSA was tracking David and Lou-Ann in order to locate Katz. But the real culprit was a clandestine monitoring operation, the Stratum Unit. The covert Stratum Unit served two masters, President Stone and Trinity's Ashton Pickering.

Following a brief call from the FBI Director, Chief of Staff, Drew Lindstrom, waited impatiently in his White House Office for one of Stratum's operatives to report. The call finally came, and it wasn't good news.

"Mr. Lindstrom. We've lost Stokes."

"Find her. I don't believe the kidnapped story she gave the FBI."

Next Lindstrom met with the President. The President deactivated the Oval Office monitoring system. She valued her personal reputation more than posterity.

"There's a problem."

"I hope not, Drew. You know how I detest bad news."

"Lou-Ann Stokes requested meeting. I stonewalled."

"Why?"

"Stratum monitored a conversation and subsequent text message exchange between Clayton and Stokes."

"Meet them. Find out what they know."

"I suspect Stokes knows you are Pied Piper's seventh child."

"The explanation is obvious. I was an innocent child. Exploited by a mad man. Thanks to my parents and a loving husband I put my life together. It's a fairytale ending."

"And that's it?"

"Yes."

"Katz has more. He has the Purple Rain folder with hundreds of files. He knows our connection to Pickering and Trinity."

"Why hasn't he released the files?"

"There's something we've missed. Something about your past."

"Nonsense. Katz is on to our plans for Zimbabwe. We'll hear from him again. He'll present demands or a manifesto. I remember Walter as a kid. He was a nervous insecure runt. Always afraid of being left behind."

"You are over-simplifying. He wants something personal."

They were interrupted by a call from the Secret Service. Lindstrom answered and scowled.

"What's wrong?" she demanded. But, before Lindstrom could respond, Katherine took the phone and gasped at what she heard and hung up.

Katherine looked at Lindstrom. "Damn it! You idiot. Clayton and Stokes are sitting outside Best's office. Didn't you alert him?"

"No."

"We have the FBI and Secret Service searching for Stokes and where is she? Sitting in the West Wing. Get over there. Call me this evening."

Lindstrom called Best's cell phone. No answer. Then he telephoned Best's office. Best's secretary answered.

"I'm sorry, Mr. Lindstrom, but Ms. Stokes and Mr. Clayton have left. I'm a bit puzzled," she said. "Mr. Best left for lunch, but never returned. He hasn't called. It's not like Mr. Best."

Lindstrom was baffled. "Please have Mr. Best call me when

he returns. This is important." *Something isn't right. Best isn't answering his cell phone. Where is he?*

✍

Lafayette Square is located across from the White House. The seven-acre common is a frequent location for political protests. A large number of visitors strolled the grounds snapping photographs of the White House and statutes of four Revolutionary War patriots. A fifth statue was a tribute to Andrew Jackson. Two tourists stood nearby admiring the view when a man approached. He nodded and walked away. The two followed.

"I can't meet you at my office. I'm the President's Chief Counsel. You two have already drawn too much attention."

"Listen Best. I could have been killed. Walter Katz is on a mission. Why didn't you tell us Katz spent months at a time behind enemy lines in Vietnam? He called in airstrikes. The guy's a goddamned survivalist," said David.

"It doesn't figure. Why withhold critical information?" asked Lou-Ann.

"It was Lindstrom's idea to bring you two into the loop." Best paused. Perspiration dripped into his eyes. "He wanted you to locate Katz and persuade him to surrender the files."

"I still don't understand why we were selected for the task," said David.

"Trust. Lindstrom believed Katz would trust Lou-Ann. He might turn over the files or come in. There's nothing else I can tell you." Best's remarks reverberated with fear.

"We know the President was part of some outrageous CIA project called Pied Piper," Lou-Ann revealed.

"Listen Best. You suspected there's a problem or you wouldn't be talking with us, now. You're shaking. Calm down," said David.

Lou-Ann instinctively rolled into "good cop-bad cop." "This conversation is totally off the books."

"I swear. I don't know the whole story. If I tell you more I could..." Best stopped cold. "Shit, a surveillance camera. The Secret Service installed them." Best turned left and increased his pace. "What does Katz want?" he asked.

"I surmise Katz wants revenge for Mary Taylor's death," said Lou-Ann. "He wants to expose MKULTRA. Most of all Katz wants justice," she added.

"MKULTRA closed forty years ago. There's little proof to substantiate the program existed. The CIA Director, Richard Helms, claimed he destroyed the records. Why, after all these years, would any one even care?" Best asked.

Lou-Ann and David looked at one another. Lou-Ann remarked, "Dakota Putnam."

"What about Putnam?" asked Best.

"Is Katz feeding information to Dakota?" Lou-Ann pressured Best.

"Does Katz have more files?" Clayton pressed his index figure into Best's chest.

Best retreated an arm's length. "I'll tell you this. The President was briefed on Katz's recent incident. Lindstrom attended the meeting. The President is not afraid of Putnam or the *Post* linking her with Pied Piper or MKULTRA."

"Suppose Putnam connects the President with Trinity International?" David put the screws to Best.

Best turned his back on Clayton.

Clayton reached out and grasped Best's arm. "Hold on, Best. If I were Katz I would want my life back. He knows he can't have it. He's beyond any reconciliation. Don't you see? Once Katz releases the files the FBI will be knocking at your door. He's got something big. Unlike Snowden, Katz is not headed for Moscow."

"He should be."

"Why?" Clayton demanded.

"The FBI suspects Katz was one of the guys who pushed Foxx to his death."

Lou-Ann interjected, "That's crap. He doesn't meet the description of either perp."

"It doesn't matter. Katz's days are numbered and perhaps yours as well. I've got to get out of here before we are spotted."

David let go of Best's arm. "The President wouldn't dare touch you, Best."

Best turned pale and frowned. *Oh, no?* He knew David was wrong.

"Look around, Clayton. We stand in the heart of sex, greed and narcissism. Do you think Katherine Stone is above it all? I do not know the President's deepest secrets. All the sex scandals and marred reputations are insignificant compared to this administration. I fear I've sealed my own future by meeting with both of you. Trinity is bound to…"

"Trinity? What is it?" asked Lou-Ann.

Best avoided her question.

"Tell us about Trinity," David insisted.

Best refused to answer. His eyes swelled with tears. "Foxx. I swear I didn't know," he pleaded.

Lou-Ann stepped in front of Best. "What happened?"

"Foxx discovered a photograph and notes in an archive. We never expected Foxx to be so passionate. We thought he was a pompous ass." Suddenly, Best focused on a woman on the corner. "I recognize her. She's part of Stone's Special Service Unit. We've been spotted."

"Who else knew you agreed to meet us?" Lou-Ann asked.

"No one." Best started to panic.

Lou-Ann dropped back to see if they were followed.

Best changed direction and walked toward Lou-Ann. "I'm trapped," he said.

Lou-Ann responded, "David walk toward Pennsylvania Avenue. I'll meet you at the Old Ebbitt Grille later. Hold my hand Best. Best managed a smile. Pretend you're cheating on you wife. Let's go."

Best and Lou-Ann strode to a huge Urn in the opposite direction. She turned and embraced Best. Lou-Ann watched the Special Service Unit tail follow David.

"Now's your chance, Best. Take a long casual stroll back to your office, but go now."

Best departed without a word.

Chapter Fifty-Four
The Old Ebbitt Grille
15th Street, NW

When David existed Lafayette Park the Special Unit agent followed. *There must be another agent trailing me. This one is too obvious.* David checked his cell phone. *I wish Lou-Ann hadn't mentioned our rendezvous location in front of Best. Best is a wreck. I never expected him to reveal such confidential detail. Best is clearly petrified.*

David Clayton was unaware of a critical dynamic. Charles Best was on the edge of a nervous breakdown. He didn't fear an indictment. He feared the complexities of his predicament. Katherine Stone was vindictive and unforgiving. There was another unknown factor – Trinity's retribution. Best had every reason to be alarmed.

As Best walked along Pennsylvania Ave he pondered his future. *Trinity controls the President. Pickering has some strange influence over Stone.*

Best recalled his anxiety following a meeting with military personnel. The usual players including the Joint Chiefs were conspicuously absent. Instead, Lindstrom and the President selected a number of junior officers. Lindstrom did most of the talking. The President frequently interjected to emphasize a point.

"I must stress the sensitive nature of this meeting. All present, along with selected civilian consultants will develop a plan we've named Operation Purple Rain," said Drew Lindstrom.

Best was bewildered by Lindstrom's presentation. *Operation Purple Rain exceeds my original recommendations. This plan may be illegal.*

Best advised President Stone: "In my opinion the President can respond forcefully to prevent serious threats to our nation's security." Best's blood pressure rose as he listened to President Stone's interpretation of Best's judgment. *She's way beyond the 'intent'. Is the President prepared to circumvent the Joint Chiefs and Congress?*

At the meeting with junior officers Stone was emphatic. "This is a contingency scenario. This is not a plan for a unilateral invasion. My intent is to test our nation's readiness to launch a rapid response to a situation anywhere on the African continent."

Colonel Charles Doering, Army Signal Corps, raised his hand. "Madame President. We have a deployment strategy in place. Isn't such a plan best left to AFRICOM?"

"I don't want another Benghazi, General."

"With all due respect, the United State Africa command is constantly reviewing contingencies," Doering responded.

"From where? Stuttgart, Germany," Katherine Stone fired back. "Bring up those projections. Let me be more specific. And please allow me to complete my presentation then we'll open it to discussion." There was no misunderstanding. Katherine Stone was in charge of the meeting.

A man approached the front of the room. He appeared to be a civilian. "I would like to introduce Colonel Robert William Lee, US Air Force, currently attached to Operation Purple Rain." Lindstrom stepped aside. The Colonel turned to the projection screen. A series of PowerPoint talking points guided his presentation.

"Our scenario deals with the deployment of Delta Force teams in country 'X'." Then Colonel Lee flashed a laser pen at the graphic. "Our staging area – Addis Ababa, Ethiopia. Our target location is here."

"Excuse me, Colonel Lee. Are we dealing with a response in Zimbabwe?" asked Colonel Doering.

The General's question stirred an undercurrent of whispered exchanges among the participants. President Stone scribbled a note and passed it to Lindstrom. "I want Doering. Bust his ass. Threaten him. Whatever. His Army career is over, if one word of this session gets back to the Secretary of Defense."

Lindstrom grimaced and nodded an acknowledgement.

"Colonel Doering. You've made an excellent point." President Stone walked to the projection screen. "Allow me to clarify my position. This scenario is my response to the Benghazi episode.

I won't tolerate American officials being gunned-down. Our ambassador was assassinated. Events are often beyond our control. I want to demonstrate to the American people I am a proactive Commander in Chief. Understood?"

"Yes, Madame President."

Two days later the inquisitive Colonel Doering was summoned to a room in the Pentagon where he met with Drew Lindstrom. Lindstrom thanked the Colonel for his service on the President's special task force. Lindstrom handed the bewildered Colonel an envelope. Doering was being transferred to Elmendorf Air Force Base in south central Alaska.

Events were happening too fast for Charles Best. Katherine Stone's swift punishment of the inquisitive Colonel Doering reinforced Charles Best's worries. *I know too much.*

Privy to Andrew Dunn's autopsy report, Best arranged for the record of the proceedings and evidence to be sealed.

It was Charles Best who first raised the issue of Trinity's potential involvement in Zimbabwe. He sensed Trinity wanted control of Zimbabwe's vast mineral wealth. Nonetheless, Best paid a high price.

He started each day with a Scotch and continued to drink until he went to bed. Best needed pills to sleep and pills to stay awake. Best's marriage nose-dived. His wife was having an affair. She sued for divorce.

⤫

Waiting at the Old Ebbitt Grill, David began to worry about Lou-Ann. He nursed his Ketel One Martini for nearly thirty minutes, a new record. He couldn't chance a second drink. Another ten minutes passed when Lou-Ann arrived. Though David declined to comment, Lou-Ann's frown portended bad news.

"What's wrong?"

"Lindstrom called me. I think he's tracking us. He warned me. More like threatened me," Lou-Ann responded

"About what?" asked David.

"David, he knows we talked with Best. He ordered me to stick with finding Walter Katz. In Lindstrom's words, 'Stay away from Charles Best. Your current path will lead to nothing but despair.'"

David looked perplexed. "Are you quitting?"

"Not exactly. I'm taking a break," Lou-Ann said.

"Lindstrom said he spoke with the President. The President acknowledged she has known Katz since childhood."

"And the cropped photos? Why did Lindstrom hold back a photo of Stone?"

"Lindstrom didn't want the investigation to influence us."

"I don't believe that. I think Foxx discovered the group photograph. Someone rushed to judgment. Who knows? In any case, Foxx is dead."

"David, don't you see? This entire affair is pointing directly at President Stone."

"Lindstrom underestimated Foxx. I remember the look on Foxx's face when he discovered we might have discovered new information."

"There's more to it. Dakota Putnam sent me a text message."

"I knew she would."

"I'm certain she has information to link Katz with the Oval Office."

At that moment David's cell phone vibrated with a text. "It's Lindstrom. 'President Stone appreciates your efforts. She requests you and Ms. Stokes suspend investigation until Secret Service and FBI complete their inquiry into Alan Foxx's death. I will contact you." David handed the phone to Lou-Ann.

"Can't you feel it, David? Best and Lindstrom played us."

"You're right. Now they hold us in contempt."

"We still have Dakota as a fall back. She may be able to help."

"Help?" asked David.

"I'm positive Dakota is miles ahead of us."

"David, swallow your pride and return her call. As for me, I've got to return to Long Island. Jack's condition is rapidly deteriorating. I want to be there."

"Agreed. We made a great team back in seventy-seven, you, Jack and me."

"Our investigation was stonewalled then and I don't want to waste another precious minute only to find out we face the same hurdle. I'll call in a few days. Call Dakota. Oh! I almost forgot. Take this. It's the cell phone Katz gave me. He'll be surprised when you answer."

Chapter Fifty-Five
The Good Bye

It was Dakota who reached out to Lou-Ann regarding Walter Katz. Over the next few days they exchanged several telephone calls.

"You and David will eventually have to meet. I'm leaving for Long Island."

There was a long silence. "I'm uncomfortable speaking with David after all these years." Lou-Ann detected sadness in Dakotas' response. "Dodge the memories. We're dealing with a critical issue."

Lou-Ann knew David would stall. *David always pouts when I talk about Dakota.*

"You have to understand, Lou-Ann. It's too painful for me," David responded.

Lou-Ann insisted and after several pleas he agreed.

The first call was brief. The former lovers both avoided the real topic – "their former relationship." David couldn't focus on their conversation. His mind flashed back to their break-up.

October 1977 seemed an eternity ago.

As David recalled it was a Friday evening. For months he ruminated over their quarrel. Now he was even sure of the day. "It had to be a Friday," he told himself. I don't know why it matters.

"I'm not ready for us to move in together, Dakota. You have a key. I need time, after what we've been through the last six months. We need to slow down. Life has been too intense."

"Then, I'm leaving. If you can't make a commitment now, you never will." Dakota walked into the kitchen, removed the apartment key from her purse, and tossed it on the counter.

David turned around to discover he was talking into an

empty room. "Dakota?" No answer. "Dakota don't be this way." The apartment door slammed. David walked to the balcony and watched Dakota's green MG-B race out of the parking lot. It was over.

They met again for the first time after the break-up at a farewell party for Robert Doyle, Congresswoman Harrington's liaison with the Senate Intelligence Committee.

"This where we first met." David discretely whispered to Dakota. He was struggling for small talk.

"A unique introduction. You spilled champagne on me," she sadly replied with a downward glance.

"I made a mess of your dress and shoes, but I met you."

"You did. And tonight it has to end."

David didn't catch Dakota's meaning. Then he spotted his rival, Bob Doyle walking across the room. *I hate that son of a bitch. He doesn't love Dakota. He doesn't respect her.*

"Well, well…David Clayton. How have you been buddy? Dakota tells me you're returning to the New York delegation. Quite a letdown after your foray with the General Accounting Office."

"I never left the delegation, Doyle. My work at the GAO was more important than the chicken shit stuff you do."

"My salary will be triple yours, old boy," Doyle retorted as he approached David.

David's fists tightened. *The bastard's going to punch me.*

Congresswoman Harrington sensed there might be tension between the two foes. She placed herself between the two rivals.

"David, happy to see you," said Harrington.

David turned to acknowledge Harrington. Doyle reached for a drink.

Harrington looked directly at David. "So glad you've decided to stay on. I need your expertise, now that my superstar has decided to move on to bigger and better things."

"Thank you, Mrs. Harrington," David replied.

" David, its time you started calling me Elizabeth."

"I'm anxious to get back to work, Elizabeth," said David.

"Wonderful. And Robert I need to speak with you for a

moment. Will you excuse us?" Harrington always referred to Doyle as "Robert" when she had a private "criticism to render."

David nodded, but this thing with Doyle wasn't finished. As they walked away Dakota approached David.

"You almost made a fool of yourself David." Dakota smiled and motioned to the waitress to bring her another champagne.

"Tell me you are not dating Doyle again. He's a shit."

"And you weren't?" Dakota laughed.

"Dakota, you're impetuous. You fall in love too easily. I'm not ready for marriage and one day you'll look back and realize you weren't either."

Dakota lifted her glass and announced, "I'm leaving the paper. You're the first to know." She moved closer.

Dakota's perfume tantalized. He was captured by the allure of her low cut dress. He recalled her playfulness. His thoughts drifted to the weekend they shared at the Three Village Inn on Long Island.

Momentarily, Dakota was distracted by an apparently heated conversation between Harrington and Doyle. "No doubt, Harrington is reprimanding Bob for making an ass of himself," said Dakota.

"Hey! You didn't hear a word I said. It's like you are a million miles away." Dakota reached out and touched him.

"Damn it. I'm sorry. For a moment I was somewhere else," David replied.

"I'll say it again. I'm leaving the paper."

He turned and said, "Yes I heard you."

"I've given the paper my notice."

"Why?"

"I submitted a book proposal. I never thought I'd get a serious response. Expected a rejection."

"You? Never. Not with investigative pieces you've been writing."

"I have an agent, too."

"Great. What's it about."

"I'm not going to bore you with the story."

"Just the plot?"

"It deals with the GOA investigation of Nazis. I submitted

the proposal with a working title, Paperclip."

"You can't be serious. Jack warned you. You could be prosecuted for revealing details from our investigation. All the documents were seized and reclassified. The United States Supreme Court refused your paper's appeal to release them. Those records will be locked up for twenty years."

"Come on, David. I'm not stupid. It's a novel."

"Someone is bound to accuse me of leaking secrets. We were in a relationship," David protested.

"My editor raised the same issue. It's with the legal staff."

"Why?" David asked.

"My publisher doesn't want the Justice Department charging him with violating the National Secrets Act."

"Dakota you are just filled with surprises. Next you'll be telling me you're back with Bob Doyle."

Dakota winced then smiled.

David stepped back. "Are you *nuts*? You are back with that narcissist."

"Do I detect a bit of jealousy?" She flashed a coy smile.

"Of course. I'm serious. That guy is no good. He is going to hurt you. He's done it before."

Doyle returned to Dakota and David. "So how's Robin surviving without Batman and the Joker?" Doyle goaded.

"Doyle, I don't like you. You're pissing me off."

"You don't have to answer. I already know. Sam Beverly quit the GAO and went into hiding after his lesbian wife died," said Doyle.

Dakota stepped between the two men and pleaded with Doyle. "Bob stop it. You've had too much to drink."

Doyle shoved Dakota aside. "I hear Jack Thompson took an early retirement. No balls. The way I heard it, you guys folded under pressure."

David stiffened. His fists were so tight his knuckles turned white. Once again Dakota grabbed Doyle's arm to calm him. "What's wrong with you?"

"You're a nobody, Clayton," Doyle slurred his angry words.

"Is that the best you can do? You're a drunk, Doyle."

Doyle turned to take a swing at David and accidentally elbowed Dakota.

"What's wrong with you, Bob? You're attracting a crowd." Doyle squeezed Dakota's arm.

"Hey you're hurting me," she exclaimed.

"Come on. We're out of here." The mix of temper and alcohol turned his face bright red. "Are you coming?"

Dakota turned and gave one last aching, desperate, but silent plea to David.

David started to respond, but abruptly stopped as Congresswoman Harrington returned. "Gentlemen, you two are creating a bit of a fuss. Enough."

"We're leaving," Doyle barked.

Dakota looked back one last time. "Enough, David. The time has come when we have to say goodbye."

David stepped back. Dakota followed Doyle to the lobby elevator.

Letting her leave with Doyle is the biggest mistake of my life.

♨

It was ten years later when on a flight to Manhattan; David sadly read that Scribner's Bookstore was closing. Among the authors honored with a book signing during the 1988 Christmas holiday was the recently published Dakota Putnam. She said she was going to do it. And she did.

Scribner's was one of David's favorite haunts when he visited Manhattan. It was a brisk windy day as David entered 597 Fifth Avenue between 48th and 49th Streets. He glanced up at his favorite spot, the second floor. He climbed the enchanted staircase to the second floor balcony and watched the customers below. *How could they be closing this beautiful building?*

A small gathering caught his eye. He checked his watch. The book signing was not scheduled for another thirty minutes. Cradling a copy of F. Scott Fitzgerald's *THE GREAT GATSBY*, David descended the stairs and walked to the center counter. "Is it true the store will be closing?" he asked the clerk.

"Oh yes. You know I've worked here nearly more than thirty years. Famous people have passed this way. We will close in January," said the veteran sales clerk.

"Sad. I've been coming here since I was a child."

"The place is a shrine. I'm here for the book signing."

"Have your read Putnam's first novel?"

"Yes. She tackles formidable topics."

The front door opened.

"Here's Ms. Putnam, now," said Janet.

Dakota was late and rushed by the counter without noticing David.

David turned away. *I'm not sure I want to go through with this.*

"Is there anything else I might help you with?" asked the clerk.

"Forgive me. Yes, I want to purchase a copy of Putnam's new novel, *DECEPTION*."

"Over there." The clerk pointed to a stack of books.

David paid for the purchases, and walked to the rear of Scribner's. He kept his distance pretending to browse the display. Dakota was seated with a number of customers discussing *DECEPTION*. After a few minutes, Dakota walked to a card table, sat down, and began signing books. David finally found the courage to get on line. When he reached the table, David placed the book in front of Dakota.

Without looking up she asked, "And is there something special you would like me to write?"

"I'll leave that up to you."

Dakota dropped the pen and looked up. "David Clayton. My god, David, what are you doing here?"

"Getting my copy of your novel signed. What else?"

"How long will you be in town?"

"Until Monday. The New York Delegation is hosting a party tomorrow night."

"I remember those parties." David caught the whimsical sound of Dakota's response.

"We did a lot of partying in Manhattan. How is Bob?"

Dakota hesitated. She motioned for David to come closer.

She whispered. "Don't you know? We divorced. I endured enough of his carousing."

David stepped back. "Divorced?"

"Nearly a year. We attended a Trinity bash at the Waldorf. Bob handled their account. His secretary, Lisa, was there. We began talking. I admired her dress. Touched the fabric. It felt lavish… We looked at each other and I knew. Damn it!"

"What did you do?"

"I left the party. Went home. Locked the doors and called my attorney first thing the next morning."

"Hey. I don't want to be rude, but I've been waiting to get my book signed, too," complained the next customer in line.

"She's right, you know. It is great to see you again, David." Dakota picked up the pen and signed his book.

David's smile was a sad smile, if that is possible. "Thanks," was all he could manage to say. He waited until he was back on Fifth Avenue before opening the books cover to read what Dakota had written. "To David. Friends forever. Dakota." David shivered. Suddenly, among the bustling holiday shoppers he felt cold and lonely.

"David, David." David turned to see Dakota rushing in his direction.

"Dakota, what the hell are you doing? It's freezing out here."

"Oh David. I just couldn't say goodbye without giving you a hug."

David blushed. "It's OK. I understand."

"If only you did, we wouldn't be standing here on 5th Avenue. It was a fun roller coaster ride. Wasn't it?"

"I'm not sure." David looked away.

"Oh come on, darling. Life isn't an ongoing saga. It's a puzzle… bits and pieces. We'll get over this."

David reached out gently touching Dakota's hand. "You're right. Life isn't a straight line."

Dakota brushed back her wind-tossed hair. "You know what they say; Get the facts right. Your heart already knows the truth."

Chapter Fifty-Six
The White House Treaty Room

Drew Lindstrom and Charles Best waited in the White House Treaty Room for President Stone to arrive. Their conversation was unusually brief and stilted. Lindstrom paged through his National Intelligence Briefing Book. Best fidgeted. From time to time he nervously scratch the back of his left hand.

Lindstrom reached into his briefcase and removed a folder. "Charles. This is a recent photograph of Walter Katz. The guy is a perennial loner with one exception."

Best studied the photograph. "Dresses like one of those silicon prodigies; T-shirt, jeans, and sneakers. The usual tech uniform."

"I'd like to get inside his head," Lindstrom remarked.

"I think a lot of people already have," Best snickered. "What's the exception?"

Lindstrom handed Best another photograph. "That's Katz's wife. Candice Wang. She's an ABC."

"ABC. What's that?"

"American born Chinese."

"I've read Katz's file. There was no mention of a wife."

"Up until six months ago she worked at the Defense Advanced Research Projects Agency – DARPA."

"Never heard of it," said Best.

"That's the point. It's top secret. I doubt the President knows," Lindstrom answered.

"What the hell do they do?"

"Wang worked for one of the DARPA divisions. They create programs and try to hack them. They search for security vulnerabilities that infiltrate the Internet."

"Let's go after her," said Best.

"She disappeared a few weeks before Katz. Intelligence believes she may be in Hong Kong or Shanghai."

"Do you think she may have copies of Katz's files?"

"I don't know. Something is up. The President is at dinner with Ashton Pickering."

"I have to tell you, Drew, this Katz affair is a time bomb. From where I'm sitting Pickering and Trinity International control the President. She's no more than their puppet on a string."

"Don't let her hear you say that Charles. I've revealed too much already."

A quizzical expression crossed Best's face.

Lindstrom abruptly ended the conversation and returned to his briefing book.

Best's comment hit upon a secret even Drew Lindstrom didn't know.

⨏

Simply put, Trinity *did* control Katherine Stone. They had since she was a child. Only a handful of people knew Katherine Grace Stone had been one of the innocent assets in a diabolical experiment concocted by Heinrich Franz and Walther Liechtenauer. As Franz's researched progressed, Trinity PharmoDynamics, with Walther Liechtenhauer's endorsement, played a greater role in the Pied Piper Project. Liechtenhauer's goal was to develop a pharmaceutical approach to alter an individual's personality.

When the CIA ostensibly abandoned MKULTRA the seven innocent children were teenagers. At a meeting with Liechtenauer, Franz agreed to try a new technique. Franz labeled the technique "twining".

Liechtenauer appeared puzzled. *I recall experiments with twins. Odd, Franz is calling his process "twining, not twinning."*

"Tell me about this so-called twining?" asked Liechtenauer.

"Can you imagine a process so seductive as to join together the souls, the minds, *the entire personalities*, of two non-related children?" asked Franz.

"Your experiment sounds like romantic nonsense, my dear Franz. It sounds to me like chemically induced 'love.'"

"All love is chemically induced," Franz replied with a faint smile. Then he added, "A-ha. I have it."

"Have what?" asked the wary Liechtenauer.

"I'll call the effect 'soul bonding'. My first two twining subjects will be Walter Katz and Mary Taylor. These two will be coupled together for eternity," he assured Liechtenauer.

"And Katherine?" Liechtenauer asked. "She is our priority. The Circle of Twelve has gone to great expense to protect Katherine Stone and her identity. The Fuhrer would be proud of your guidance, Franz."

"I am convinced that one day she will be an invaluable asset," he assured Liechtenauer.

Franz's next twining paired Andrew Dunn and Katherine Stone. Liechtenauer was the only witness. In a subdued, but formal procedure, Franz hypnotized Katherine and Andrew. The pair was sedated to erase future memories of the ceremony. He joined their hands.

"Listen to me. With your permission, I am going to take you to a safe place. I will count from ten to one. Very slowly we will descend a staircase. Imagine a beautiful beach. Listen to the waves. Smell the salt air. You are safe here."

Franz's rhythmic voice caught Walther Liechtenauer off guard. He stepped back and forced himself not to fall under Franz's spell.

Franz continued. "With your permission, I want you to imagine a very warm, peaceful place near the water's edge. Your bare feet feel the warm damp sand. It's so peaceful. So comforting. Andrew. I want you to hold both of Katherine 's hands. She is beautiful. She is intelligent. Combine those gifts with tenacity and Katherine could rule the world."

Andrew turned and looked at Katherine. They were infinitely symbiotic. Only death could separate them.

The stage was set. Katherine 's character, her very essence was programmed to be the alpha personality. Andrew was destined to be the beta mate.

Three weeks later Franz proposed an entirely different procedure that he referred to as "brain change". Trinity's lab in Argentina supplied Franz with "LA-3", a psychotropic drug.

"We must use restraint, Franz. Our technicians warn that this is a powerful drug. We don't want to kill our subjects," Liechtenauer cautioned.

"I agree. We are entering uncharted areas of the human psyche. We don't know the altering effects on perception, or behavior," said Franz. The potential for brain manipulation obsessed Franz.

"Have you selected your subjects?"

"Yes. Ray Wood, Ed Jablonski, and Bill Hess, the troublesome boys," Franz responded.

"Isn't it odd that after all these years, not a single parent has questioned our work or the effects on the seven?" asked Liechtenauer.

"I have often wondered about that myself," Franz admitted and then shrugged.

Preparations were made for the upcoming experiment. "I've gained the confidence of the superintendent at a local psychiatric facility not far from here," Franz informed Liechtenauer.

"The superintendent will be well-rewarded. Of course, there will be no record of the experiment," Liechtenauer insisted.

"He has already agreed to that stipulation," Franz replied.

"And the parents?"

"I will assure them this is a harmless procedure to deal with the boys' increasingly unruly behavior," replied Franz.

Two weeks later and with their parents' consents, Ray Wood, Ed Jablonski, and Bill Hess were driven to Kings Park.

The boys were led into three individual padded cells. The process did not go well, initially. Franz needed two additional sessions before he was satisfied.

"I've decided to increase the "LA-3" from twenty to sixty milligrams," Franz told Liechtenauer.

Glaring lights intensified the sessions. Powerful loudspeakers screamed through the night. The boys all reacted in a similar fashion. They huddled in a corner of their cells curled in a fetal position. The room smelled of urine and feces.

"Are you driving these children insane?" asked Liechtenauer.

"Perhaps. I've only just begun to understand what actually transpires in the victims' brains," said Franz.

"They will have no fear, no conscience, no sense of right and wrong. When called upon they will kill. Their lives will appear normal, but their psyches will be in constant turmoil. Sublimation will be a challenge. Nevertheless, one day they will be on call for service," Franz continued.

"Something or someone could set them off," said Liechtenauer.

"Yes. It is a possibility, unfortunately. They will need lifetime professional supervision and medical attention."

"And, Katherine? No harm must come to her. I need your assurance."

"Andrew will protect Katherine," Franz assured Liechtenauer.

"From what you've told me, all seven assets have prompts to control their behavior. Are they all the same?"

"No. I'll share them with you, in time."

Liechtenauer frowned.

I've planned a subtle prompt, but with a safeguard. Katherine's trigger, the word "green", will only activate when associated with the color green."

"Why green?" asked Liechtenauer.

Franz snickered and said, "It's my favorite color. Now you share the trigger. Be careful. The final stage of Katherine's programming went amiss. It's all Bruns' fault."

"What happened?"

"Bruns and his damned electromagnetics." Franz suddenly exploded into a violent rage. "I warned him. Katherine was the only child who didn't suffer the headaches. Katherine began treatments before she was six years old. The others were in elementary school. Wood, Jablonski, and Hess received intensive psyche programming."

Liechtenauer was alarmed. "You've created three monsters, Franz. I never approved excessiveness. What safeguards do you have?"

"None for Wood, Jablonski, and Hess. Perhaps, I could program them to self-destruct. They could vanish, but that sounds like a Trinity concern."

"I don't like the possibility of the boys going haywire," said Liechtenauer.

"I wouldn't be concerned about Dunn and Katz. They never experienced the brain change experiment. Wood, Jablonski, and Hess are the ones to monitor."

Something did go wrong for Wood, Jablonski, and Hess. Eventually, they were abandoned without future medical attention. Years later, all three suffered from untreated multiple personality disorders. Ultimately, all three were incarcerated for murder.

Prior to his death, Walther Liechtenauer passed the remnants of MKULTRA and the disbanded Pied Piper project to his successor, Ashton Pickering.

Chapter Fifty-Seven
The White House Residence

President Katherine Stone sat in front of her vanity carefully applying the final touches of eye shadow. She felt depressed. The white wine and two five-milligram diazepam tablets did seem to help. *This eye shadow doesn't complement my eyes. It simply draws attention to my wrinkled complexion.* For the last few weeks Katherine had been considering injections to erase the increasing number of wrinkles. *I never have enough time for myself. What's happened to me? Lately, I am overwhelmed by a sense of impending doom. What good is being President when I feel miserable?* She glared at her reflection in the mirror. *I loathe growing old.*

"Damn it!" she screamed. Katherine furiously swept her arm across the marble top. Her cosmetics flew across the room and crashed on the tile floor. *My meetings with Ashton Pickering intensify my anxiety.* Katherine inhaled deeply. Then with a long moan she pushed away from the vanity and tiptoed around the broken glass. She had less than an hour to dress for her dreaded dinner meeting with Pickering.

Contrary to her predecessors, early into her Presidency, Katherine Stone had made the decision not to have a personal valet. Nixon brought his personal valet with him when he entered the White House. Katherine 's fixation on privacy was the imperative. This evening Katherine regretted her decision as she walked into the master suite's huge wardrobe closet.

Katherine's wardrobe was meticulously arranged. She pressed the control button and the revolving rack displayed her evening apparel.

White, navy blue, and black dominated her wardrobe. The President rarely enjoyed down time from public scrutiny.

Consciously, she preferred pastels for casual wear. For some troubling reason she always felt compelled to wear a shade of green when meeting with Pickering. *The Director always compliments me on my selection.* And he did later that evening at dinner.

❧

"Green is my favorite color, Madame President," said Pickering with satisfaction as Katherine entered the dining room. The debonair Pickering kissed the President's hand.

The President's wary expression changed with the phrase -"green is my favorite color". Now, she appeared to be daydreaming as she acknowledged Pickering's compliment. "Thank you, Ashton."

Pickering smiled.

The President dismissed her staff. "I hope you don't mind. The meal will be simple. Elegant I assure you, but we need our privacy."

"I agree, Katherine. Now please fill me in on this Walter Katz business." His faint smile disappeared.

Katherine hesitated. *Ashton is testing me. I suspect he knows everything.* She appeared to brood. "I will get down to business. Walter Katz smuggled thousands of top-secret files from the DOD. I'll be specific."

Pickering interrupted. "Trinity's tech guys at Bland Corporation in South Carolina monitor Chinese and Russian intrusions into the DOD system. We watch them in real time. We follow every detail involving shipments of rare earth materials. And they didn't know?"

"Exactly. I was informed Katz arranged a maze of computer servers and directed traffic to his personal server."

For the first time during their relationship it was Pickering who appeared frantic. He began to nervously tap his index finger on the table.

"Katz monitored the DOD bid lists. Then he went after those vendors with vulnerable servers," said Katherine.

"Katherine, I cautioned you the DOD system was vulnerable. Bland Corporation has a backdoor into all of your servers. They send me regular reports."

"But Walter Katz was one of your contract guys," Katherine argued.

"So you gave him free access?" Pickering scowled.

"He tricked vendors to open malicious e-mails with embedded malware. That's how he managed to get into their servers."

"Ashton. You bear responsibility, too. I'm not taking the fall alone."

Katherine saw the fury in Pickering's eyes. "How many files?"

"Katz claims he has thousands of files."

"Critical?" demanded Pickering.

Katherine nodded. "Yes, I'm afraid so. We've compiled a list by category. There's as many as three hundred thousand files and e-mail exchanges."

"Are WikiLeaks or Edward Snowden involved?"

"No."

"Katherine, do you realize the impact if Katz releases those files to the media? It could finish your Presidential days. I can't imagine facing the Circle of Twelve. Do you grasp their financial investment in your presidency?"

"I told you. Katz hasn't released the files. The Secret Service searched his Georgetown apartment. They have the server. It's been sanitized. He must have the files on some damn encrypted cloud."

"I scanned Katz's personnel jacket. He married a few years ago."

"Yes. Chinese-American. She disappeared several weeks before Katz. We believe she is somewhere in China, perhaps Hong Kong.

Pickering appeared to drift deep into thought. He was known for his slow, but concise decisions. "There must be more bad news."

"Indeed. Dakota Putnam is back in the picture," Katherine said.

The absent look disappeared from Pickering's face. "Ms. Putnam is shrewd."

"Katz is feeding Putnam information. His signature name is Black Coffee. My Special Unit monitors every aspect of Putnam's life. She's writing a new book. Putnam contends my administration is connected with Trinity International."

"Pure speculation, Katherine."

"I don't think so. I've seen her column for tomorrow. She knows about Blue Sapphire, your rare earth venture in California. She quotes a geologist's report."

"And?"

"The survey discovered hundreds of thousands of gallons of toxic wastewater leaked from unlined storage ponds. The plume has contaminated a huge aquifer. A major source of California's drinking water is at risk. Is this true Ashton?"

"Yes. The report places Blue Sapphire and Trinity in an awkward position," said Pickering.

"Putnam's article purports Trinity and its California minions suppressed the findings."

"Putnam is cunning. It is true. Trinity needs rare earth minerals. Don't play naïve Katherine. You must appreciate the significance of Operation Purple Rain. A California court injunction will close us down. Trinity needs those abandoned mines in northern Zimbabwe. Otherwise we remain at the mercy of the Chinese. They have the monopoly on precious resources."

"Ashton, you constantly talk down to me. I'm no fool. The objective of Operation Purple Rain was to promote an insurgency. Mugabe's human rights violation and policies contributes to regional instability."

"Your plan is crumbling, my Dear Katherine. Last evening Mugabe's representative contacted John Strauss at Trinity's Headquarters. Mugabe received a warning from South Africa."

"I never informed South Africa."

"Mugabe fears you and the British are about to invade his country. The agent claims Mugabe has proof the CIA is financially supporting the opposition."

"This CIA provided the intelligence sources. Nothing more." Katherine fumed.

"You never consulted with me. It was never Trinity's intention to undermine Mugabe or topple his administration," Pickering responded.

"You just said Trinity craved control of rare earth resources. Where better than Zimbabwe? We've discovered a wealth of rare earth elements in the Marange diamond fields in Eastern Zimbabwe. Mugabe sent his troops into the region to seize control. His troops murdered at will. The region is filled with hostility."

"Military intervention isn't the answer, Katherine."

"I disagree."

"We just can't have our forces occupy the region. Other African nations will be outraged. My staff spent months putting an African business coalition together to support you."

"There is an even greater predicament. Kurt Strauss, Trinity's CFO, is promoting his son, John, as his successor. John has been micromanaging the rare earth project."

"Why?"

"Nanotechnology. Trinity needs to circumvent the Chinese monopoly."

"All the more reason to supply arms to dissidents in the Chiadzwa district."

"We can't have another Iraq."

"Nonsense. The timing is perfect."

"Katherine, you are in deep trouble. When word of this leaks to the press, your availability to run again will be shaken. No one will trust you."

"Hold on, Ashton. Now I understand. It's not about me. You're afraid of Kurt and John Strauss. John is in. You are out."

"You're naïve, Katherine. Without Trinity's support your administration will fold. The Circle of Twelve will destroy you."

Katherine peevishly tossed her napkin on the table. "What does the Circle of Twelve expect of me?"

"End your scheme to invade Zimbabwe," Pickering demanded.

"And the deal with the California environmental groups?"

"It is vital the Environmental Protection Agency and the Bureau of Mines reassure Californians their water is safe to drink. Trinity requires plausible deniability," Pickering insisted.

"So there we have it. I amount to a disposable pawn. *Follow orders or else.*"

Pickering was troubled. *What's wrong with Katherine? I've never seen her so upset.* "Katherine, your administration and Trinity both face Armageddon if Katz releases those files."

"In the end you leave me no choice but to agree."

"And Katz?" asked Pickering.

"Katz wants revenge. He doesn't care about Zimbabwe."

"Revenge?"

"Yes, for Mary Taylor. Taylor was one of my fellow participants in a research project."

"MKULTRA's Pied Piper?" asked Pickering.

"Yes. But haven't spoken to Walter Katz in thirty years. Then one afternoon, I received a mysterious text message. Only ten people have the direct number to my personal phone."

Katherine stammered. "The message read: 'j383132.'"

"Did your geeks figure out how he got your phone number?"

"Something about a backdoor and unauthorized access. We aren't talking about my computer. He got into my cell phone."

"What did the message mean?"

"This is wacky. It is from the Book of Job. Roughly, God can stop him, but we cannot."

"A religious nut?"

"Who knows? But he called again. This cyber spying frightens me Ashton. National Security Agency tracked the call through Germany. The code j383132 is a group of hackers. They have discovered a way to exploit a flaw in the mobile communications network, Signal System Seven. It's mumbo jumbo to me. Katz claims he can track me any place."

"What's the bottom line?"

"He was brief and caustic. He demanded the name of the CIA personnel who ran the Midnight Climax Operation in San Francisco."

"What the hell was Midnight Climax?" asked Pickering.

"Katz asserts it was a clandestine operation. We have no idea if it was officially authorized," Katherine responded.

"Be specific."

"Mary Taylor participated in the covert operation to blackmail foreign officers at several consulates."

"Prostitution?" Pickering looked worried.

"Mary was an intelligent, beautiful woman. Her advanced programming made her defenseless. Katz claims when the psychiatrists finished, Mary was a zombie. When the operation closed down, Mary was cut loose. Katz located her living in an abandoned psychiatric hospital on Long Island. Mary and Katz were twined soul mates. Franz did it. Now we will pay the price." Katherine scowled at Pickering.

"Who else knows?" asked Pickering.

"I think Foxx knew. He's dead. Katz may have told Lou-Ann Stokes. Drew Lindstrom has a piece of the puzzle. I confided in Charles Best. I counted on his counsel, but now he's falling apart."

"Is he vulnerable?" asked Pickering.

"Very. I'm afraid we'll have to deal with him," said Katherine with a downcast glance.

"Did Katz say anything else?"

"Yes. He will release all the Trinity Files unless I resign. He demands amnesty and safe conduct for his wife."

Pickering snickered. "Katz thinks I'm a pimp with a stable."

Katherine laughed.

"Listen carefully, Katherine. We need to stonewall the media. Find a reason to void Putnam's press credential. Leave Clayton and Stokes alone for now. We have to rein-in this mess. I must fly to Lake Como immediately."

"I feel sorry for you, Ashton. You think you are powerful, but you're nothing but a puppet."

"Save your breath, Katherine. It's easy to berate me, but this could mean my job and yours, Madame President. You have the Joint Chiefs in an uproar over Zimbabwe." Pickering shouted, red-faced.

"Don't threaten me, Ashton. I'm their Commander in

Chief." Katherine smiled arrogantly as she struggled to regain her composure.

"One question before you leave, Ashton. Did Trinity have a hand in Foxx's death?"

"That's unfair Madame President. Alan Foxx was about to compromise one of the Circle's most valued commodities." Pickering forced a smile. "Your Special Unit at Stratum had Foxx right in their grasp. He almost got away. I'll leave the rest to your imagination. As for Charles Best, you deal with him."

"All these machinations amount to nothing more than the Circle of Twelve's obsession to control the world's resources."

Katherine scowled and was about to leave the room when Pickering remarked, "Katherine, you look stunning in *green*."

Chapter Fifty-Eight
The "Right" Thing

The Treaty Room presidential clock chimed. Charles Best and Drew Lindstrom obediently waited for President Stone to finish her dinner engagement with Ashton Pickering.

"Good evening, gentlemen," said President Stone as she entered the room.   She was dressed in a lime green dress.

Both men stood. "Good evening, Madame President," replied Best.

Lindstrom gave a wistful smile. *She's been with Pickering. She always wears a shade of green for those occasions.*

Katherine looked at Lindstrom. She felt his eyes caress her neck and cleavage. She relished toying with a younger man who hungered for her.

"Please sit down, gentlemen. Let's get on with the briefing." Stone's face was expressionless and pale. "Charles. You've been terribly indiscreet."

Best looked puzzled.

"You met with Stokes and Clayton. Are you insane?"

"As for you Drew, Pickering spilled his Martini when I told him about Katz and the files. I wouldn't want to be in his shoes. He has to inform his superiors," she said. Katherine would never dare to reveal the existence of the Circle of Twelve.

Both men looked alarmed.

"Pickering will take it from here. Trinity is going after Katz and his wife. We seem to have one problem after another. "

"Stokes and Clayton?" asked Lindstrom

"We have to find a way of taking them out of the picture. Pickering suggests we discredit them for starters. Clayton's weakness is Dakota Putnam."

Lindstrom opened a second folder. "I received this brief a

few hours ago. Lou-Ann Stokes is on her way to Long Island. Jack Thompson's health is failing. ALS. Our text intercepts reveal he has only a few weeks left."

"Jack Thompson? I don't recall the name."

"Thompson was part of the original GAO inquiry back in 1977."

"My god. He's still around? He's old enough to be Stokes' father."

"And David Clayton?" asked the President.

"He's a predicament. Stokes put Clayton in touch with Putnam. No meetings, yet," Lindstrom assured the President.

"But he will," the President responded. Then she turned to Charles Best. She paused. "Drew, please give us a few minutes alone."

Lindstrom placed the random folders into his briefcase and began to exit the Treaty Room into the main hallway. "Excuse me Drew. Use this exit." She pointed to a paneled door on the far end of the room. Lindstrom tilted his head and nodded in agreement. It was an entry to the Lincoln Bedroom.

"Charles, what's happened to you?"

Before Best could respond she continued, "I have tremendous respect for you. Few people have demonstrated such loyalty. Your years as station chief in Beirut demanded awesome sacrifice. You've guided me through a number of dangerous situations. Sadly, I'm afraid it's time."

"Time?"

"You need a rest, my friend."

"I can't. What will I do?"

"I'm certain you'll do the right thing."

Best's eyes glistened. "You're asking me to fall on my sword?"

The President moved to where Best sat. She gently touched his shoulder. "I was too young to recall much about CIA Director Richard Helms, but I've read about him. He played a significant role in MKULTRA just as you have in Operation Purple Rain."

"What's the connection?" Best sobbed.

"Helms had a job to do. He did what he thought best. He protected his colleagues."

"I did my best for you, Madame President."

"You have. But there's one more task." The President walked behind Best and placed both hands on his shoulders.

"A last task?"

"I believe you understand what it is. Richard Helms once said 'Let's get on with it.'"

The President's hands fell to her side. "Good night, Charles." She paused and repeated, "I know you'll do the right thing."

A pathetic Best looked at President Stone for the final time. *Her voice echoed a gentle reaffirmation – "Yes, I want you to fall on you sword."*

Best didn't reply. He was overcome by disillusionment as he watched the President enter the adjoining bedroom.

❧

"I want you to stay tonight, Drew," said the President.

Lindstrom was caught off guard. *Our interludes always open with a prescribed routine. Katherine sets the tone. She points to the bed. When she's satisfied, she simply dismisses me.*

Tonight was different. The President risked Drew's presence in the residence overnight. Nevertheless, an air of tension filled the room.

Why the Lincoln Room? Something warned Lindstrom the President was frightened. He tried to lighten the mood. It was a mistake. "You should have invited Charles. He looked despondent."

"Are you mocking me?"

"Mocking you? No. Teasing you? Yes."

"Stop! I feel strange. Pickering has some odd influence over me. My head aches as it did when I was a child. Pickering dominates my thoughts. He lurks in the back of my mind. I don't like the sensation," Katherine complained.

"No. I imagine not." The mood grew somber. "It may be your Alpha personality conflicting with his."

"You don't like Ashton," Katherine said with a demure smile.

"Not particularly. I've only met him on business occasions."

"Are you jealous, Drew?"

"I'm uncertain." Drew undressed. "Have you slept with him?"

Katherine avoided the question. "Let's freshen up first." She took his hand and led him to the adjoining bathroom. The scene was quite matter-of-fact. They showered. Drew sponged her gently. Katherine didn't react.

As they stepped from the shower Drew whispered, "Your relationship with Pickering mystifies me. Perhaps I am jealous. You looked so enticing in the green dress."

Katherine spun around and shoved Drew into the sink.

"Wow, that hurt," he exclaimed. *What did I say wrong?* Drew was baffled. *Was that a playful request to roughhouse?*

Drew watched Katherine walk toward the bed. She tantalized him. The rosewood bed was high off the floor. Katherine needed to use the bed footrest. Before she reached the step, Drew rushed from behind. With one brazen move he lifted Katherine and tossed her on to the mattress.

"Stop it, Drew. I'm in no mood. I asked you to stay. Does that have to mean sex?"

"What? I'm puzzled, Katherine . You ask me to stay the night. What's going on?"

"Slide under the covers."

"Drew pulled the blankets up to his waste. Propped a pillow and said, "Now what?"

"There are times when I simply don't know who I am. Tonight's one of them. Slide down. I don't want to have sex. I simply want to caress you." Katherine ran her fingers along his chest.

"And Agent Kevin Goodman the new head of your detail?"

"What does Goodman have to do with us? He's on duty," Katherine responded.

"On duty? Come on, Katherine. Be honest with me."

"Stop it Drew."

"In other words, Goodman is part of your stable, just like me."

"Don't even mention Goodman's name again," Katherine warned.

Drew turned on his side to face her. "Katherine, I'm devoted to you. I've sacrificed my career and I suspect my reputation is shattered."

"You made that choice, Drew. I never forced you."

"That's easy for you to say, Katherine."

She stared at Drew for a moment. Then she shoved him away.

The shocked Lindstrom tried to sit up, but to no avail. She wrapped her hands around his throat.

"Stop it your hurting me." Drew pushed her away and rolled on top. "What's wrong? You've never behaved this way."

They grappled. Katherine marshaled tremendous strength. She mounted Drew again. He grabbed her wrists. She fell forward against his neck."

"Damn it," Drew hollered. "You bit me."

Katherine laughed. She taunted him and bit him again.

"I'm not a beggar," Drew bellowed. "This isn't lust. This is anger." He pushed her away. He forced her arms back and rolled on top.

"Stop this Katherine . It's crazy."

"Hit me. Go ahead and hit me. I dare you Drew," she jeered. "You're revolting."

"Hit you. Why would I hit you?" Drew fell back against the headboard. He was exhausted. "You used me, Katherine. I don't know what happened tonight, but I've made it too easy. And now you explode with contempt. What the hell did I say that triggered all this? Was it was my compliment after we showered that angered you. Now, anything I say fans the flames. Why are you so damned agitated?"

Suddenly Katherine 's eyes widened. Her expression glazed. Her body tensed. "I want you to leave, Drew. Get out of here. Alert security that you are leaving."

"OK. Please, just calm down," he said.

Drew dressed and prepared to leave. He looked at Katherine sitting in bed. She trembled and appeared oblivious to his presence. He couldn't figure out what prompted Katherine's vicious behavior. He felt the desire to comfort the sobbing Katherine, but he was too confused from their encounter.

❧

Drew Lindstrom turned in his pass and exited into the White House parking area. The President's Chief of Staff has optional limousine service. Drew opted out in favor of personal privacy. The White House does not have valet parking. Drew walked to his black SUV. Staff skeleton crews work the night shift. He pressed the car remote. The lights flashed as the doors unlocked. Drew was about to get in when he caught a sight of Charles Best sitting in his Honda Civic. *Why the hell is Best hanging around?* Drew gave a casual wave, but he doubted Best noticed. Furthermore, it wasn't a pleasant evening for either man. Lindstrom faced another dilemma. *Should I go home?* Drew acknowledged White House Security as he exited the grounds. It was an agonizing drive home.

Chapter Fifty-Nine
Time To Make Amends

It was a heartbreaking evening for Charles Best, also. The President just humiliated him in front of Drew Lindstrom. He once trusted her. Best considered himself a loyal confidant. And now the President had asked him to "do the right thing." The message was clear and direct. He began to sob as the President and Lindstrom abandoned him in the Treaty Room. He returned to his office and typed his resignation letter. Next he opened his diary and typed a series of comments. The last entry read, "I've allowed myself to become corrupt. I've promoted a culture of power where illicit money and bedroom capitulations replaced love of country."

Best walked to his car tossed his brief case in the trunk. It was nearly three AM. He sat behind the steering wheel contemplating his next move.

Best opened the center console and retrieved a pint of Scotch and a plastic bottle of diazepam. He sipped the Scotch then swallowed several pills. Best turned on the car engine and lowered the window. White House security patrols the parking lot in a golf cart. The watchman never heard the bottle break nor did he notice the despondent White House Counsel.

It is time to make amends. Who can I trust? I have no one. He opened the glove compartment. Felt inside. Smiled and slammed the glove compartment door closed. The security logs noted Best's departure at 3:22 AM.

Instead of driving North toward his Silver Springs apartment Best turned on to E Street then south along an uncommonly-deserted Route 66 toward Centerville. He telephoned David Clayton several times. His call went directly to voice mail after the first ring. Best left a voice message. He fumbled with the phone in an attempt to text Clayton. The Scotch, pills and phone calls consumed Best's dulling awareness. He failed to notice the silver Toyota Highlander tailing him. He gave one last desperate call to Clayton. "Clayton. Please call my cell phone. It's important." Clayton had apparently silenced his phone for the night.

Somewhere near Centerville Best's faculties seemed to rally. A car's bright lights reflected in Best's rear view mirror. He drove for another mile. Best looked in the review mirror. A black Suburban was still following. *I'm being tailed.*

Best accelerated. The Suburban's driver accelerated, too. He was dangerously close. Best frantically cut across the highway at Route 29. The Suburban remained in pursuit. Best slowed down hoping to catch a glimpse of the driver. It began to rain.

Best decided to continue south toward Route 66, again. "Damn it," he shouted. "My Honda is no match for the Suburban."

Best's desperate scramble led along Bull Run Drive and the National Park. Best made a sharp left onto a dirt maintenance road, but to no avail. He feverishly turned and looked back. The Suburban had stopped a short distance behind. Best looked for an escape route, but the road ended a few hundred feet into the woods. *My god, I have no way out of here. I'm trapped.*

❧

Clayton set his alarm clock for 5:30 AM. The alarm never sounded. A brief power outage had reset the clock to an ever-blinking 12:00.

"Shit. I forgot to replace the battery back-up." He rushed to the kitchen to check his cell phone. It was nearly 6:45. There were several voice messages. *I'll have to listen to them on the way in to DC.* His coffee maker was flashing that same 12:00. *No coffee either?* He scrambled to shower and dress. He was about to leave the apartment when he remembered the second phone; the one Katz initially gave to Lou-Ann. He snatched it off the counter and dropped it into his suit pocket.

It had been raining for days. Today was no exception. The I-495 interchange at Tyson's Corner was backed up for miles.

Now it was at a complete stop. *I'll miss my 8:30 appointment at the Library of Congress.* Resigned to his predicament he called ahead and requested a late morning appointment. Then David listened to his voice mail. There were eight messages including three from Charles Best. *He sounded desperate. Why call me?*

David decided to contact Lou-Ann on Long Island. "Best called. Sounded frantic. I've tried returning his calls with no success. Traffic is snarled. I'm on my way in to the Library of Congress."

"What do you expect to find there?" Lou-Ann asked.

"I want to run through the catalog at the Research Division. A documentary on PBS caught my attention. It focused on narcotics traffickers operating as a business. The show emphasized the research available at the Library of Congress from an economic perspective."

"I still don't get the connection to Walter Katz or Alan Foxx's death," Lou-Ann replied.

"The filmmakers focused on the exploitation of globalization and new technology. These are high-tech business operations. Katz, the computer maven, was a trusted operative of the Bland Corporation. Bland develops computer programs and other digital technology. Bland is a subsidiary of Trinity International."

"Just be careful, David. We both know Trinity can be dangerous when confronted."

"I agree. Trinity is powerful. Our GAO investigation essentially exposed them in 1977. Trinity leveraged the Justice Department and the Feds terminated our investigation. Think about this. All the significant players are gone. Our report was buried," said David.

"Not all. You and I haven't quit. Pickering is still out there," Lou-Ann replied.

"We don't know the new players, Lou-Ann. Katz is out there some place."

"This is risky business. I need a rest, David. I can't be much help to you. I hope you understand."

"I understand. I'll be OK. I'm convinced I will eventually find Walter Katz or he'll find me. He's bound to reach out to me. I have to do this. I'll call you when I find him."

Chapter Sixty
The White House Oval Office
11:30 AM

President Katherine Grace Stone sat alone in the Oval Office. Her calls were on hold. She did not want to be disturbed. For the last hour or more she stared out the window and ruminated. The persistent migraines debilitated Katherine. She was frightened. There were episodes when she went into her private bathroom, turned the lights off, and rested on the cool ceramic tiled floor. These were the attacks of which her late husband complained. She was haunted by cloudy recollections of dreamlike incidents. She leaned forward and held her aching head between her hands. There were violent moments as well. Last evening's encounter with Drew Lindstrom troubled Katherine.

I felt a compulsion to strangle him. Why? She began to sob. *This has got to stop. What's happening to me? I'm losing control.* She spun around and looked into the empty room. Then she picked up the phone and spoke with her secretary.

"Call Lindstrom. I want to meet with him in thirty minutes."

"Mr. Lindstrom's been sitting here. You had an appointment scheduled for an hour ago."

"Send him in."

Drew Lindstrom entered the Oval Office and stood almost at attention in front of Katherine's desk.

"I apologize for keeping you waiting Drew. Do you have my daily brief ready?"

"Yes, but there are two items I must bring to your attention."

"Why so formal, Drew. Are you OK?"

Drew could not believe the contrast in the President's demeanor from last evening.

"Stratum has been monitoring David Clayton's calls. Earlier

he called Lou-Ann Stokes. Clayton is at the Library of Congress."

"What is he looking for?"

"I suspect he is searching for clues to substantiate his theory."

"And what might that be?" Katherine petulantly asked.

"He suspects a connection between the Pied Piper project, Trinity and you."

"Me?"

"Yes."

"And what was the other important news?"

"Charles Best is dead. Heavy torrential rains and flash flooding kept the National Park Service ranger from making his usual rounds. Best's personal car, a Honda Civic, wasn't discovered until around eight this morning. The ranger radioed for assistance. He found Charles' body a short distance away. He'd been shot."

The President's face was void of surprise. Her gaze made Lindstrom feel transparent and uncomfortable. *Is she incapable of feeling?*

"What else has been reported?"

"Once the local authorities determined Charles' identity the FBI was called in."

"Damn it, Drew. Dispatch Agent Kevin Goodman immediately. We have to keep this under control."

"Was it a suicide?"

"I don't know. I saw Charles sitting in his car when I left the parking area around two or so. I waved, but he didn't acknowledge me. You two spoke briefly in the Treaty Room last night. Did you have a clue he was despondent?"

"No, of course not. I encouraged him to take a few days vacation. He'd been working too hard. That's all."

"You were harsh during our meeting. Who knows? Charles was vulnerable. He felt he let you down. You seemed to reinforce the impression."

"Are you implying I triggered his death?"

"I did not say that. The authorities haven't released a preliminary report. Allow events to evolve. Earlier the police speculated it might be a robbery."

"Skip the morning security briefing. I want a detailed report from Goodman. Do you understand?"

"Yes, Madame President." Lindstrom forced a smile and turned to leave the Oval Office.

"Drew. I want you to search Best's office and computer. You may discover some detail to aid in the investigation. You understand where I am coming from?"

"I do."

The President watched Lindstrom's shoulders slouch as he acknowledged her orders. *I feel sorry for men like Drew. He has a sexless marriage. It affects every aspect of his life. It obliterates his confidence. The emotional agony is destroying him. It may be time for me to find a new lover.*

It was late afternoon when David Clayton learned of Charles Best's death. Following protocol the Virginia state authorities isolated the scene. The investigation was hampered by another bout of rain. Rumors proliferated in Washington. By late noon, anonymous sources close to the investigation were speculating that Best's death was a suicide.

The White House had a different perspective. When agent Kevin Goodman arrived at the Manassas scene, two police officers were on watch waving rubberneckers away.

"I'm sorry, sir. Until we get further orders, this area is considered a crime scene," the sergeant informed Goodman.

Goodman flashed his shield and scowled. "This is official business. Now do you let me through or do I have to call your supervisor?"

Reluctantly, the sergeant lifted the yellow police line tape that cordoned the maintenance road. Goodman passed the two local police officers and walked the few hundred feet to the Honda Civic.

The trunk of Best's car was open. Rainwater pooled over several folders. Goodman slipped on a pair of latex gloves and picked up the soaked folders. *Nothing here.* Next, he scanned the immediate area for Best's personal effects. In the distance he saw two detectives searching beyond a fallen tree. The preoccupied pair didn't notice Goodman searching Best's car.

Ironically, the detectives had failed to thoroughly check the Honda's glove compartment. Feeling for a minute particle, Goodman was stunned to find an overlooked narrow plastic box of .22 caliber bullets wedged into the compartment. Ten rounds were missing from the pack of fifty. *I can't believe Best was so stupid. He never got rid of the bullets.* Goodman hefted the plastic case and grinned.

The two detectives caught a glimpse of Goodman. "Hey," called one of the detectives. "This is still a crime scene. Stay out of the car."

"You got it." He smiled and tossed a casual salute of recognition. He dropped the cartridge box into his rain slicker pocket and walked to the main road.

"Thank you," Goodman told the two cops guarding the entrance. "Looks like everything is under control." Goodman climbed into his black Suburban and headed for the White House.

Kevin Goodman was pleased with himself. He drove about 5 miles before he began dropping one .22 bullet at a time out the car window. Not far from the White House he stopped the car and got out. He walked to the curb. He sneered. He crushed the plastic box with his foot and kicked it down a nearby culvert. It was an awesome day's work. *I wonder if the President will have a special reward?*

Chapter Sixty-One
The Arrival Gate
Long Island MacArthur Airport.

The arrival gate at Long Island MacArthur Airport was packed with passengers. David Clayton moved to a far wall to avoid the fray.

Where is she?

He was apprehensive or better yet, ambivalent with the reunion at hand. He had been rehearsing his opening words for days. The parade of passengers, baby carriages and children clogged the narrow corridor. A baby's cry startled David back into the present moment. He felt a tap on his shoulder and turned with surprise.

"Dakota?"

"No welcoming hug or peck on the cheek for an old friend?" she asked. Dakota recognized David's befuddled expression.

"Wow! Am I that wrinkled? Have I aged so much?"

Dakota smiled and hugged David. She loved his awkwardness.

"Damn it Dakota. I practiced my opening lines over and over and I screwed them up." He regained his composure and with an embarrassed blush said, "You look great. I'm the one who has aged. I had a thirty-inch waist back then. Forgive me. You know me; too little and too late."

"Yes, I remember exactly how you…we were."

"Welcome to Islip. Not exactly the Hamptons. I have to warn you it takes as long to get the luggage as it did to fly from Denver."

Dakota laughed. She felt more at ease.

"And how was the flight?"

"Awful."

David paused. He struggled, but the words finally came out. "Well, you made it. I'm really happy you're here."

"Me too, David. We have a lot a 'catching-up' to do."

"Your call blew my mind. I assumed you'd eventually check in with Lou-Ann."

"I did. But first I needed to substantiate a hunch. Three weeks ago I was in Germany on assignment. I called Lou-Ann when I returned."

"Germany?"

Dakota was apprehensive. "I'll tell you all about my trip once we are on the road."

"Why the trip to Laramie?"

"Another mystery. I still can't figure it out. I'm afraid it was a wasted effort."

"I'm eager to hear about your adventures."

"They weren't exciting. Believe me." Dakota ran her fingers through her hair in that carefree way that still aroused David.

"I'm sorry to learn Jack died. How is Lou-Ann dealing with it?" Dakota asked.

"She's doing as well as can be expected. Jack struggled with ALS for years." David cast his eyes toward the luggage carousel. "Let's get your bags. We can talk in the car."

"I wonder if Jack ever forgave me for the piece I wrote about the Watergate Affair. I had no idea he was so ill. I've been out of touch with everyone," Dakota added.

"Well, let's make the best of it. I'm just happy to spend time with a famous author. Two friends," David said as they left the airport.

"Where are you staying?"

"A Hampton Inn in Farmingville. I'm due back in Washington on Monday. I'll drop you at Lou-Ann's. Would you like to go to dinner this evening?"

"Sure, but shouldn't we invite Lou-Ann?"

"I think she'll understand."

I used to imagine living on Long Island, David. I cherish the weekend we shared at the Three Village Inn. But that was so long ago."

"We had fun."

"This is a hell of a reunion," Dakota said. "Maybe it's for the best. I don't want to fool you, David. You may not be so happy when I tell you about my trip to Germany. Lou-Ann already heard the abridged version. Truthfully, she urged me to fly to Long Island and meet with you."

"And all along I thought this was your way to rekindle our relationship."

A prolonged silence enveloped the car. Dakota gazed out the passenger window to suppress unexpressed feelings.

"Hey. Is something wrong?" David asked.

"No. Nothing. I'm fine."

David decided this was not the time to pursue a conversation.

Dakota broke the ice and asked, "So what was it like to be on President Stone's staff?"

"Actually, I wasn't. I left soon after she moved into the White House."

"Stone is strong-willed. Some say she is vicious."

"She has her temper, but I rarely worked with her. Her moods took their toll on Andrew and the marriage. She's a driven woman."

"Some say possessed."

"Katherine Stone had a powerful influence over Andrew. Can you imagine the pressure of being married to the President?"

"A bad marriage generates anger. It is no secret Stone has a demeaning behavior. I can picture times when he felt ignored or neglected. Anger undermines a relationship. I hated Bob for humiliating me. I wanted to kill him." David looked over at Dakota. She scrunched her face."

"Hey lady, slow down. That's behind you," David remarked.

"There was a brief time when I blamed myself. I considered suicide. I wonder if Dunn felt the same way?"

"Maybe we should shift gears. I am still struggling to get over his death."

"And how about you Dakota?"

"You probably guessed I was pregnant before Bob and I were married," Dakota replied. "I blame myself. You were right.

He was a bastard."

David looked at Dakota, but didn't respond.

She accepted his silence as a "yes". Dakota pause then said, "Bob and I rarely communicated. I mean we never talked about things beyond the news and weather." Dakota gazed out the passenger widow. "Honestly? There was no intimacy. The relationship crumbled. After Robbie was born Bob absented himself more and more. Women!"

"Lou-Ann told me your son is an assistant district attorney in upstate New York."

"Yes he is. I'm proud of him. It was tough being a single parent with a career. As for Bob, I run into him from time to time. Our conversations are brief." Dakota's mood changed as she wiped away tears. "The bastard is still a lobbyist with a K Street firm. He represents your old adversary, Trinity PharmoDynamics."

"They aren't my opponents, Dakota. I just don't like the way they do business."

David turned left off Montauk Highway and drove along River Avenue until he arrived at a group of condos along the river's edge.

"Lou-Ann lives in the second building. I don't see her car." David pulled into the parking lot and glanced at his watch. She'll be along in a minute. Tell me. What took you to Germany?"

"A woman named Eleanor Giles. I want you to meet her. She lives in St. James. It's not far from here."

"What a coincidence. St. James is a stone's throw from Trinity's former headquarters. And how did you meet Miss Giles?" asked David.

"Its Mrs. She's a widow. She contacted me through my publisher. Her letter convinced me Giles wasn't fabricating a story. I met her a short time later."

"What story?" David asked.

"I want you to hear it from her, but I'll share this much. She claims her father was an OSS agent during World War Two. He rarely talked about his work. Later he worked for the CIA and the Justice Department."

"Thousands of people worked for the OSS during the war."

"I checked her father's name against recently declassified documents. He was the real thing."

"OK. Then what?"

"Her father died in a plane crash in 1977. His name was William Robert Mallory. Several months before his death Mallory told his daughter a story only an insider could know."

"Hold on. Are you telling me Eleanor's father was my informant, Robert?

"She's credible. I trust her. I'm not dealing with an anonymous source like you were back in 1977."

"David, you once told me Robert's calls suddenly stopped in April 1977."

"That's right."

"Robert Mallory died in April 1977. He was on a flight to DC when the DC-9 crashed. They flew into a violent storm. Rain and ice damaged the engines. I read the report."

"Mrs. Giles' story must be compelling. She convinced you to fly to Germany?"

"She told me something few knew."

"What?"

"Her father recounted a bizarre story about a baby born in Germany at one of Himmler's Lebensborn. Eleanor's reference to the Lebensborn caught my attention. I remembered the tattered brown card we found during the 1977 investigation."

"Yes. It was in one of the passports we discovered. Initially we had no idea it was a birth registration. Once we learned its significance we tried to find the official records in Germany."

"Our embassy reported the Lebensborn records were destroyed. It's not true. Many of those records exist. The Russians have records, also. After the war lots of mothers abandoned their children. Some were adopted with new identities. Others were left to state care. I've read horrifying stories of neglect and child abuse in those institutions."

"A number of survivors' stories are posted on the Internet. I corresponded with two individuals who discovered their history. Access to the Lebensborn records is limited to individuals with legitimate claims. Initially, I was denied. I could not remember the number stamped on the card or the mother's name. Municipal authorities refused to take my calls."

"Alan Foxx located the Sunrise Files and our evidence stored in a Justice Department Warehouse. I searched the records inventory. There are thousands of boxes with coded catalog numbers. We would have to search every box," said David.

"I needed the Lebensborn card number. I telephoned Eleanor Giles."

"And she had the number?"

"Yes. I can't imagine why she didn't tell me right from the beginning. A reporter with the LA Times covered the Lebensborn story. The files are supposedly in Berlin, but I discovered they are scattered among several locations. A contact at the International Tracing Service in Bad Arolsen agreed to help, but only if I flew to Germany."

"But you went to Hamburg. He used the name Grubb. He lives in Hamburg. Grubb is a retired archivist. He worked with the Federal victims compensations unit."

"Not the Lebensborn children?"

"No, but get this. Grubb was born in Norway in a Lebensborn. The Norwegians punished woman who collaborated with German soldiers. His mother gave him up for adoption. His adoptive parents brought him to Germany after the war. Years later he wanted to learn about his biological parents. After many inquires he found numerous records existed. Eventually, Grubb discovered the name of his biological mother."

"You make it sound so easy, Dakota."

"It wasn't. I flew from Dulles to Frankfurt and then on to Hamburg. Frankfurt is a hub and tremendously busy. I purchased a coffee and located my departure gate. I felt someone was watching me."

David smiled.

"I'm serious. There's more. Grubb called my cell phone as I deplaned." Dakota related a mysterious chain of events.

"Do you have the numbers?" Grubb asked.

"Yes, I have the registration numbers."

"But you do not have the original card?"

"No."

"Please confirm the number," Grubb requested.

"SS-1-3128."

"Meet me tomorrow at St. Michael's Church. Four o'clock sharp. Sit in the fifth pew near the pulpit, on the left."

"No sooner?"

"These matters take time. I work a few hours a week for the municipal government."

"You said you thought someone was watching you at the airport," David said.

"Yes. I caught a glimpse of him again, but then he disappeared.

"I took a taxi to Barcelo, Hamburg, a hotel near the Rathaus, the municipal center. I gave the receptionist my passport. In turn, the receptionist took the passport to the manager's desk."

"That's standard. Someone always checks the guests' passports," said David.

"I was suspicious. The pair appeared to scrutinize my passport. At first I thought,

'It's my imagination. I'm tired. Just want to get the Lebensborn documents and get the hell out of here.' I just wanted to get to my room. I walked to the lift. As the door closed, I spotted the stranger from the Frankfurt terminal. He *was* following me."

"You must have felt vulnerable," David remarked.

"I did."

Just then a tap on the car window interrupted Dakota's story. Lou-Ann had arrived home.

"What happened to the guy who followed you?" David asked.

"You'll learn more when we meet with Eleanor Giles in the morning," Dakota said in such a way as to encourage David's curiosity.

As Dakota got out of the care he asked, "Are we still on for this evening?"

David smiled. "No business. I promise."

"Great. The rest of the story can wait until tomorrow."

David watched Dakota follow Lou-Ann into the condo.

∽

Dakota's unfinished story of her visit to Germany had all the makings of a spy thriller. Dakota arrive on the fifth floor. There was an eerie stillness. She unlocked the door, hastily walked in, and locked the door, again. With a disapproving glance, Dakota tossed her carry-on bag on the bed, used the bathroom, and departed for the Rathaus, Hamburg's city hall. She hoped to get a glimpse of Herr Grubb. Dakota decided to walk rather than take a taxi. Lou-Ann needed the fresh air and exercise. She paused just before arriving at the Rathaus. Instinctively, Dakota turned. *I sense I'm being followed.*

The following afternoon Dakota took a taxi for the ten-minute ride to St Michaels.

St. Michaels is a Baroque style building. Some consider it the most famous of Hamburg's churches. She looked up at the bronze statue above the entrance, St. Michael defeating the devil.

She arrived on time and found the pew where Grubb was to meet her. He didn't show for another fifteen or twenty minutes.

"I apologize for being late. I arranged an early dinner hour, but my coverage was delayed." Grubb was a frail man. He moved slowly, almost painfully. Dakota noticed his hands as he held on to the pews to sit down. They were distorted perhaps from arthritis.

"Did you bring the documents?"

"No, but I have the information. You have no experience with the Lebensborn files, but you appreciate the secrecy."

"It seems to involve a lot of cloak and dagger suspense."

"You are quite right, especially in the case of SS-1-3128."

Grubb noticed two men enter the church. They sat in a pew darkened by an overhead balcony. Dakota noticed Grubb's apprehension.

"The files may not be photocopied without risk. I memorized the information." Grubb's voice lowered to a whisper. I've written the details. He placed an envelope on the pew and slid it to Dakota.

"You said the file is unusual."

"It is not unusual –it's exceptional. I've seen a number of records, none like this. Listen carefully. SS-1-3128, a female was born at Steinborg, Himmler's first Lebensborn. The biological mother was Anna Bruns."

"Is the mother still alive?"

"Please Ms. Putnam, I don't have a lot of time. Allow me to finish. The record shows SS-1-3128 remained at Steinborg for a number of months." Grubb turned. The two men in the rear pew were gone. "The child was released into the custody of a German naval officer, Manfred Bartel and his wife, Gertrude. Lieutenant Commander Bartel, a German naval officer, served on Admiral Dönitz staff in 1943. The Bartels are listed as "guardians".

"Not adoptive parents?"

"No. Strangely enough, they listed an address in Berchtesgarden. Bartel's was stationed in Berlin when Dönitz relocated to the Naval Academy in Flensburg."

"What makes the record for SS-1-3128 unique?"

"The order to release the child was signed by Hitler's secretary, Martin Bormann. Bormann, along with Hitler and other top officials built estates at the Berghof compound."

"Do you think the child lived with Bormann?"

Grubb thought for a minute and said, "I don't know, but to have a directive from Bormann was almost tantamount to a Fuhrer order."

"Perhaps someone in Hitler's household?"

"I have no idea, but here is another disturbing note. I was curious and searched the central registry records of government employees during the war. I discovered Anna Bruns worked as a clerk typist in Munich. She was granted a UK visa following the war. Anna Bruns Mueller was murdered in the mid-seventies."

"Murdered?"

"I have no other information Ms. Putnam. I must return to work." His voice trembled. That was the last time Dakota ever talked with Grubb.

❧

The Riverside Inn
Patchogue, Long Island

Dinner was a casual affair on a beautiful summer evening.

"This is a wonderful location, David. I love watching the boats on the river. I'm glad we chose to sit outside." Dakota paused. David's dreamy expression was a dead give-away. Her touch on the back of his hand brought him into the moment.

"I'm sorry, Dakota. I was thinking about our last evening in Stony Brook."

"David, let's be honest with one another. Look around. What do you see?"

"Boats. This is a marina," he said half-heartedly.

"I see people having an enjoyable evening. See the couple standing near the bar? How old are they?"

"Maybe in their mid-forties."

"Where are you going with this?"

"We aren't in our forties. Years have passed between us. You once told me I was impetuous and fell in love too quickly."

David frowned. "I remember."

"I know myself better now. I feel a sense of emotional security. We have a history. When we were together I was always comparing you to Bob. You resented the comparisons."

"I felt you were trying too hard to make our relationship work. It was your way or else we were finished," David replied, defensively.

"We both needed our space and time. We struggled to establish our careers. I found my identity through work. And you did, too. We never created time for true intimacy."

"You're right. I always described myself by what I did, my work. Now I am confronted with who I am."

"I refused to accept your imperfections, your faults, because I needed to be perfect. I needed you to be perfect. Looking back I regret our break-up."

"Me too," he smiled.

"I hope I am not assuming too much."

"No. This is important."

"I'll share my feelings. My marriage failed. I trusted Bob Doyle. When the honeymoon ended he destroyed my trust. At this point in my life I'm reluctant to begin a relationship. Do you understand?"

David's eyes looked down at his glass of pinot noir as though to avoid her question. "When I was young I viewed life as if it was a cheap wine." He swirled the glass and watched a thin film of wine on the surface. For a moment he gazed at the running lights of a passing boat. Then he looked at Dakota. "It takes time to appreciate wine, the aroma, the color, and eventually with maturity the bouquet."

Dakota tilted her head wistfully to one side. *Where's he going with this?*

"I understand," he assured Dakota. "Let's go slow and see what awaits."

Chapter Sixty-Two
Operation Paperclip

The next morning David arrived at Lou-Ann's condo. Lou-Ann greeted him. They hadn't seen each other in several weeks. Lou-Ann gave David a hug. They looked at each other for a moment.

Lou-Ann looks woefully tired. David forced a smile, but he couldn't disguise his feelings. He gave her another hug then stepped back and said, "How are you holding up?"

"I'm OK. Some trouble sleeping. Waking up each morning is the hardest part of my loneliness. I miss Jack. Hey, don't look so bleak. I'll make it. It's great to see Dakota again."

"Yes. We talked for several hours last night. It was kind of like only a few weeks had passed rather then all those years."

Just then Dakota walked into the living room carrying a canvas bag and a travel mug of coffee. "I'm set. I called Eleanor. She is expecting us."

The drive to St. James took about thirty minutes. Eleanor lived near St. Philip and St. James Church just off North Country Road.

"Take the next left. It's that cottage on the right." Dakota pointed to a small home.

The house looked out of place compared with the more luxurious properties.

"Eleanor's husband worked for an aircraft data systems company until he died about ten years ago. There she is."

Eleanor waved. She was playing with her dog in the front yard. David parked the car. Dakota was a bit nervous. She sensed David's skepticism.

Eleanor Giles was an attractive woman with a casual, cordial manner. David could see the natural rapport between Eleanor and Dakota. He didn't waste time on small talk.

"I'm curious why you contacted Dakota? You've known your father's story for years."

Dakota gave David one of her scornful looks. "David, please go easy. Give Eleanor a chance."

"Come on inside. May I offer you a cup of coffee?"

"No thank you," David' gruff response irritated Dakota.

"I'll have a cup, thanks," *What's gotten into David?*

Eleanor poured Dakota's coffee and said, "I admire Dakota. I've read her two books and follow her columns. She received a lot of negative criticism for one of her articles on the Obama Administration failing to halt payments to Nazis."

"You see, David. I do have some devoted readers."

"Yes. It is apparent the President and Congress wanted the episode to go away," David replied.

"There's more to it." Eleanor walked to the counter and returned with a folder.

"What makes you so sure?" Dakota asked Eleanor.

"I clipped a number of the articles. Even the current administration avoids dealing with the historical implications. They attempted to discredit Dakota by accusing her of having an ax to grind."

"You've done your homework," David conceded. "Why?"

"Mallory, that's what I called my father. He approved. I think calling him Mallory still lingers. I'm still ambivalent about our relationship. Anyway, Mallory believed the Paperclip Operation was a monster. It may have had patriotic intentions but broke the law. I think he felt conscience-bound to expose the underside. Tell me Mr. Clayton, how does one destroy a monster without becoming a monster?"

The question caught David off guard. He shrugged. "I've never thought about it.

Perhaps one doesn't recognize one is turning into a monster." David said.

"That was my father's predicament. The dilemma weighed heavily on his conscience."

Eleanor smiled. "I'll be more specific. Among my father's

papers I came across newspaper accounts of the Church Committee hearings. I found a number of articles about the MKULTRA program. I was surprised to find a story about the General Accounting Office's inquiry into Operation Paperclip. The reporter mentioned you in the story. My father had circled your name."

"You definitely have an understanding of the scope of the CIA's activities during that time. Did your father share other information?" asked Dakota.

"My father was a secretive and moody man. He rarely shared his feeling or displayed emotion. He seldom mentioned my mother, especially after he remarried Linda. If it hadn't been for Linda, I wouldn't have an inkling into Mallory's story."

"Dakota may know a bit about your backstory, but she hasn't share it with me."

"Surely you encountered Erskin Young."

"Yes."

"Erskin Young was my stepfather. My mother and father divorced when I was a child. When my mother died, Mallory retained full custody. Erskin and Mallory agreed I should be enrolled in a Catholic girl's school, St. Hallvard's in Virginia. Mallory owned a small farm a few miles away. I was thirty-two years old when Mallory died."

"And your stepmother?" asked Dakota.

"Linda was a child psychologist. According to Mallory, they met while he was working on Long Island for the Justice Department. She died in 2001."

David began to ask another question when Eleanor interrupted him. "Perhaps it might be best to tell you what Mallory shared with me."

"Of course," David replied.

For the next two hours Eleanor recalled the final months before her father's death. "He made frequent trips to DC." Eleanor related her father's references to several journals.

"Where are those journals, now?" David asked.

"I destroyed them. Mallory worked for several agencies. I'm surprised you do know how disciplined a field agent is when it comes to detailed reports. My father did not want reputations destroyed or the names of agents revealed."

David didn't respond. He removed a notebook and pen from his jacket.

Eleanor looked at Dakota and said, "We had an understanding…no notes or tape recorders."

"I agreed, David. I should have told you," said Dakota.

"No notes. No documents. All we have to go on is Eleanor's recollection. How do we corroborate?"

"Listen to the story and try not to interrupt," Dakota said.

David scowled.

"Mallory's story started in Germany before the Second World War ended." For the next two hours David and Dakota were entranced as Eleanor shared what she knew of Mallory's clandestine life.

The Lebensborn child was a significant part of the account.

When Eleanor finished, Dakota said, "I was denied access to the one thousand or so Lebensborn files," Dakota said. "The children's identities are a closely guarded secret. I do believe the child existed and may still be alive. I met one source in Germany. He confirmed my suspicions."

"Perhaps the child is a Soviet agent?" David speculated.

"My father didn't know what became of her after the early sixties. Allegedly the records were destroyed."

"Being the daughter of a spy must have impacted you," David remarked.

"I followed my father into the agency. Strange, don't you think?"

"You were a spy?"

"No. I was an analyst for a brief time. I didn't have the correct mind set. The experience gave me insight into Mallory."

"What really motivated you to come forward?" David asked.

"Americans distrust their government and leaders. They view politicians as weak and greedy. Reform through legitimate means seems beyond the average citizens grasp. Mallory knew the risk he was taking when he revealed information about Operation Paperclip. He violated the national secrecy laws. Remember my question about destroying a monster? A country's desire for safety and security can turn into an evil monster. There's another at large. I'm confident the letters "TI" in my Mallory's notes represented Trinity International. I feel certain they had some role in this drama."

"Without his notes, we will never know for sure," David, responded.

"It's getting late," Eleanor said and abruptly pushed back from the table.

"Mallory would not have wanted me to hurt innocent people."

"We will protect your identity. You have our promise," David assured Eleanor.

"This may be painful, but I am going to ask. Do you think your father's death was untimely?"

"No. My father was ill. Doctors gave him inside of a year to live. If you are thinking he may have been assassinated, I thought so at first. Now I have changed my mind. Erskin Young and Mallory despised one another, but Young would never have ordered Mallory's murder. I'm convinced it was an accident."

"May I call you, if I need clarification?" Dakota asked.

"No. I prefer this be our last discussion. I've given you all the help I can."

∽

As the car turned on to North Country Road, Dakota asked: "So, what do you think?"

"I don't know. She has too many details. The missing link is the document Alan Foxx insisted I see."

"What do you think he wanted to show you?"

"My gut says it was a photograph and maybe some other piece of key evidence. It's only a guess."

"Where was he when he called you?"

"His office at GAO."

"I met Foxx on a few unpleasant occasions. Bob married Foxx's sister. It didn't last long. I suspect Foxx made copies. He'd never surrender the originals."

"It never occurred to me, but you may be right. He was insecure, almost paranoid."

"His office. The FBI probably searched it. Perhaps they overlooked something."

"You may be right."

"We'll never know unless we search for ourselves."

"We have to find a way in and while we are at it..."

"Yes, his apartment and car, too."

Their conversation was interrupted. Dakota's cell phone rang. "It's Lou-Ann."

"Where the hell is David? I've been calling for the last hour," complained Lou-Ann.

"We turned off our phones. What's up?"

"Carol Dean called. She said she's been trying to contact you. Any message?"

"She didn't want to leave a message."

"That's bad news. I'll call. Thanks."

David called Carol Dean. The news was shocking. Dean wanted David to have a "heads up". "David. The authorities released a preliminary report. There should be a White House statement by mid-afternoon."

"You sound distressed. Dakota Putnam is with me. We are on speaker. Are you OK with that?"

"Sure," Carol Dean answered. "David, it's another suicide. A .38 caliber pistol was discovered where Best's body was found. One round was fired. Sound familiar?"

"Tell me more." David's interest was piqued.

"First, Andrew Dunn commits suicide and now the Chief Counsel. It's too much of a coincidence. Picture this. Best drives to the Bull Run battlefield on a stormy night to kill himself."

"Best tried to contact me. He sounded scared."

"Initially, the Virginia authorities suspected Best's car was forced off the road. There was extensive damage to the rear bumper and a large scrape on the passenger side of the car."

"I called a friend on the state police. The toxicology report shows Best was legally drunk and using drugs. Here's the kicker.

The .38 caliber revolver was found several feet from the body. I can picture the piece falling from his hand or spinning a bit from recoil. My friend insists the forensics team measured the distance. It was 40 inches away."

"Has Katherine Stone's staff gone mad or is there more to it?"

"Has the Press Secretary released a statement?" Dakota asked.

"No. My source told me the President left for Camp David before the Virginia authorities released their statement. Get this. President Stone will undergo a complete medical checkup on Monday. I think she's ill."

"Anything else?"

"No. You have enough to keep busy."

"I'll be at the GAO on Monday. The Inspector General provided me with a cubical to use as a temporary office. Call me, if you need me," David said.

"Sounds like Dean is quite concerned about you. A little something special?"

David laughed. "Dean and I aren't. I'm not sleeping with her, if that's what you are hinting. She's twenty years younger and married to her career."

"Hmm. Sounds a bit evasive to me. Honestly, David, you are always tantalized by strong-willed woman."

"You should know. Now let's get back to the matter at hand, Eleanor Giles' story.

"I sense Eleanor persuaded you that her father's story is true."

"Yes, but we need something substantial. If we could find Foxx's documents they may help. On another point, I'm begging you not to draw me into your article. The story is yours. Anything you publish has to be from interviews and open source intelligence. Agreed?"

"Yes. I promise not to involve either you or Lou-Ann," Dakota agreed.

Chapter Sixty-Three
Connecting the Dots

When David returned to the White House West Wing the security guard handed him an "eyes only" envelope. Inside was the letter he had anticipated. David was assigned as White House liaison to the GAO Inspector General. Clayton was replacing Alan Foxx.

David smiled. While casual observers might be fooled, David knew his reassignment was simply done to create a favorable impression. He was being phased out. He was certain Drew Lindstrom was behind the move with the President's tacit approval. The President underestimated David. He still had time left and would make the best of it.

David went right to work. He searched the DOD and Justice Department databases for even a minute record of a submarine sunk off Long Island in early May 1945. *I'll go blind if I don't take a day off.* He was about to call it quits when he discovered an obscure reference to a wreck diver, Edward Savage.

Savage was a retired Suffolk County Police Officer and avid wreck diver. The Justice Department employed Savage to investigate the wreck of a trawler off the South Carolina Coast. The fishing vessel was scuttled during a US Coast Guard interdiction operation south of Georgetown. Allegedly, the trawler was involved in human trafficking. South Carolina police believed the kidnapped victims were taken by speedboat to the waiting trawlers and later transferred to container ships headed for the Middle and Far East.

David took the information and began an expanded search. He cross-referenced Savage with U-boats and Long Island. Sure enough Savage's name appeared. Savage was an expert wreck diver with a particular interest in the U-853. Others were interested as well. Several divers died exploring the vessel.

Savage's last known address was in Bay Shore, Long Island. Savage was married to Diana Sandoval, a freelance writer. Sandoval received national recognition for her exposés of human trafficking along South Carolina's Grand Strand. Sandoval was shot in a shopping center parking lot. The assailant was never apprehended.

David telephoned Lou-Ann on Long Island and explained his hunch. Savage may hold the key to the mysterious U-boat and William Mallory. I can't locate Savage."

A few hours later she returned his call. " I made a few calls. Savage lives in Cabo San Lucas, Mexico. From what I've discovered, he and his wife dropped out. Some guy tried to kill her."

"Thanks. I'll check TSA and Customs. They probably have a lead. How are you doing?"

"I'm surviving. Gets a little easier with each passing day. I miss Jack. I'm starting to think it may be time for me to get back to work."

"I can use your help, but take your time."

"Thanks, David."

⌘

Several nights later David received a text message with a number to call in Mexico.

"Hola."

"My name is David Clayton. I'm calling for Edward Savage."

"You got him," Savage replied.

"I'd like to speak with your about your dives on the U-853."

"Not over the phone," came the terse response.

"This is important, Mr. Savage."

Savage paused. *I want no part of any CIA intrigue.*

"There are other divers. Give one of them a call. I'm no archeologist."

"I know you are one of the divers who searched for the U-853 log."

"No. I looked for historical artifacts. Never specifically

looked for the log. Wreck divers frequently recover a trophy. I never sold a relic. Gave them to a historical society in Rhode Island. There were other divers. I didn't do any professional airlifting."

"You were a contractor for the Justice Department. Did they ever employ you to search the U-853 for the log or Enigma code books?"

"This is an open line Mr. Clayton. I answered your question." *This guy is too unsophisticated to be CIA.* "End of conversation Mr. Clayton."

"Hold on Savage. Don't hang up," David pleaded. "I'll fly to your location."

"Civilian flight Clayton. I don't want anything to do with Uncle."

"I'll text you. I'll need authorization," replied David.

It took two weeks for the Inspector General to grant authorization. *I wonder if the Inspector General informed Lindstrom?* David flew to Cabo via Delta. A taxi was waiting. David glanced at his phone. It was noon. He expected a text from Savage. It didn't arrive.

David knew Savage lived in an expatriate community on the heights above Cabo. Savage insisted for their initial meeting they rendezvous at a location away from his home.

As the taxi entered the highway to Cabo, Savage called.

"There's a large resort overlooking the Sea of Cortez. It's called Playa Grande."

"I'm staying there," said David.

"That makes it easier. I'll meet you in the lobby near the bar. Seven sharp."

David checked into the resort and spent the afternoon lounging near the pool. He checked his email several times. He suspected Savage might change the rendezvous. He didn't.

David walked into the lobby a few minutes early. The bar was packed. A Latin jazz band performed. Savage failed to show at seven. David walked to the far end of the lobby and sat down. He watched people enter the lobby. A tap on his shoulder startled him.

David looked up.

"Clayton, your surveillance skills need work."

Clayton stood up. "You caught me by surprise. You look different from your passport photo."

"It's a couple of years old."

Nevertheless, Savage appeared physically trim with closely cropped hair.

The two men exchanged a few comments. They never shook hands. Savage nodded a few times to acknowledge David's remarks.

"My car is in the parking garage. Let's go."

They drove a short distance from the marina into the suburbs. Savage stopped the car near an intersection and observed the traffic on the street to his right. Then he approached a driveway a few hundred feet away. A large wrought-iron fence surrounded the home. Savage tapped a code into his cell phone and the gate rolled open.

"Just a precaution," he assured Clayton. He opened the console and removed a Sig Sauer pistol. He looked at David's startled expression. "Take it easy Clayton. Relax."

Savage pulled into the garage. "The entire house is wired with state of the art electronics. All these safeguards are a pain in the ass and frighten the shit out of my wife. But…" He didn't finish. The two men walked inside. The home resembled a nautical museum. Large glass displays enclosed ship models and relics from wreck dives.

"I've given a lot of the stuff away. Some museums auction it off. I'll hold on to my personal collection for now."

Savage excused himself. He returned with his wife.

"My wife, Diana." Diana Sandoval was a gorgeous woman with a dark complexion to match her deep brown eyes. Her trim figure revealed a woman who enjoyed physical activity.

"Good evening, Mr. Clayton."

"Pleased to meet you."

"Your inquiry must be important if it brings you all this way."

"David smiled."

Diana turned to her husband and said, "I left your U-853 dive logs on the table." She pointed to the nearby pool.

"I'll leave you two alone." As Sandoval turned to leave, David notice a prominent scar along the left side of her neck. Sandoval caught David's glance. "It's nasty," she said, as though reading David's mind.

Sandoval changed direction and pointed to a large discolored patch on her rear shoulder. "This one really hurt."

"I'm sorry. I didn't mean to stare."

"Every one does," Diana said as she walked back into the house.

"Let's sit by the pool," called Savage.

Savage handed David one of his diving logs. "I record every wreck dive. Leaf through it."

David was impressed by the clear script and concise anecdotes. For the next hour or so David listened to Savage's tales of wreck diving.

"You still haven't answered an important question, Mr. Savage. Did you or another diver find the U-853's log from the final voyage?"

"That's it?"

"Let's start there."

"No. As far as I know, the log was never recovered"

"Divers retrieved other artifacts, spoons, a pistol. I'll bet a ton of stuff is sitting in someone's closet. I read a skeleton was removed," David remarked.

"Let's get one thing clear, Mr. Clayton. I want to help you, but no condemnations. I wasn't involved. Clear?"

"Agreed," David said.

"There was some airlifting."

"Airlifting?"

"It's like a vacuum cleaner. The U-853 is loaded with silt. It's dangerous. Disturb the bottom and the silt fills the area, impossible to see. At least two divers died searching the U-853. I assume you know its history."

"Somewhat. The U-boat is a mystery. Too many stories, gold

bullion, Hitler's escape submarine. Do you put any credence in the stories?"

"If there was bullion on board, I didn't find any. I've talked with other divers. They all tell the same story. No gold. Thinking about it now, I did find one thing unusual. The captain's quarters."

"How so?"

"His quarters were smaller. There were two small quarters forward of it. Never saw that before. I thought they were for additional storage.

"Could they have held a couple of improvised bunks?"

Savage shrugged as he walked around the swimming pool. "A former OSS officer speculated the U-853 carried secret weapons. The guy died a long time ago." Savage looked down at the Marina lights. "Take a look Mr. Clayton."

David walked to the pool's edge to stand by Savage.

"Your home is beautiful."

"Designed it myself. I love the way it surrounds the pool. My wife loves it here. Against my wishes she still free-lances. Diana's obsession with human trafficking nearly cost her life. But she still pursues the bad guys. Me, I just want to take life easy. As for the U-853, let it go, Clayton. Nothing good will come from you pursuit. Like my wife, you could get hurt."

David looked toward the bar at the far end of the pool.

"A drink, Mr. Clayton?"

Both men smiled. The conversation had been obscure and evasive. David was tired.

"I sense your urgency, Mr. Clayton. I'll be blunt. My sources tell me you are a Nazi hunter."

"Not exactly."

"What is it you really want Mr. Clayton?" asked Savage.

"I want the log from the U-853. I suspect the log will open new insight into World War Two history. I suspect the Captain's log exists"

"The log was never recovered. Hard hats went down to inspect the U-boat when it was sunk. They opened the main hatch and pulled out one body. The divers never entered. The U-853 is surrounded by unexploded depth charges, maybe two hundred. The Captain refused to surrender and doomed his crew in 120 feet of water."

"I've seen the photos. I believe the U-853 was destined never to survive. Not allowed to surface. Another U-boat surfaced two weeks after the war ended. It wasn't strafed or sunk."

"Who knows? I can tell you this. The Enigma codebooks were recovered. I saw them. A team discovered them in the galley, of all places. The divers were airlifting. They uncovered three skeletons below the mud. They must have been prepared to exit through an escape hatch. All three wore their escape lungs.

"What about the Enigma books?"

"Given the circumstances the books were in fairly good shape. The mud may have saved them from marine life."

"Seems amazing."

"I immediately noticed something so unusual."

"What?" David asked.

"I've seen several other Enigma code books. The U-853 books were unique. They printed in German, but under various portions were hand written English translations."

"Were there any signs civilians may have been on board?"

"Never thought about it. By now it would be impossible to tell. Moreover, it's against the law to explore the U-853. It's a war memorial. Why are you so interested in civilians on board?"

"Just a hunch, Mr. Savage. I'm tracking the log. Perhaps the log was retrieved from the sub's safe."

"Are you sure the log was in a safe? I've been inside several U-boats. Never found a safe. Possibly your informant meant a locked desk drawer. That's where the U-boat commander kept important dispatches and perhaps a pistol. All the firearms were kept in a secured locker. I've never found a safe."

"You told me a pistol was retrieved from the U-853," David said.

"Yes, along with personal possessions and debris which surfaced during the depth charge runs. The attack was so intense one of the US ships was temporarily put out of service."

"The reports I've read speculate many of the crew were

prepared to use escape hatches and breathing lungs to reach the surface."

"Agreed. The U-boat was about 130 feet below the surface. I spoke with the diver who claimed to have discovered three crewmember's remains in the galley. I doubt they drowned. They most likely died from concussions. The one body the Navy did retrieve supports the theory. The autopsy revealed he died from a concussion rather than drowning. The U-boat took a direct hit."

"Savage, some consider you the expert on the U-853. I'll ask one last time. Was the log discovered?"

"You seem to think so, Mr. Clayton."

"I've told you. It is a hunch. Here's the bottom line. I need you to do one last dive into the Captain Fromsdorf's quarters."

"Now I get the picture. You said, I not 'we.'"

"Does the GAO know where you are headed with this theory?"

"I've told my superiors I believe there was a log. Still, everywhere I turn I meet denial or resistance."

"May 1945 is long gone, Mr. Clayton. Some things are best left submerged."

"Like the U-853?"

"Only you can answer the question."

"You can help. One final dive into the U-853."

"No. First it's against the law. And second the U-boat is a death trap. Forty years ago it was a risky dive. Just getting through the main torpedo hatch presented issues."

"I've seen recent photographs. Perhaps you could enter through one of the gaping holes."

"Absolutely not. The dive would require a team. There is a maze of wires and pipes. One false move could bring clouds of silt up into the compartment, zero visibility. It's insane. I am not doing it."

David clearly had provoked Savage. "It's nearly midnight. Please call a cab," David requested.

"I'll drive you to the Playa Grande. It's no trouble," Savage responded.

Neither man spoke the entire ride back to the resort.

The car passed through the gatehouse and drove a few hundred feet. Ed pulled into the parking garage.

"Thanks. Please give my request more time, Ed. I need to know if the log exists. You could alter the past and have a significant impact on the future."

"What does that mean?"

David didn't respond.

"You are adding to the myth, David. Take my warning to heart."

"Sounds ominous."

"I was on Long Island a few month ago. I have a friend who owns a marina in Montauk. He's into a little bit of this and that. Rents boats, engine overhauls, fishing charters. He told me about some easy money, a cash advance on a rental. It was a dive boat."

"What is unusual about that?"

"These folks had an archeological permit to enter the U-853. It takes months to get a sanctuary permit to enter a sunken vessel like the U-853."

"Maybe it's legitimate."

"My friend watched them load airlifting equipment. Now, that's a 'no-no'. They were intent on vacuuming the sub."

"Relics?"

"Hold on. My friend did some checking on his own. Capital Maritime Reclamation employed the divers. CMR is based in the Bahamas."

"Sounds like a big operation."

"Window dressing," Ed scoffed. "It's a cover story, David."

"I don't understand."

"First of all, the foreman paid my friend in cash. The U-853 is a sanctuary. Airlifting is outlawed. They're searching for something specific."

Ed Savage's grim expression was a dead giveaway.

"They want U-853's log. But why take the risk of getting caught?"

"Exactly. The search didn't last long. They packed it in after two days."

"My friend said they left in a hurry."

"Damn. Maybe they weren't authorized."

"It may have been a bootleg operation. A daring mission like that required financing."

"If not the Feds, who else could it be?"

Ed turned off the car engine and looked at David with intensity. "A few years ago Diana was researching a controversial case of human trafficking and the international sex trade in South Carolina. Clearly, it's a subject no one wants to talk about it."

"I've read newspaper accounts. They are bloodcurdling."

"Diana learned the hard way. These guys don't mess around. Surely you noticed the scar on the left side of her neck."

"What happened?"

"Diana was part of a research project. She just finished a presentation. As she approached her car a white van pulled up. The side door opened and two guys grabbed her. She cried out for help and tried to fight." Ed's face reddened with anger. "One of the attackers punched Diana and broke her nose. Her screams alerted several patrons. Diana struggled. One of the guys waved a handgun. She grabbed his wrist. The gun went off and struck her in the neck. Missed the carotid artery. Then he kicked her in the face. As she fell, he fired. The bullet ripped through her shoulder. It left that ugly exit wound."

"Did they catch the bastards?"

"No. The patrons were so terrified they never got a plate number, only a sketchy description."

"Thank God Diana is OK."

"I thought she was going to die," Ed confessed.

"They're depraved."

"No they are not. They are greedy. These guys are brazen, David."

"Did Diana go back to reporting on human trafficking?"

"Yes. That's why I'm warning you to stay away from the U-853."

"I don't understand."

Ed fixed his eyes on David. "Human trafficking is no small operation. It's a ten billion dollar business here and abroad.

Diana's source claimed an international corporation was pursuing favors some place in southern Africa. I'm guessing. Maybe mineral rights."

"Bribes?" asked David.

"Influence peddling, David. Don't be naïve. We call it lobbying and campaign contributions. Diana's source claimed in one case an order was placed for a young American female."

"Somebody places an order for a girl or a boy in return for helping a company gain influence? Never heard of such a thing," replied David.

"Yes. And the request may be a very precise profile."

"I still don't see the connection between the U-853 and sex traffickers," David insisted.

"Capital Maritime Reclamation. CMR is owned by Trinity International."

"I don't believe Trinity would risk running brothels," David countered.

"Brothels?" Ed laughed. "Diana was on her way to meet an informant when she was shot. He claimed he just returned from a country in southern Africa. He told Diana a powerful international company was exploring mineral rights worth billions."

"Did the source name a specific country?" asked David.

"No. But we have a hunch."

"Diana's source said a number of international corporations are vying over mineral rights. Something about rare earth elements."

David looked wide-eyed. "What else did he tell you?"

"Our only domestic source of these minerals is some place called Mountain Pass mine. There were environmental issues. Diana spent weeks checking out her source's claims. He was right on the money. Most Americans have no idea. The United States defense technology depends on rare earth elements. These components go into jet engines, communications equipment, complex targeting devices and missiles. There's no end to the list. China has a monopoly. Our military relies on Chinese markets. The Chinese now have a foothold in parts of Afghanistan, too.

Oh yes! The Russians, as well."

"Let me get this straight. Are you talking bribery? In exchange for a young woman or man, a government official grants favors?" asked David.

"If that's the demand."

"Did the informant tell Diana how the operation worked?"

"In one case a government official demanded a young American male. Spotters profiled the victim during college spring break and snatched him off the street in broad daylight. They took him by speedboat about 50 miles off shore to a fishing trawler. The trawler worked its way to a prearranged rendezvous with a freighter headed for Africa."

"How do they avoid the Coast Guard and other international marine authorities?" David wanted to know more.

"These guys aren't your ordinary Somali pirates. They are sophisticated organizations with intelligence sources and complex communications. They own cargo planes capable of landing on temporary airfields as well as international freight terminals. These guys aren't looking for ransoms. They are after the cargo. They also provide special delivery. The deals are brokered," Ed Savage insisted.

"And Diana thinks she knows who is involved?"

"There's more than one, but Trinity International tops her short list."

"Trinity is powerful. They have a number of affiliates in southern Africa including Zimbabwe. There is so much turmoil, disease and poverty. A powerful conglomerate can easily curry favors."

Savage saw David's grim facial expression.

"Trinity is only one tentacle of an invisible empire more powerful than the Davos group." David sounded fatalistic.

Ed Savage nodded in agreement. "My sources tell me you ran into Trinity back in 1977."

"It was a controversial investigation. Our own Justice Department closed us down. Seized every bit of evidence, every scrap of paper. Sealed it. Stamped it top secret."

"Then you know who you are dealing with," Ed warned. "Is

it worth risking your life? Diana nearly paid with her life. I don't want to lose her. You have to understand."

There was a brief silence. Then Ed said, "I will offer you this. Give me the name behind the hit on my wife and I'll make one dive on the U-853."

"Honestly, Ed. I don't have a clue. Ashton Pickering is the Director for Trinity International and Trinity PharmoDynamics. That doesn't mean he's your man. It could have been a rogue operation. I'm not defending Pickering. Listen to me. President Stone is Commander in Chief. Do you think she is aware of all the special operations within the military or the CIA?"

Ed shrugged. "Who knows? Maybe the same people who control Trinity control President Stone."

"Be sensible." David grimaced. "That's a conspiracy theory, Ed."

Ed Savage was adamant. "You give me the name, I make the dive."

David hesitated, then he reluctantly agreed. "I'll do what I can."

Ed started the car and drove to the front entrance of Playa Grande. Neither man exchanged a farewell.

Chapter Sixty-Four
Stratum Monitoring Center
Sterling, Virginia

Ambrose Ross was a twenty-two year old high school dropout who existed on Big Macs, fries and shakes. He never quite fit in with his classmates. He never had a girlfriend or any close friend for that matter.

"Yes, you're different," his mother told him. "Different in a special way."

When his mother died Ambrose shuttered the house and tinkered in the garage with his deceased father's heirloom, a Ham radio. Electronic gadgets fascinated Ambrose. No one knows exactly how Ambrose Ross ended up as a contractor with the National Security Agency, but he did. And now he sat alone in a NSA satellite building marked Stratum Monitoring Center.

In New York City, Ashton Pickering sat behind his desk reading the morning financials. The blue cell phone on Pickering's desk vibrated.

"What is it?"

"Mr. Pickering, David Clayton is on the move again."

"Where to this time?"

"Mexico. Cabo San Lucas to be exact. I have the address."

"And?"

"Clayton met with a wreck diver named Ed Savage."

"Any connection?" Pickering asked.

"Yes," said Ross.

"Ross, why do I have to drag these things out of you?"

" I don't know why, Mr. Pickering."

"Get on with it," ordered Pickering

"I cross-checked Savage with Trinity's human resources files.

He is married to Diana Sandoval, a freelance writer. Sandoval has made a number of inquiries into Trinity's transactions in Africa. I suggest you read the Incident Report data.

"Never heard of Savage or Sandoval. I'll check into it." Pickering entered Sandoval's name into Trinity's worldwide security database. *This can't be.* "Who the hell was so stupid to order a hit on this woman?"

"I believe it was you." Ambrose's staccato response was matter of fact.

"Are you certain?" *Talking to this guy is like talking to a robot.*

"The directive originated in your office, Mr. Pickering."

"Ambrose, what's your take on the situation?"

"I don't understand your question, sir."

"Give me an analysis," Pickering demanded.

"It's quite obvious. First, Clayton met Savage. Savage is a U-boat specialist. I can find no intentional effort on Clayton's part to involve Diana Sandoval."

"Second, since…"

"Stop. Tell me about the database compromise," said Pickering.

"Yes, Mr. Pickering. Regarding the Sandoval intervention, Trinity's Deputy Financial Officer, John Strauss, has accessed the read-write incident reporting partition within the database on numerous occasions."

"Impossible," said Pickering. Only two people have the password, his father, Kurt Strauss, the Chief Financial Officer, and me."

"It is puzzling. Since you did not authorize the Sandoval intervention, I would speak with John and Kurt Strauss. The other possibility is an unauthorized intrusion. You've been hacked. "

"Thank you." Pickering ended the call and returned to Trinity's database. He was baffled and angry. Within minutes he discovered the obvious coincidence. Or was it simply a coincidence?

❧

Clayton returned from Mexico determined to discover the mystery of the U-853 with or without Ed Savage's help. Lou-Ann was eager get to back to work, also. They met at the Old Ebbitt Grill.

"I need a way to gain entry into Foxx's office at GAO," he told Lou-Ann.

"Your office is on the same floor."

"The police sealed Foxx's office."

"What's so important?"

"I believe Foxx may have hidden copies of the documents he planned to show me.

"In his office? I'm sure the FBI did a thorough search."

"I recall a trick Jack used. He said the best place to hide something is out in the open. He taped several documents from our first inquiry to the inside of his desk behind the drawers. Erskin Young's moving crew took the entire desk. The papers may still be in their hiding place. Perhaps Foxx did the same."

"Seems too simple. The trick is getting in to the office."

They discussed several contingencies. "Please, David. This black bag job must not become another Watergate caper. I don't want to go to prison."

"Here's the good news. Except for my office and Foxx's the entire floor is under renovation. Painters and carpenters are busy all day until around 3:30. The electricians work at night. "

"Do we need to take the risk?"

"Dakota has the story. We need more evidence."

"I don't like breaking the law, but I have your back. When will we do it?"

"Tomorrow. Security changes shifts at 4 PM. They usually spend a few minutes bullshitting over a cup of coffee. We'll have an hour. The tough piece will be resealing the door."

"I'll come up with something."

Lou-Ann arrived at David's office around 3:30 the next

afternoon. David rode the elevator to the basement command post. Sure enough, the night crew had changed into their uniforms and sat around drinking coffee. David returned to the fourth floor. The pair walked to Foxx's office. Lou-Ann opened her tactical knife and slit the yellow sealing tape. She remained in the hall while David searched in the obvious places. He felt behind the steel gray filing cabinet and found a brown envelope taped to the lower half. It was in an awkward place and difficult to retrieve without being a contortionist. He shoved the cabinet. It wouldn't budge. He lowered to the floor and reached behind the cabinet. Pain shot through his right shoulder as he stretched to free the envelope.

"David, hurry up. You are taking too long. This is too dangerous."

David stood up. He slipped the envelope behind his back and inside his belt. Lou-Ann was already assembling her part of the caper.

"What are you doing with those cans?" David whispered.

"I'll show you." Lou-Ann took a few rags from a hodgepodge of paint cans. "Smell these. The painters tossed them here last weekend." Lou-Ann kicked a few cans to the floor and lit the rags. "Now, get back to your office."

David scurried to escape being discovered. Suddenly he smelled smoke. The building fire alarm sound followed by Lou-Ann screaming 'Fire!'"

When the first watchman arrived via the stairway he was panting from the climb. At that point Lou-Ann was attempting to extinguish the blaze with a hall fire extinguisher. "I'll take it from here, Ma'am," he ordered. "Head for the stair case."

The watchman banged on David's door. "Hey there's a fire. Get the hell out of here. Follow me."

The sidewalk was crowded with evacuated employees when the fire department arrived. David found Lou-Ann waiting across the street. "Let's get out of here. There's so much chaos, we will never be missed."

"Do you have what you were looking for?"

David grinned. "I've got something. I just don't know what it is."

Late the same evening the building security chief called David and questioned his absence from the checkpoint during evacuation. David explained he was concerned for Lou-Ann and drove her home. The security chief accepted David's explanation with a caution. "Until you answered your cell phone we could not account for you. In the future please follow the drill."

"Was there much damage?"

"No. Ironically, the police gave us the authority to open the office this weekend. Now we have to paint the hallway and replace the door."

The incident never came up again.

David and Lou-Ann drove to Lou-Ann's suite at the Hampton Inn.

"I'm anxious to see what you found in Foxx's office," said Lou-Ann.

David carefully opened the envelope. Inside were two photocopies. "I was certain Foxx was going to show me a photograph. This is a death certificate for a Katherine Grace Stone, dated March 1945."

"A death certificate?"

"Yes, for a three year old girl. It was registered with the Town of Brookhaven."

"That's the President's name."

"I'm baffled. This has to be more than a coincidence," said David.

The second document equally flabbergasted both of them. David handed the paper to Lou-Ann. "I can't believe it." Lou-Ann read the identification number, "SS -1- 3128". Her voice trembled. This is a copy of the Lebensborn birth registration card. You were right, David. Foxx did find Erskin Young's Sunrise Files."

"What's the connection?" David asked.

"I'm certain Foxx discovered the link and that is why he was murdered. The original documents may have been incinerated when Foxx fell on the transit tracks. His body was charred."

"Dakota has the information we need."

"But not the official documents. Everything is circumstantial."

"I'll run the death certificate through the public records database. By chance it may have been recorded somewhere," Lou-Ann said.

❧

The following morning Lou-Ann and David found the GAO's fourth floor off limits due to the previous day's fire. David telephoned Dakota. She was waiting at LaGuardia Airport for her flight home to Myrtle Beach.

"I promised my publisher an outline. I'm obligated to the *Tribune* for a series on the U-boat."

"Tread lightly. I'm troubled. We may have tripped over a sleeping tiger."

"Come on, David. Be real. Are you warning me I must avoid investigating a U-boat sunk more than sixty years ago? I'm already up to my ears in this story. My publisher has invested money. I've spent time."

"We aren't talking about a can of worms. We may have stumbled upon something substantive. Can't you hold off publishing until we have something substantial?"

"No, I can't. I'm sorry David. I have to go with what I have."

Two days later, the *Tribune* along with 24 other major newspapers published Dakota's series, "The CIA – U-boat Connection". Reporters clamored for a response from the CIA Director. He issued a brief statement. "The Agency never comments on these matters." He referred inquiries to the White House.

"Ives, I want you to deal with the press. Stall them. We need time to respond," President ordered. "And stop with the bewildered expressions when I ask you to do something. There's more to your role than sipping Martinis."

The next morning, Venal complained of the flu. His spokesperson held a brief press conference. "Nobody wants to embarrass a former president or his administration for actions he may have taken for national security. That some connection existed between an agency of the United States and Nazi German is fiction. Putnam's speculations are an example of how the media frames events from their own perspective. These assertions will boost the cable news networks' audience and Ms. Putnam's future book revenues. They are laughable."

Later in the day, President Stone's spokesperson, Paul Basset, took a different tact. Addressing a small group of 'select' reporters he said, "Historically, there have been a number of purges at the Central Intelligence Agency. The Church Commission and several other oversight committees have investigated similar allegations. Ms. Putnam's assertions are unproven. No one can seriously believe these claims, although they *would* make a great novel."

Sue Williams, a reporter for the *Times*, raised her hand. "Mr. Basset. Your statement reflects sarcasm. It resonates through the administration."

"And what might that be?" Basset asked.

"You're implying the public will only accept honesty if it is labeled fiction. A secret agreement between the US and Nazi Germany is compelling news. The use of children and other innocents for research on mind control deserves investigation and public scrutiny. Historically, a pattern of cover-up emerges."

Basset opened a folder and leafed through several pages. "Let me be perfectly clear. In the mid-70's Richard Helms, then-director of the CIA, testified before Congress. Project MKULTRA was thoroughly investigated by the Church Committee." Basset held a document in the air and waved at the television cameras. "This a portion of the Church Committee's report." Basset read the last paragraph. "Pending the Congressional hearings, CIA Director, Richard Helms, ordered all MKULTRA files destroyed. Helms conceded MKULTRA existed by having the files destroyed. We'll never know the true objective or the identities of the participants."

Basset looked directly at the reporters and asked, "Is there a sunken U-boat off the coast of Rhode Island? The answer is yes. It never surfaced and official Navy records support the entire crew of fifty-two men perished. Yesterday, the CIA categorically dismissed Ms. Putnam's allegations." Basset pointed to another reporter.

"Jeff Murray, *Advance*. My question deals with Putnam's claim that an international pharmaceutical company played a key role in the MKULTRA program."

Basset rubbed his chin and grimaced. "All sorts of allegations circulated regarding the Agency's use of LSD and other drugs on unsuspecting subjects. Several cases have been authenticated. This administration does not condone such practices." Two more questions and we'll wind this up.

"George Butler, *The Review*. Mr. Basset, just prior to this news conference I listened to a PBS interview with Dakota Putnam. Ms. Putnam asserts President Stone revoked her press credentials. Can you explain the President's rationale?"

"The recent death of Charles Best, the President's Chief Counsel, has delayed a number of items soon to be presented to the Attorney General. I am not at liberty to go into the details, but I am authorized to concede to a request for an investigation into how Ms. Putnam obtained background information for several previously published stories. Simply put: Did someone in our government violate the official secrets act? One last question."

"Todd Finch, *CNN*. "In the closing paragraph of Ms. Putnam's article she asserts 'the ramifications of MKULTRA and powerful financial interests have altered the course of America's mission.' Are you absolutely positive the practices described in Putnam's MKULTRA expose were stopped when the records were destroyed?"

"Mr. Finch. Stop. We have no records to confirm the extent of MKULTRA. CIA Director Colby confirmed a number of practices might have circumvented the Agency's charter. Until Ms. Putnam reveals her sources, her columns make great fiction. Perhaps Hollywood will purchase the screen rights."

"The Justice Department could subpoena Putnam. The congressional over-sight committee and GAO have subpoena power," countered Finch.

"Why, Mr. Finch. I'm shocked a fellow journalist would suggest we compel Ms. Putnam to give us the names. Of course that might prove the President's contention that the national secrets act was violated. No, Mr. Finch, not at this time. This is nothing more than an unsupported conspiracy theory. Don't you agree, Mr. Finch?"

Finch was about to respond, when Basset's assistant stood and announced, "Thank you, everyone." Basset turned and exited the pressroom.

⁂

Lou-Ann and David watched the conference. They were both discouraged.

"Well, Dakota has blown this investigation wide open. I expect a call from Drew Lindstrom or the Inspector General telling us we are dismissed." Lou-Ann turned off the television and slumped back into her chair.

David joked. "It isn't funny, but we serve at the 'displeasure' of the President."

"Looking back, Lindstrom never expected our search for Walter Katz to snowball, like it has."

"Katherine Stone is driven, but what propels her? She's brazen and clearly controls her staff by fear. We are missing a piece of the puzzle. Now what do we do?"

"We wait. Say, what do you know about Zimbabwe?"

"Nothing, really. Why?"

"Ed Savage told me his wife, Diana Sandoval, was shot while investigating human trafficking. The case remains open, but Savage suspects Trinity might have sponsored the hit. Diana was tracking a kidnap victim. Diana's informant alluded to rich mineral deposits in Zimbabwe."

"Are you giving me a homework assignment, Mr. Clayton?"

"Of course not. I'm suggesting you look into Trinity's Zimbabwe investments. President Mugabe is in his late eighties. He rules the country through intimidation. Years ago he seized land from the white farmers who remained behind. He gave land to a number of his supporters. In recent years members of his political party have defected. Zimbabwe is suffering one of its worst economic crises in years. Banks have run out of cash. The government is struggling to pay its workers. We don't read of the riots and protests because the news is forcefully controlled.

The country is primed for a civil war. It's a risky investment for Trinity unless they are on the winning side. Russia and China will rush to support the rival sides."

"Perhaps Trinity is working with all the interests. I'm not clear on the link between Walter Katz and mineral wealth in Zimbabwe?"

"Trinity International," David asserted.

David's perception intrigued Lou-Ann. "You're serious."

"Absolutely. Follow the money."

Chapter Sixty-Five
West 57th Street
New York City

Kurt Strauss, Chief Financial Officer, was Trinity's last remaining charter board member. He was a disgruntled man. He hoped the Circle of Twelve would appoint his successor at its next Lake Como meeting. Strauss recommended his son, John, for the position. Strauss viewed his recommendation as a legacy appointment rather than nepotism. The elder Strauss groomed his son to take over. John had an intimate knowledge of Trinity's complex financial assets. On this morning John was meeting with several African trade groups.

Kurt Strauss sat in his electric wheel chair near the huge window overlooking Manhattan. A writing board cluttered with an assortment of financial statements rested on the wheel chair's arms. Strauss reached for his glasses and several folders fell to the floor.

"Damn it," the old man shouted. The documents would have to wait for John's arrival. It was Saturday. Strauss's personal secretary, only a few years Kurt Strauss's junior, no longer worked weekends. Strauss's aide waited in the outer office sipping coffee and reading the *Wall Street Journal*.

Strauss' mind wandered to his last meeting with the Circle of Twelve in Italy. This year he would not make the journey. In deference to Strauss's age and frailty the group agreed to a consolidated gathering limited to Strauss's presentation. Unlike the Davos Group's fanfare with the gathering in Switzerland, the Circle's members traveled anonymously to dodge the media. Trinity's security division cautioned against a teleconference in light of the Katz controversy. The top floor conference hall of Trinity's West 57th Street headquarters was seldom used. John Strauss worked for days supervising arrangements. Ashton

Pickering was first to arrive. He met with John Strauss hoping to gain a brief insight into the elder's report. John remained silent.

The Circle's members, now more than twelve, considered themselves the guardians of the world's financial stability and the power of family dynasties. Soon it would be time for the Circle to replace Kurt Strauss and, conceivably name a successor to Ashton Pickering. After a brief social hour the participants entered the huge conference room and found their designated places. Kurt Strauss assisted by an aide entered the room. John Strauss walked to the podium on the far side of the room from which he directed his father's carefully choreographed presentation. Kurt Strauss looked at the first projected slide, paused and spoke in a low almost inaudible voice.

"Friends, and I call you friends with deep sincerity. I feel today will be my last annual report. You each have a copy of my detailed evaluation. Our holdings are solid though we face a number of worldwide challenges." Strauss continued.

First, he detailed an emergent concern for the Chinese economy. The Chinese privatization program is faltering. They face an inverted social welfare triangle with fewer men and woman entering the work force the aged will become a burden. They have over-extended their military commitment with the construction of defensive gestures in the South China Sea. The leadership has no choice but to cut back on social programs and slowly reduce the size of the military budget.

"I envision a new nationalism and anti-west propaganda program to divert public attention. Will it work with an emerging middle class? As their economy falters, we see huge Chinese investments in the United States and other targeted regions, including several African nations and Afghanistan. The Chinese strive to control rare earth elements. Their endeavor will threaten Trinity International's holdings."

Second, Strauss noted Putin's continued moves to reinstate his vision of an imperial Russia. He clamors for controversy with NATO and the United States. "President Stone's administration has been inept in dealing with Putin and we will pay the consequences. I'm sure you see the need for reassessment."

"Third, the Japanese have expanded their sphere of influence into Zimbabwe. The 2016 Harare-Tokyo accords have strengthened President Mugabe's political position."

A member asked, "How does that influence Mugabe's relationship with North Korea? They have been allies. The North Koreans received Zimbabwe uranium in exchange for arms."

"I am concerned about Japan's reinforcement of Mugabe's personality cult. Japan's Prime Minister called Mugabe the most revered patriarch of Africa, an honor previously bestowed upon Kwame Nkrumah, Ghana's first Prime Minister. Nkrumah is the so-called father of Pan-Africanism."

"Dealing with Zimbabwe presents a complex issue," the member replied. Then Strauss continued.

"President Stone's administration is surrounded by political controversy. I have to be blunt. From my perspective, Ashton Pickering and Trinity have lost control of the situation. Even as we meet I have confirmation that General Longfellow, the Chairman of the Joint Chiefs is meeting with the other Chiefs."

"What precipitated the meeting?" asked a senior member at the far end of the table.

"According to our intelligence a retired Colonel, Charles Doering, exposed President Stone's Operation Purple Rain."

"Will Longfellow pull the Delta unit from Zimbabwe?" one director inquired.

"He'll undoubtedly confront the President first and demand she extract the team. Then all hell may break out."

"Will he go public?" asked another member.

"I doubt it. He respects protocol. After all, Stone is his Commander in Chief. He might go to the Justice Department or Congress," Strauss replied.

With that, Ashton Pickering rose from his seat. "Kurt, I've been diligent as Trinity's Director. The Presidency of Katherine Grace Stone was an experiment. I presented the risks years ago as her political availability increased. President Stone is out of control. I brought in Trinity's security to temper the problem. They exacerbated the situation with zealous responses."

"Andrew Dunn's death nearly collapsed Stone's Presidency.

We had to respond to protect Trinity's interests," said John Strauss stepping out from behind the podium."

"Nonsense. Walther Liechtenauer's Pied Piper project backfired. The first female President of the United States is in a meltdown."

Strauss pointed a finger at Pickering. "Ashton, you were in charge."

"No. A madman named Heinrich Franz was in charge. Now look at our inheritance," Pickering responded.

"Gentlemen please stop this bickering. What's done is done. We have return to our mission."

"Agreed," responded another member. "The Davos Group is focused on their New Global Context. You know they view the old order as corrupt and socially exclusive. We live in a world of imploding institutions. The Circle of Twelve is the protector of international stability. We must continue to control the world's resources."

Strauss smiled at the member's comments. "Gentlemen, we must get our house in order. We face a Presidential election with fortunes at stake. We can't allow the United States to be governed by public interest polls. Ashton, time is running out. Get this administration under control. We can maintain control of government through political influence. We must do everything possible to prevent governments from restraining our inherited wealth and resources. We are compelled to rethink Katherine Grace Stone's nomination for re-election."

Ashton Pickering was stunned. He considered Kurt Strauss a mentor and friend. He looked at the faces of the conference members. They appeared to avoid eye contact with him. *Strauss has betrayed me.*

The video screen went blank and the cross talk began. Kurt Strauss faced the attendees and said, " Thank you Gentlemen and God bless our endeavors."

Ashton Pickering scowled and stormed out of the room. The gauntlet was thrown.

✺

President Stone kept Chairman Brent Longfellow and his

fellow chiefs waiting outside the Oval Office for nearly twenty minutes.

"Let them work off some steam," Stone told Lindstrom.

"This meeting is a mistake." Lindstrom's voice trembled.

President Stone scoffed at his criticism. "I don't want the Secretary of Defense or any cabinet members present. Emphasize my position when we meet Longfellow. And I don't want ultimatums."

"I have no idea what to expect. Will you tell Longfellow the extent of the Katz break-in?"

"DOD knows some of it."

The intercom light on President Stone's desk flashed. Lindstrom answered.

"Drew this is Pickering."

"This is a bad time, Mr. Pickering. The President is preparing for a conference."

"Put her on the phone immediately."

The President waved Drew off. There was a brief silence and then Pickering screamed into the phone, "Damn it Katherine. Take the goddamned call. This is a matter of your life or death."

Katherine grabbed the phone and shouted back, "What is it?"

"I don't owe you shit, but I have to save my ass, so here goes. You and your administration are in jeopardy. Two hours ago I left a meeting at Trinity's New York headquarters. Kurt Strauss told the Circle of Twelve attendees your leadership threatens several critical economic interests."

"That's bullshit. Trinity owns my administration."

"Yes and Kurt Strauss believes you are out-of-control."

"That bastard. I am what Trinity made me."

"Right again. And they recognize the nightmare. I'm warning you Katherine. Get control of yourself. Listen carefully. Carol Dean has been talking with Dakota Putnam. She may be digging into Andrew's death."

"Is she implicating me?"

"It's part of a bigger picture. She's on to Pied Piper," Pickering insisted.

"And you, my dear Ashton? You'll run with your tail between your legs."

"On the contrary. I've been ordered to deal with your predicament. Then I'll retire. Your candidacy for re-election is finished."

Katherine Grace Stone, the first female President, dropped the phone. Her body stiffened as though petrified.

Drew Lindstrom picked up the phone. "Pickering, are you still on the line."

"Yes. Did that bitch toss the phone?"

"No. She's catatonic. I'm serious. She's stiff as a board. The Service Chiefs are waiting for a meeting."

"I'm telling you, she's gone crazy." Pickering persisted. "Get her to a psychiatric facility before she implodes. Wait! Airlift her to Walter Reed. Isolate her from the general population. Double the Secret Service protection. No reporters. We face an economic and a political crisis." Pickering seethed.

"What else can I do?" Lindstrom pleaded.

"Initiate a press black out until you have a handle on the situation. I'll get back to you. My god! I have to deal with Ives Venal."

"Venal isn't President, yet, " Lindstrom said.

"There is a growing concern within Trinity and the Circle of Twelve. Trinity's chief financial advisor speculates you will face a Congressional investigation."

"For what? I've done nothing illegal."

"Be prepared. I don't have time to elaborate."

Drew suddenly imagined his destiny. He walked to the President's desk and placed the phone in its cradle. There was a loud thump. He turned to find President Stone on the hardwood floor. A pool of blood oozed from her head.

Drew ran into the outer office and called "Help. The President collapsed."

Kevin Goodman rushed to Stone. Goodman called into his radio, "Activate Code Blue. Sandpiper down."

A team of Secret Service and White House medical responders rushed to the Oval Office. Goodman turned to

Lindstrom. "Camp David?"

"No. Evacuate to Walter Reed, the Presidential Suite. Alert the neurological staff. I want their top psychiatric staff assembled, too. Then isolate them. Understood?"

Goodman nodded acknowledgement, but he grimaced in disbelief. "Psychiatric staff?"

"Do it," Lindstrom ordered with an authority he hadn't felt in months.

The Service Chiefs along with the President's secretary watched in horror.

"Looks like this meeting is postponed," said General Longfellow with an obvious distain. Without another word Longfellow turned and exited the office.

⋘

President Stone's detail assembled and she was evacuated to Bethesda. Drew Lindstrom remained behind. It was his responsibility to set the Constitutional succession plan in motion. He telephoned Vice President Venal first.

"I'll go to Walter Reed as soon as possible. I hate helicopters. I'll drive."

Venal relished in the notoriety and mystery surrounding motorcades. Venal's press secretary leaked a statement: "President Stone was rushed to Walter Reed Hospital several hours ago. Vice President Venal is in route to the facility."

Within minutes the Marine helicopter arrived at Walter Reed. Goodman called the White House. He informed Lindstrom that security was in place.

"I've established three security perimeters around the president. The Presidential Protective Division is covering the inner shield."

"And President Stone?" Lindstrom asked Kevin Goodman.

"She is isolated near the Presidential suite, but not in it. The ambassador from India was allowed to use the accommodations for his heart surgery. The ambassador will be moved to another suite."

"Before we go further put this call on speaker."

"Yes, sir," said Goodman.

"Now, And where is Vice President Venal?" asked Lindstrom.

"His motorcade will arrive within the hour."

"Paul. You're the Press Secretary. Keep Venal away from the reporters." Paul Basset looked at Goodman, nodded in agreement and rushed off.

Several minutes later Basset called Lindstrom. "Drew, I'm afraid it is too late. Venal wants to meet with the media. They are gathering in the hospital's auditorium."

"Damn you, Venal."

❦

Back at the White House Drew Lindstrom was horrified by Ashton Pickering's warning. Lindstrom took a notepad and made a checklist of notifications and calls he needed to make as soon as possible.

Lindstrom called the hospital administrator, General Harvey Petty. "No one other than the attending physician and his staff are to be with the President. No press releases. Warn your staff." Lindstrom rushed to Bethesda. He arrived ahead of Venal.

When Lindstrom' arrived at Walter Reed Hospital he was escorted to General Petty's office. Petty, a gruff combat surgeon, scowled as Lindstrom entered his office.

"I detest publicity," he carped. "The press turns everything up-side-down." Petty blew cigar smoke in Lindstrom's face. "Ives Venal is a showman. Be careful Mr. Lindstrom. I don't want Walter Reed Hospital turned into a circus."

Lindstrom gave the General a hostile look, but remained silent.

"Dr. Greaves is waiting for you." Petty laughed. He picked a pen off his desk and began reviewing paperwork.

Lindstrom left Petty's office and walked through the secured hallway to the Presidential suite. He had never visited the complex before. The Presidential suite was a self-contained emergency room. Unpretentious paneled walls slid open at the touch of a button revealing a miniature operating room. *This is some setup.*

A team of neurologists waited for Dr. Greaves' direction. Down the hall a psychiatric group assembled.

"The President has lapsed into a comma," Dr. Greaves, told Lindstrom.

"Did you know President Stone named you as her health proxy?"

"No. Are you positive Dr. Greaves?"

"I've reviewed her records. You were named health proxy after her husband died. You have quite a responsibility. She never told you?"

"I am surprised, but President has no other relatives."

"President Stone's personal physician is attending a conference in London. I will confer with her. We need to plan. I'll be meeting with staff in thirty minutes. I will brief you as soon as Vice President Venal arrives."

"Venal?"

"Agent Goodman told me to wait for the Vice President's motorcade."

"No. Brief me now." *I can't allow Goodman to assume a leadership role. Is he switching his loyalties to Venal? I don't trust the son-of-a- bitch.*

Dr. Greaves walked to the President's room. "We adhere to a strict procedure. Follow my lead," he said.

An airlock separated the Presidential facility from the hallway. Dr. Greaves and Lindstrom removed their shoes and dressed in paper surgical gowns. Several nurses attended the President. Lindstrom entered the suite and walked to the President's bedside. Dr. Greaves waited in the air lock for his colleagues, a neurologist, and neuropsychiatrist.

Greaves huddled with Lindstrom. He motioned for the two specialists to join. "Mr. Lindstrom requests a diagnosis before he meets with Vice President Venal."

"President Stone is stable. Her condition is in part due to the fall. There are neuropsychiatric concerns from TBI cross a broad spectrum." The neurologist sounded evasive.

"TBI?"

"Traumatic brain injury."

"I didn't see the President fall, but I heard her head strike the floor. She must have hit her head on the corner of a table and then the hardwood floor."

"There's more to the President's condition than the fall, I'm afraid," said the neurologist.

"I concur," added the neuropsychiatric specialist.

"There's more than a simple contusion. Have you noticed a personality change or behavioral difference? Has the President complained of headaches?"

"Yes. I've been with her when she suffered debilitating headaches."

Then Greaves walked to computer monitor and typed the President's code.

"These are the MRI images."

The neurologist pointed to a second screen. "This CT scan was done when President Stone was admitted."

Lindstrom began to feel overwhelmed. "Please make your explanation as simple as possible."

"The President has multiple bilateral hemorrhagic contusions of the medial orbital frontal lobe and anterior temporal lobe. Now I'll show you a similar CT of a recovered patient. The initial CT's are similar."

"What are you telling me?"

"It may be months before President Stone is fully functional. Patient "X" recovered in several months and returned to work. Katherine Grace Stone is the President of the United States. She is perhaps the most powerful leader in the world," insisted the neurologist.

"She must be fully recovered before she is ready to lead," Dr. Greaves added.

"Another significant medical question has arisen," said the neuropsychiatrist.

"What is it?"

Dr. Greaves walked to the President's beside.

"This is an initial diagnosis, of course, but we believe President Stone has a history of brain stimulation therapies. The scans suggest electric shock therapy."

"We also discovered traces of lesions similar to ones created by chemical stimulation. The Oval Office injury complicated the President's condition."

The neurologist returned to the monitor. "I suspect the faint scar tissue resulted from electronic or chemical applications during adolescence. We still don't know the full impact of brain stimulation. Years ago it was used to change a patient's behavior. Subjects may not show the effects for years. The procedure has changed many an individual's personality."

"The medical term is somatization disorder. Simply put, the normal, unconscious process by which an individual's psychological distress is expressed as physical symptoms," said the neurologist.

Lindstrom was bewildered. "The President must return to the White House as soon as possible," Lindstrom insisted. "We have a team of specialists stationed there." Lindstrom began to pace. He walked to the window. Flashing lights and sirens announced the Vice President's motorcade. *What the hell is going on?* Lindstrom saw Kevin Goodman walk across the courtyard and stand under the portico. *Goodman should be stationed outside this suite.*

"Mr. Lindstrom we need to return to the matter at hand," insisted Dr. Greaves. "There is no way President Stone will be able to travel."

"Do you understand the 25th Amendment?" Lindstrom glowered. "We are addressing presidential succession, Dr. Greaves."

"This is not a political decision Mr. Lindstrom," Dr. Greaves replied.

⤜⤏

Ives Venal moved swiftly. He called Drew Lindstrom to a meeting in one of the hospital's offices. Kevin Goodman was present.

"Drew, I need the President's signature on a letter of temporary disability."

"Is it necessary? President Stone is in a coma. Dr. Greaves informed me the President would remain on a respirator for several more days. As the brain swelling decreases the President's medication will be reduced. Once her vital signs are stable she will be brought out of the coma."

"Be reasonable Lindstrom," said the Vice President.

"I am."

" I don't want to start a Constitutional crisis by demanding Congress implement Section Four. We have a team of physicians standing by," Venal replied.

Lindstrom turned his back on the Vice President. "I can't discuss this further with Goodman in the room."

Goodman didn't budge.

"It's all right, Agent Goodman. We need a few moments alone."

Lindstrom looked at Goodman and then turned to Goodman. *What the hell is going on with Goodman?*

"You know as Vice President I have the authority to request Congress to invoke an declaration of disability. It makes the President look bad and her team worse. I am not forcing the President from office. For the next eight hours I am assuming the duties of the Presidency. Then I want the letter sent to Congress. I'm leaving you a window of opportunity to save President Stone."

Lindstrom shrugged submission. "I'll leave it to you."

❧

The next morning regularly scheduled radio and television broadcasts were interrupted. The camera zoomed in on the face of Vice President Venal.

"Good morning, fellow Americans. Yesterday, President Stone fell in the White House Oval Office. She received a life threatening concussion. She is a patient at Walter Reed Medical Center. Though stable, the President remains in critical condition. Under the terms of the 25th Amendment I have assumed the duties of the President. A panel of physicians has been appointed by Congress to monitor the President's physical and emotional health. President Stone is disabled and unable to perform her Constitutional duties. Rest assured, as Vice President I will continue to deal with the business of our country. A panel of experts will monitor the President's condition. Every American looks forward to President Stone's recovery and return to the White House. God bless Katherine Grace Stone and God bless America."

The deed was done. Now it was time for Ives Venal to place his stamp on the Presidency. The calls of support flooded the White House switchboard. Venal knew better than to occupy the Oval Office, at least not immediately. He held court in the Eisenhower Executive Office Building surrounded by a triad of Secret Service personnel. Agent Kevin Goodman appeared to be in charge of the transition.

The call came on Venal's personal cell phone. It caught him by surprise.

"Vice President Venal. Forgive me, President Venal this is Ashton Pickering." There was an obvious condescending tone."

"Oh no! I'm Vice President Venal. Haven't taken the oath and I hope I will not have to.

"Of course. And I stand corrected Mr. Vice President. As you know, Trinity International has maintained a close working relationship with the US government," said Pickering.

"I'm not surprised you had access to my personal cell phone number. You are a powerful man. What do you want?"

"You get right to the point, Mr. Vice President. I admire that quality in a leader. Please don't feel put upon or intimidated. It is imperative that we act as soon as possible."

"I'm not interested," Venal responded.

"Don't be foolish Mr. Vice President. Your future tenure depends on our mutual cooperation."

"Sounds hostile to me."

"Mr. Venal. I'll call again tomorrow. You are under a lot of pressure. Perhaps you will be more amenable, tomorrow. Please reconsider your recalcitrance."

Chapter Sixty-Six
The Vice President's Residence.

Ives Venal prided himself on his physical and mental discipline. He never smoked and was particularly careful to avoid being photographed with a glass of anything in hand. Over the years Venal savored his reputation as mean and unforgiving. Yet, as he finished his late-afternoon cocktail, Venal was certain something sinister lay ahead. He couldn't let go of the menacing innuendo in Pickering's voice.

"Are you finished with your Martini?" asked Janice Brodski, his longtime personal assistant.

"Janice, I might enjoy another. Ask Chef to postpone dinner a bit."
"Of course."

Janice returned with a fresh Martini. "Dinner will be ready at six thirty. Is there anything else?"

Venal didn't acknowledge Janice. He focused on his wife's portrait over the fireplace mantel.

"I'll be here if you need me." She waited for a response, but Venal didn't reply. "I'll say goodnight then, Mr. Vice President. She closed the French doors. *The Vice President is under a lot of pressure. The only other time I served him two Martinis was his first night alone after Mrs. Venal passed away.*

❧

The next morning Venal's chief of staff awakened him.
"This envelope arrived by courier from Langley."
Venal opened the envelope and removed four photographs.
"Shit," he screamed. "Get Goodman here immediately."
When Kevin Goodman arrived he found Venal huddled on his bedroom floor. Four photographs were scattered at his feet.

"Sir, what's wrong?"

Venal pointed to the photos. "You must have known about these, Goodman."

"You'll have to discuss the matter with Mr. Pickering."

"So that's how it works? You are the hired gun for Pickering."

"No sir. I work for Mr. Pickering's employer."

"Trinity?" Venal whimpered.

"It doesn't matter at this point. Take my advice and follow Mr. Pickering's lead." Goodman bent down and gathered the photos. "Your stepdaughter is an attractive woman, sir."

Venal nodded. He cast his eyes at the floor and sobbed. "I was so lonely after my wife died. Who else knows about this?"

"I don't know. Certainly Pickering wants to be discreet. No one wants a scandal. Photos of you in compromising positions with your stepdaughter spell disaster for your future administration."

"And raise havoc for Trinity," Venal added with distain.

"I would be cautious. Your stepdaughter is a successful TV personality with three children and a devoted husband. I've read the file."

Goodman turned and tossed a pillow from the bed at Venal's feet. "Cry into this. Miss Brodski and the household will be alarmed if they hear you. Let me warn you. There are cameras everywhere. You are under constant surveillance. Forget suicide. It will complicate matters. I assure you, Trinity will destroy your stepdaughter's family. Get dressed. When Pickering calls, tell him you're a player."

"I can't believe what I'm hearing."

"Being President is easy, sir. The same forces that control the world's resources direct Trinity. Sit back and let Trinity take charge. President Anderson was stubborn. He resigned. Katherine Stone could have owned the world. She refused to cooperate."

"How is Stone?"

"She'll be fine. She underwent a surgical procedure this morning. I'm sure Mr. Pickering will fill you in."

"Get dressed. I'll call when Mr. Pickering is ready to meet with you."

Venal looked up at Goodman. "You are a son-of-a-bitch."

"It's my job, sir," said Goodman as he left.

Venal buried his face in the pillow and screamed.

⁊

Ashton Pickering pointed a remote control at the far wall of his office. A white board slowly descended from the ceiling. With his hands straddling each side of his waist and posture erect, Pickering stood in front of the blank board and inhaled deeply. The day of reckoning had arrived. In the middle of the board he drew a triangle. *Here we have Clayton, Savage and Sandoval and their puzzling connection.*

Next he listed the names of the provocateurs: Clayton, Putnam and Stokes. On the top he printed Walter Katz. *Katz is my target for now.* He circled the name as though to emphasize his commitment to get Katz. Pickering smiled and began to walk away. He stopped and returned to the board. *A piece of this puzzle is missing. I just need time to figure it out. I am determined to retire from Trinity on my own terms. I'll be damned if I let Kurt Strauss force me out.* He returned to the board and furiously scribbled "Strauss".

Pickering returned to his desk. He called for his secretary. "Claire, get Kevin Goodman on the phone."

"Yes, Mr. Pickering."

Pickering gazed across the room at the whiteboard entranced by the names. The phone rang. "I have Goodman on the line, sir."

"Thank you, Claire."

"Ah, Goodman. First, we'll deal with Venal, Stone and Lindstrom. Next, it's time to settle accounts with Mr. Katz and finally, the incidentals. I'll be in Washington later today. The aircraft hangar at Dulles. Have everyone waiting."

"Yes, sir."

Once again Pickering turned to the white board. *It's time for a bloody purge. Wipe the board clean. And then I will deal with my rivals within Trinity.* Pickering laughed. The thought amused him.

Chapter Sixty-Seven
The Meeting

It was mid-afternoon when Ashton Pickering's private jet touched down at Dulles International Airport. The runway noise was deafening. Pickering quickly disembarked. Two security guards waited on the tarmac and escorted him to a waiting SUV. It was a short drive to Trinity's aircraft hanger. The chauffeur pulled close to the rear entrance.

The two security guards exited the SUV and scanned the area. They escorted their chief inside. Ives Venal, Drew Lindstrom and Kevin Goodman were waiting.

"Gentlemen, thank you for being on time. I'm running a tight schedule. Looks like we are in for a bit of bad weather. I scheduled a conference in Manhattan this evening.

"What's this meeting all about?" demanded Lindstrom. "Why haven't I been allowed to visit with President Stone?" Lindstrom paced the room.

Pickering gestured with his index finger for Kevin Goodman to respond.

"Very well. Let's start with President Stone. At 7:30 this morning President Stone underwent a medical procedure known as a therapeutic lobotomy. A small incision was made through her right eye orbit. The operation went well. Unfortunately, President Stone is suffering from Transient Global Amnesia (TGA). She is disoriented. Quite frankly she may not remember you. Give her some time.

"You bastards. You punched a hole in her brain and killed her memory," shouted Lindstrom.

Pickering interceded. "Calm down, Drew. The surgeons never intended over-kill. Do you want to see a babbling Katherine Stone?"

Lindstrom rushed at Goodman. Goodman stepped aside and collared Lindstrom throwing him to the floor.

"Now stay there!" Goodman ordered. "Listen to me. Stone was experiencing uncontrollable life threatening seizures. She had violent outbursts. Too much is at risk. Pickering ordered the lobotomy. We had no choice."

Ives Venal moved towards the door. "Sit down Ives," ordered Pickering. "Goodman, please help Mr. Lindstrom back to his chair. Gentlemen, this entire business is out of hand. There's no need to resort to fist fighting. Goodman, from now on you will address Ives as Mr. Vice President. I'll not tolerate otherwise."

Goodman sneered.

Lindstrom wiped blood from his from his face. "I think my nose is broken."

"I just want this to end," Ives Venal pleaded.

"It will, Ives," said Pickering.

"As for you, Lindstrom, here's the plan. President Stone has suffered a debilitating stroke. Venal is the President. Accept it. Someone must bite the bullet for Katherine Stone and that's you. Tomorrow you will issue a press release. Later in the day Vice President Venal and you will appear at a White House briefing for the media. Vice President Venal's press secretary will issue a brief update on President Stone's condition. Then it's your turn, Drew. Everett Stans, from the *Journal*, will raise his hand. Acknowledge him."

"What? Stans is hostile towards Stone," protested Lindstrom.

"Stans will inquire about reports circulating the Pentagon."

"Oh no. Not Zimbabwe?" *Pickering is tightening the noose around my neck.*

"He will ask about a rogue operation inside Zimbabwe. You will disclose Stone's attempt to circumvent the Joint Chiefs by inserting ground forces into Zimbabwe."

"Is that wise?" asked Venal.

"We have no choice," Pickering responded. "We need to get our version of the story out there before Putnam."

"Pay attention, Drew. You will insist the executive order to enter Zimbabwe was a mistake. Stans will insist on further clarification. You'll decline noting a possible investigation by the Department of Justice and Congress. Now here's the catch. You will accept full responsibility for not stopping the President or warning the Joint Chiefs and Congress. Emphasize Vice President Venal was not informed and did not participate."

"I refuse," Lindstrom shouted. Blood spurted from his nose.

"Be reasonable. You did participate in the planning. You have no choice."

"Are you telling me to plead guilty to a serious crime during a press conference?"

"Exactly. Venal will grant a full pardon within two years. Trinity will provide significant restitution for your loyalty."

"And if I don't?"

"You'll accept the consequences."

"What does that mean?"

"Oh, you'll survive, but one by one, your family will die. Understood?"

Lindstrom sank back in his chair and cupped his hands over his eyes.

"And you, Venal. You coward. I can't imagine you as the President of the United States. Then again, you are the perfect choice. You lack integrity. You're greedy. You fit the profile. Relax, Ives. The Circle of Twelve calls the shots. Get yourself together."

Venal's jaw dropped. He sat on the edge of his chair staring at the floor.

Pickering walked toward Venal. "Ives, look at me." Pickering reached under Venal's chin and gripped his jaw.

Venal winced.

"Stay away from your stepdaughter," Pickering demanded. His clasp tightened. "Ives, did you hear what I said?"

Venal acknowledge Pickering with an agonized nod.

"Good," said Pickering with an insidious laugh. "I look forward to your press conference," Pickering mocked.

Goodman left the room and returned with four security guards. "Gentlemen. Your cars are waiting."

Once Lindstrom and Venal had left, Goodman asked, "Sir,

what do we do about President Stone?"

"For now, lock her up at our Long Island retreat. I don't really care, Goodman. She's your problem. I have faith in you, Goodman. I want the Katz affair brought to closure. Are you up to the task?"

"Yes, sir. As we speak I have people searching Hong Kong for Katz's wife. Hong Kong is a huge area. They've narrowed the search to Hong Kong's Aberdeen region. It's a vast area, but they have a number of leads."

"Wonderful. I'm disgusted with the entire mess. Don't let me down, Goodman."

❧

Seventeen hundred miles west of Washington, DC a bitter man watched the choreographed performance by the Vice President and President Katherine Stone's Chief of Staff, Drew Lindstrom. The televised press conference only increased Katz's anguish and guilt. *It's my fault. I shouldn't have waited to release the files.*

Earlier in the day, Walter Katz intercepted an encrypted text from China. It was brief and direct. "Hwamei," terminated.

"Hwamei" (Chinese for Melodious Thrush) was Candice Wang's code name. Walter Katz was stunned. He began to cry as he walked out onto the cabin's front porch. *Candice is dead. Candice didn't have access to my cache of files. She insisted on safeguarding one of the two keys to my cloud vault, a hand-carved jade Buddha, on a simple braided horsehair necklace. I should never have involved her. She insisted she would be safe with her relatives.*

Suddenly, Katz screamed, "*No!* What have I done?" and fell to his knees.

Katz, an already condemned man, knew Trinity and the US government were desperately searching for him. Each day Katz remained on the loose the greater the probability he would release his cache of files. Candice had an extended family still living in China. She had made previous trips to China over the last two years as a US representative of the Defense Advanced Research Projects Agency. It was time to move. She used her passport and visa to enter China then disappeared on board one of the more than 600 junks in Hong Kong's Aberdeen Harbour.

Within days, of Candice's arrival in China, Trinity's hunt was on. The intercepts revealed Kevin Goodman had reached a near panic with his effort to find Candice. The Chinese operatives referred to Candice as "fighting bird".

I was helpless to intervene. One mistake might have betrayed her cover. What have I done? It was clear more than one organization was in pursuit of his wife.

Katz understood and feared Trinity's omnipotent power. Katz's mind and body were beginning to spin out of control. *I have to battle my brain to remain consciously in control.*

This morning's intercept between Trinity and a Chinese official over-whelmed Katz. Candice's mangled body had been found in the parking lot of a car dealership near Aberdeen Harbor. Ironically, the necklace and jade Buddha were still around her neck when the body was discovered.

As the day wore on Katz's headaches increased with the intensity of his despair. He feared the seizures. Despairingly, collapsed into a chair. *My autonomic nervous system will terrorize and betray me.*

Chapter Sixty-Eight
Centennial Wyoming

In its time Centennial Wyoming held a huge promise of mining wealth – gold… until the Great Depression. Those days had passed. Now the region was a vast ranching area. The closest community of any size was Laramie.

Sitting outside the small ice cream store, Bobby-Lee Brown looked up at the hillside road. Each day the collection of RV's dotting the overlook increased. He scanned the homes on the hillside. *It's getting too crowded. Too many new people.* He pulled his soiled wrangler's hat forward. It cast a shadow across his scarred face.

"Where the hell is Walter?"

A portly man with melting ice cream on his hand turned and looked at Bobby-Lee.

"Sorry, man. I'm just talking to myself. I'm wired different." And he was. Bobby-Lee laughed. Bobby-Lee sat down again and checked his cell phone. No calls. Once again, he looked at the hillside across the street. *Seems like some of those fifth-wheelers squeezed among the lower rows of cabins are here to stay. I hate those interlopers.*

Bobby-Lee Brown was born in Centennial. His mother, Wachiwi, was an Oglala Sioux. Legend has it Wachiwi was an ancestor of Akecheta, a US Cavalry scout and sole survivor of the bloody battle of Fort Kearny. Eighty-one soldiers died in an ambush led by Red Cloud and Crazy Horse.

Bobby-Lee's skill with his ash bow and bowstring made from bison tendons convinced Wachichi her son was guided by Akecheta's spirit.

Bobby-Lee's father, Terrance Brown, was an Irish immigrant, drawn to Centennial hoping to discover a new vein in one of the nearby abandoned mines. He never did. One afternoon word arrived in Centennial. A shaft collapsed and trapped Terrance along with two others. Their bodies are still down there.

Wachiwi eventually found work at the Sullivan ranch. Clint and Sue Sullivan converted a small out-building into a modest cottage where Wachiwi and Bobby-Lee lived. Over the years Bobby-Lee worked on the ranch herding stray cows down off the mountains of Medicine Bow National Park. Bobby-Lee knew the park as well as any mountain man.

Owning a cattle ranch is a tough business. Bleak winters and dry summers, volatile market prices and government regulations are trials ranchers face.

"The world is closing in on us," Clint told Bobby-Lee. "The young people want to move to the cities. Our way of life may not last much longer. Sometimes it feels like there were more bad years then good ones." The Sullivans, like many of their neighbors, were independent folks. Clint could always count on Federal regulations increasing costs and cutting profits. *Thank god Washington, DC is a world away. Laramie's got all we need.*

"One day those wild mustangs will be a real problem," Clint complained.

"The government doesn't listen," Sue replied. Those herds are growing like a wild fire."

Clint and Sue weren't about to sell the family ranch. Clint's great grandfather owned the ranch. Sue's parents owned the neighboring ranch. The Sullivans were proud people. They kept their one regret to themselves. They never had children. Then the Browns came along.

Bobby-Lee attended Centennial's small school. Bobby-Lee's classmates were not as accepting of the dark-skinned boy as were the Sullivans. Mean pranks and bullying intimidated Bobby-Lee. He disliked school.

One afternoon Bobby-Lee took a beating that changed his life forever. The Cloon boys jumped him. When the incident was over, Bobby-Lee lay crying and bleeding in the dirt. That's where Clint Sullivan found Bobby-Lee when the boy failed to show for supper.

"No use calling Early Cloon," said Sue. "I've known him since grade school. He's lazy and useless as tits on a bull. And those two boys of his are criminals."

Clint laughed. "You're right. But the kid needs some help."

"He's all yours," said Sue. "Just make sure his mom agrees."

Bobby-Lee's survival training began that evening. As Bobby-Lee and Clint strode into the barn, Clint smacked the boy across the back of his head. He shoved him to the floor. "Now, don't ever turn you back on your opponent. Stand up."

Bobby was stunned.

Clint walked to an empty stall and grabbed a length of two by four. "Listen son. Don't let the Cloon boys catch you alone. Those guys are twice your size."

Clint grasped the board in his right hand. He smacked it against the palm of his left hand. "Stalk 'em like a wolf. Wait until they're apart. Then strike." Clint's passive smile turned to a scowl. Without warning Clint turned and slammed the board against the stall gate. The wooden gate broke at the hinge.

Several weeks later Early Coon, Jr. was found unconscious behind the general store.

"Honest. I can't remember a damn thing."

"Or maybe you don't want to admit someone got the best of you," his old man said.

"Serves you right for taking a piss behind the store in broad daylight."

Junior weighed fifty pounds more than Bobby-Lee and stood six inches taller. Bobby-Lee never told Clint about the encounter, but rumors spread through Centennial. Naturally, no one imagined the culprit was scrawny Bobby-Lee.

Bobby-Lee smirked a bit as he took in the gossip. *That two by four came in handy.*

Nonetheless, the old man was outraged when young Elmo disappeared for two days. Park rangers found Elmo hiding along the abandoned railway tracks just outside Albany. "I don't remember how I got here. Someone hit me in the back of the head."

It didn't take long for the Cloon boys to take revenge on at least five innocent classmates they caught gossiping about the incidents. But that was years ago.

Wachiwi died the summer Bobby-Lee graduated high school. He enlisted in the Army. That's where he met Walter Katz.

❧

They served together in Vietnam or, more specifically, Laos in an operation the United States government claimed never existed. Katz and Brown were members of a long-range reconnaissance unit. They manned an observation post. Katz radioed reports of enemy troop movements. Bobby-Lee was a sniper.

One night, their camp came under fire. A sniper killed the first sergeant. Bobby-Lee swore to avenge the sergeant's death. They suffered heavy casualties without hope of evacuation. They were doomed if help didn't arrive. Walter Katz knew from the radio dispatches, that they were on their own for at least another day. The sniper struck again. His target, a Second Lieutenant, had been in country for only two weeks.

That evening Bobby-Lee crawled to the camp's perimeter. He readied his bow. Then he covered himself with foliage. He was certain the sniper would strike again. At sun- rise Bobby-Lee lay motionless. He didn't move all day and into that evening. He felt certain his adversary would return. During the passing hours Bobby-Lee never sipped water. Then he heard a scurry on the path. He took a deep breath and prepared to strike. Instinctively, he sat up, bow in hand. His rival was startled. It was too late. Bobby-Lee released the arrow. It pierced the sniper's throat. Bobby-Lee rolled to his side and crawled to the dying enemy.

"For god's sake. It's a woman."

She reached to touch his hand. He pulled away. Her last breath gurgled through the blood spurting at Bobby-Lee. He turned and crawled away.

The sniper's death didn't end the battle. The enemy returned again that night. Two enemy sappers tossed their charges blowing a path through the wire. A dozen or so more North

Vietnamese soldiers rushed through the opening. They tossed phosphorous grenades. Bobby-Lee caught the worst of it. "Phosphorous," he screamed and rolled in the dirt. Katz rushed to Bobby-Lee. Katz dragged Bobby into a small bunker. White phosphorous is nasty. It burns to the bone. Katz tore off Bobby-Lee's fatigues. Bobby-Lee screamed.

At first light the siege was over. Bobby-Lee was burned raw. Thankfully, four courageous chopper crews rescued them.

There was no unit citation or visit from the battalion commander. They were expendable. The operation never took place.

Bobby-Lee returned home soured. His charred face frightened children and adults alike. And Bobby-Lee liked it that way.

Walter Katz finished his enlistment and eventually went to work for the Bland Corporation, a subsidiary of Trinity International. Vietnam and Laos were thousands of miles away and forty years ago. For many, the war was a lingering memory, best forgotten. Bobby-Lee held those folks in contempt. As time past, Walter Katz returned to Centennial several times a year and eventually built a small log cabin retreat on private land bordering the Medicine Bow National Park.

The two men had formed an inseparable bond.

✍

Bobby-Lee's musings ended abruptly. He looked at his watch. "Where in the hell is Walter?" he mumbled.

"What's that?" asked the man with the ice cream cone.

Before Bobby-Lee could answer the man, he heard Katz yell, "Hey, Bobby-Lee. Let's go."

"You're late," Bobby-Lee shout back. "I was about to give you up for dead." He flipped Katz "the bird," and climbed into the rundown pickup. "Next time you ask to borrow my truck, remind me to say *no*," said Bobby-Lee.

Suddenly, Katz's expression turned sour. "Get in. We need to talk."

"Where are we headed?"

"The trails."

Fifteen minutes later they pulled into a parking area. No one will notice us with all these tourists.

"This must be serious," said Bobby-Lee.

Walter rested his head against the steering wheel and sobbed. "Candice is dead."

Then Walter revealed a secret his friend had never known.

❧

Late into the night Walter paced his kitchen. Walter continued to second-guess himself. *Maybe I shouldn't have involved Bobby-Lee? It's too late.* Perhaps it was his anger, but whatever it was Walter Katz's next move sealed his fate.

At 2:00 AM he emailed the compressed files to Dakota Putnam. When Dakota checked her email, she recognized Katz's user name, "Black Coffee." To her disbelief the attachments were not encrypted. It was as though Katz were taunting anyone who might intercept the seventy-six files. Dakota telephoned Clayton.

"These files are a bombshell, David. They link a reckless government research program with Trinity International."

"We need specific details...names, dates."

"I think we have the missing piece."

"What?"

"The U-853."

"We have Katz's files. It's all here. There are references to William Mallory and the U-853. Walther Liechtenauer and Heinrich Franz signed invoices dating back to the early sixties."

"We need to find the U-boat's log. Without it we're just blowing smoke," David replied.

"David, there's more. Katz holds the key to Trinity International's hacking the DOD's Logistics Agency. Now I understand."

"It's too early in the morning. Just give it to me straight."

"A while back I sent Katz an inquiry. Why did Trinity target the Logistics Agency? He sent a cryptic response. 'Amateurs talk strategy, professionals talk logistics'. Now I understand," Dakota declared.

"What does that mean?"

"Trinity International wants to control the supply and demand of rare earth elements. Their next objective is Zimbabwe's abandoned mines. They've discovered a process to turn hundreds of years of slack into priceless rare earth resources. It's worth billions."

"Sounds great, but how do we tie it all together?" asked David.

"We don't. Katz will. Something has set him off."

"Have you shared this information with Lou-Ann?"

"No, not yet."

"Dakota, please don't involve her. She's been through enough. I have to update the GAO. We could face criminal charges for impeding an FBI investigation. I'll delay until you publish, but not a minute longer. I have no intention of spending the rest of my life in prison or worse yet, the Moscow Airport."

"They already know. The most recent emails weren't encrypted. Something has gone wrong. Katz is acting out of character. These emails defy Trinity and the government."

"He's a dead man. That frightens me."

"Why?"

"Don't be naïve. They may come after us. Will the next UPS delivery man be an assassin and fire an Uzi through my front door?"

"Stop! You're scaring me, David."

"You should be scared. There's no turning back."

"I'm not changing my mind. Katz has given me a proviso. I have until mid-afternoon to publish the story. Then he plans to release thousands of pages to the media. You are taking one hell of a risk. Someone will attack your credibility."

"If only I had the U-853's log."

"That's unrealistic. Ed Savage made a number of dives on the U-853. If there's a log, no one has found it."

"We'll talk later. It's my first scoop since Watergate. Katz gave me a five-hour head start before his bursts the files. I have a deadline."

Chapter Sixty-Nine
Centennial
5:00 PM Mountain Time

Later the same day, Walter Katz was spiraling on a descent into an abyss. *I have to be careful not to jeopardize innocent people.*

At 5:00 PM Katz fired a series of files at worldwide media outlets. He routed emails via a myriad of IP's and Internet connected appliances. The files overwhelmed a number of providers. The underground service, *Snicker,* was down for nearly an hour. Most companies attempted to hide the violations.

The six o'clock news announced a possible state sponsored attack on East Coast providers.

Back in South Carolina, Dakota Putnam sipped a Cosmo waiting for the shoe to drop. For the first time in years, Dakota Putnam beat a deadline.

The story began -

"Is there a monster roaming the White House?"

This morning an anonymous source released seventy-six compressed files. The source claims these are the first of thousands downloaded from classified US agency and Department of Defense databases. The source plans to flood Internet providers and social media with thousands of files.

These documents purport to unmask a surreptitious plot to subvert the Executive, Congressional and Judicial branches of our government. The sender points to a secret plan by a group to do something unlawful and harmful to the United States. Its roots are deep within the economic and political fabric of our nation's most trusted institutions.

I love our nation. Americans must honor our moral and ethical responsibility to uphold and protect the Constitution. Even so, I am committed to journalistic integrity.

Three Chief Executives have occupied the White House in the past three years.   It is without precedent in our nation's history. President Kevin Andersen resigned after a series of heart attacks. Vice President Katherine Stone replaced Andersen. She selected House Speaker, Ives Venal to be her Vice President.

Stone underwent brain surgery. She is convalescing at Trinity's Retreat on Long Island's north shore. With one year remaining for Stone's first term, Ives Venal occupies the Oval Office.

It seems fair to ask, "Is a monster lurking in the White House?"

A series of tragedies struck President Katherine Grace Stone's brief tenure.

1. Andrew Dunn, President Stone's husband, committed suicide in the master bedroom of the White House private residence.

2. Charles Best, President Stone's Chief Counsel was found dead near Manassas, Virginia. The coroner ruled his death was a suicide.

3. Late yesterday afternoon, following a televised news conference, Drew Lindstrom, Stone's Chief of Staff, was found hanging in his home. The preliminary report points to suicide. Lindstrom was due to appear before the Armed Service oversight committee. They are investigating a clandestine US intelligence gathering operation in Zimbabwe. Lindstrom was subpoenaed to appear before a Federal grand jury next month.

4. Early this morning, Kurt Strauss, the Chief Financial Officer for Trinity International and a major Stone fundraiser, fell to his death from the terrace of Trinity's Manhattan headquarters. Strauss' son, John, released a brief statement noting his father's on-going battle with Parkinson's disease.

5. Each of these individuals is referenced in the documents I reviewed. Our nation has endured

several traumatic presidential campaigns. In part private email servers, classified documents, and state sponsored hackers fueled the bitter exchanges that diverted voters from critical issues confronting America. I don't subscribe to conspiracy theories. This is not my intention. In 1928, Justice Louis Brandeis wrote, 'If the government becomes a lawbreaker, it breeds contempt for law; it invites every man to become a law unto himself; it invites anarchy.'

"It's time to cage the White House monster."

Chapter Seventy
FBI Headquarters
Washington DC
4:00 PM Eastern Standard Time

The official government response to Dakota Putnam's piece was almost instantaneous. The FBI blamed the Chinese for the initial email leaks. "Pure fabrication. They are fakes."

Several conflicting reports were leaked to the press.

"Putnam is a sensationalist. President Stone pulled Putnam's press credential, again."

Attention turned to the Russians. "We're months away from electing a new President. Once again the Russians are interfering with our elections, " said President Venal's spokesperson.

The Secretary of Defense cautioned President Venal, " Deny the possibility of a traitor within the Defense Logistics Agency. We can't afford to reveal any vulnerabilities."

A DOD spokesperson insisted the newly released emails were assembled via open-source intelligence. In response to Dakota Putnam's column the spokesperson responded, "Anyone with persistence could dig up apparently incriminating documents. We have no reason to believe these files are authentic. Ms. Putnam did not act in the best interest of this country by referencing unauthenticated documents or releasing classified documents."

A press aide stepped forward. He covered the microphone with his hand. There was a brief exchange with a Justice Department official. The press aide waved his arm. "Ladies and Gentlemen, I have a brief statement. I won't be answering questions at this time. The Justice Department has informed the President that thousands of pages of classified material have been released via the Internet by *Prurient,* the social media outlet. The Justice Department has initiated an investigation. They have a court order demanding Putnam surrender all documents in her possession."

The pressroom was chaotic. Reporters demanded more information. "I'm sorry. No questions at this time." The press aide and the Justice Department official exited the room. The briefing was over.

Chapter Seventy-One
Timber Point
Suffolk County Golf Course
Great River, NY

Matt Nagle and his golf partners played every Friday weather and time permitting. Matt was retired. Once school started their outings were limited to nine holes plus a round of Martinis. When it was Matt's turn to pick the course, he always chose Timber Point.

"For god's sake Matt," complained Sandy Nevins. "With all the courses closer to home, why the hell do you always pick Timber Point?" Sandy was a ball buster. "Jim, grab the bags," Sandy ordered.

Jim Lowe, Sandy's shadow, pulled the golf bags from the trunk and waited for Sandy's next command.

The third guy, Doc Clawson, the newest member of the Friday foursome, smiled. He'd listened to the same Mutt and Jeff routine dozens of times before. Oddly, Sandy was a bit more out of sorts than usual. Doc didn't care where they golfed because Matt always insisted on driving.

Matt laughed at Sandy's irritability. *Sandy would have made a great undertaker.* Jim was constantly parroting Sandy's comments. *His head bobs up and down like a flamingo sipping water.* Matt liked Doc Clawson. Clawson, a recent retiree enjoyed discussing politics. There was a bite to some of his comments. Matt attributed Doc's sarcasm to Clawson's Vietnam experience about which Matt knew little. Still, he enjoyed playing golf with Clawson while he simply tolerated Sandy and Jim.

Today, Sandy was struggling around the greens.

At some point Jim began a conversation with Matt. "Hey, I see the government is out looking for Nazis, again," Jim remarked. "Did you catch the story on the news?"

"What now?" Matt asked.

"Oh, this time it's a sunken U-boat off Block Island."

"Steer clear of Nazis," said Jim with a laugh. He recalled Matt's article in the *East End Advance*. "Didn't you claim the government had a Nazi working on Plum Island? They test all those viruses there. Right?"

Matt forced a laugh, but Jim's remark hit home. "Let's not go there. I haven't thought about Nazis in years," Matt replied.

Doc tuned in on the conversation.

"I can laugh about it now, but it wasn't too funny back then," said Matt pulling a putter from his bag.

"Hey, is this a bullshit session, Matt, or are we here to play golf? Now stand back," Sandy barked.

Matt backed off the green. *Screw you Sandy.*

"Sorry Sandy," Jim whimpered. He nervously tapped the ball and came up short.

No one noticed the surprised look cross Doc's face at the mention of Nazis. *I wonder what Nagle knows. I'll wait until I have a better opportunity to speak with him. Should I tell him about my meetings with Jack Price? Maybe. I'll feel him out first.*

As the round ended, Sandy and Jim drove their cart directly to the parking lot. Matt and Doc followed. Sandy tossed his bag in the trunk and then Jim's. "You take the cart. I'll meet you over there," said Sandy. Jim sheepishly climbed back into the golf cart and drove away.

"Aren't you guys going for a drink?" asked Matt.

"I'm not into it," said Sandy as he drove away.

"What pissed them off?" asked Doc.

"Who knows? Got time for a drink?"

"Sure," Doc said. He looked at Matt. They both started to laugh.

"My treat, but just one. I promised Liz I'd take her to the movies this evening. Eight-forty-five show." Matt pointed to his wristwatch. The two walked across the parking lot to the bar and ordered drinks. Matt sipped his Martini. Doc squeezed a lemon slice into his Coke.

"So what's this about you and Nazis?" Doc asked.

"Back in the seventies I aspired to be a writer. Don't get me wrong. I had a great job as a teacher, but something inside said I was born to be a writer."

"Fiction?"

"Yes. We all have a novel some place inside."

"I don't know about that. So what's with the Nazis?"

" A friend told me about some weird stuff on Plum Island. It raised my curiosity. Got myself into an incredible mess. Nearly cost me my life."

"It couldn't have been that bad."

"It was. I feared for my wife and kids, too. The rest will bore you." Matt motioned to the bartender.

"Sir?"

With a smile Matt pointed to his glass. "You shorted me an olive," Matt said with a smile.

Doc looked at Matt. "What's that about?"

"Oh. Three olives bring good luck."

Doc shook his head. "We all have our little quirks."

Matt lifted his glass. "To our quirks. So what's up with your interest in Nazis?" Matt asked.

"There's your story, now." Doc pointed to the TV over the bar.

It was a brief report. "Syndicated columnist, Dakota Putnam, called on the Defense Department and Congress to reopen the controversial investigation regarding sinking of the U-853. Putnam claims to have read files to support her request."

"Probably nothing to it."

"I don't know. She's been in the news quite a lot, lately," said Doc.

"TV news is nothing more than talking heads reading a script. No reporting. Twenty minutes of news. Ten minutes of pharmaceutical company ads."

"I don't know about that," Doc answered. "But I do know something about the U-853."

"What? You're kidding. Right?"

"Decide for yourself. You're the first person I've told."

"I'm listening," Matt insisted.

"A while back I met a man. He knew a lot about U-boats, especially the last one sunk at the end of World War Two."

"The one Putnam's writing about?"

"That's the one," said Doc.

"The papers speculated it was Hitler's escape sub loaded with bullion. Who knows? None of the crew survived."

Doc looked at his watch. "Oops," he said. "I've kept us talking too long. We better get out of here. I don't want your wife to be angry with me."

"Nonsense," Matt said. *You bet she will be angry. So what else is new?*

"O'Neil just walked in," Doc said. "He lives up the street from me. I'll hitch a ride with him. Drop my clubs off tomorrow. While you're at it, I have a better idea."

"What's that?"

"Give me a buzz in the morning. I have something to show you."

Matt nudged Doc. "Give me a hint."

"Nope. I'll show you tomorrow."

Matt agreed, waved to the other guys and left. *This could be an interesting story.*

∽

Matt was running late as he drove past the Bayard Cutting Arboretum. *Damn it. Why can't I let go of this Nazi thing?* He pulled the car to the side of the road. There was still time to call George at the *East End Advance*. He dialed. After six rings, George answered.

"East End Advance," said the deep-throated voice.

"George, it's Matt."

"Hey Matt," replied George Wait, the owner. "What's up? Haven't heard from you in nearly a year."

"I need a favor."

"Just like you, Matt. Never ask about the family or me. Right down to business."

"Sorry George. Listen. You ran a number of stories about the General Accounting Office investigation of Plum Island operations."

"How could I forget? I foolishly published your story. First the Feds descend on me, and then your wife. She's a pit bull. She frightened me more than the Feds."

"Agreed. I caused a ruckus."

"Speaking of the Feds this may be a coincidence, but they were in town last week."

"They were? Why?"

"They rented a dive boat."

"And?"

"Never used it."

"Are you sure?"

"Positive. One of them came in. He flashed his ID. Asked to see our World War Two files."

"He leafed through a few files and left. Never thanked me."

"He didn't ask to go view your microfiche?"

"No. I thought that was odd."

"Me, too," said Matt.

"Have you returned to freelancing stories about Nazis and Plum Island?"

"I'm not writing a story George. I just had a drink with a guy. Do you recall a U-Boat that sunk off Block Island?"

"Sure. Souvenir hunters on a dive boat brought up the skeleton. The German government raised all sorts of hell."

"That's the one, George. This is important. Check your files. Send me some background material."

"Don't you learn, Matt? For god's sake, let it go," George said.

"It's OK, George."

"Please Matt. Watch yourself. No wild goose chases. Enjoy retirement. Play golf. Get a hobby."

"Call me back on my cell phone. I don't want to alarm Liz."

"Like hell. You know she'll kill you if she finds out."

"Just call my cell phone."

"It's your funeral, Matt."

Matt tossed the phone on the passenger seat and drove toward Patchogue. He knew Liz would be pissed. Almost everything he did these days upset her. *These aren't the golden years I expected.*

❧

Matt was right on. Liz was waiting in the kitchen, sipping a glass of wine. As soon as she saw him she went at him.

"Matt, you promised you would be home by six thirty. You know how impatient Sylvia is." Sylvia and Mike Sloan were Liz's friends from the bridge club. Matt hated bridge and he didn't care for the Sloans.

Matt cringed and hurried to their bedroom. Matt undressed, dropped his clothes on the floor and took a shower. He never heard his cell phone ringing in his pants pocket.

"Matt your cell phone is ringing," Liz called from the bedroom.

A soap-covered Matt headed for the phone before Liz could answer.

"George Wait called. Matt why is George Wait calling?" Liz threw a stern look at Matt not unlike the ones he received from his third grade teacher for chewing gum in class.

"I called him to say hello. I cancelled lunch a while back and wanted to see if we could set something up."

"You expect me to believe that? I know you're up to something. Whatever, but stop leaving your dirty clothes on the bedroom rug."

Matt grabbed a towel and returned George's call.

"I think I have a lead for you. Dakota Putnam is behind the push to reopen the U-853 inquiry."

"George, that's no lead. Putnam's been in the news all week."

"There's more. The Feds are back in town."

"What for?"

"Maybe it's a coincidence, but they brought a dive team. Now here's the strange thing. They never left port."

"How do you know?" Matt's voice rose a couple of decibels with excitement.

"It's a small town. I hear just about everything. It's my job. Remember?"

"Really? I'm certain they're interested in the U-853."

"Are you sure?"

"Right after you called, two GAO investigators walked in. Here's the strange part. They specifically asked for my father's articles on the U-853."

"Maybe it is a coincidence."

"My dad got in trouble for one of his stories. He claimed the U-853 sinking was overkill. According to him it was quite a media event."

"I'll bet he got in trouble for that."

"Great talking with you, Matt. Do me a favor, wait another year before you call."

"But George, I *love* talking with you."

"I'm running a small town paper. We print good news. Once in a while we're forced to print newsworthy copy. Good news, Matt. You know what I mean?"

"Bye, George. Hey don't forget to send me those clips." Matt laughed and tossed the phone on the bed.

⌘

Matt awoke around 5:30 the next morning. While the coffee was perking, he walked to the far end of the house. A pull-down staircase opened into the attic. He climbed the stairs and reached for a cardboard box containing all that remained of his notes from his original story about Plum Island. Liz had begged him to dump the boxes of notes and files, but to no avail. Matt removed a spiral notebook and blew the dust away. *Where had all the years gone?*

Matt walked back to the kitchen. He poured a cup of coffee and paged through the notebook. He finished his second cup of coffee and glanced at the clock. It was after seven. Max walked to the garage. He reached up and placed the notebook behind some old paint cans on a shelf. Then he quietly slipped back into the bedroom.

Damn, Liz still looks great. He quietly slipped back into bed and began massaging his sleeping wife's shoulders. It was her favorite foreplay.

"Come on, Matt. Not now. You just can't let me sleep."

By now he realized it was useless to protest. Matt pouted. *Well, so much for that.*

❧

Matt sat in the family room reading while Liz slept until around nine. The phone rang. Matt scrambled to the kitchen, but not before the answering machine picked up.

"Matt, this is Doc. I'm headed out. See you around noon."

Around eleven-thirty Doc called out, "Liz, I'm going to Doc Clawson's. Be back in a couple of hours."

❧

Doc leased a one-bedroom apartment just off River Avenue near the Great South Bay.

Matt arrived as Doc was unpacking the groceries.

"Coffee or water?" Doc asked.

"No thanks. I'd really like to see what you have on the U-853."

Doc walked into the living room and took a leather-bound book off the table.

"Here you go."

"What do we have here?"

"I guess you can call it anything you'd like. You have it."

Matt looked at the first few entries. "Looks like pages have been removed."

"I removed them to conceal the name of the guy who wrote it." Doc said.

"What do you mean?" asked Matt.

"You're holding a translation of the U-853's log."

"But it's in English."

"I told you. It's a translation. I never said it was the original."

"What happened to the original?"

"Locked safely away."

"And what are these?" Matt pointed to comments penciled in the border.

"They belong to the man who gave me the journals."

"The U-853's log was written in German. It was damaged."

"What do you mean?" asked Matt.

Doc began to answer when Matt interrupted. "I think I will have that cup."

Matt squinted. "I need reading glasses. I can hardly read these notes"

Doc poured the coffee. "Milk and sugar?"

"No, I take it black." Matt picked up the journal and asked, "Who gave this to you?"

"Matt, I trust you. Don't pressure me. The man is dead. His name was Jack. For now, that's it. Be satisfied."

Matt hefted the book. "This is a historical document. If it's legit, people will want to know how you got it. It's priceless."

"Settle down, Matt. You haven't read it. Don't jump to conclusions."

Matt's face reflected Doc's admonishment. "Sorry Doc. You're right."

Over the course of the next hour Matt examined the journal. "If the log is authentic, the Navy will have to rewrite its account of the U-853," said Doc.

"This journal is a ticking time bomb," Matt insisted.

"I don't follow you."

"The captain writes that he left Norway with a crew of fifty-five plus four passengers, three adult men and an infant. Doesn't that seem strange to you?" Matt scratched his head and asked for more coffee.

"Sounds right for a U-boat crew. Except for the passengers," Doc answered.

Matt closed the journal. "You believe there were?"

"Yes."

Then Matt took a risk and confronted Doc. "They didn't go down with the U-boat."

"I'm not sure."

"You're holding back."

Doc glared at Matt. "I'm not ready to share those pages with you," Doc asserted.

"Well you better keep them safe. If this story is true, a lot of people will want to get their hands on the real log," Matt cautioned.

"They've searched the sub before and come up with relics, but no log."

"Someone found the log or you wouldn't have it."

"Honestly. I don't know that part of the story. I think the original owner paid a lot of money to a wreck diver for it. Jack got possession when the owner died."

"The wreck diver must have been paid a tremendous amount. And after all these years he never bragged about finding it?"

Matt winced and rubbed his knees. His old motorcycle injuries kicked in as the tension between the two men increased.

"What are you getting at?"

"Nobody alive keeps a secret this long. The diver is dead. Don't be naïve."

"It's a complicated story. Bottom line?"

"Make it simple."

"I promised Jack I would return the log to the U-853."

"What? You can't destroy it. You owe it to the crew. And what happened to the passengers? You have to determine if the log is authentic."

"Who else knows you have the U-853 log?"

Doc hesitated. "Presley, Jack's aide."

"Has Presley tried to contact you?"

"No."

Matt slid the journal across the table. "I have to leave. Take my advice. Don't tell anyone else. The government brought a number of Nazis into this country when the war ended. Gave them critical defense jobs. Back in 1977 the GOA was on the verge of apprehending a rogue Nazi when the investigation was shut down."

"Suppose there were three passengers on the U-853. Maybe. But an infant, too? It sounds far-fetched."

For a moment Doc appeared to agonize. Doc picked up the journal with his right hand. A quizzical expression momentarily crossed his face. "The likelihood would be hard to swallow. Who would believe it?"

Matt sensed Doc already knew the answer.

Chapter Seventy-Two
The Decision

Over the weekend Matt grappled with his curiosity. *The journal piqued my interest. Does Doc have the actual U-853's log? What should I do? Can I trust Clawson? Go easy Matt.*

Trust? Matt wasn't upfront with Doc. He never told Doc about the call to George Wait, the east end editor. *I know a lot more about the U-853.*

Matt's head ached. *I remember George Wait's editorial protesting airlifting on board the sunken vessel. It caused an international fury, but that was years ago. Now wreck divers may be out there, again. Why are the Feds involved?*

Realistically, Matt faced a tough decision. *Should I pursue my interest in the U-853 and risk another confrontation with Liz? She'll kill me. I promised, no more intrigue.*

Matt recalled Liz's anger with the Plum Island episode. *You're meddling. You're a teacher not an investigative reporter. Someone tried to kill you. And what about the children and me? Matt, you are putting us in harms way. I'm warning you. I'll take the children and leave!*

Matt anguished through the night imagining different consequences. Finally, he made a decision. *This isn't 1977. I'm not risking my family. The kids are grown and married. Liz and I are retired. We do our own thing.*

Their empty nest amplified the unspoken restlessness they both felt. Their relationship was in trouble.

One late afternoon just before dinner Liz poured a glass of wine and announced, "I need my space. I don't want to be tied at the hip." Her attitude hurt Matt.

"What brought this on?" Matt asked. "What the hell does that mean?"

Liz ignored the questions. "Let's eat at 6:30," Liz said, and walked away.

❦

The next morning, Matt lay in bed thinking about his marriage and Liz's bitter comments the previous day. From time to time, with Liz's approval, they shared a brief interlude. But all in all, married life had become work, exhausting and monotonous for both of them. Once Matt had made the mistake of confiding in Sandy Nevins during a round of golf.

"You're not telling me anything new," Sandy said. He dropped his cigar on the green and tapped the ball into the cup. "Birdie," he shouted.

Matt laughed.

"Matt, I'm on my third divorce. I can't get it right. You need to play more golf. Get yourself a man cave in Florida. Separate vacations. You don't have it so bad. Hey, three square meals a day and a roof over your head. At your age…well forget the rest of the crap."

"That's not what I'm talking about, Sandy. I know the excitement and sex is about gone in my marriage. I still love my wife."

"Hold on, Matt," said Sandy as he walked back to the green to pick up his cigar.

"Sandy, forget the sex and food. I need someone to pay attention to me. Don't you feel that way, at times?"

"What?" Sandy exclaimed. "I have a new girlfriend. She's twelve years younger, and a super cook." Sandy rubbed his stomach. "I've put on twenty pounds since we started dating and the sex is almost killing me. I've got all the attention I need."

"Thanks Sandy," Matt said as he returned to their cart. Matt shrugged. *Confiding in Sandy was a mistake.*

Matt quietly rolled out of bed so as not to awaken Liz. He skipped his Sunday morning routine of eggs and bacon. Instead he made a pot of coffee and headed out to the garage. He reached behind the shelf filled with old paint cans.

"My notes." Matt's wide-eyed expression said it all. *It's time for an adventure.*

❧

On Monday morning Liz headed for the gym. She'd be gone for at least two hours. At ten o'clock Matt called the number on Clayton's business card. No luck. Then he called the General Accountability Office's general number.

"I am calling to speak with Mr. David Clayton."

"I'm sorry, sir. The GAO doesn't acknowledge who works here," replied the man.

"Have you tried the Directory?" the man asked.

"No."

"It's a comprehensive listing of government employees maintained by the Office of Personnel Management."

"Is it accessible to the public?"

"Yes, the basic OPM search engine is The Directory. You might discover Mr. Clayton's profile there. It lists everyone from Congressional staffers to Cabinet members."

"Thanks," Matt replied.

Next, Matt flipped the card over and called the number Clayton had penciled in years ago. Matt squinted as he fumbled with the cell phone keypad.

"Hello. You've reached the number of David Clayton. If that's the number you're calling please leave a message. I'll return your call as soon as possible."

"Mr. Clayton. This is Matt Nagle out in Patchogue, Long Island. We met years ago. You interviewed me about Plum Island. I need your help. Please call me at 651-555-1362. It's really important. Thanks."

"Matt, I'm home," Liz called from the garage. "Give me a hand with the groceries."

"I'll be right there, dear." He quickly placed his notes on top of the refrigerator.

"Is someone here?" Liz asked.

"No. Why?"

"Whom were you talking with?"

"I was talking out loud," he responded defensively.

"Cut it out. Folks will think you're nuts."

Once the groceries were unpacked Liz said, "I think I'll read for a while."

Matt waited for Liz to settle-in. Then he placed his second call. He knew it was a long shot, but he called Dakota Putnam's publisher and left a message with the public relations office. "You might try Ms. Putnam's email address. It's at the bottom of all her columns. It might be a faster way to contact her." And it was.

By chance, Dakota was scanning the email responses to her recent column. Dakota scrolled past Matt's e-mail. *Matt Nagle. I recall that name from years ago.* She moved the cursor back up the page and opened the e-mail.

Matt's note was brief. "I have discovered something related to your recent columns. I left a message on Mr. Clayton's answering machine, but he hasn't returned my call. This is very important. Please call. This is urgent."

Dakota replied with her own e-mail. "Thank you. I will be in touch."

Dakota was intrigued, but cautious. She called David on his cell phone. "Hey, have you checked your home answering machine?"

"My bad," David admitted.

"Remember Matt Nagle, the professor on Long Island?"

"Sure."

"Check your answering machine. He wants to speak with you."

"You talked with him?" asked David.

"No. I called you first."

"I'm on my way to Denver."

"What?"

"Walter Katz gave Lou-Ann a cell phone. He said when the time came he'd contact her. It's been charging on my kitchen counter. Katz called during the night. He wants to meet me in Laramie."

"Oh, forget it. I got the same request. He never showed," Dakota warned.

"Sometime later today, Katz will release more files. I asked him about the Pied Piper Project and William Mallory," said David.

"And?"

"He claims to have tons of files related to MKULTRA. It will take him time to sort. It doesn't matter. I have a flight to Denver this afternoon."

"Be careful, David."

"Will you be able to meet with Nagle?" David asked.

"Yes."

"OK. Please get back to me when you do."

Next, Dakota telephoned Matt Nagle.

Liz answered.

"Hello. My name is Dakota Putnam and I'm calling for Mr. Matt Nagle.

"Putnam, the author?"

"Yes. Is this Mrs. Nagle?"

"You bet your ass it is. Hold on I'll find the son of a bitch." Liz slammed the receiver on the kitchen counter and screamed, "Matt, Dakota Putnam's on the phone." Liz stormed upstairs.

Dakota and Matt talked for about twenty minutes. He told Dakota about his meeting with Doc. "I don't know if he really has the genuine log. I've never seen it. I've read the so-called translation. I will caution you, Clawson told me he removed a number of pages from the translation. Seems he promised to safeguard the journal and the log. We'd need an expert to authenticate the log."

"Clayton won't be able to meet with you, Matt. He is on another assignment. Maybe a week or more. I'm in South Carolina. Don't misunderstand. I sense you are on to something. I have a few commitments here. I'll fly to Long Island later in the week. Can you arrange a meeting with Mr. Clawson?"

"I'll try to persuade him. I'll get back to you."

"I have someone in mind who may help us confirm it's the U-853 Log."

"Sounds like you already know of the log."

"Oh no. It's pretty much accepted that the log is still on the U-boat or maybe destroyed by the its captain."

"Believe me. The story is sensational, if it's true."

⊷

Liz was still fuming as she prepared supper. "You're up to something, Matt. That woman, Putnam, pressured me for an interview in 1977. She's a reporter. She doesn't give a shit about us. She's after a story. What's wrong with you?"

Matt didn't respond.

"We agreed. No more investigative reporting. You are crazy."

"Liz, it's something I want to do. I'm not writing a story."

"What is it?"

"I don't know, but once I find out, you'll be the first to know."

"You're insane. I'm going for a walk. You can clean up."

When Liz returned she found Matt sitting in front_ of the computer. Lost in thought, he didn't see her.

"You aren't being honest with me, Matt. I can't trust you." Liz frowned and left.

Matt recalled George's warning. *Don't go off on another wild goose chase, Matt. Remember what happened last time?*

Liz appeared to be sleeping when Matt turned in after midnight. Matt slid under the covers. "I'm sorry," he whispered.

She turned on her side. "Forget it. You aggravate me," she replied. "And here we go again."

"This time it's different. Nothing is going to happen to either of us. I promise."

⊷

Matt wasn't fooling anyone. He was involved in a situation best left to a skilled reporter or better yet, the FBI. *I've done it again.* The next morning he telephoned Doc Clawson. "We have to meet. Something's come up."

"Where?"

"Bob's Luncheonette. You know it?"

"Patchogue."

"Breakfast. Tomorrow morning. Bring the journal," Matt said.

"I'm not sure I want to do that." Doc responded.

"I'm not asking to see the original, at least not yet."

"Matt, are you sure you want to get involved?"

"I'm already involved, but before I go further we have to talk."

The two met the next morning in a booth at Bob's. Doc was already sipping his second cup of black coffee when Matt arrived. They ordered.

"Take your time," Matt told the waitress.

"Did you bring it?" Matt asked.

Doc lifted a brown paper bag and scowled.

"I have been truthful with you, Doc"

"I'm listening."

Matt revealed his phone conversations with George Wait and his attempt to contact David Clayton.

"Why involve Clayton? You should have told me first."

"That's what I'm doing. I need to examine the journal, before we go any further."

"I'm not certain I want to pursue this thing, Matt. It's eerie." Doc opened the paper bag and handed Matt the journal. And the pages you removed?"

"They are safe."

Matt began to leaf through the leather bound book. "I've been in touch with Dakota Putnam, the author."

"Why?" Doc looked perturbed.

"I'm convinced she can help us authenticate the log."

"And what about Clayton?"

"We can trust Putnam and Clayton."

"Why go further?" Doc paused and stirred his coffee. "I should never have shown you the journal."

"Well, you did. You didn't show me the original Log."

"I trust you, Matt. OK, call your people. I still don't understand how they can authenticate the log. Get back to me,"

Doc said reluctantly.

The two shook hands.

"One last thing," Matt cautioned. "The U-853 is surrounded by controversy.

We don't know who else might be interested in the log. The government might want to bury it. The official Navy inquiry concluded the captain refused to surrender."

"We don't know that for sure."

"I suspect you do, Doc," said Matt.

Doc smiled. "You've overlooked something. Suppose someone else wants to get their hands on the log. You and I could be in danger."

"I don't subscribe to conspiracies, Doc."

"Be honest with yourself, Matt. You're fascinated by this mystery. Its taken hold of you."

"Maybe it has," Matt admitted.

"Imagine if the U-853 was involved in something sinister. Are you so intrigued you would risk your life? And what about Liz?"

Matt looked confused. "No, I wouldn't want Liz harmed. Still, my life seems so frivolous these days. I feel a need for some excitement and grit. I just can't let go of my dream to be a published writer."

"You have been published. And look at all the trouble it got you into."

Chapter Seventy-Three
No Turning Back

It was an uncomfortable flight from DC to Denver. David Clayton was feeling sluggish as he headed for the car rental pick up. An hour later he was about to exit the Denver airport when the cell phone alert sounded. It was a text message from Walter Katz. The message read Pegasus 444. *What the hell does that mean?*

A second or two later the answer appeared in the form of an application on the phone's homepage. Then a second text message arrived. "Use the Pegasus application in place of GPS."

When David activated the app it required a three-digit pin code. *I'll try 444.* The application opened and a grid filled the screen. A third text message arrived. "I will forward grid coordinates when you arrive in Laramie."

Rather than stay overnight in Denver, David decided to drive directly to Laramie. He registered at the Hampton Inn and then walked several blocks to Roxie's on Grand Ave.

"What will it be, darlin?" asked the waitress.

"I can't decide. What do you recommend?"

"I'd suggest our bison burger to start."

"And a tall draft?"

"Sure thing, sweetheart," she said.

It had been three hours since Katz's last contact. *I hope this isn't another wild goose chase.* David glanced at the cell phone several times. He knew Katz's chances of being located increased with each text message. David compared the signal on his personal cell phone with Katz's phone. They were both weak.

"Here you go, darlin." The waitress placed David's order on the table and handed him a roll of paper towels. "These are way better than napkins. Enjoy."

David laughed. As he bit into his bison burger a hand grasped his left shoulder. He was startled. He turned and looked up. What he saw was even more alarming.

"Clayton?"

"I'm Bobby-Lee Brown. Black Coffee sent me."

"Look, I don't want to sound weird, but who the hell are you?"

"I told you, Black Coffee sent me."

Black Coffee is Katz's signature ID. But this guy is something else. One half of his face is gone.

David's surprised expression didn't faze Bobby-Lee. "Don't bother returning to you motel room. It's too risky." Bobby-Lee pointed a finger at Clayton. "Where's the cell phone?"

David tapped his jacket pocket.

"When I leave, open the app. Memorize the grid. Destroy the phone. Then walk back to the motel parking lot. Any questions?"

"Yes. How do you fit into all this?"

"It doesn't matter. Follow the instructions on the grid."

"And Katz?"

"Soon enough. Oh, one last thing. Katz wants you to know there's no turning back. You've placed your life in danger." Then a sad expression gripped Bobby-Lee's distorted face. "Katz's wife is dead. He's gone a bit mad with grief, so be careful."

David waited for Bobby-Lee to leave then he opened the phone application. The grid coordinates were simple. David memorized the route. He glanced at his watch. *Better get back to the motel.* He was about to destroy the phone when his own phone rang.

"Hello."

"David, I just spoke with Ed Savage. He doubts the U-853 log exists. This guy Clawson may be a sensationalist. On the other hand, if the log checks out Savage contends World War Two history could be changed. Savage wants in. He'll fly to Long Island ASAP."

"What does Nagle think?"

"He is convinced Clawson is no charlatan."

"And what do you think?"

David paused. *Is someone following me?* He looked around. Grand Avenue was deserted. Yet, he couldn't shake the feeling he was not alone.

"Hello, David are you still there?" Dakota began to panic.

"I'm here. Thought I was being followed," David said.

"I don't believe in coincidences, but something tells me there's a story here."

"I'm confused. What do you mean by coincidences?" David asked.

"I've been tracking Trinity and Ashton Pickering for years. You and Lou-Ann have been searching for Walter Katz for months. Unexpectedly, Matt Nagle finds a guy who claims to have the very piece that may complete our puzzle," Dakota replied.

"I still don't follow you, but there is no time now. Tell me about Nagle," David insisted.

"I trust Nagle. His wife is really pissed that Nagle contacted me. She suspects he is on to something."

"That adds a bit of credibility. Savage is willing to help us? What changed his mind?"

"Savage agreed to examine the log. He thinks it would only take a few hours to authenticate."

"After all these years?"

"Yes."

"David, are you alright? You sound like you are winded."

"I'm walking at a pretty fast pace. Have to dump Katz's cell phone. Be careful, Dakota. Ed Savage is a bitter man. He's hunting the people who shot his wife. He suspects Trinity and Pickering ordered the hit on Diana."

"He told you?"

"Yes. I told him about the U-853's connection to Pied Piper."

"Does he know about Walter Katz?"

"No. But once he reads the log, he'll put the pieces together."

"David, are you in trouble?"

David paused. "This is scary shit, Dakota. We may be in over our heads. You have to persuade Clawson to show you the pages he removed from the translation. Most of all, he has to produce the log. Your lives are in danger. Only one thing can save you."

"What?" Dakota asked.

"Go public. Release portions of the log. It's a long shot, but it may be the only way to save yourself and the others."

"I can't do that until I know the log isn't a hoax," Dakota protested.

"Dakota, we've talked too long. This call may be tracked."

"David, please be careful," she pleaded.

Suddenly the call dropped.

David entered the motel parking lot and stepped behind a Dumpster next to the building. He took one last look at the smart phone's app. He smashed the mobile phone against the concrete building and let the parts fall to the ground. He crushed them with his foot then tossed the pieces into the Dumpster. He felt a sharp pain in his chest. Suddenly, his head swirled. He fell back against the building and slid to the ground.

"My god. I'm going to be sick," he said loudly. His body quaked. He gagged and vomited the undigested bison burger. He heaved again. He sat there for several minutes hoping the chest pains would subside. He recalled Bobby-Lee's warning. "Don't return to your hotel room." *Feels like I'm having a heart attack or a very bad case of nerves.* David's sight grew dimmer. He no longer felt the cold macadam as he fought to remain awake.

"Hey, mister, are you OK?" came the echo of a distant voice. David looked up at what appeared to be a blurry figure moving in slow motion. It was the motel's night custodian. He had stepped out of the rear entrance to have a cigarette. David struggled to get to his feet, but the best he could do was crawl.

"Mister, I think I should call the rescue squad. You need a doctor."

"No. Don't do that. Please just help me to my feet."

The custodian helped David stand. "If you won't go to the hospital, at least come inside and warm up."

David nodded in agreement.

The custodian pulled David to his feet and guided him into the utility room.

"What happened out there?" the man asked.

"'I have no idea, but thanks for helping me."

"You staying in this motel?"

"Yes, but I have to leave for a few hours."

"I don't think you should be driving."

David's complexion was pale. "I feel cold, but I'm perspiring. What time is it?"

"It's after midnight." The man handed David a bottle of water and a wet rag. "Don't dehydrate."

"Midnight? Oh no. I'm screwed," David gasped. Just then a man passed the utility room and exited the motel.

"That's odd," said the custodian.

"What?"

"I came on an hour early tonight." The custodian pointed to the utility room window. "See that guy who just walked out?"

"I see him."

"This must be the fourth time he's walked around the silver Mustang in the far row."

"That's my rental," said David.

"Well, that guy sure likes it."

David looked again, but the stranger was gone.

"You recognize him?" asked the custodian.

"No, but I only caught a glimpse," David grimaced. *That guy is after me. I better get my ass out of here.* David's chest pains lessened. *I've got to meet Katz. It's now or never.* "Thanks for helping me," David blurted. He looked down the hallway. *All clear.* David ran to his car.

As the Mustang sped off, the persistent stranger rushed into the parking lot. "Damn it!" he shouted. He reached for his cell phone.

"Central, this is Goodman. Clayton is on the move. There's a ballpark not far from Snowy Road and Route 130. Have the chopper meet me. Route 130 is a direct route to Centennial. He'll be easy to find."

A voice from Central Command responded, "Sir, we are

experiencing wind shears. The wind conditions are causing up to thirty-minute delays for arrivals and departures."

"I'll give you thirty-minutes. After that disregard the tower. You have a military clearance." There was a brief delay. "Acknowledge?"

"Affirmative, sir."

Goodman slid the cell phone into his jacket pocket and felt for the object in the small of his back. Then he returned to the motel. He walked to the utility room. The night custodian was sitting behind a card table sipping coffee and reading a magazine.

"Excuse me," said Goodman.

The custodian looked up. "Hi. May I help you?"

A man just drove off in a Mustang. Did you happen to speak with him?"

"I did. Odd guy. He shouldn't be driving a car."

"So you talked with him?" Goodman asked, again.

"Yes, sir. I did." The custodian nodded and smiled.

"Thanks," said Goodman as his right hand reached under his jacket and grasped the High Standard pistol. "One last thing," said Goodman.

The custodian looked up at Goodman.

Goodman's first round punched the man alongside his nose throwing his head to one side. Goodman instinctively fired a second headshot.

Goodman looked around. The coast was clear. He stepped back into the hallway and closed the utility room door. His cell phone vibrated.

"Sir. The chopper is on its way."

"Full compliment?"

"Yes sir. Fifty calibers in each door as requested."

"It will be nearly sunrise. I need you here forthwith."

"Affirmative, Sir."

Chapter Seventy-Four
Route 130 North
Laramie, Wyoming

David drove north along a dark and deserted Route 130. He looked in the rear view mirror for the headlights from another car. *I can't believe someone isn't on my tail. The chest pains are returning. My right arm tingles with a strange sensation. I feel dizzy. I've got to stay focused.* The speedometer blurred. David pushed the accelerator pedal to the floor as he struggled to remember Katz's directions. He was losing the cover of night as daylight slowly approached. *Don't panic. Take deep breaths. Get control of yourself.*

He passed his first waypoint, the Vee Bar Ranch. *I'm confused. I think the next intersection should be Route 11.* The Mustang was now traveling in excess of ninety miles an hour.

David began to talk to himself. "Slow down. You are searching for Route 11 on your left. Remember? I'm trying to. Damn it." At the last moment he saw the intersection straight ahead. He hit the brakes hard, but the Mustang had a mind of its own. The car surged ahead as the brakes squealed. The car veered hard to the left, but it was too late. David lost control. The Mustang spun in a circle and then hurled another 180 degrees before it came to a stop. The engine stalled. The impact smashed David's head against the window. *Thank god the airbags didn't activate.* The stench of burned rubber drifted into the car. *I could have been killed.* He unbuckled his seat belt and rested his head against the steering wheel.

David's throbbing headache and adrenalin rush masked the chest pains. Once again he had lost track of time. He started the Mustang and continued west on Route 11. His destination was Albany, a tiny community near the Medicine Bow National

Park. David drove several miles when a pickup truck pulled out from a dirt road and began to follow him. The truck's driver flashed his lights several times. David ignored the pickup's signals. *It could be a trap.* He drove on until he saw the sign for Albany, population 55.

Look for a general store on your left. There it is. David turned off the road. The pickup truck pulled behind him.

"Clayton," called the man from the truck. It was Bobby-Lee. He pointed toward a dirt road behind the store. "Park down there. Get your gear and come with me."

"It's all back at the motel."

"Don't worry about it. Park the car. We have to get out of here."

David drove a few hundred feet down the dirt road and scurried back up the incline to the pickup truck.

"Where's the fire, Brown?"

"You'll find out soon enough. Trinity is searching for you, Clayton. Let's go." Bobby-Lee ground the clutch into first gear. "This truck is on its last legs, but I love her. Now grab that shotgun we may have to use it."

"I've never fired a shotgun."

"Simple. Rack it and fire, like in the movies."

The pickup bumped along the ever-narrowing road. Bobby-Lee made a sharp right next to an abandoned railroad bed.

"Where the hell are you taking me?" David demanded.

"Years ago, a railroad ran along here to Centennial and beyond. Serviced the gold mines west of Centennial. It all took a dump years ago. The veins petered out. The Great Depression finally killed it."

"How did you find this place? I've been hunting here since I was a kid. Walter is the brain behind the idea. And now..." Bobby-Lee stopped in mid-sentence.

"And now what?"

"And now it's all coming to an end."

"What does that mean?" David rubbed his left hand across his chest. *The pains are returning.* He felt uneasy and confused.

"I'll let Walter fill you in."

"From the look on your face, it can't be good news."

The pickup truck traveled for about two miles along the railroad bed until Bobby-Lee made a hard right. "Hold on." The truck rolled forward and down what appeared to be no more than a path. Bobby-Lee accelerated and double clutched down into first gear as the old truck crash-banged its way across a tiny stream and up an incline.

"We're here."

David looked around. "We are?"

"Bring the shotgun." Bobby-Lee stepped on the running board. He opened a utility box in the truck bed. "Take this," he ordered. He handed David an AR-14 Bushmaster. "I'll carry the supplies." Bobby-Lee gripped a backpack and several other canvas bags. He adjusted the pack and pointed to a clearing. "The lodge is just over the rise."

It was only a short distance, but David fought to keep up with Bobby-Lee. Finally they approached a small log cabin facing south along the ridge.

"This place is hidden away," David gasped.

"What's wrong?"

"I'm not feeling so well," he admitted.

"Probably altitude sickness. Some rest and food will help."

"As far as this place goes, it's not as secluded as you think. Walter has surveillance cameras all over the place with motion sensors. We still have a problem. Look up."

David looked at the blue morning sky. "What am I looking for?"

"Anyone with half a brain could come in here with a chopper, if they were determined to get us. It wouldn't be pretty. I guess we all have our day of reckoning," Bobby-Lee snarled.

Bobby-Lee took the lead as they approached the cabin. The place reminded David of several self-sustaining homes he visited in the Arizona desert. *Survivalists.* Several solar tubes dotted the roof. Gutters and leaders directed water into barrels. Solar panels lined the south edge of the building. Two satellite dishes completed the array of what appeared to be an electronic survivalist's retreat.

The cabin door opened and a man stepped forward. He was thin and his face was drawn. His deep-set eyes revealed a man who had not slept in days.

"Clayton, I'm Katz. Come on in," he called.

David entered the cabin.

"Let me take those from you," said Walter Katz reaching for the two long rifles.

"Bobby-Lee, were you able to get all the supplies?"

"Everything," he responded with a thumbs-up. "I've got business to look after." With that he headed out the back door carrying the heavy backpack.

"Bobby-Lee is my babysitter." Katz smiled. "Sit down Clayton. You look bushed."

"I'm feeling nauseous."

"You'll recover. We have a lot to discuss and I suspect we don't have much time. First things first." Katz walked to the far side of the room and pulled up a carpet covering a trap door. "This place was built over an abandoned mine. This is one of the shafts."

David walked to the entrance and looked down into the opening. A wooden ladder led to a dark abyss. There's a tunnel that comes out a few hundred feet down the hill. Got it?"

"What's next? A suicide pill, just in case?"

"Don't melt down on me Clayton."

"Bobby-Lee suggested we could face a catastrophe from an aerial attack."

"Yes, but we have a fighting chance. Bobby-Lee picked the spot years ago. I never imagined this place could be a fort. The cabin makes a perfect safe house. We've stockpiled food and water and the mineshaft gives us an underground shelter."

"What's in the other rooms?"

"Come on. I'll show you."

The two walked into the room on the far right near the kitchen. Against the far wall was a long table holding an array of computer monitors. "This is my station," said Katz. "What you see is sophisticated electronic surveillance system."

"You tapped into DOD, the Russians, and the Chinese from here?"

Katz grinned. "I accumulated most of the files at work.

My method was simple. I attached the files to dummy invoice confirmations and forwarded them to a cloud."

"Wasn't that risky?"

"No. Security was searching for thumb drives and chips. I never cared for them. My way was chancy and so obvious that no one checked. Odd, but as security intensified it became easier to revert to basic hacking."

"The systems are so vulnerable?"

"I held a top security clearance. Once I discovered the software design flaw I circumvented oversight. Bingo! I had access to all the resources at DOD including the Defense Logistics Agency. The only systems I couldn't access were the antiquated disk drive computers on in-house networks separate from the Internet."

"Floppy discs?" David looked surprised.

Katz laughed. "You bet, but here is the real surprise. The network administrator is accountable for network security. You don't think a network administrator is going to admit to an intrusion, do you?"

David scratched his head. *Katz talks so heedlessly indifferent. He's committed serious crimes. He helped Trinity steal electronic parts and other rare earth components.*

"I know first-hand that the Chinese wrote the program. They called it Putter Panda. US intelligence sources tracked Putter Panda to a Chinese military unit stationed in a building in the PuDong section of Shanghai."

"In other words, Putter Panda searches for a flaw, a vulnerability in the system."

"Yes. It's called a 'zero day' vulnerability. It's present in the original software. It cost a lot to repair. Sometimes the creator doesn't discover the flaw until it's too late."

"So it's kept a secret? Never fixed." David asked.

"Correct. That's how I found an opening, a backdoor. I exploited a major supplier, Emporium International Shipping (EIS). Their field office is located in Chungking, China. EIS conducted their business and notified the Defense Logistics Agency prior to shipment. Once I acquired a bill of lading, I notified Trinity's subsidiary, the Bland Corporation, in Florence, South Carolina.

"The Defense Logistics Agency never discovered the delivery discrepancies?"

"No. There were no discrepancies. I generated new shipping dispatches and routed the material via Hawaii rather than San Francisco. The Hawaiian shipments took longer and eventually went through Los Angeles. There was never an overlap."

"And Bland Corporation?" David asked.

"To the casual observer it's a simple electronics research facility. Warehousing powerful magnets created a challenge. Who would suspect a maze of warehouses two stories underground?"

David prodded Katz for more information. "So you decided to copy the transaction files and blackmail the government?"

"Not exactly. I inadvertently discovered the constant traffic between Trinity International, the Chinese, and the Russians. My curiosity was aroused when the communications between Ashton Pickering and President Stone intensified. Suddenly, the interest turned from magnets to troubles within the Stone Administration."

"So you began filtering the transmission and copying files?"

"Yes. Several weeks later I made an even greater discovery. There was a power struggle within Trinity International. Kurt Strauss and his son, John, are pushing out Ashton Pickering. It's nasty."

"And that was the turning point for you?"

"Exactly. Bam! I had the bastards. It was payback time."

"It's all about payback?"

"In the beginning I wanted revenge for what they did to me and the others. They used us. We were nothing more than laboratory rats. They messed with our minds. My life has been wrecked. We were harmless children – innocent assets."

"You broke the law."

"I never planned to sell the information to a foreign nation. I'm not a traitor. I'm a patriot. The government committed the crimes. I didn't. I want the people behind

MKULTRA and Pied Piper to be held accountable."

David didn't respond.

"I can see from your deadpan expression, you don't believe me."

"You took classified files," David argued. "You are a wanted man. You helped Trinity steal millions."

"Yes. And I'm ready to go to jail. But what happens to the people calling the shots? They are untouchable. Clayton, I was certain you would understand. I am telling the truth," Katz pleaded.

"There are other ways to expose the administration and Trinity. The people you are after died years ago."

"And you think that's why the government and Trinity are hunting me?"

"I'm confused." David responded.

"Don't be naïve, Clayton. The government and Trinity are collaborators. They have greater concerns than pilfering from the Defense Logistics Agency. They want to stifle the publication of the Sunrise Files."

"You accessed Erskin Young's records?"

Katz frowned. "They revealed diabolical connections between Trinity and an number of government agencies as far back as World War Two."

"Were they digitized?" David asked.

"Yes, but the originals were stored in a Justice Department Warehouse."

"Alan Foxx discovered the secret. It cost him his life," David replied. "What else did you discover?"

"At first, I was astounded by what I read. Now it all makes sense. Powerful financial interests are heavily invested in the upcoming Presidential election. Ives Venal is sure to win."

"Are you talking about the Davos group?" David asked.

"No. The group I discovered is century's older and far more powerful. They control the world's resources. The file refers to them as The Circle of Twelve."

"Bullshit. No one is that powerful. You're promoting a conspiracy myth. The legendary Illuminati lurk behind every damn conspiracy theory. I don't believe it."

"Most people deny the truth."

"And that's your version of the truth? "

"Agreed. The idea is frightening."

"Give me one example to prove your allegations." David demanded.

Katz continued. "Operation Pied Piper was an extension of Franz's experiments into eugenics and mind control under the Nazi regime. He selected seven orphaned Lebensborn children and performed similar, but less sophisticated, research at the Goering Institute. He named each of them. After Franz was smuggled back into the United States, the Goering project was secretly transferred to Walther Liechtenauer, the CEO at Trinity International. Years later Liechtenauer came to the United States. He helped fund Pied Piper. "

"Slow down. Are you telling me those Goering subjects are still alive?"

"Yes."

"Do you know their names?"

"No, not for sure. I've intercepted several email exchanges between John Strauss, a deputy financial director at Trinity and Ashton Pickering."

"And?"

"They refer to "GG"."

"I struggled with the initials. Now, I'm convinced that it is none other than Anatoly Ivanovo," said Katz.

"Russia's President? It can't be."

"You look stunned, Clayton."

"In Russian, Ivanov means 'God's grace'. Franz's caustic sense of humor at play."

"Katz, if you've read the Sunrise documents you must know Project MKULTRA is history. Except for Katherine Stone, your classmates are either incarcerated or dead."

"Her brain finally short-circuited. Her behavior was uncontrollable and unpredictable. Katherine was a liability for Trinity. She had to be incapacitated."

"Listen to me, Katz. The Pied Piper Project was a mistake, but the principals are dead. Erskin Young, the agent-in-charge of Pied Piper, died in 1977. We have no credible witnesses. Kurt Strauss, the last surviving member of the original Trinity International board, died several weeks ago."

"Naturally. He conveniently fell to his death from the top floor of the Trinity Building. For god's sake Clayton, Strauss was confined to a wheel chair. You don't get it. Strauss was murdered. Trinity is cutting its last connections to MKULTRA."

"And that's the story the Circle of Twelve wants to suppress?"

"It's obvious. I've pissed them off and they are going to make me pay."

Clayton nervously paced the room. *This conversation distresses me.* He could feel his heart pounding.

"How do the Russians and President Ivanov come into play?"

"I don't know the answer."

"This is incredible. It ranges beyond a conspiracy theory. You are right, Katz. No one will believe you. The government will discredit you. They will contend you are fabricating the entire episode to avoid prosecution."

"Now you are getting the picture, Clayton. I assure you, The Circle of Twelve controls Ives Venal and the White House. He's running for re-election. With the Circle of Twelve's backing Ives Venal will win."

"We have to find a way to alert Congress without releasing the files to the media."

"Are you crazy, Clayton? I told you. I'm a dead man, but there is still time to save yourself and your friends."

From around his neck Katz removed a small jade Buddha dangling from a horsehair necklace. He handed it to Clayton. "On the table is a smart phone. There's an "app" on the homepage similar to the grid you used before."

Clayton picked up the phone.

"You swipe the Buddha across the application. It points to my cloud vault. Same pin number – 444. It will take months to go through them."

"And the Sunrise Files?"

"As long as you hold access to my vault, they are safe and so are you."

"Shit! I told Dakota to publish portions of the U-853 logs if they are authentic."

"Never! Don't reveal the log's existence."

"Why?"

"My wife was senselessly murdered. Do you want that to happen to Dakota and the others? Stop her now."

Katz retrieved a second phone from the table. "This is a satellite phone. Call. Warn your friends. It will take the NSA several hours to track the call."

David telephoned Dakota. She didn't answer. He left a message. "Dakota do not publish the log. Don't release any information until we talk. Trust me."

David turned to Katz and said, "I'm not feeling well. I need to lie down."

"Of course. Try calling Putnam later. You need some rest. Use the small bedroom. I'll wake you, if she calls."

"Thanks. This whole thing sucks. I feel so helpless," David lamented.

"It doesn't matter now. There is something greater than both of us at stake," Katz insisted.

"Tell me your…" Clayton didn't finish his question. Suddenly he swayed. His words slurred, and he turned a clammy grey.

Katz reached out help Clayton. "What's wrong?"

"I need to sleep."

Katz helped David walk into the bedroom. David kicked off his shoes and fell back on the bed.

❧

A few hours later Katz was in the kitchen preparing a meal for David when the alert sounded on his two-way radio.

"Base, we have a recon group about a mile down the road. They tripped the sensors."

"Hunters?" Katz asked.

"Negative. Bandits. Four of them are on foot. They just dismounted from a military-style Humvee. The driver is in the vehicle. They have firepower."

"What's your take?"

"Let them proceed." They'll wait until dark."

"Don't take any risks. We have to get Clayton out of here."

"Base, there has to be aerial surveillance. They'll come in tonight."

"One task at a time. Stay safe, buddy."

"Roger." Bobby-Lee lay prone on a bluff overlooking the dirt road below. He shivered with a thrill of excitement. For an instant his mind drifted. Suddenly, it was 1969 and Bobby-Lee was back in Laos observing the enemy. The approaching reconnaissance team halted. The Humvee pulled off the road.

"Base. Our visitors have taken positions in the tree line. They haven't spotted my truck. Have you picked up any talk?"

"No. I'm scanning frequencies."

"Base. It's time for you and your guest to vacate. The cabin is vulnerable. These dudes would never come after us from their current position." Bobby-Lee searched the horizon for a plane or helicopter.

"Stay put. We hold the high ground."

"Clear out," Bobby-Lee pleaded. Katz didn't respond. He placed his radio on the kitchen table and rushed to awaken Clayton.

"Clayton, get up. We have to move."

Clayton rubbed his eyes and search for his shoes. Clayton opened the closet and removed two shotguns and an M-14. "Follow me," he shouted. Clayton scrambled to retrieve his missing left shoe from under the bed.

"Damn it Clayton. Get a move on it," he ordered. "Take the camouflaged jacket hanging on the door. Let's go."

Katz stopped. "Hear that rumbling?"

"No," David responded.

" It's a chopper. We'll use the tunnel. You go first. I have to set the charges. I'll blow the place. It may give us extra time. Bobby-Lee has the road covered."

"David rushed to the opened the trap door."

"Get going Clayton," Katz shouted.

David swung one of the two packs on to his back. He

trembled as he started to climb down the ladder.

"Hold on, Clayton," Katz shouted. He ran to the kitchen table and returned with his satellite phone and a two-way radio.

"Take this radio. Plug in the earpiece. Listen, but don't transmit unless it's an emergency." Katz knelt by the trap door and handed the radio to David.

"This is my satellite phone. Once you are clear of the mine, turn it on. It will search for a satellite. I have waypoints for an escape route programmed."

"Katz, I'm no Ranger. I've never fired a rifle. I've never used a satellite phone. What the hell will I do once I get down there?" Katz looped a rope through the slings on the three weapons.

"Wait at the bottom of the ladder. I'll lower the rifles. I'll join you in a few minutes. If something happens follow the tunnel. You can work your way back to where Bobby-Lee left the truck. With any luck they didn't find it. Bobby-Lee will cover your retreat."

The roar of the helicopter grew louder. "Now, move," Katz, shouted, again. *They'll open up soon.* "They're directly over head."

"Listen, it's leaving," David called back as he climbed down the ladder.

"Bullshit. They're scouting the terrain. Clayton, I told you to move."

"Base. We have a UH-60 on the approach," came the call from Bobby-Lee.

"A Black Hawk? What the hell? Military?" Katz shouted as the chopper neared.

"Can't tell. There are no insignias or numbers. She's fully armored. They aren't going to wait until dark. Walter, get out now."

Before Katz could respond a burst of 50 caliber rounds ripped through the wall of the building.

"Damn it!" Katz shouted. The blast tossed him like a wet rag across the room. Debris slashed his face. He crawled across the floor searching for the two-way radio.

"Base, we have four bandits moving up the hill. I can handle it." Bobby-Lee crawled along the ridge to find a better position. He pointed his M-21 sniper rifle towards the distant figure. *I'll take him first.*

Bobby-Lee zoomed the auto-ranging scope until the marks on the vertical crosshairs showed the best line to the top of the invader's head. *Hold for the wind. Breathe. Pull the trigger.* The distant target turned and fell unobserved. Bobby-Lee quickly moved along the ridge. *I want to create the impression the cabin's parameter has several defenders.* He heard the Black Hawk returning. It whizzed overhead at about 110 knots then turned for a second pass."

"Base." Katz didn't answer. "Base, the chopper is turning. Get out now. I need you out here. They may be preparing for an insertion on the far side of the ridge. I need you to cover my back." The radio static increased. Katz didn't reply. "Walter, come in."

Inside the cabin, Katz painfully crawled to the trap door and shoved it closed. Exhausted, he slumped against the wall. "Clayton, get going. I'll catch up. Clayton did you hear me? Acknowledge."

"I heard you," David called back.

"Bobby, are you still there?"

"I'm on the move. Stay put," came Bobby-Lee's reply.

"Hey buddy, that burst of 50 caliber shit did a number on my arm and face." His voice was weak. His two-way radio fell among the debris. Katz momentarily lost consciousness. As he became cognizant he tried to move his right leg. Finally, he managed enough strength to reach across his body and grab the antenna with his left hand.

"Bobby, no way I'm getting out of here under my own power. My right leg is broken."

"I told you, stay put. I'll work my way to you." Beyond the trees a second figure emerged. Bobby-Lee rolled over and waited for the man's approach. He fired. The suppressor did its job. Through his riflescope Bobby-Lee watched his opponent's eyes widen with surprise as the 7.62 round shattered the intruder's jaw and exited behind his ear.

"Bobby, cover Clayton. Don't worry about me."

Before Bobby-Lee could respond, the chopper's door gunner opened fire and sprayed the area with fifty caliber rounds. Katz'

SUV was parked behind the cabin. The vehicle exploded. A second burst tore into the center of the cabin cutting the roof trusses.

"I'd hate to be on the other side of that wall," the gunner called to the pilot. "One more pass and the whole place will collapse." It didn't take another run.

Inside the cabin, Walter heard the roof groan a second before it collapsed. He was helpless to move as part of a truss fell like a pendulum and smashed through the adjacent wall. Walter struggled to stay conscious. He looked at his contorted left leg. His pant leg was shredded. Shattered bone stuck out of his flesh.

"Walter, I haven't spotted Clayton. What is your condition?" Bobby-Lee called into the radio. With that Bobby-Lee slid from cover and moved closer to the cabin. A third figure emerged from the woods. The intruder worked his way to the far side of the cabin then lay prone. "Walter, you have Charlie on the north side of the cabin. Do you read me?"

Walter lay trapped under the debris. "Bobby, I'm done for. I'm going to blow the cabin. Stay clear. It's Clayton's only chance."

"Negative, Walter. Stay put. I'm working my way to you."

"Clayton's in grave danger, Bobby."

"I'm not abandoning you Walter."

"That's an order, Sergeant. Did you hear me?"

Bobby-Lee used a small berm for cover as he crawled toward the cabin. The chopper made a third attack spraying the cabin. The random sweep reached into the underbrush thrashing the operative hiding near the cabin. Bobby-Lee nodded with satisfaction.

A few yards off the road below, the Humvee driver crouched behind the vehicle waiting for an opportunity to run into the woods. Suddenly on the far left the fourth foot soldier exposed his position. Bobby-Lee twisted his body, took aim and fired.

In the mine tunnel below the cabin, David frantically listened to Bobby-Lee and Katz deal with the ensuing onslaught. David lifted the M-14 and one of the shotguns and slung them over his shoulder. He hefted the other pump shotgun and desperately recalled Bobby-Lee's instructions. *It's a pump shotgun. That button is a safety. Push it or the gun won't fire. You have five shots. Rack it and fire. Reload it here.* David called into the radio. "Katz, I'm headed out."

"Damn it," came a response from Bobby-Lee. "Stay off the radio."

The brief distraction with the radio diverted Bobby-Lee's attention from the Humvee driver. The driver darted across the road and into the wooded area behind Bobby-Lee.

The chopper swooped in low from the north and set down in a clearing about 1000 feet from the cabin. The chopper's dust covered the driver's advance behind Bobby-Lee.

"Ah shit, Walter. The chopper set down in the clearing below the cabin." Four figures dressed in black leaped to the ground and deployed into the woods. The sun was setting.

"Clayton, hold your position. It will be dark soon. Use the satellite phone's GPS. Follow the waypoints marked. You're on your own, pal. Good luck."

David huddled near the tunnel's entrance. The chopper, its twin engines running, was perched in a tight clearing about 500 feet away.

David felt faint, again. He fell to his knees. *How did I get myself into this mess?*

He set the two long guns against the tunnel wall and rummaged through the pack. He began talking to himself. "I'll stick with the shotgun," he said stuffing shotgun shells into his jacket pocket. He discovered two nutrition bars tucked into the side pocket along with a bottle of water. Next, he checked the phone Katz gave him. *No signal.* He fought the urge to leave the tunnel to test the phone. *There's nothing I can do until dark.* Over the radio he could detect the increasing desperation in Bobby-Lee's voice as he tried to work his way to the cabin. Then the radio went silent.

From his vantage point Bobby-Lee saw a pointman emerge from a cluster of trees and rush the rear entrance of the cabin. The others waited anticipating a signal to advance. It came within a minute when the pointman stepped onto the rear deck. He raised his right arm and gave the hand signal. "All clear. One prisoner down."

Bobby-Lee watched with increasing alarm. *Son of a bitch,*

they're mercenaries.

A second man emerged from cover. The man hefted his rifle and rushed to the cabin, but there was no resistance.

As the second man entered the cabin the pointman aimed his rifle at Katz and said, "Sir, he's not going to make it." Katz lay sprawled against the cabin wall. A wedge of splintered pine pinned Katz's left shoulder to the wall.

"Walter Katz, at last. Walter, you are such a pain in the ass," said the second man pulling off his ski mask.

"I might have known it was you, Goodman," said Katz. "I underestimated you."

Goodman laughed. He walked toward Katz. "You're arrogant, Walter." With that Goodman kicked Katz's mauled leg.

Katz screamed.

From their hiding places Bobby-Lee and David could hear the exchange broadcast by Katz's open transmitter.

"Walter, I want the files. Pronto."

"They're beyond your reach, Goodman. I've secured them."

"I doubt that." Goodman kicked Katz harder.

Katz screamed louder.

Bobby-Lee lay powerless behind a small berm listening to his friend being tortured.

"Listen to me Walter. You are going to die. I can leave you here to bleed to death. Some hungry creature is bound to catch your scent. You do have an option," offered Goodman.

Katz struggled to suppress the pain. Blood oozed from his ears. "What's the option?"

"You give me the files or the pin numbers to the cloud and I promise to fire a bullet into your ugly mangled head. It's quick. It beats being mauled to death. Fair exchange?"

Katz appeared to agonize. Then he replied, "Deal. But, first you tell me something. It doesn't matter, I'm a dead man anyway."

"Katz you are mad. What do want to know?"

"Andrew Dunn. How did you manage to murder him?" Katz asked.

"Congratulations, Walter. How did you know? I baffled the Secret Service."

"Katherine Stone wasn't programmed like the rest of us. Andrew and Katherine were bonded. I suspected it had to be someone else with access to the White House residence." Katz coughed and spit blood.

"I almost got caught." Goodman chuckled.

"Katherine was sleeping with you?"

"Among others. She used sex as weapon, a reward system for the bad boys in her stable. Stone's behavior was becoming erratic. Trinity was troubled when she started breaking ranks, acting on her own. Ashton Pickering ordered the scenario. I drugged Katherine, but it wasn't enough. The gunshot sent her into a rage. I was lucky. Her hysteria diverted attention and gave me enough time get away."

"How?" Katz could barely whisper.

"The tallboy on the far bedroom wall conceals a servant's staircase. Grover Cleveland replaced the door with a sliding panel. He enjoyed the pleasures of the private entrance. I used it on a number of occasions." Goodman responded arrogantly.

"And I thought you were a buffoon," said Katz. He struggled to lift his head. "I know why you murdered Alan Foxx."

"You do?"

"Foxx discovered the Sunrise Files weren't destroyed."

Goodman smiled. "There's more to it. Richard Helms told the Congressional Committee he destroyed the MKULTRA files."

"We know he didn't. The Inspector General found a batch of files and released them," Katz mumbled.

"That's what Congress concluded. Foxx was too smart for his own good. He was determined to make Clayton and Stokes look like amateurs. He was angry with the White House, too. Professional jealousy, I guess. Then he discovered the Pied Piper documents. That's when his conscience got the best of him."

"You mean he wanted to show me the file." Katz struggled to speak. Every breath brought excruciating pain.

"Foxx found a group photograph of the seven. He planned to show it to Clayton. Foxx had to be eliminated."

"But why kill Charles Best? He was harmless. He trusted Trinity and adored Katherine Stone."

"Best fell apart."

"Did you kill him?"

"You bet I did," Goodman bragged. "Best was gutless. Even Stone cut him loose."

"And Drew Lindstrom?" Katz asked.

"As for Lindstrom, I never touched him. The poor bastard was devastated. He simply tossed a rope over a garage beam and kicked the chair away. Never could figure out why he did it. Pickering offered Lindstrom a lifetime retirement."

Blood was beginning to pool on the floor beneath Katz' shattered leg.

Goodman drew his pistol and pointed it at Katz. "Now buddy-boy it's time."

"You win," Katz mumbled. "I have a flash drive in my vest pocket."

Goodman moved closer and pressed his pistol against Katz's head. "Go easy, Walter. No tricks."

Katz fumbled with his vest pocket. The throbbing pain in his left shoulder increased as he retrieved a small rectangular plastic object.

"What the hell is that?" shouted Goodman as he stepped back and fired a .40 caliber round into Katz' head. But it was too late."

Katz pressed the detonator button just as Goodman fired. Six charges detonated simultaneously. The pointman standing directly over one of the explosives simply vanished. Goodman, barely alive, lay on the floor near Katz's shredded body.

The strength of the blast launched fragments in all directions. Bobby-Lee was less than one hundred feet from the cabin when it exploded. He buried his head in the dirt. Debris rained down. From a distance the Humvee driver saw Bobby-Lee's predicament. The driver rushed at Bobby-Lee firing his rifle on full auto. Bobby-Lee shifted his body and rolled over the berm desperately searching for cover. He felt the initial shock of the round striking his buttocks. A round ricocheted and pounded his side. Suddenly, the pain spread from his throbbing ass to his testicles. *You bastard.*

Bobby-Lee held his rifle close as he rolled down the embankment. The firing stopped. He reached between his legs. A hot liquid flowed into his hands. He pelvis was on fire. The agony reached into his stomach. *Oh God. I'm finished.*

The Humvee driver stood at the embankment aiming his weapon for one last round to finish his prey. There was a loud blast. The man tumbled down the hill coming to rest a few feet away from Bobby-Lee.

Bobby-Lee painfully raised his head to see David Clayton screaming as he rushed insanely down the ridge. David came to an abrupt halt over the driver, racked his shotgun and fired, again. Then David turned, dropped the shotgun and moved to Bobby-Lee's side. He knelt next to the dying man. Bobby-Lee's eyes glazed. "Shit, Clayton. I never thought this would happen," he whispered. The wounded man winced.

Clayton remained silent. He cradled Bobby-Lee's head in his lap.

"Dying ain't easy, Clayton. I wish it would come," he gasped.

From the landing zone on the far side of the hill the pilot saw the cabin explode and shouted into the radio, "Saddle up." The two mercenaries still in the woods scrambled on to the Black Hawk. Its four blades whirred.

The co-pilot cried out, "Look at that. It's crazy."

Slowly, what remained of the cabin began to shift. With a sudden shudder what remained of the structure dropped into the mine below.

"Sir, what about Goodman and the others," called the crew chief.

"I was just thinking the same thing," answered the pilot over the intercom. The chopper rose and peered down at the huge debris-filled opening which moments ago had swallowed the cabin and its three occupants.

The pilot flipped the ready switch to arm the Hellfire missiles.

"Sir this side of the mountain is nothing but dead pines. It could turn into an inferno. It will be days before the forest service controls the fire."

"Exactly." He fired a missile into the mine. Next he targeted the Humvee below. It vaporized. Both sides of the dirt road burned furiously.

"If you ask me, Medicine Bow needs new growth," the pilot barked. With little remorse for Goodman and their fallen comrades, the Black Hawk sped for home at Trinity's secret Denver facility.

The impact of the first rocket knocked Clayton unconscious. As the wind shifted the fire began to burn down the hillside. And then as though awakening from a dream state, David heard a voice calling. "Wake up. You've got to get your ass out of here. The fire could trap you."

It was dark, but the burning mine shaft lit the sky like an erupting volcano. David looked to his left. Bobby-Lee had managed to roll a bit and was laying a few feet away. "Clayton, Katz bit the bullet for you. Now get your ass out of here while you can still make it."

"I can't leave you here," David moaned. He ears rang from the missile's   concussion.

"There isn't enough time. I'll cover you." Bobby-Lee racked his .40 caliber pistol and said, "Now get your ass out of here. I'm done for."

Several of the burning pine trees began to explode sending flares into the air. David looked around and decided it was time to move out. "Thank you Bobby," was all David could muster. He turned and rushed toward the path that led to Bobby's truck. Then David heard a single shot coming from behind. Clayton was frightened to look back. Bobby-Lee had just ended his agony.

Now I'm on my own. David was overcome with trepidation. He reached into his jacket pocket for Katz's mobile phone. *I can't find Katz's phone.* He searched his other pockets frantically tossing the shotgun shells on the ground. "Oh shit. I've lost it," he exclaimed. He touched his neck. *I still have the jade Buddha.*

Chapter Seventy-Five
The Peril

The fire rushed down the hillside in pursuit. *I'm not going to make it.* Both sides of the narrow trail were engulfed in flames. Just as the trail broke into a small clearing, David saw the pickup truck. David started to run, but the fire sucked the breath from his lungs. He made it to the truck and climbed in. The keys were still over the visor. The engine turned over twice, but wouldn't start. On the third try it started. David eased the clutch gently into first gear.

He slowly circled the clearing and drove back to Albany along the abandoned railroad right of way. As he approached the general store, David stopped and stared down the road for his rented Mustang. All that remained was a burned out shell. *The sun is coming up. In a few hours a search team will arrive. It won't take long to discover I'm still alive. They will come for me.* Then he recalled Katz's warning. "As long as you hold the key to my files, they won't kill you. But, eventually they will get the data."

David tried calling Dakota on his own cell phone, but there was no signal. *I have to speak with Dakota.* He pressed the accelerator hard to the floor, but the old truck refused to go faster. *The downhill run along Route 11 requires a degree of experience, especially in this old Ford Truck. The brakes feel soft.* David ran the stop sign at the Route 130 intersection and swung south toward Laramie. The speedometer slowly climbed to 65 miles per hour.

David began to feel the chest pains returning as he approached Laramie. He rubbed his eyes. *My vision is blurred.* David was becoming more desperate by the minute. He reached for his phone, again. There was a signal. He called Dakota.

She didn't answer. He tossed the phone on the passenger seat. Several minutes later Dakota called.

"David, where are you?"

"Outside Laramie. They are all dead. It's awful. Katz is dead. It was Goodman."

"You aren't making any sense."

"Goodman murdered Katz. Goodman was here on the ground. He directed the operation. My God, a helicopter destroyed Katz's cabin and set the area on fire."

"David, please calm down. It sounds like your were in a war zone." Dakota pleaded.

"I was. Dakota, listen to me. Where are you?"

"I am at Lou-Ann Stokes' condo. Ed Savage is here. So are Matt Nagle and Doc Clawson. We have the notebook and the U-853's log. Savage believes the log is authentic. I'm going to publish a column."

"No! Don't do that. Don't let anyone know you have the log. Your lives depend on it. Trinity will come after you and your families," David protested.

"That doesn't make any sense, David. I'm going to put you on speaker phone so the others can hear you," Dakota answered.

"Katz warned me. The log is the link between Trinity and the Presidency. They will kill to get the log."

"David, I have an obligation to publish the story."

"Goodman bragged about killing Foxx and Best. And…he murdered Andrew Dunn. They will come after you."

Lou-Ann took the phone. "David, find an out-of-the-way motel. Get some rest. You've been through a grueling experience."

"Lou-Ann, I am not delusional. Goodman bragged how he got away with it."

"Katz is dead. How do we recover Katz's files?"

"We can't, Lou-Ann."

"Then all we have is hearsay and circumstantial evidence. We have no choice. Dakota needs to publish excerpts from the U-853 log," Lou-Ann replied.

"Katz told me there's a power struggle within Trinity

International. Ashton Pickering is frantic to hold on to his position. Desperate men do desperate things. Nine men died last night. By now Pickering knows I'm alive. Damn it Dakota. The files are lost."

"What?"

"I lost Katz's satellite phone during the firefight. I needed to activate a pin number on the phone to have access to his cloud account. All this bloodshed was for nothing."

"So the log is all we have? The American public and the world need to know the truth."

"Damn it. You're placing your lives in jeopardy."

"The five of us agreed to publish portions of the log. We can't stop now. There has to be a reckoning," Dakota persisted.

At that very moment David looked toward the horizon. "Dakota they've made me."

"What?"

"I spotted an RQ-1 drone. One of those unmanned reconnaissance drones."

"Are you sure?"

David didn't respond. A loud blast of what sounded like a ship's horn boomed over the phone.

"That's a blast from an 18-wheeler's air horn," said Ed Savage.

"Oh no!" David cried. In a moment's distraction the pickup wandered across the narrow divide into oncoming traffic. An 18-wheeler sounded its ear-busting air horns. There was the sound of grinding brakes and a series of resounding rumbles and finally a loud explosion. The phone went dead.

"Now what do we do?" asked Matt Nagle.

The answer was at hand. There was a pounding on the front door. Lou-Ann hurried to respond.

From the living room the others heard, "Goddamn it. Where is he?"

Before Lou-Ann could answer, Liz Nagle brushed her aside and rushed into the room. "You bastard. Turn on your cell phone. You told me you'd be at Clawson's."

"We changed locations at the last minute. What's wrong?" Matt protested.

"I asked you. No, I begged you. Please don't get involved in this nonsense. Nazis and conspiracies are all you think about. I'd cut your balls off, if you had any. Matt, how could you do this?"

Liz opened her email and pushed the phone in Matt's face. "This is our granddaughter." Liz dropped the phone on the table. Loud-Ann picked it up and gasped.

The e-mail opened with a voice-over. "Good morning Mrs. Nagle. Sources inform me that you husband is in possession of important documents. I want them. I am a fair man. In exchange for the documents I will not kill you granddaughter. Fair?"

"What the hell is he talking about?"

"Quiet. There's more," ordered Lou-Ann.

"One caution, Mrs. Nagle. I will present you with your granddaughter's head if the documents are published. I need your assurance the documents are safe."

Liz sneered at Matt. "You bastard. You've jeopardized our family. What's wrong with you?"

Dakota tried to intervene. "Mrs. Nagle, no one thought it would come to this."

"You're all assholes," Liz screamed. She snatched her phone and threw it at Matt.

"Let's go home," said Matt.

"Home? Don't come home. We're through." Liz picked her phone off the floor. She glared at the group and stormed out of the condo.

Matt ran after her. "Please Liz, wait. I knew I was taking a risk. But so was continuing to live a boring life."

"Boring?" Liz shouted from the car and drove away in a fury.

"Hold on, Matt. Come inside," Lou-Ann called. "Give Liz some time. She needs to cool down. We need to talk."

"Lou-Ann's right," Ed agreed. "Doc, give me a hand. I'll make coffee. Lou-Ann and Dakota, help Matt make sense out of what just happened."

After a few minutes the coffee was ready and the five sat around the kitchen table. Dakota's phone sounded. It was an anonymous text message.

"A Virginia man was critically injured when the pickup truck he was driving ran off the right side of the roadway and landed in a ditch outside of Laramie. David Clayton, of Manassas, Virginia, remains in critical condition, according to a Central Hospital spokesperson.

The Wyoming Highway Patrol spokeswoman said the crash happened early this morning at the intersection of Snowy Road (Route 230) and Route 130. He was the only person in the vehicle. Clayton was not wearing a seat belt. This incident remains under investigation."

Dakota gasped and handed the phone to Lou-Ann. "Read this text out load, so everyone can share it."

Lou-Ann slowly read the text message. The group looked at each other in horror, but no one spoke. Dakota crossed the room and sank into the sofa. "I need time to think," she told the others.

A few minutes later, Dakota's phone rang.

"Dakota Putnam," she answered.

"Ah, Ms. Putnam. Let's set the pleasantries aside."

Dakota recognized Ashton Pickering's voice. "Get on with it Pickering."

"I know your group is in possession of a U-boat's log. Its contents could prove quite embarrassing for my employers. The log comes at a high price. Wouldn't you agree?"

"Pickering, I know you are at the end of your tether."

"Do not publish the U-853 log." Pickering warned.

"And Katz's files?" Dakota asked.

"I imagine they were lost when Katz died. I understand the entire Wyoming business was quite unpleasant."

"And David Clayton?"

"He is a victim of his own curiosity," Pickering laughed. "It was a case of the wrong man in the wrong place at the wrong time. I never intended to have Clayton executed. I needed him alive to lead Goodman to Walter Katz. And now?"

"Clayton is all yours, Ms. Putnam, with one proviso."

"Proviso?"

"Stay out of my business and Clayton will live. Pursue me and Clayton dies. I must have the log, Ms. Putnam," Pickering stipulated.

"I'm not sure I can do that."

"You *must* convince the others to agree. Your time is running out. I need your answer this afternoon. Tread carefully, Ms. Putnam. Many lives depend on you."

When the exchange ended Dakota walked into the guest bedroom and sat on the bed for nearly an hour. She felt a sense of despair and ambivalence. *I don't know what I should do.*

Lou-Ann knocked on the bedroom door. "Hey. Is everything OK?"

"No. Ashton Pickering wants the log. Where are the others?"

"Nagle is sulking in the living room. Savage and Clawson are in the kitchen."

"Let's get everyone together. I have to share Pickering's demands."

Lou-Ann walked into the living room and motioned for Nagle to follow her into the kitchen. Clawson was sipping coffee.

"Where is Savage?" Dakota asked.

Clawson ran his index finger around the brim of his coffee cup, but didn't respond."

"Are you deaf? Where's Ed?" asked Lou-Ann.

"He's gone," Clawson declared.

"Doc, please tell me you didn't give him the log."

Doc nodded and said, "He has Price's notebook, too. I also gave him the stopwatch Price gave me. A diver removed it from the sub years ago. I promised Price it would be returned along with the log."

"Why? Pickering warned us he would kill Nagle's granddaughter, if we didn't surrender the log."

"Ed and I agreed it was a risk. We have a greater chance of surviving if Pickering doesn't have the log. Once he has the log, we are liabilities. We are expendable."

"You had no right gambling with our lives," Lou-Ann shouted, exasperated.

"Perhaps you are right. Nevertheless, we made the decision. There is no turning back," said Doc.

"And what do I tell Pickering?" asked Dakota.

"Don't look so despondent," said Doc. "We have nothing to lose."

"I'm angry and disgusted," said Matt. "My granddaughter's life is on the line." He tossed his coffee mug into the sink shattering it into a hundred pieces and walked outside.

For the next two hours Lou-Ann and Dakota rehearsed different replies when Pickering called. None of the responses seemed right. It was nearly four o'clock when Pickering called.

"Well, Ms. Putnam. What has your group decided?"

"We didn't make a decision."

"What? I warned you of the consequences."

"We don't have the log."

"I didn't know it when we talked. Savage has the log and a notebook, too. He disappeared more than an hour ago."

The signal dropped. Dakota redialed but Pickering didn't answer. The others stood by anxiously awaiting Dakota to relay Pickering's response. Her facial expression echoed bad news.

Dakota looked at the others and said, "Pickering ended the call. He sounded furious. I feel certain there will be all sorts of hell to pay. We're emotionally drained. I've had enough for today. I have a column to write."

"Not about the U-853," Matt insisted.

"No, Matt. Not about the log. Maybe the story will appear as my obituary, but I hope that's a long way off. Do yourself a favor, Matt."

"What?"

"Go home to your wife. Right now you need each other."

Matt looked grim. "I'm not ready."

"You know Matt, I think I'll skip the column. I have to book a flight to Laramie. David needs me."

"It is time we all left," Doc added. "I feel a sense of relief knowing Savage has the log. I hope he can deliver on his promise to safeguard the log and the notebook."

"Before everyone leaves I need to share my sense of pride having known you," said Lou-Ann.

Lou-Ann stood in front of her condo and watched the others walk to their cars. A pall of despondency descended upon them. There were no parting assurances that everything would work out for the best. One unspoken question tormented Lou-Ann: *Where is Ed Savage and the U-853's log?*

Chapter Seventy-Six
Skippy's Marina
Montauk, Long Island

Skippy's Marina, in Montauk Harbor, is one of the least-fashionable sites in this tourist town. Bennett "Skippy" O'Brian inherited the boatyard from his deceased father-in-law before the Great Recession. Skippy's wife died a few years ago. Estranged from his two children, the retired Suffolk County Police Sergeant hit the bottle. Now he wore a cheerless expression under an unkempt beard. His long, stringy, tangled hair underscored Skippy's distaste for showers.

The marina, not far from Gosman's Restaurant, pretty much ran itself. The only thing Skippy cared about was his thirty-five foot Maine Coaster with twin 200 horse power Volvo diesels, the *Adventure III*. For years Skippy ran wreck divers to the Andrea Doria shipwreck off Nantucket or the U-853 off the coast of Block Island.

Skippy prided himself on the Adventure's economy of operation and durability. She was the perfect charter with one exception. Skippy no longer chartered the *Adventure III*. It was his home and the only woman he still loved. Early risers could find Skippy cleaning the teak or polishing the chrome. Each season he hosted a couple of Irish kids. They split their time working for Skippy or working at one of the local pubs. Skippy depended on the kids.

Skippy spent most afternoons sleeping at his desk in a dilapidated shop crowded with scuba accessories and fishing gear. He made it a rule never to drink until lunchtime. By two he was napping in a dilapidated easy chair. Skippy neglected his business and without the vigilant summer help the place would have gone bankrupt.

The phone rang. Skippy shouted for one of the summer kids to answer it. "Damn Irish," he cursed under his breath. He stretched for the phone and grumbled, "Skippy's. How can I help you?"

"Skippy, you old fart. How are you?"

"Who is this?"

"The guy who backed your bullshit story for running aground off Davis Park."

Skippy paused. "Shit man. Is that you, Deco?" Only Skippy called Ed Savage "Deco."

"None other."

"Where are you?"

"Patchogue. Just got in. We split our time between here and there."

"I suspected as much when the guys told me you split from Cabo and left no forwarding address."

"That's another story."

"So what's this call about?"

"Listen, man. You know I'd only be calling if I needed a favor. Right?"

"Come on. Do you have to be so honest?"

"Diana and I are headed your way next week. I need a favor for a day. No more than two."

"I thought there had to be a hitch."

"Are you sober enough to remember?"

"If it was any one else I'd tear their head off. It's none of your damned business. Before I hang up, what's the favor?"

"I need to charter the *Adventure* for a day, not more than two."

"A dive?"

"Yes. Don't ask and I won't tell."

"You need federal authorization to dive the U-853."

"Skippy, don't ask. I need the Adventure. Can I have her?"

"I'll kill you, if you get caught and my boat gets impounded."

"I understand. I need her outfitted and ready to go next Tuesday."

"Why Tuesday?" "It looks like an open window. Fog has been heavy for July."

"We'll see you mid-afternoon on Monday, Skippy. I'll need

equipment, too." Ed ended the conversation abruptly.

Ed turned and looked at Diana. "Skippy thrives on imposition. Why the weary look?" Ed asked Diana.

"I feel uneasy about this entire plan," Diana said.

"We've been over it a million times," Ed argued. "I have to do this with or without you. And I really need your help."

"I'm here," she conceded. "Ed, I know you're an expert wreck diver. You relish not knowing what's around the bend. We have to be careful. I love you. I don't want to lose you because of a promise to return the damn U-853 log."

"I understand. I can't explain my compulsion, but I am driven," Ed replied.

"You told me men have died making the dive. Now, you are going to return to the U-boat alone. The interior is loaded with silt. What happens if you get entangled in all the hanging cables and broken debris? You'll be trapped."

"You're right. Once we tie in, I'll have to be careful not to get disoriented. Please don't worry. I'm not going to dive without reviewing my sketches and available drawings of the interior. We have the next five days to plan the dive. The last time I went inside I squeezed through the forward torpedo hatch."

"Are you sure it's safe?"

"No. I'll have to make that decision once I'm down there. Remember the Navy dropped eleven mines and 180 depth charges on the U-boat. Recent U-853 photos revealed large portions of the hull had fallen away. It may be safer to enter through the forward torpedo hatch."

"Will you be able to see?"

"Yes. I'll have two lights with me and a lead to find my way back out."

"Oh, Ed. It sounds so risky."

"I'm not going to take any unnecessary risks, Diana. I trust you at the helm."

"There is no way I can change your mind?"

"Diana, I'm determined to go through with it."

⌁

It was about two in the afternoon as Ed and Diana passed Amagansett on their way to meet Skippy.

Diana gazed out the passenger window. The couple had hardly talked all day.

"OK, Diana. What is it?" Ed asked with a tinge of exasperation.

"I'm worried for you."

"This is no time to turn back. We are almost at Montauk. I'm starting to worry about you, Diana. I'm depending on you to run the boat and take charge topside."

Diana remained silent. There are no reassurances that she felt confident with Ed's decision to return to the U-853 after all these years.

When they arrived at the dock, Skippy was sitting outside the store.

"I hope he isn't drunk," said Ed.

To Ed's surprise his former partner Marine Division was sober. Skippy walked to their car.

Without a greeting or a simple "hello", Skippy said, "Hand me the suitcase. You grab the gear bags. We have a lot to do."

"Nice greeting, Skip," remarked Ed.

"I think you're insane. Why return to the U-853?"

"And yes. This is my wife Diana. Diana this is Skippy."

Diana smiled. "Is there some way we can ease the tension between you two"? She asked.

"Yes. A couple of beers would do, but not today. I'm determined to stay sober until you guys head out."

Diana looked puzzled.

"It's simple. I don't want to blame myself for helping kill your husband, if this solo dive turns into a disaster."

Diana grimaced. Her puzzlement turned to fear.

"Thanks, partner. You are a champ. You've eased Diana's fears. Now let's cut the bullshit and load this gear on board."

Skippy shrugged and led the couple to the *Adventure III*.

"She's beautiful, Skippy."

"Don't let anything happen to her, Ed. She's all I've got."

The trio boarded. Skippy pointed to a rack of scuba tanks. "I've filled your tanks,

'104's'. Low pressure steel tanks. Thirty-two per cent Nitrox mixture."

"Nice," said Ed as he surveyed the boat's staging area. "I need you to show Diana how the up-line reel and decompression line are controlled."

"That's a new lift bag in case of an emergency."

Diana felt the tension dissipate as they dealt with the hands-on aspect of the pending dive.

"Last year a team of divers from Rhode Island surveyed the U-Boat. She's in worse shape than others. Watch yourself around the periscopes."

Diana walked forward to the helm. Then she surveyed below. "Skippy, thank you for letting us borrow the Adventure. I can tell she means a lot to you."

Skippy smiled. "OK. She's fueled and ready to go. When do you leave?"

"About an hour before sunrise. This isn't a pleasure trip, Skip. I'm in and out."

"Fine by me."

"Now let's head over to Gosman's. My treat."

✍

The Adventure III arrived over the U-853's location about thirty minutes after sunrise. There was a slight breeze, but the ocean was nearly as smooth as glass. Ed struggled a bit with his dry suit. Diana helped him with the two tanks and the rest of his gear.

"I'll survey the hull," he assured Diana. "There's a huge hole from a depth charge."

Diana touched Ed's arm. "I'll be careful," he assured her.

"Here are the log and notebook." Diana handed Ed a sealed plastic bag. In turn Ed dropped the package into a net bag suspended from his weight belt. He walked to the dive platform and jumped in. He descended slowly to a depth of about 120 feet. There she was – the U-853. Ed made the tie in. Then he surveyed the hull. His time was limited. He swam to the forward torpedo hatch. *I've entered this way before. I'm a few pounds heavier, but I'll give it a try.*

Diana had lowered two additional lines. One line was for the emergency lift bag. The other had a basket attached. The basket held a net bag and a length of hose. Ed retrieved a fifty- foot hose with regulator fitting from the basket. He attached it to his tanks. The other end was attached to a mouthpiece. He clipped the net bag to his belt. Next he carefully squeezed through the forward torpedo hatch and cautiously swam aft following the beam of his light. The U-853 was listing more to the portside then when he was last inside. Wires hung dangerously low. A diver could easily become ensnared.

Finally, Ed located the radio room. *The captain's compartment will be on my left.* It was. He moved warily to his left. As the beam of light surveyed the small compartment Ed felt uneasy. He reached into the net bag and removed the watertight package. *I'll leave it here.* Ed looked around the compartment one last time. *I wonder what really happened. I guess no one will ever know.* With ever so slight a push the bag floated down into the silt. *I've kept Doc Clawson's promise to return the log to the U-853.* Silt began to shift as the bag settled.

Oh no. It can't be. The displaced silt revealed a skull still wearing an escape lung. For a moment Ed was bug-eyed. He backed away. *The poor bastard never had a chance.*

Startled by the sight, Ed began to breathe rapidly. *Control your breathing, Ed.*

Ed worked his way back and exited through the torpedo hatch. He gathered the hose and slipped his tanks back on. Ed felt an adrenaline rush. *Calm down. I can't become reckless.*

It was time for the critical ascent. He monitored his decompression meter. *I have to time myself.* Ed slowly ascended until he reached his final critical stop before surfacing.

⁓

It was mid-afternoon as Ed stood on the bow and Diana docked the Adventure III. Skippy tossed Ed a dock line.

521

"Welcome back," called Skippy. Diana killed the engines and walked to the rear of the yacht.

Skip walked along the dock to greet Diana. "Toss me a line, Skip."

Ed made his way aft. "How did it go, Ed?"

"Without a hitch. It's a relief."

"Well, I hate to spoil your day but…" Skip hesitated.

"But what?" asked Diana.

"Two suits showed up earlier today."

"Suits. Yes. They came on like Feds, but something didn't fit."

"They're private security. Are you in trouble, Ed?"

"Let's put it this way. I'm not sleeping well."

"I told them you chartered the Adventure for three days. Expected you back on Thursday. I sense they didn't believe me."

"Ed we better get moving. We don't want to get trapped on Montauk Highway."

Diana went below and gathered the gear.

"Don't bother with the gear, Diana. Just hand me the suitcase. The gear's yours Skip. Send me the bill for the fuel."

"It's on me. I don't have your address."

"Neither do we right now."

Diana gave Skippy a huge hug. "Thank you, Skip."

Skip laughed. "The hug is just what I needed."

"Thanks, Skip," said Ed.

"Be careful, Ed."

Epilogue
Santorini, Greece

The two-seater helicopter hovered above the *Trinity Corinthian*. The *Corinthian* was a three hundred foot motorsailer, moored near the island of Santorini. The copter's brief flight combined business with pleasure. Ashton Pickering, a licensed pilot, insisted the waters surrounding his yacht be policed. He felt a responsibility for his guest's security. Pickering also enjoyed his routine flight especially while maneuvering the craft back on to the ship's tiny landing pad. The vessel represented a high point for Pickering. He helped design the yacht.

Diesel-electric motors enhanced the five computer-operated sails. The motorsailer was designed for long-distance cruising. The *Corinthian's* interior layout accommodated six staterooms, including Pickering's suite. The spacious guest compartments were extravagantly decorated. Pickering contended he owned the only motorsailer with a luxurious spa. The stern was designed to accommodate jet skis, scuba diving and snorkeling. Onboard his three hundred foot yacht Pickering enjoyed all the amenities a wealthy corporate director and his guests merited. One guest commented, "I know there are twenty crewmembers on board, but they seem invisible."

The *Corinthian* followed a course from Athens on a leisurely sail to the island of Santorini. Along the way they visited a few islands. The captain was ordered to always be in port by nightfall.

He once confided in his head of security, "It's strange, Chief. I never quite understood my reluctance to sail after dark."

Ashton Pickering was a valued employee of the Circle of Twelve, Lake Como's powerful consortium. The previous evening, Pickering surprised his guests with a quiet celebration and a brief announcement.

"I want to share a special announcement. I will soon relocate to my home over-looking Lake Como, a generous retirement gift from Trinity International. I love living on board the *Corinthian*.

This will be my second home."

The sound of corks popping as the stewards poured champagne encouraged the guests to briefly cheer and offer a toast. He chatted with the group. After a round of drinks his party went ashore to continue the celebration. The party lingered beyond midnight. Pickering left the restaurant with the musicians. He was the lone passenger in the gondola as it descended to the harbor.

At sunrise the *Corinthian* set sail for Athens. The wind increased. Whitecaps kicked up. The captain instructed the helmsman, "We'll seek the shelter of Mykonos."

It was midday when they arrived. An afternoon of watersports and beachcombing ended with a lavish lunch. At some point, Pickering met with the Captain.

"Captain, call ahead. We'll stay at the marina in Mykonos for the night. I know my guests will appreciate the visit."

"Yes sir, Mr. Pickering." The captain gave a casual salute.

It took less than three hours to motor to a mooring in the harbor near the marina. After a few more cocktails Pickering's guests boarded a launch for the dock. While his guests partied on shore Pickering remained on board. Pickering walked to the ship's bow. Then he turned toward the stern. He pulled his two-way radio off his belt and paged the security chief. He looked toward the helicopter resting on its pad. He hadn't made his routine flight.

"Is everything secured Chief?"

"Yes, Mr. Pickering. I'll be on deck until the last guest returns."

"Very well. I'll be in my cabin, Chief." Pickering slipped the radio back on to his belt. He walked down the stairs to the lounge below. Near the starboard windows the chief steward was speaking with a woman.

"Good evening," said Pickering.

"Good evening Mr. Pickering. I didn't hear you enter, sir."

"That's quite all right." Pickering walked toward the two.

"This is Ms. Diana Gonzales," said the steward.

"Ah yes. Good evening Ms. Gonzales," said Pickering with

a smile. He looked directly at the dark-skined, petite woman. "I've been eager to meet you." *This creature is beautiful.*

Pickering motioned for the steward to leave.

"Thank you for the gift, Mr. Pickering," she murmured. "I was surprised." She smiled. "It's a beautiful print."

The sheer sensual snake-print kaftan loosely draped her body. Diana's fingers played with the ruffled neckline to accentuate her subtle breasts. Ashton sat on the edge of the couch admiring her skin.

Diana could see anticipation in his eyes. She knew he was aroused. She began to stand.

"Oh no. Please stay where you are. May I call you Diana?"

"Of course," she replied.

Pickering slowly turned and gently touched the side of her neck. The tilt of her head exposed a scar. She placed her hand over the spot and glanced down to avoid his eyes.

"Forgive me, but I am curious. How did you get the scar?"

Diana didn't respond. She dropped her hand from her neck to the cushion. Pickering continued to caress the nape of her neck. Then he kissed the scar. Her hand touched Pickering's thigh. They looked into each other eyes. Pickering was about to embrace Diana.

"Please wait. Can't we go to your suite?"

Pickering's fingertips paused at her cleavage. He whispered, "Shall we go?"

Diana followed Pickering along the narrow corridor.

She is amazing. Pickering recalled the day he first saw her waiting on the dock in Athens. One of the crew called in sick. Diana was her replacement. The Chief relied on the dockmaster's recommendation.

Coincidently, two days before Diana was hired, the *Corinthian's* divemaster abruptly quit. The Chief was glad to be rid of him. The man was a philanderer. Luckily, the dockmaster who recommended Diana knew of an available replacement.

"He arrived in Athens about a week ago looking for work. He's certified for international scuba diving. Don't take my word for it. Check him out," the dockmaster told the Chief.

"I will." The Chief ran his name through Trinity's security database. After a brief interview the Chief said, "Your credentials check out. You're hired."

"Thank you. I'll have my gear on board in the morning." Everything was falling into place.

Ashton Pickering wasn't thinking about the newly-hired dive master as he led Diana into his suite. She needed little coaxing. Diana walked to the starboard windows. She pulled the sheer curtain open and looked out on the harbor. The light from the other yachts glistened off the calm dark waters.

"This is beautiful. I've never experienced such luxury." Diana opened the balcony door and stepped outside. It was a warm evening with a gentle breeze. Diana turned at the sound of a cork popping.

"Dom Perignon 2003 Rosé." Pickering filled two flutes. He handed a flute to Diana. Their glasses touched. The understanding exchanged minutes before in the ship's lounge was nearing fulfillment.

Pickering caressed Diana's hand and gently led her to his bed. She paused. Pickering unbuttoned her dress. It fell to the floor and the pair tumbled on to the bed. Diana moved on top of Pickering and guided his hand.

The moment was interrupted by a noise on the patio. "Did you hear that?" asked Pickering.

"No. Please don't stop."

Pickering paid no attention to her appeal. "Please get off me." He abruptly pushed Diana. She rolled off the bed and backed into the shadows of the room.

Someone is out there. "Who's there?" Pickering called. Instinctively, Pickering rolled to his left and reached toward the nightstand. The top drawer held his loaded nine-millimeter Sig Sauer. It was too late. Pickering felt swift blow to his extended right arm. Then the pain registered. His arm dangled alongside the bed. He looked down.

"My wrist is shattered," he shouted. He gagged at the sight of his bone-pierced skin. Blood spurted on the sheets.

"Shit. Chief, help me!" Pickering screamed. He rolled back to his right. He braced for another hard hit, but it didn't come.

A hand covered Pickering's mouth. He felt the warm barrel of a pistol firmly pressed against his head.

"Please be quiet, Mr. Pickering. No sense enduring more discomfort. Your Chief won't be responding."

Indeed, the Chief's body was slowly sinking below the water's surface behind the Corinthian's stern. A short length of cord ended the unfortunate steward's curiosity. They were the only security on board. The rest of the crew had departed for a night on the town. They weren't due back for hours.

Diana stepped from the shadows. She slid the patio door closed. Then she turned on the accent lighting over the suite's bar.

Pickering's vision was blurred. Vomit filled his mouth. He spit. "I know you," he cried. "You're the new hire, the diver."

"My name is Ed Savage, Mr. Pickering. We've never met, but you and your henchmen have been a big part of my life. Your thugs tried to kill Diana. You've created a lot of havoc in our lives."

"What are you talking about? I don't know you. Why kill me? There's some mistake," Pickering begged.

"Diana is my wife, Diana Sandoval. Trinity ordered a hit on Diana after she published a story about a South Carolina kidnapping and human trafficking."

Pickering looked at Diana. "Oh…" he moaned.

Ed turned to Diana. "It's time for us to leave."

Pickering moaned in pain. He struggled to sit up in bed. "Who sent you?"

Ed stepped back and raised his pistol.

"No. Stop!" Pickering ordered. "Diana, please. Stop him. I'll do anything. Pay any amount. This is insane."

Diana silently stepped back into the shadows. Silence filled the room.

The expression on Pickering's face turned lifeless as though he was resigned to his fate. Then, in a woeful tone he asked, "Tell me again. What have I done?"

"Greed," said Ed.

"I am not a greedy man. I've worked hard. I followed orders just as you do."

"It's time, Mr. Pickering. Someone must hold you accountable for the innocent people you and your employers have hurt."

"Innocents? In the end aren't we all innocent assets?" Pickering scoffed.

"You may be right," said Ed.

"Ed, it's time. We have to leave," Diana cautioned.

"No, wait," Pickering begged.

"Take a deep breath Mr. Pickering, please."

"Tell me. Who hired you?" Pickering demanded, again.

Ed's eyes focused on Pickering. "There's no conspiracy, Mr. Pickering. No one hired me. Someone had to hold you accountable."

"Hold me accountable? No one is blameless. We all know the reality, but are afraid to speak out," Pickering scoffed.

"And what is your reality, Pickering?"

Pickering sneered. "You are powerless. Don't you see that? Kill me and you and Diana will never enjoy a moment's peace. You are challenging powerful corporate interests. They run our government. They control the world's resources."

Ed gave a shrug of acceptance. He raised his pistol. Pickering waved his left hand as though to repel the inevitable sentence.

The bullet struck Pickering in the temple. His body shuddered. It was over.

Ed and Diana looked at one another and then glanced back at Pickering.

"Our lives will never be the same," said Diana as they swiftly headed to the stern of the ship.

A canvass covered two small backpacks. Ed opened the hatch to the diving platform. He pushed an inflatable raft into the water. Diana handed the backpacks to Ed. A favorable breeze aided their retreat to the island. They disappeared into the night.

Many of the guests returned intoxicated and exhausted from their night on Mykonos and most slept late the next morning.

The crew noticed the security chief and steward were absent from breakfast. The room steward discovered Pickering's body.

"Captain, this is Eldridge, Mr. Pickering's room attendant. We have a 'Code One' in the master suite."

"Affirmative, Eldridge. Maintain radio silence. We don't want to alarm Mr. Pickering's guests."

"Yes, sir."

Several minutes later the Captain secured Pickering's quarters. Then he radioed Trinity International with the news and requested authorization to notify the authorities. Within minutes the Captain received his orders.

"Captain, this is John Strauss speaking."

"Yes sir."

"I want you to cooperate with the local authorities. A team of Trinity attorneys will arrive tomorrow. This is a very delicate matter. Avoid public statements. Please inform your guests of Mr. Pickering's unfortunate death, but give no details. Trinity International will make travel arrangements for them to return home."

"Any questions, Captain?"

"No, Mr. Strauss."

Five days later an inquest was held. The autopsy report was sealed. John Strauss, Trinity's newly appointed Director, released a simple statement.

> *"It is with deep regret that Trinity International must announce the death of Ashton Pickering. Mr. Pickering served as Director of our subsidiary, Trinity PharmoDynamics, since 1977. He died of natural of causes while vacationing in Greece. Ashton Pickering played a vital role in the growth of Trinity PharmoDynamics. He will be missed."*

Some secrets are best left to rest.

Endnotes

(1) MKULTRA was the code name assigned to the Central
Intelligence Agency's technical research. The designation was
changed to MKRESEARCH. The early research investigated
the use of drugs, chemicals, and drugs. The impetus was
motivated in part by psychological and physical interrogation
methods used by the North Koreans to extract information
from American prisoners of war during the UN Police Action.
Documents released in 2001 identified corporations and
educational institutions that collaborated in the MKULTRA
research. The names of administrators and personnel were
redacted.

(2) Project MKULTRA, the umbrella operation, encompassed
several facets of mind control. Young's initial assignment was
labeled Project Artichoke. First, recruit Heinrich Franz. Second:
enlist selected universities and hospitals to investigate the
effects of Franz's research on a wider population of children. A
recently discovered internal legal opinion challenged scope of
Heinrich Franz's research. The anonymous author writes: "The
1947 Nuremberg Code was used to judge German scientists who
performed similar experiments. Experimentation with innocent
human subjects (in this case children) would be morally and
legally unacceptable."

(3) The Nuremberg Trial affidavits reveal Admiral Dönitz insistence
"nothing compromising" should be included in U-boat log
entries. Commanding officers were ordered to make every
sacrifice to insure U-boat logs were not surrendered. Unedited
U-boat logs might reveal deliberate violations of the Geneva
Convention. As the tide turned against Germany a number of
disabled U-boats were scuttled rather than abandoned. In turn
U-boat logs were frequently recovered. Dönitz was angered
by increased reports of "insubordination" among his U-boat
commanders. He issued the following order: "I demand from
Senior Commanders that they should take just as ruthless action
against any commander who does not do his military duty."

(4) In 1940 gold was valued at nearly forty-four dollars ($33.9) per troy once. One gold bar weighed twenty-seven and one half pounds. Each bar was valued at nine hundred and thirty-five dollars.

(5) According to official Kriegsmarine Naval Warfare records a number of Type IXC/40 U-boats were stationed at Stavanger, including the U-858 commissioned in September 1943. The U-858 would play an important role in U-853's destiny.

(6) **Time Line for April 29, 1945 – May 6, 1945**

April 29, 1945: Adolf Hitler and Eva Braun exchange wedding vows in Adolf Hitler's underground Berlin bunker.

April 30, 1945: Adolf and Eva Hitler commit suicide in the Berlin bunker. Joseph and Magda Goebbels follow suit, murdering their six children before taking their own lives. Soviet Union forces capture the Reichstag.

May 1, 1945: Admiral Karl Dönitz, Adolf Hitler's handpicked successor, establishes a government in Flensburg to control Nazi Germany following Adolf Hitler's suicide.

May 2, 1945: Some 490,000 German soldiers in Italy lay down their weapons. May 3: Red Army units link up throughout Berlin as German resistance ends, completing the capture of the capital of the Third Reich. Hamburg, Germany, and Innsbruck, Austria, fall to the Allies.

May 4,1945: German troops surrender en masse throughout northern Germany and the Netherlands.

May 5, 1945: Admiral Dönitz orders all U-boats to return to base. Admiral Donitz later orders all U-boats to scuttle. Order rescinded. All U-boats ordered to surrender under a black flag. According to the US Coast Guard inquiry, U-853 did not receive that order, or may have disregarded it.

May 5, 1945: Operations Seahawk ends. The clandestine operation to secure Otto Bruns and carry SS – 1 – 3128 out of harm's way completed.

Cast of Characters

1. Admiral Karl Dönitz. Supreme Commander of U-boats and mastermind of Operation Drumbeat in the Battle of the Atlantic.

2. Agent Kevin Goodman. The newly appointed head of President Stone's personal Secret Service detail. Trinity PharmoDynamics and the Circle of Twelve secretly employed him.

3. Ambrose Ross. Directed Stratum Monitoring Center's illegal monitoring operation.

4. Andrew Dunn: A Bay Grove prodigy. One of Pied Pipers' innocent assets. The husband of Katherine Stone.

5. Ashton Picker. Kurt Liechtenhauer's successor and the second Director Trinity PharmoDynamics.

6. Bobby-Lee Brown. Close friend and Army veteran. He was a sniper in the military and an expert with a traditional bow.

7. Carol Dean. In charge of President Stone's Secret Service Detail.

8. Charles Best. Served as Chief Counsel to both President Anderson and President Stone.

9. Donald Price. Price was an adventurer. Trinity International retained him after Ansgar

10. Drew Lindstrom. Severed as Chief of Staff for President Anderson and President Stone.

11. Edward Shaw. Lieutenant Commander, US Navy Reserve. Assigned to Operation Sunrise as assistant to Erskin Young. Later Shaw became Erskin Young's deputy.

12. Eleanor. Mallory's Daughter

13. Elizabeth "Beth" Collins. Mother of Margaret Collins and mother-in-law of Robert Mallory.

14. Heinrich Franz. Code name – the Pied Piper. Conduct

extensive research in behavior modification and brain change on a group of seven children.

15. Helen Scott.   Second-in-command of President Stone's Secret Service Detail.

16. Helmut Fromsdorf, the twenty-three-year-old commander of the U-853.

17. Henry Beck. Fromsdorf's executive officer.

18. Ives Venal. Former Speaker of the House. He became Katherine Stone's Vice President when Stone became President.

19. John Strauss. Deputy Financial Office, Kurt's son, and heir apparent.

20. Katherine Grace Stone. (Lebensborn: SS -1-3128). Born during the Nazi era never told of her parents' roles in the Third Reich.

21. Kevin Andersen. US President resigns position. Katherine Grace Stone was his Vice President.

22. Kurt Pokel, US citizen conscripted into German Army. Volunteered to escort baby Edith (Lebensborn: SS -1-3128) from Norway to the United States on board the U-853. In return, his wife Ingrid was guaranteed safe passage to US after the war.

23. Kurt Strauss. Chief Financial Office for Trinity International.

24. Lieutenant Walter Kappe. Cummings' case officer in Berlin was.

25. Linda Wilson: A trained clinical psychologist. Employed as Assistant to Heinrich Franz for initial Pied Piper research project.

26. Manfred Bartel and his wife, Gertrude. Temporary guardians for Lebensborn baby SS-1-3128.

27. Mary Taylor. A Bay Grove prodigy. One of Pied Pipers' innocent assets. Later recruited by CIA for Operation Midnight Climax.

28. Mikkelsen. Code name for Danish Freedom Council partisan who aided William Mallory on his mission to negotiate the Hitler Fuhrer Order.

29. Paula Evans. Worked at the Patchogue Hotel. Sean Cummings' girlfriend.

30. Presby. Jack Price's personal assistant.

31. Ray Wood, Ed Jablonski, and Bill Hess, The three Special Seven men convicted of murderer.

32. Richard Klein and wife Sonja. Managed Martin Bormann's Estate.

33. Sean Cummings. IRA trained German spy and saboteur. Recruited by the Abwehr to spy in the United States.

34. Stephen Stone and Virginia Stone. Retained by the CIA to raise Katherine Grace Stone.

35. Theresa Murk, OSS will become Assistant Director of the Research Division at CIA

36. Timothy "Doc" Clawson. The keeper of the U-853 secret.

37. Walter Katz. A Bay Grove prodigy. One of the Pied Piper's innocent assets. Walter was a perennial loner and electronics wizard. Twined with Mary Taylor

38. Walther Liechtenauer. The first Director of Trinity PharmoDynamics and later Trinity International.

39. Wilhelm Hoff, Commander Germany Navy (The Kriegsmarine), and Admiral Dönitz's aide-de-camp.

40. William Robert Mallory. Code name, "Robert." He was an OSS agent. A passenger on the U-853. He later supervised the Bay Gove based Pied Piper Project.

Bibliography*

Abraham, David S. The Elements of Power: Gadgets, Guns, and the Struggle for a Sustainable Future in the Rare Metal Age.

Albarelli, H.P. A Terrible Mistake: The Murder of Frank Olson and the CIA's Secret Cold War Experiments.

Dobb, Michael. Saboteurs: The Nazi Raid on America.

El-Hai, Jack. The Nazi and the Psychiatrist: Hermann Göring and Dr. Douglas M. Kelley.

Hayden, Michael V. Playing to the Edge: American Intelligence in the Age of Terror.

Huddle, John. Locked In: My Imprisoned Years in a Destructive Cult.

Hunt, Irmgard A. On Hitler's Mountain: Overcoming the Legacy of a Nazi Childhood.

Humphries, Marc. Rare Earth Elements: The Global Supply Chain.

Jacka, Tamara and others. Contemporary China.

Jacobsen, Annie. Operation Paperclip: The Secret Intelligence Program That Brought Nazi Scientist to America.

Kelly, Barry. Shades of Justice.

Lewy, Guenter. The Catholic Church and Nazi Germany.

Nolan, Keith. Ripcord: Screaming Eagles Under Siege, Vietnam 1970.

Palmer, (Captain) Bill. The Last Battle Of The Atlantic: The Sinking of the U-853.

Ross M.D., Colin A. The Cia Doctors: Human Rights Violations By American Psychiatrists.

Russell, Jan Jarboe. The Train to Crystal City: FDR's Secret Prisoner Exchange Program.

Simpson, Christopher. Blowback: America's Recruitment of Nazis and Its Destructive Impact on Our Domestic and Foreign Policy.

Strasser, Todd. The Wave. A novel dramatizes in incident in a California school in 1969.

Thomas, Gordon. Secrets and Lies: A History of CIA Mind Control and Germ Warfare.

Vete, David. Mind Control: MK-Ultra, Project Artichoke, and the Jonestown Cult.

Woodward, Bob. The War Within: A secret White House History 2006-2008.

Documents And Other Interesting Sources.

"After Nazi Surrender, A Final Battle Off U.S. The Final Hours of the U-853." Newsday, Thursday, May 2, 1985.

"Mining And Exploitation of Rare Earth Elements in Africa As An Engagement Strategy in US Africa Command." Eugene V. Becker (Lt. Col, USAF) National Defense University Joint Forces Staff College – Joint Advanced Warfighting School.

"Project MKULTRA, The CIA's Program of Research in Behavioral Modification: Joint Hearing Before The Select Committee On Intelligence and the Subcommittee On Health and Scientific Research Of The Committee On Human Resources United States Senate." Select Committee On Intelligence and Committee On Human Resources.

"Report of The National Commission For the Review of The Research and Development Programs of the United States-Unclassified Version." May 29, 2013. United States Intelligence Community.

"U.S. National Security and Military/Commercial Concerns With the People's Republic of China: Unclassified Version." Select Committee United States House of Representatives. January 3, 1999.

**The material used for writing this novel was collected from open-source intelligence (OSINT): intelligence collected from publicly available sources. In the intelligence community (IC), the term "open" refers to overt, publicly available sources (as opposed to covert or clandestine sources).*